Murder

in the
Holy City

Murder
in the
Holy City

Simon Beaufort

ST. MARTIN'S PRESS ✹ NEW YORK

Design by Victoria Kuskowski

Library of Congress Cataloging-in-Publication Data

Beaufort, Simon.
    Murder in the Holy City / by Simon Beaufort.
        p.   cm.
    ISBN 0-312-19566-4
    1. Crusades—Fiction.   I. Title.
PR6052.E2226M8   1998
823'.914—dc21   98-18710
                                        CIP

First Edition: December 1998

10 9 8 7 6 5 4 3 2 1

TO MICHAEL THOMAS

Murder

in the
Holy City

PROLOGUE

S ir Guibert of Apulia's head snapped up from the ground, and
he was alert instantly as he heard the cry outside his tent.

"Saracens, Lord, Saracens!"

Snatching up his sword, Sir Guibert threw open the flap to
the tent. The darkness was broken only by the low-burning fire
and the streaks of light in the sky preceding dawn. Guibert
quickly took in the scene.

His small camp was being attacked from all sides. If the sen-
tries forming the triangle outside the camp were therefore already lost, only his sergeant, Adhemar, and the other nine men
of his party of fourteen were left. He could not tell with certainty, but there appeared to be at least fifty Saracens pouring into
his camp.

"Draw closer together, and stand back to back," Guibert
yelled to his panicking troops. Adhemar and two of the men
formed a small cluster, but it was already far too late. Awakened
from deep sleep after a rapid and thirsty march, his weary force
was unable to form an effective defense and was being quickly
overwhelmed. Guibert had bivouacked miles away from the
guarded supply routes, because his delicate mission had demanded both secrecy and haste. Out here in the desert, there was
no help and no retreat.

"Apulia!" Guibert yelled the war cry of his house and waded

into his enemies, sword in one hand and dagger in the other. His prodigious fighting talents, which had earned him the nickname "Guibert the Two-Handed," allowed him to drop four of the enemy as he slashed his way toward Adhemar. But, with blows falling from all sides, his light chain-mail shirt, which he had worn because it was less cumbersome than a full set of armour, was rent by several determined thrusts. He saw his sergeant and the last of his men fall, and then Guibert himself was struck down by a blow to the neck.

As he crumpled to the ground, his last thought was that he should not have braved the dangers of the Saracen-infested desert wearing only a mail shirt and leather leggings. Such light protection enabled him to ride with far greater speed, but what use was haste when he would not live to see his mission accomplished? And then the pale light of dawn was blocked by the Saracens who fell upon him, and he knew no more.

CHAPTER ONE

JERUSALEM,
JULY 1100

The small band of soldiers glanced around uneasily as the scream rent the air a second time, clear and piercing. One or two fingered the hilts of their swords as they marched, and all were tense and wary. Although the street was deserted in the blazing midday sun, whispered voices and flickers of movement came from the huddle of houses that stood in an unruly line along the side of the road. Further ahead, a babble of hysterical voices exploded into the silence, and a dog began to bark furiously. Sir Geoffrey Mappestone exchanged a glance with Will Helbye, his sergeant at arms, and raised his hand to bring the soldiers to a halt. Nervously, the men shuffled to a standstill behind him, and Geoffrey heard the discreet rasp of steel on leather as weapons were drawn.

"I suppose we should investigate," muttered Helbye, not looking at Geoffrey, but scanning the street with eyes alert for the signs of an ambush, "although I would sooner head straight back to the citadel. The men are exhausted after two weeks of desert patrol, and so am I."

Geoffrey nodded in agreement, but led the way toward the cacophony of voices, his men falling in behind him. Their feet kicked up small clouds of dust as they walked, adding to the layers of yellow-white powder on their boots and powdering their faces and hands with a familiar grittiness. Geoffrey reached the end of the road and stopped a second time.

To the left, a small alley ran downhill, disappearing into the deep shadow of shabby buildings that had been built so close together that they almost met to form an arch overhead. To the right was a wider street, where larger, grander houses suggested that this area had once been home to some of Jerusalem's more wealthy citizens. In the middle of the road, a woman stood, swathed in black from head to toe and clutching a long curved dagger in both hands. The dagger, Geoffrey noticed immediately, was bloodstained. Other people had formed a circle around her and were chattering in loud, excited voices.

Gesturing for his men to remain where they were, Geoffrey strode forward, with Helbye at his heels. Seeing heavily armed soldiers bearing down on them, the crowd parted quickly to allow them through, and the babble of voices died away.

"What has happened?" asked Geoffrey in Norman French, addressing his question to the woman, since she was obviously the cause of the incident.

She gazed at him with frightened eyes until someone in the crowd translated the question into Greek. She glanced at the interpreter and forced herself to look at Geoffrey again.

"There is a dead knight in my house," she said, her voice low and unsteady. She looked down at the knife in her hands, as if seeing it for the first time, and flung it away from her in horror. It clattered at Geoffrey's feet. Someone relayed her response to the onlookers, and a thrill of excitement rippled through them. All eyes turned expectantly to Geoffrey.

"Oh Lord!" breathed Helbye in Geoffrey's ear. "The woman has done away with a knight, Sir Geoffrey. Now what do we do? After two weeks of chasing infidel robbers in that hell they call the desert, you would think we could go home quietly to rest and drink cool wine. But no! We are confronted with a killer of knights. Is it a trick? If we arrest her, will we be attacked?"

Geoffrey did not answer, but looked beyond the crowd to see whether he could detect any telltale signs of activity that might forewarn him of an ambush. Helbye was right to be suspicious and reluctant to become involved. It was only a year since Jerusalem had fallen to the Crusaders, and thousands of its people had been massacred in a way that still made Geoffrey—a hardened and experienced soldier—sick with disgust. The city, despite so few of its inhabitants having survived the sack—or perhaps because of it—was uneasy, and there were pockets of resistance to Crusader occupation everywhere.

"What is your name?" Geoffrey asked the woman in Greek. She looked startled to hear him speak to her in her own tongue, and it was some moments before she replied.

"Melisende Mikelos," she replied in a low voice.

"Show me this dead knight, Mistress Mikelos," he said, fixing her with a hard stare. He gestured with his hand that she was to precede him back into the house. Her eyes opened wider still, and she backed away from him in terror.

"No! Please!" she cried. "Please don't make me go back in there!" She looked as though she might run away, but the spectators hemmed in close and allowed her no escape.

"Do you live here?" asked Geoffrey, watching her closely. Warily, she nodded. "Then you will have to go back inside at some point. Unless you wish to abandon your house to looters."

She gazed at him pleadingly. "I would rather wait here until you have removed the . . . body from my home," she said. "I will enter again when it is gone."

"You must enter now, with me," said Geoffrey, his patience beginning to fray. The longer he stood negotiating in the street with this woman—who may well have committed murder—the longer he put his men in unnecessary danger. When she did not move, he stepped forward and took her firmly by the arm. She struggled automatically, but he was strong, and she desisted as soon as she realised she could no more escape from him than fly.

Helbye motioned for three of the soldiers to enter the house with Geoffrey, while he stayed outside with the remainder, arranging them in two groups to make an ambush more difficult. Geoffrey's fat, black-and-white dog found a patch of shade and flopped down in it, its sides heaving vigorously and its long pink tongue dangling out of the side of its mouth.

It was cool inside the house after the intense heat of the sun, and dark, too. Geoffrey paused to give his eyes time to adjust, and looked around him. The house was no different from many he had visited since arriving in Jerusalem, where the luxury of even the poorest houses provided a stark contrast to the hovels on his father's manor in England. The floor was paved in stone of attractively contrasting colours, and furniture was sparse, but elegant: a narrow couch, some stools, a large table. A large jug of water stood near the door, and a shelf revealed cooking utensils of pewter and pottery, all spotlessly clean. But there was no dead knight. He turned to Melisende Mikelos with raised eyebrows.

"Upstairs," she said in a whisper.

Still maintaining his grip on her arm, Geoffrey propelled her toward the stairs and pushed her in front of him. Slowly, after throwing a tortured glance at him, she began to ascend. The house was simple: just one room below, and a second, for sleeping, above. The upper room had wide arched windows, draped with patterned cotton to allow a cooling breeze in and keep the burning sun out. The floor was of pale wood, and the only items of furniture were a bed, strewn with brightly coloured covers, and shelves on which various items of clothing were neatly stacked. Like the lower room, it was perfectly tidy—except for one thing.

The dead knight lay on his stomach, and the back of his grimy grey shirt was red with the clotting blood that had trickled to form a dark, irregular circle on the wood beneath him. Melisende inhaled sharply and turned away. Geoffrey saw her begin to cry. He looked back to the body, recognising with dismay the fair hair and delicate features of Sir John of Sourdeval. Geoffrey's stomach knotted painfully, and he found himself unable to move. Then the moment of shock passed, and Geoffrey rubbed his chin with his thumb and forefinger and looked away. John, a soft-spoken, thoughtful Norman, had been a good friend;

Geoffrey had often sought out his company when the other knights had become too rowdy and debauched.

"How did he come to be here?" Geoffrey asked, taking a deep breath and hoping Melisende Mikelos was too wrapped up in her horror at the body to be aware of his own. He went to the window to see whether it was possible to climb up from the outside. It was not.

She shrugged, her back still turned to him. "I do not know. I went out to visit my uncle, who lives near the Church of the Holy Sepulchre and came back a few moments ago, intending to rest until the heat of the day was past. I drank some wine downstairs, bathed my feet, and then came up here to lie down. He was there . . ." Her explanation was concluded with a sob.

"Do you know him?"

She shook her head, turning slightly so she could look at Geoffrey without seeing the dead man. "I have never seen him before," she whispered. "And I do not know how he came to be here. The door was locked, and my neighbours have just told me they saw no one enter." She gazed at him with enormous gold-brown eyes. "You must believe me! What reason could I have for a knight to be in my sleeping chamber?"

Geoffrey could think of one, but said nothing. He studied her intently. Younger than he had first thought, she was wearing the black that indicated she had been widowed, probably in the carnage of July 1099, he thought, when so many had been killed—Christian and Moslem alike—as the Crusaders took Jerusalem.

Nodding to one of his men to ensure Melisende did not run away, Geoffrey bent to examine John's body. The young knight was most assuredly dead, and his stiffened limbs and the dryness of the blood around the wound in his back indicated that he had been so for some hours. Geoffrey made a slit in the shirt, and looked at the single puncture mark that had killed him. It was a wide wound, and it could very well have been made by the curved Arab-style dagger Melisende had been clutching in the street.

Geoffrey sat back on his heels and reflected. Knights were not popular among the citizens of Jerusalem: it had been the knights who had led the slaughter that followed the city's fall. But while there were many knights who bragged about the number of people they had butchered, John was not among them. And besides, that was a year ago—if the motive were revenge, why should a killer decide to strike now?

Geoffrey glanced up to where Melisende regarded him with huge eyes that brimmed with tears. Her hands were stained with John's blood—either from the dagger she had been holding in the street, or from when she had murdered him.

"I did not kill this man," she whispered. "Please believe me."

"What I believe is irrelevant," said Geoffrey, trying to ascertain whether she was lying. "I am merely a knight. It is the Advocate you will need to convince. John was a favourite of his." And of mine too, he added silently, looking down at the lifeless body in front of him.

"I see," said Melisende, her voice suddenly hard. "You are yet another Norman incapable of independent thought, unless it is for repressing the local population. You are undoubtedly a nobody, some penniless younger son of an equally insignificant knight, who thinks to make his fortune from our land."

Geoffrey met her eyes, but did not answer—her accusation was true, at least in part. He was the youngest son of Sir Godric Mappestone, a knight who had followed William the Conqueror to England in 1066, and who had been rewarded for his bravery at the Battle of Hastings with a manor on the Welsh border. But, unlike most men in his position, Geoffrey cared little for making his fortune—indeed, he was generally indifferent to amassing wealth, and he usually found looting was more trouble than it was worth. Geoffrey's motive for joining the Crusade had been that it afforded him an excellent opportunity to travel. He had set out in high spirits, dreaming of the great libraries of the Arab world, and of an entire new culture of philosophy and literature about which he might learn. It was not a motive approved of or understood by his fellow knights, however, and Geoffrey had been regarded as something of an oddity from the outset.

John de Sourdeval had understood, though and had spent many hours discussing Arab writings with the scholarly English knight. Geoffrey's glance slid down to Melisende's bloodstained hands. Was she telling him the truth? Or had she murdered his gentle, honourable friend?

He shook his head impatiently. Now was not the time for speculation, not with his men travel-weary and a potentially hostile crowd gathering around. He grabbed a blanket from a neatly folded pile near the window, wrapped John in it, and told his men to carry the body downstairs. He glanced around quickly, but there was nothing else in the sparsely furnished chamber to give him any further clues. There was only one way into the room—up the stairs the way he had come—and if John had had any belongings with him when he was dispatched to meet his maker, they were not with him now.

Geoffrey took Melisende's arm again and led her out of her house into the street. His first thought was to find the knife she had hurled away from her, but there was no sign of it. He glanced at the crowd and was not surprised. The dagger had been a fine weapon with a jewelled hilt that looked valuable. It would doubtless fetch a good price at the market.

Sergeant Helbye was haggling with a scruffy-looking fig seller for the loan of his cart to transport John's body back to the citadel on the other side of the city. The citadel was where the Advocate, Jerusalem's military leader, had his headquarters, and where many of the knights, including Geoffrey, chose to live.

The crowd in the street was becoming larger with each passing moment, despite the searing heat of the early afternoon sun. Geoffrey saw his soldiers' increasing alarm: two had unslung their bows and had arrows at the ready. He overrode the indignant protestations of the fig seller and heaved John's blanketed body onto the cart. Seizing Melisende by the wrist, he shouted orders to his men and set off, the disconsolate fig seller trotting along beside them, bewailing the fact that his fruit was being crushed.

The crowd parted to let them through, but Geoffrey sensed a resentment that had not been there earlier. A small child darted forward and tried to press a knife into Melisende's hand. People became ominously silent, and Geoffrey was aware of his soldiers preparing themselves for a fight. Here and there, a flash of steel caught the sunlight as men in the crowd drew an odd assortment of concealed weapons from their clothing—kitchen knives, sticks, and even a discarded horseshoe. The silence of the crowd was now a tangible thing, sinister and menacing.

"Let me go," said Melisende in a low voice to Geoffrey. "It is because you are taking me that these people are angry. Let me go, and you will be allowed to leave unmolested with your men."

"If you are innocent of this knight's murder, as you claim, then you have nothing to fear," said Geoffrey, not slowing his pace.

The woman snorted in derision. "Who at the citadel will believe me?" she said. "You do not."

This was true, Geoffrey reflected: he did not. One of his men gave a sharp yelp and put his hand to his head.

"Keep moving," said Helbye in a calm voice to the jittery soldiers. "They are only throwing stones. You are wearing mail; they cannot harm you."

"Not much!" muttered the soldier with the bleeding head, but he kept walking. Geoffrey handed Melisende to Ned Fletcher, a slow but reliable soldier in his forties, and drew his sword. The crowd was following them along the street, hurling a hail of stones and other missiles after them. As the soldiers rounded the corner, the throng broke into a trot, and Geoffrey yelled for his men to run. His dog, true to character, had sensed the menace in the onlookers and had long since fled. Several of the soldiers fumbled to fit arrows to their bows, but Geoffrey ordered them to stop. Such an incident could turn into a bloodbath within moments, and he had no wish to be responsible for a skirmish that would cause the deaths of the women and children he could see among the crowd, or of his men.

A stone struck him hard in the chest, and a roar of approval went up from those at the front of the advancing mob. His chain mail and padded surcoat protected him from injury, but the force of the throw made him stagger. He collided with Helbye, who was close behind him, and before he could right himself, his leather-soled boots had slipped in some of the figs that had fallen from the cart, and he was down. With a howl of delight, the mob rushed forward, and Geoffrey struggled in vain to clamber to his feet. He yelled to Helbye to run, but saw him stand firm with his weapon drawn, preparing to protect his fallen leader.

Geoffrey closed his eyes in despair. What a stupid way to end his life, after the trials and torments of the gruelling three-year journey to Jerusalem from England! He did not usually dwell on the manner of his death, but on the few occasions when it had come to mind, he imagined himself falling in battle or dying peacefully in bed in his dotage. That he would be ripped from limb to limb by a horde armed with sticks and stones after he had slipped on some figs had never occurred to him.

The sun was blocked out as the furious citizens converged on him, but just as quickly returned. Geoffrey felt, rather than heard, the thud of horses' hooves on the beaten earth of the road, and the street erupted into chaos. Yells and screams combined with the terrified whinnies of war-horses as the crowd and the mounted monk-knights of the Order of St. John Hospitaller clashed. Geoffrey covered his head with his hands to protect it and tried to stand, but was knocked down again by a man racing to escape the Hospitallers' whirling swords and maces.

As quickly as it had started, it was over, and the commotion faded away. Geoffrey felt someone take a firm hold on the back of his surcoat and haul him to his feet. Dusty, bedraggled, and deflated, he was not pleased to find himself face to face with Edouard de Courrances, a man Geoffrey detested above all others. Courrances was trusted adviser to the Advocate—the man who had been crowned as official ruler of Jerusalem the previous year.

"My men?" Geoffrey gasped, peering through the clouds of settling dust to try to see whether any were injured.

"Running away, as ordered by their leader," replied Courrances nonchalantly, sheathing his sword. "You were lucky we happened to be passing, or you would not now be alive to rally your motley gang together."

Geoffrey said nothing, irritated that it had been Courrances of all people who had witnessed the ignominious skirmish and who had effected his rescue. The monks of the Order of St. John Hospitaller ran the great hospital in Jerusalem for needy pilgrims, but recently, some of the monks had abandoned their policy of nonaggression and had taken up arms to protect themselves and their property. Over his monastic habit, Courrances wore a surcoat of black with a white cross emblazoned on the back, and Geoffrey had seldom seen him without the arsenal of weapons he carried. Ten or so similarly clad warrior-monks were with Courrances now, mounted on sturdy war-horses and armed to the teeth.

Geoffrey glanced about him and saw that several of the mob lay dead or injured, and were being carried away by friends and relatives. One was the small boy who had tried to press the knife into Melisende's hand. The Hospitallers sat astride their restless horses, their weapons still unsheathed, clearly itching to fight again. The crowd gathered their fallen comrades and slunk away, hatred and fear burning in their eyes.

"These were unarmed people," protested Geoffrey, turning to Courrances angrily. "We are under orders to maintain the peace, not massacre civilians!"

"Oh, well said, Sir Geoffrey," responded Courrances with maddening serenity. "Would you rather I let them kill you? And let us be honest about this—you had antagonised them into rioting long before I arrived on the scene, so do not seek to blame me for the deaths of these people. If anyone was at fault, it was you."

Geoffrey scowled, aware that Courrances was right. He should have let Melisende go, and then sent soldiers for her later when there was no crowd to witness her arrest.

"John of Sourdeval has been murdered," he said, changing the subject and squinting against the sun to look Courrances in the eye. He was gratified to see the soldier-monk blanch. "Stabbed in the back. That is how Sir Guido of Rimini died three weeks ago, is it not?"

"A second knight murdered?" asked Courrances in a low voice. He drummed his long, well-kept fingers on the pommel of his saddle. "This is grave news indeed."

"Did you see Guido's body?" asked Geoffrey, watching as his men, under Helbye's direction, began to reassemble on the opposite side of the street. Fletcher still had Melisende in tow, and John was still wrapped in his blanket on the cart. The fig seller was nowhere to be seen, and Geoffrey felt sorry: the cart was probably all the man owned, and its loss would have serious consequences for him. Geoffrey's fat, cowardly dog, back again now that the danger was over, began to gorge itself on the unattended fruit.

"I saw it," said Courrances. "And I am told that the weapon used was a great carved dagger with a jewelled hilt—you know the kind I mean? Wicked looking things, but cheap and gaudy. They can be bought in the marketplace."

Geoffrey rubbed his chin thoughtfully and looked at Courrances. "Almost as if the murderer did not want to use his own weapon?"

Courrances gazed back at him. "Quite. As if he wanted to ensure that there was nothing that could connect him to his victims."

"I trust you were suitably grateful to Edouard de Courrances for his timely arrival," said Sir Hugh of Monreale, settling himself more comfortably by the small fire in Geoffrey's quarters. It was not cold, even within the dank, thick walls of the citadel, but Geoffrey liked a fire when he was in his chamber: it provided him with light should he want to read, and it offered some degree of homeliness in a room devoid of most comforts.

Geoffrey snorted in disgust. "He killed unarmed people."

"There is no such thing as an unarmed person," mused

Hugh. He flexed his fingers at his friend. "Hands that can punch, twist, gouge, and scratch." He gestured to his legs. "Feet that can kick and trample." He pointed to his mouth. "And sharp teeth that can rip and puncture. There is no such thing as an unarmed person. You are a soldier, Geoffrey—you should know that. Anyway, from what you say, those unarmed people were going to kill you."

Geoffrey studied Hugh through half-closed eyes. They had met on the long, gruelling journey across the deserts outside Constantinople. Hugh, like Geoffrey, was a landless younger son of a Norman noble. He had been born in Sicily and had been in the service of Bohemond, one of the leaders of the Crusade, since childhood. Unlike Geoffrey, Hugh was still bitter at the twist of fate that gave his eldest brother more lands and wealth than he knew how to handle, but had left Hugh empty-handed. But Hugh was not a man to languish in self-pity, and like many Normans, he saw the Crusade to the Holy Land as an opportunity to take for himself what had been denied by his birth. And there had been plenty of opportunity to amass a fortune as the great Crusading armies had sacked and looted their way from the West into the Holy Land. Most knights had chests of booty in their possession, and Hugh, who was not given to drinking, whoring, or gambling, had a chest that was larger and fuller than most.

"A letter arrived for you today," said Hugh languidly. He held it up. "It is stained with grass, and the handwriting is appalling, so I draw the inevitable conclusion that it is from your father at his noble castle on the manor of Goodrich in England."

Geoffrey scowled at him and snatched the letter from his hand. The parchment bore signs of its long journey from the Welsh borders, and the spiky, ill-formed handwriting was that of his father's clerk—a man whose employment depended on the fact that Geoffrey's father was illiterate and wholly unable to tell good script from bad. Geoffrey broke the seal with a mixture of foreboding and curiosity, for his father had written to him only twice since he had been sent away to commence his knightly training almost twenty years before—once to tell him that his younger sister had died, and once to inform him that a new flock of sheep was thriving on the manor.

He smoothed out the cheap parchment and strained to decipher the words, reading them aloud to Hugh. "My son Godfrey," he read. Geoffrey sighed and wondered whether it was really too much to ask that between them, the clerk and his father might get his name right. Hugh spluttered with laughter.

"What news from the land of sheep and rain?" he enquired, his eyes glittering with amusement. "Are all the ewes in fine breeding form? Are the slugs still a trial to the cabbages? Does your mother still wail that you failed to become a priest as she intended?"

"My brothers send me their greetings," said Geoffrey, turning the letter this way and that in the firelight, trying to read the spidery text.

"I should hope so!" exclaimed Hugh. "You did them a great service when you allowed yourself to be dispatched to France in the service of the Duke of Normandy at the age of twelve! Had you stayed in England, your avaricious brothers would be in constant dread that you would be attempting to wrest their paltry inheritances from them!"

Geoffrey shot Hugh another unpleasant look, but knew he spoke the truth. Geoffrey's mother had determined that the youngest of her four sons should become a monk, but while Geoffrey enjoyed the study, he proved himself wholly unsuited to a life of monastic obedience. Seeing that Geoffrey at twelve years of age was taller, stronger, and distinctly more intelligent than his older brothers, his father hastily dispatched him to France to train as a knight. This had the twofold advantage of providing Geoffrey with a vocation, and of keeping him away from home—Geoffrey's father considered he had enough trouble with three sons waging a constant battle over the eventual division of Goodrich manor, and he was more than relieved to rid himself of a fourth.

"My sister-in-law has died," said Geoffrey, peering at the letter. "But he does not say which one. And the black bull called Baron has also gone to meet his maker . . ."

Hugh roared with laughter again. "Your family are priceless! They describe the bull and give its name, but do not provide the same service for your sister-in-law! You owe your father a great debt of gratitude by sending you to Normandy, my friend. Or you might have ended up like your brothers—greedy, petty, and thinking only of livestock!"

"I did not want to become a knight," said Geoffrey, looking up from his letter and watching the humour fade from Hugh's face. "I wanted to go to Paris—to the university to study. I ran away from the Duke of Normandy several times, but was always caught and taken back."

"A scholar?" asked Hugh, shaking his head and smiling indulgently. "So you would rather be living in squalid, cramped quarters in some seedy hall, teaching snivelling youths about Aristotle than enjoying life as a Crusader knight?"

Geoffrey eyed him askance and gestured around his chamber. "Where lies the difference? Here are squalid, cramped living quarters, and there are snivelling youths aplenty among my men. And yes—I would rather be teaching them about Aristotle than how to set up an ambush. At least in Paris, I would not be forced to kill anyone."

"Rubbish!" spat Hugh. "There is nothing so dangerous as a man of learning, and the streets of Paris are more treacherous by far than the streets of Jerusalem. But this is reckless talk, Geoffrey. What would our fellow knights think if they heard of your qualms?"

Geoffrey shrugged. "I do not care what their opinions might be. Most of them have held me in deep suspicion ever since I chose books over gold after the siege of Antioch. That these texts are worth ten times their weight in gold anyway—quite apart from the brilliance of the learning contained within them— seems a concept quite beyond their grasp."

"I have often wondered what led you to choose to come

Crusading in the first place, given that you seem to abhor killing and are indifferent to looting. You must have guessed how such a venture might have ended."

Geoffrey stared into the fire, his letter forgotten as he remembered the events leading to the day when he had learned of the Crusade. "Once I realised I would not escape from the Duke of Normandy to become a scholar, I settled down to life as a knight in training. I still read as much as I could find, and eventually was sent as tutor to Lord Tancred in Italy. He was fifteen and far more interested in developing his physical abilities than his intellectual ones, but despite our differences, we came to respect each other well enough."

"You are too modest," said Hugh. "Tancred does more than respect you. He trusts your judgement absolutely, and thinks highly of your skills—both as a knight and a scholar. You have been invaluable to him throughout this entire Crusade, and he considers you his most worthy adviser."

"Hardly," said Geoffrey, startled. "He mocks my learning constantly, and his uncle, Bohemond, is actively hostile to it."

"But Bohemond is no fool," said Hugh. "As you know, I have been in his service since I was a child, and I have come to respect him like I respect no other man, except perhaps you." Geoffrey looked away, embarrassed at Hugh's blunt expression of friendship. Hugh saw his discomfort and smiled before continuing. "Bohemond might gripe and bluster, but he knows how useful you have been to his nephew. He is quite resentful that the Duke of Normandy assigned you to Tancred, and not to him— he would dearly love to have you in his retinue. But all this has not answered my question. Why did you agree to come on Crusade in the first place?"

Geoffrey sighed as he recalled events that had occurred three years before. "Tancred and Bohemond were besieging Amalfi— a wealthy merchant town that had found itself on the wrong side of Bohemond. One day, Tancred and I saw groups of men riding past with red crosses sewn onto the backs of their surcoats. Tancred's brother was among them, and he told us that the Pope had called for all Christians to set out for the Holy Land to free it from the infidel. Bohemond and Tancred alike saw an opportunity to gain a fortune and lands beyond their wildest dreams. They abandoned the siege of Amalfi that same day and set about raising their troops so that they might lead the Crusade. You, I take it, were among them?"

Hugh nodded. "I was on Bohemond's business in Germany at the time. But when I heard the Pope's call, I knew Bohemond would rally to it. I hastened to him as fast as I could get a horse to carry me, and we were off toward the Holy Land within the month. But you are being obtuse with me, Geoffrey. Why did you follow Tancred? Surely he would have agreed if you had asked to be left behind in Italy?"

Geoffrey gave him a look of disbelief. "He most certainly would not! When young Tancred left his home in Italy, he knew he would never return. It is his intention to carve out a kingdom for himself in the Holy Land—just as Bohemond means to do and Tancred wants me with him. And I was willing enough, because I had read a little of Arab philosophy and medicine, and I saw it as an opportunity to learn more."

"So that was your motive?" asked Hugh. "Learning and books?" He smiled suddenly. "I had guessed as much, knowing you as I do. And have you discovered what you hoped to find?"

"I have not!" said Geoffrey vehemently. Hugh looked startled at the force of his words. "I have found bloodshed, massacres, disease, flies, dust, and hatred. And we are so concerned with the basics of our survival here that there is little time for learning."

"Come now," said Hugh, still smiling. "It is not so bad. You are learning Arabic, I heard, so you are at least achieving something! But we are growing maudlin here, by your fire. We need some diversion. Continue reading your father's letter. That should suffice."

Geoffrey dragged his thoughts back to the home he had not seen for years, and tried to concentrate on his father's disjointed letter. "He has hanged three Welshmen who he believes were stealing his sheep. Lord help us, Hugh! The man is a fool! I doubt very much he has the real culprits, and he is likely to bring the fury of the hanged men's relatives upon himself with such a rash act."

"And what would you have done?" asked Hugh, stretching his hands toward the fire, although the room was not cold.

"Tried to parley with the villages I believed were stealing," said Geoffrey. "Or set a better watch over the sheep during vulnerable times to prevent the thefts in the first place."

Hugh snorted in derision. "Your father was right when he sent you away from his flocks! You are far too soft to be the lord of a manor!"

"And now we come to the real purpose of my father's letter," said Geoffrey, ignoring Hugh and reading on. "He observes that I am careless for riches, but asks that I remember that Goodrich Castle is in sore need of stone walls, and there is a fine ram in the next village he would like to own."

Hugh laughed softly, while Geoffrey crumpled the letter and thrust it into the fire. It hissed and sizzled, sending a shower of sparks up the chimney. Geoffrey leaned forward to prod at it, while Hugh replenished their goblets with the sour wine that Geoffrey had begged from the citadel's cellars. Hugh allowed his long, graceful body to recline on the hard bed, and sipped carefully at the wine.

"Devil's brew!" he exclaimed, wincing at its sharpness. "Do you have nothing better?" He eyed his friend resentfully and placed the goblet on the floor. Geoffrey's dog padded over to it with interest, but walked away in disdain after the briefest of sniffs. Hugh watched it, his fair hair flopping over one bright blue eye. "So, what did you do with this woman you arrested this afternoon? You were far from kindly with her!"

Geoffrey shrugged, still poking the fire. "She seemed too shocked at Courrances's murderous tactics for further conversation with me. I handed her over to the Advocate's men. But then the Patriarch asked to question her because apparently two monks were murdered at the same time as Sir Guido three weeks ago. The Patriarch seems to believe that they may be connected. Since the Advocate is away in Jaffa, Melisende Mikelos was transferred to the Patriarch's palace for questioning, and she will be brought back here to the citadel when the Advocate returns."

The Advocate of the Holy Sepulchre was the impressive title adopted by Godfrey, Duke of Lower Lorraine, who had been the leader of one of the Crusader armies that had left France to reclaim Jerusalem; now he was in overall command of the city. Meanwhile, the Patriarch—an ambitious Italian called Daimbert—was the head of the Latin Church in the Holy Land. There was a constant power struggle between these two men and their supporters, and knights like Geoffrey and Hugh often found themselves drawn into their disputes. Geoffrey's lord, Tancred, and Hugh's, Bohemond, both powerful leaders themselves, were firmly allied to the Patriarch, a fact that made the Advocate wary of knights like Geoffrey and Hugh, who lived in his citadel.

"Why did you arrest this woman at all?" asked Hugh, breaking into Geoffrey's thoughts as he, too, poked at the fire. "No one arrested the monks at the Dome of the Rock who found the body of Sir Guido of Rimini."

"I had the impression she was not telling the truth," said Geoffrey with a shrug. "And poor John lay dead on the floor in front of her. Would you wish his murderer to go free?"

"Of course not," said Hugh soothingly. "You knew John much better than I did. But you must not allow friendship to cloud your judgement. What was he doing in her house anyway?"

Geoffrey had been wondering the same thing, but said nothing.

"You may have condemned her to death," continued Hugh idly. "It is possible she had nothing to do with the death of John, as she claimed, but she may pay the price regardless."

"She was holding the murder weapon, Hugh. What woman would stride over to a dead knight—according to her an unexpected and most unwelcome guest on her bedroom floor—hoist the dagger from his back, and run outside with it?" Geoffrey stood abruptly and began to pace in the small room. As he walked, he was aware that his legs were tired and stiff from his exertions on desert patrol, and he knew that he should rest. He was exhausted by the constant need for vigilance and the sheer physical grind of walking in the heat wearing chain mail and surcoat. Most knights rode, but Geoffrey found horses unsuitable for patrolling in the ferocious heat, and so he usually walked with his men.

"You are too inflexible in your thinking, my friend," began Hugh. Anticipating a lecture, Geoffrey sat down and closed his eyes wearily.

Hugh, undaunted by his friend's clear lack of interest, continued. "You say she had been out visiting her uncle, and she had only arrived back a few moments before she discovered the corpse. This means that she had walked across the city at the hottest time of day. She would have been sticky and tired. She said she drank wine and bathed her feet before going to rest. She must have been telling you the truth, because what woman admits to a man such personal details as washing her feet?

"Now, imagine her wearily climbing the stairs, longing to lie down in the coolness of her sleeping chamber, and what does she see? A bloodied corpse on the floor! You are a soldier used to such things, but she is a young woman who is not. Her reaction would have been one of disbelief. She would have touched the body to make certain her long walk in the sun had not made her hallucinate, and she would have touched the dagger. She did not say she hoisted it from his back: that was an assumption you made with no evidence to support it. Perhaps the dagger was lying on the floor next to John. So, she picked it up from its bloody pool in horror at her discovery, and then fled outside. You heard her scream. She then flung the knife from her when she realized that she still held it after you began to question her."

Geoffrey eyed him thoughtfully. "The knife had disappeared when I thought to look for it later, which was unfortunate. If we had it, we could compare it to the dagger that killed Sir Guido."

"True. And if the woman you arrested is executed as a murderer, and another knight is killed, we will know that she was innocent."

"I am sure she will be pleased to hear it," said Geoffrey dryly.

"But it is none of our concern. The Patriarch's clerks are investigating the matter now, and then the Advocate will decide what should be done with her when he returns."

"The Patriarch has a difficult task," said Hugh with sudden seriousness. "He is here to wrest control of Jerusalem from the Advocate and hand it to the Pope. Meanwhile, the rioting of today underlines that the Greek Church bitterly resents the superiority of the Latin Church, and will rebel against it at every opportunity. Then there is the Latin Church itself—the Benedictines control the Church of the Holy Sepulchre, but the Augustinians and Cistercians feel they should be in charge, and they petition the Patriarch about it constantly. Meanwhile, the Hospitallers, headed by your friend Edouard de Courrances, are supposed to care for sick pilgrims, but Courrances is as good a fighter as I have seen, and he parades around the city letting everyone know that he is more warrior than monk. And to top it all, the real enemy—the infidel—laughs at us as we fight among ourselves."

Geoffrey smiled. "True enough. To be honest, I wonder whether it is time to leave here, and be away from all this bickering."

"But you are in the employ of Tancred," said Hugh. "How would he manage without you? You are his eyes and ears in this pit of intrigue."

Geoffrey looked at him in horror. "Is that what you think? That Tancred sees me as his spy?"

Hugh made a dismissive gesture. "Not in a sinister way, but no one can deny you are useful to him. But you are right, Geoffrey. The time for soldiering is over: perhaps we should leave the city for the diplomats and politicians to haggle over."

"And kill for," said Geoffrey. "Like John and Guido."

Hugh scrubbed at his smooth cheeks and stared into the fire. When he looked up again, Geoffrey was asleep, long legs stretched out comfortably, the flickering light making shadows of the etched lines about his mouth. Hugh leaned back in his chair and studied his friend's soldierly features: brown hair cut short in

Norman fashion, clean-shaven chin, and strong, long-fingered hands. He was about to rise and go to his own bed in a chamber on the floor above, when there was a sharp knock at the door. Geoffrey was on his feet with his sword at the ready before Hugh could even reply. The fair-haired knight made a motion of disbelief at Geoffrey's distrust, even locked up safe for the night in the citadel, making Geoffrey grin sheepishly.

Geoffrey opened the door and admitted Helbye.

"Lord Tancred asks that you attend him," Helbye said, his words chosen hesitantly, for he was a fighting man, not a messenger, by nature.

"Now?" asked Geoffrey in disbelief, glancing at the darkness through the open window. "It is well past the curfew."

"Now," said Helbye. "He is a guest at the Patriarch's palace tonight." He paused, looking at the glowing embers of the fire. "I think he wants you for more than desert duties this time. A priest has just been found dead. The man who found the body says that the murder weapon was a curved dagger with a jewelled hilt."

CHAPTER TWO

Geoffrey walked alone through the dark streets toward the handsome palace that the Patriarch had requisitioned for himself and his sizeable retinue. Although it was only a short distance from the great, square keep of the citadel, Geoffrey was wary. The roads were empty after the dusk curfew, but his sharp eyes detected shadows flitting here and there, and at night the city seemed even more uneasy than during the day. It was late, and all God-fearing people should have been abed, sleeping after an exhausting day of honest labour under the Holy Land's blazing sun. But the city did not sleep, and Geoffrey was painfully aware that his progress through the shadowy streets was watched with interest by more than one onlooker.

He forced himself to think about the business at hand. He was aware of the wild rumours that flew around the Crusader community regarding the murder of Sir Guido of Rimini three weeks before. Why anyone would want to kill the quiet Italian was a mystery to all, and his untimely death at the hands an Arab-style scimitar had been blamed on all manner of people: on wicked Greek priests from the Eastern Orthodox Church; on the aggressive Order of Benedictines, who bickered for power with other monks; on the little Jewish community who lived near the towering western wall and who tried to keep as far away from the squabbling Christians as possible; and on the handful of Moslems who had miraculously survived the massacre when the Crusaders had taken Jerusalem the previous year.

So which of these rumours was true? Or were they all wrong, and was there something even more sinister afoot? Geoffrey narrowed his eyes in thought as he walked. The Crusaders had set out on a golden cloud of piety and hope to rout unbelievers from the most holy place in the world. But the rot had begun to fester within days: Crusaders from one country refused to cooperate with those from another, and their leaders were all in desperate competition for power and riches. By the time the ragged, disease-depleted, greedy, undisciplined rabble had reached Jerusalem three years later, any illusion that this was a just war fought by God's heroes had long been shattered.

Geoffrey jumped as a dark shadow glided across his path, and forced himself to relax when he saw the dull gleam of a cat's yellow eyes. He was relieved when the dim lights of the Patriarch's palace came into view. There were always lights burning at the Patriarch's headquarters, as there were always candles glimmering at the windows of the citadel, where the Advocate lived. Geoffrey headed for the wicket gate in the huge bronze-plated door at the front of the palace, and knocked. It was opened at once—and slammed shut as soon as he had been ushered inside.

He was led through a maze of tiled corridors, off which doors of distinctive eastern design led. He had been in the palace on several occasions, but never at night and never further than the great state room in which the Patriarch conducted his public business. Now he was escorted to a small chamber on an upper floor, where he was furnished with a goblet of spiced wine and then abandoned. He looked around him. The little room was a far cry from the sumptuous hall below: worn carpets of faded colours replaced the glorious mosaic of the hall floor, and instead of the fabulous gilt-painted murals and Byzantine pillars there were plain whitewashed walls. Under the window was a roughly made table, piled high with parchments and scrolls. Naturally curious, Geoffrey unrolled one and began to read.

"Do you possess a knowledge of astronomy, as well as your other skills?"

Geoffrey turned with a smile of greeting to Tancred, and replaced the scroll on the table. Tancred, like his uncle Bohemond, was a formidable figure—tall, broad-shouldered, and with massive chest and arms. He kept his fair hair unusually short for a western knight, and like Geoffrey, he was clean-shaven. He came toward his old tutor with a welcoming grin.

"I heard you returned today from the desert. Any news?"

Geoffrey shook his head. "We found several abandoned camps and were attacked twice, but we uncovered no evidence that Arab forces are massing in the east. I suppose an attack, if there is one, will come from the Fatamids in Egypt."

Tancred shrugged. "You are probably right, but it is best to be sure. You were gone so long, I wondered whether you were coming back."

Geoffrey looked at him sharply, wondering whether this intelligent, perceptive young man was aware of his misgivings about remaining in Jerusalem. Most of the Crusaders had gone already—either back to their homes in the West or to richer pickings in lands more prosperous than the parched, arid desert around the Holy City.

He raised his hands in a shrug. "Perhaps it is time to be thinking of returning home."

"Home?" echoed Tancred. "Home to what? Your sheep-farming brothers, who regard you with such suspicion, because they think that you have come to wrest away their meagre inheritance with your superior fighting skills? To those monasteries and their dusty books?"

"Why not?" asked Geoffrey, irritated that the younger man should be questioning his motives. "I am tired of trudging around baking deserts weighed down with chain mail looking for phantom Saracens. I would not mind sitting in the cool of a cloister reading mathematics or philosophy." He paused. "And I miss England. I find myself longing for the green of its forests, and the heather-clad hills of autumn."

Tancred gaped at him in disbelief. "My God, man!" he breathed. "Have you become a poet all of a sudden? Where is your manhood?" He gestured with his hand. "There are riches for the taking in this land, and you hanker after the wet trees and flowers of England! You have not even lived there for twenty years!"

Geoffrey felt his temper begin to fray. He was tired from his patrolling, and his reasons for embarking on the Crusade had already been well and truly aired by Hugh that evening. He had no wish to be ridiculed a second time within the space of an hour.

"I do not want riches, and I grow sick of the slaughter here."

Tancred made an exasperated sound. "And here we reach the nub of the issue: the slaughter. You were always squeamish about such matters. I have heard how you declined to slay the infidel when we took Jerusalem."

"The infidel we found were mostly women and children," objected Geoffrey hotly. "And, besides, not all who were slain were infidels—many were Christians. In the frenzy of killing, even some of our own monks and soldiers were slaughtered. The massacre was so indiscriminate that it included anyone unable to defend himself. What man would want to take part in so foul a business?"

"Most of your colleagues," said Tancred dryly. "Why not, when the rule of the day was that plunder belonged to the man who killed its owner?"

"It is exactly that kind of lawlessness that I find repellent," said Geoffrey wearily. "Perhaps you are right, and I have lost my spirit. But I have had enough."

"Come, Sir Geoffrey," said Tancred dismissively. "You are a knight, trained to fight since childhood. What else would you do? There is nothing for you on your father's manor in England— that is why he sent you away in the first place, is it not? Where would you go? Despite your monkish tendency toward books and scrolls, you are too independent a thinker to become a priest. You would not survive for a week, before you were thrown out for refusing to be obedient. Look at you now, questioning me, your liege lord!"

Guiltily, Geoffrey looked away. He was fortunate that Tancred tolerated his occasional bouts of insubordination. Bohemond certainly would not have done so. In his heart of hearts, Geoffrey knew Tancred was right. If he forswore his knighthood, there was little else he could do. He was too old to become a scholar, and he had no intention of taking a vow of chastity to become a monk.

Tancred walked to the table and picked up the scroll Geoffrey had been reading. "This is a treatise on why shooting stars can be seen at certain times of the year and not others," he said, changing the subject. "By an Arab astrologer. Are you familiar with his work?"

Geoffrey nodded impatiently. "I have read his theories on shooting stars," he said. "But I believe them to be fatally flawed. These heavenly bodies are seen in the summer months, but not in the winter, and I think it must have something to do with heat."

"You believe the Earth can influence the movements of the heavens?" queried Tancred. "Archbishop Daimbert would say that is heresy, Sir Geoffrey. The heavens are ruled by God, not the Earth."

Geoffrey sighed. "I did not say the Earth causes the stars to fall only in the summer," he said, trying not to sound patronising. "Perhaps they fall all year, but conditions on the Earth are such that we can only see them in the summer."

Tancred chewed throughtfully on his lower lip. "That is an interesting concept," he said, smiling suddenly. "You are among very few here who possess scholarly knowledge." He raised his hand to preempt Geoffrey's objections. "Oh, the priests are educated and know all manner of things, but they do not think as you do. And they do not speak the languages that you can— French, Italian, Latin, and Greek. Do not think of returning to your sheep yet, Geoffrey. I have need of you here. Helbye tells me you are learning Arabic?"

Geoffrey frowned, discomfited that his men should be telling stories about him. "It is a way of unlocking some of the secrets of Saracen knowledge," he answered carefully. "They are far ahead of us in so many ways: medicine, astrology, mathematics, architecture . . ."

"I understand your admiration," said Tancred sharply, "although I do not share it. But by your own admission, there is much with which you can satisfy your insatiable yearning for knowledge here, especially if you master Arabic. Stay and learn— I will release you from desert patrols if it makes you happy. And while you learn, you can solve a riddle for me."

"What riddle?" asked Geoffrey suspiciously, anticipating a trap.

"The deaths of these two knights," said Tancred. "And three priests. I thought perhaps you had solved the case when you brought that Mikelos woman here earlier today, but even as I questioned her, her innocence was being proven, as a fifth victim was killed using these carved daggers. Thus, the killer could not have been her, and it seems she is what she says: an honourable widow whose house was chosen at random for John of Sourdeval's murder."

He perched on the edge of the table and looked solemnly at Geoffrey. "I know I often ask you to do things well beyond any obligation, but our comradeship has benefitted us both at times. And now I need you again. These two knights—Guido and John—were in my uncle Bohemond's service. Their murders represent an attack against the Normans in Jerusalem, and that includes both you and me. You are good with riddles—you solved the mystery of those thefts back in Nicaea when all the priests and scholars were at their wits' end. That shows that you can get to the bottom of affairs such as this. You can be subtle, wily, and dare I say, even devious, to find out what you need. I would like you to serve me again and to solve these murders."

Geoffrey ran a hand through his hair. He could hardly refuse Tancred—despite his reluctance to undertake such duties, he was still in Tancred's service and would be until Tancred agreed to release him. He was vaguely amused to note that Tancred was asking, rather than ordering, him to help. In this way, Geoffrey would be his willing agent, not merely a hired hand, which would eliminate any resentment that might have interfered with Geoffrey's solving of the case. He smiled suddenly, out of respect for Tancred's transparent, but effective, cunning.

"What do you know of these murders?" he asked.

Tancred grinned back, aware that Geoffrey had seen through his ruse, but also aware that he had won his former mentor's cooperation. He sat on a stool and gestured for Geoffrey to sit next to him. "Little, I am afraid. Five men have died in similar circumstances so far: the two knights and three priests. The three priests seem to have been murdered with a weapon identical to that which was used to kill the knights."

He paused for a moment and chewed at his thumbnail. "The first victim was Sir Guido of Rimini, whose body was discovered about three weeks ago under a tree in the gardens of the Dome of the Rock. The second was a Benedictine monk, Brother Jocelyn from France. He died two days after Guido, and his body was found *inside* the church at the Dome of the Rock. The third was a Cluniac, Brother Pius from Spain, who was found dead in the house of a Greek butcher. His body was discovered the same morning as Brother Jocelyn's. Then there was John of Sourdeval—a friend of yours, I believe—whom you found in a house in the Greek Quarter earlier today. And news came a short while ago that a Greek priest named Loukas has been killed in the Church of the Holy Sepulchre. So, the priests are not from the same Order, not from the same country, and not even from the same Church, because Loukas is Greek Orthodox and the others are Latin. But both knights were in Bohemond's service."

"Surely the Patriarch is investigating these priest's deaths?" asked Geoffrey. "After all, they are under his jurisdiction—not yours, not the Advocate's, and not Bohemond's."

Tancred's eyes flashed briefly at this impertinence, but his temper cooled as quickly as it had flared. "The Patriarch is having no success at all. I discussed this business with him tonight, after news came of the last killing. I see the murders of these men as a direct attack on our authority here. How do we know it is not a diabolical plan to expose our vulnerability in Jerusalem and to incite our enemies to attack us? We are surrounded by hostile forces, and yet we are so full of factions and rifts that, if struck in the right place, the fragile alliances with our fellow Christians might shatter like glass. And then we will all die, ripped apart by an enemy who is watching constantly for such holes in our armour. There is more at stake than the deaths of two knights and three monks: I believe this business might affect our very survival in the Holy Land, let alone the possibilities of establishing other kingdoms."

And there we have it, thought Geoffrey. Young Tancred—who only a few short months before had become Prince of Galilee—wanted a kingdom of his own. And Tancred could never have a kingdom unless Jerusalem was safe.

Unaware of Geoffrey's reservations, Tancred continued. "Since the first victim was killed, the Patriarch has had two clerks investigating, but they have come up with nothing. I have acquired a copy of their report, so that you might study it at your leisure." He handed Geoffrey a scroll. "You may question the clerks further if you wish. Their names are Brothers Marius and Dunstan, and they work in the Patriarch's scriptorium."

Tancred rose, and sensing the interview was at an end, Geoffrey also stood. Tancred gave another sudden smile, one that made him look even younger than his twenty-three years, and gently touched Geoffrey's shoulder.

"I am grateful to you for doing this," he said. "I believe it may be more important than either of us can know."

For some reason, his words struck a feeling of cold unease in the pit of Geoffrey's stomach.

His mind teeming with questions, Geoffrey made his way back through the deserted streets to the citadel. He had not gone far when he thought he heard a noise behind him, and he immediately sprang into the deep shadows of a doorway, dagger drawn, to wait. He stood immobile for several moments before thinking he must have been mistaken, and cautiously eased himself out into the road again. He looked carefully in both directions, but the street was as silent and still as the grave, and not even a rat disturbed it. Forcing himself to relax, he walked on again, faster this time, and with his dagger still drawn.

Moments later, he thought he heard a sound again—the soft slither of leather soles on the parched, dry dust of the street. He turned abruptly into one of the many narrow alleyways that turned the city into a labyrinth, and he cut sharply left, then right, and waited. Sure enough, there were footsteps behind him, running, desperate to catch up with him before he became invisible in the complex catacomb of runnels. He listened hard, eyes closed in concentration. Not one set of footsteps, but two, or possibly three. Who could be following him so intently in the middle of the night? It could not be casual robbers: first, his padded surcoat with its faded Crusader's cross sewn on the back identified him as a knight, a trained warrior whom robbers would be hard pushed to best in hand-to-hand conflict; and second, his pursuers were being remarkably persistent for a chance attack.

Still listening, Geoffrey weighed his options. He was armed with a short sword and a dagger, and he was skilled in the use of both. He also wore a light mail shirt under his surcoat, and so was reasonably well protected, while still able to move unhindered by heavy body armour. He was in no doubt that he could take on three opportunistic thieves, but not three knights trained like himself. He decided caution was the order of the day, and sank back further into the shadows.

Within moments, three men shot past, fleet-footed and confident. One skidded to a halt so close that Geoffrey could have stretched out his hand and touched him. The man glared up and down the empty alleyway as if just by looking he could tell which way Geoffrey had gone. The others, seeing their quarry lost, came back shaking their heads, panting hard, and bending over to regain their breath. Geoffrey held his, afraid even the soft sound of his breathing might give him away, and he felt his heart begin to pound in protest.

He strained his ears as the men began to talk in low voices. He could not hear what they were saying, but he could hear isolated words, and the language they spoke identified them as Greeks. He released his breath slowly as the three men walked back the way they had come, the last one, judging from his angry gestures, furious that they had been so easily fooled.

Why was Geoffrey being followed by Greeks? They obviously did not intend to kill him, or they would have done so earlier and avoided the trouble of following him. Were they the murderers of the hapless knights and monks, aware now that Tancred had charged Geoffrey with solving the mystery? But that did not make sense either, for Tancred would not have told anyone what he intended to ask Geoffrey to do, especially because he believed that the murders were threatening his own interests.

Geoffrey waited some time in the shadows before slipping out and making his way stealthily back to the citadel. He did not go by the most direct route, back the way he had come, but took a tortuous journey along the dingy alleys where the traders lived, stopping every so often to listen. Once or twice, he heard sounds, but the first time, it was a scrawny cat scavenging among some offal, and the second it was the furious cry of a hungry baby demanding to be fed.

At last the citadel loomed ahead of him, the huge Tower of David a black mass against the dark sky. The citadel, called the Key to Jerusalem, was a formidable fortress. It was surrounded by a pair of curtain walls that were each several feet thick, and that were pierced by two gates. The first entrance was the great fortified barbican at the front that led outside the city walls, and the second entrance was a sally port that led onto David Street inside the city.

Within the lower of the two curtain walls was the outer bailey, where the common soldiers camped, while the more secure inner bailey was located inside the taller curtain wall. It was in the Tower of David in the inner bailey that Geoffrey had his quarters. While many knights had opted to live in sumptuous houses appropriated when the Crusaders had taken the city, others, like Geoffrey, preferred the security and convenience of life in the citadel. It was overcrowded, smelly and noisy, but it was well protected against attack, and there were no neighbours to complain about the peculiar hours working soldiers kept, or the incessant clang of blacksmith's forges as weapons were honed and armour mended.

The citadel was rigorously guarded by the Advocate's soldiers. As Geoffrey approached, basically unidentifiable in standard surcoat and helmet, there came the sound of arrows being fitted to bows by archers along the wall, and the captain of the guard called out for him to identify himself. Geoffrey pulled off his basinet so they could see his face, and told them his name. The captain thrust his torch near Geoffrey's face to satisfy himself that the sturdy knight who had been walking Jerusalem's streets in the dark was indeed the English-born Geoffrey Mappestone. There was a certain amount of unpleasantness in his manner, for the captain was a Lorrainer and had no love for the Normans—like Geoffrey and Hugh—who lived in the citadel. Eventually, Geoffrey was allowed past, only to go through a similar process at the gate that separated the outer bailey from the inner bailey.

The Tower was always rowdy, as would be expected in a building filled with warriors, and even now, in the depths of the night, there were guffaws of laughter and triumphant shouts from some illicit game of dice. Geoffrey, being relatively senior in the citadel hierarchy because of the regard in which Tancred held him, had his own chamber, a tiny, cramped room in the thickness of the wall overlooking David's Gate. It served Geoffrey as an office as well as a bedchamber and, on occasion, even as a hospital if one of his men were ill and needed rest away from the smelly, cramped conditions of the tents in the outer bailey.

Gratefully, he pushed open the stout wooden door to his

chamber and stepped inside. It was dark, and only the faint shaft of silver moonlight glimmering through the open window offered any illumination. The room was sparsely furnished: a truckle bed that could be rolled up and moved into the short corridor that led to the garderobe; a table strewn with parchment and writing equipment; a long bench against one wall; and a chest that held spare bits of armour, some clothes, his beloved books, and some less intellectual loot from Nicaea. His dog, stretched out in front of the window to take advantage of the breeze, looked up lazily as Geoffrey entered. It gave a soft, malevolent growl, and went back to sleep.

Without bothering to light the candle that was always set on the windowsill, Geoffrey unbuckled his surcoat and removed the chain-mail shirt, hanging them carefully on wall pegs. No warrior who valued his life failed to take good care of the equipment that might save it. He tugged off his boots and, clad in shirt and hose, wearily flopped down on the bed.

And immediately leapt up again.

"God's teeth!"

Pinned to the wall above his head was a heart, dark with a crust of dried blood. And it was held there by a curved dagger with a jewelled hilt.

In the cold light of morning, Geoffrey could see quite clearly that the dagger was not the same one that had been used to kill John of Sourdeval in the Greek Quarter the previous day: the blade was chipped and bunted, and the hilt was adorned with roughly cut pieces of coloured glass rather than jewels. But it was similar, and its message was clear: someone knew exactly where Geoffrey had been that night, and what he had been told to do. It was a warning that he should not meddle. But it also told him that someone in the citadel was involved in the murders. Security was tight at the Advocate's stronghold, and no one was allowed in unescorted. And certainly no one was allowed in the

knights' rooms on the upper floors. What little cleaning th[ ]
place was performed by foot soldiers, not by local labou[ ]
only people who could have gained access to his chamber, tnere-
fore, were Crusaders.

But what of the heart? What was its significance? Geoffrey
frowned as he poked at it with his dagger, turning it over to try
to gain some clue as to its origins. The dog watched with greedy
attention, licking its lips and salivating on the floor.

"The kitchens," announced Hugh, eyeing dog and heart
distastefully from the window seat. "Where else could it have
come from?"

"It looks like the heart of a pig," said Geoffrey, still prodding
it. "Pigs are not common here. The Moslems and Jews consider
them unclean, and we have learned by bitter experience that
their meat becomes tainted quickly in the desert heat. There are
simply not many pigs around."

"Well, go to the kitchens, and ask whether a pig has been
slaughtered recently," said Hugh, becoming bored by the conversation. "You will probably find that they killed one to make blood
pudding or something, and parts of the carcass were left over."

Geoffrey shook his head. "That is unlikely. Food is not so
abundant in this wilderness that we can afford to discard it carelessly. I imagine all parts of any animal slaughtered will be used,
even the bones to make soup."

Hugh rose languidly from the window seat. "All this talk of
food is making me hungry. It must be time to eat."

Abandoning the grisly warning, Geoffrey followed Hugh
down the spiral stairs that led to the great hall on the second floor
of the Tower of David, with the dog at his heels. On the way,
Hugh banged hard on the door of Sir Roger of Durham, an
English knight who had elected to stay in Jerusalem after the rest
of his contingent had left. The remainder of the knights, about
three hundred in all, were mainly Lorrainers in the pay of the
Advocate; however, there were also substantial numbers of Normans who were in the retinues of Bohemond—like Hugh and
Roger—and Geoffrey's lord, Tancred.

Roger emerged from his chamber, and followed them down the stairs. He was a huge man with cropped black hair and a brick-red complexion, and was the illegitimate son of the powerful Prince-Bishop of Durham. Roger was a simple man, blessed with a north country bluntness that Geoffrey assumed he must have inherited from his mother, who had been the Bishop's robemaker. Roger had no time at all for the politics and intrigues in Jerusalem, and was always the first to volunteer for expeditions where he would be able to use his formidable fighting skills. Roger's prodigious strength and honesty, coupled with Hugh's lugubrious cynicism and Geoffrey's quick intelligence, made them a force to be reckoned with in the citadel hierarchy. John of Sourdeval, Geoffrey recalled with a pang, had often made a fourth, his gentleness and integrity repressing some of Roger's and Hugh's wilder acts.

"I heard you had a heart delivered last night," said Roger conversationally, pushing past Geoffrey to be the first to arrive at the meal in the hall. "Do you want it? I have not eaten a heart since I left Durham."

"You would be in competition with half the flies in Palestine for it," drawled Hugh. "It stinks like a cesspool."

Roger grinned, showing strong brown teeth. "Picky Frenchman," he said. Hugh smiled back, while Geoffrey wondered how they could be so complacent about such a breach in security.

Geoffrey watched Roger clatter down the stairs in front of him. Roger was not a man Geoffrey would have imagined he would have forged a friendship with—he was coarse, loved fighting, and despised anything remotely intellectual. Yet English knights were a rarity on the Crusade, and Geoffrey found himself first drawn to Roger for the simple reason that they were countrymen. Later, however, he had come to respect other qualities in Roger: his honesty, a certain crude integrity, and an absolute loyalty to his friends—chiefly Geoffrey and Hugh. Although Geoffrey had more in common with the quick-witted, sardonic Hugh, Geoffrey admired Roger and felt himself fortunate to have two such friends, regardless of the difference in their personalities.

The great hall was already heaving with men. The window shutters had been thrown wide open, but the air inside was thick with the smell of unwashed bodies, Jerusalem dust, and oiled leather. Geoffrey immediately felt the prickle of sweat at his back, and pulled uncomfortably at his clothes. Even within the great walls of the citadel, the knights wore armour—mostly light mail tunics over their shirts. When they left the citadel, they wore heavy chain-mail shirts that reached their knees; over the shirts, they donned padded surcoats emblazoned with a Crusader's cross on the back and their lord's insignia on the front. Added to this were thick mail gauntlets, a metal helmet with a long nosepiece, and weighty boiled-leather trousers.

The hall was a rectangle, so large that there were two—not one—hearths to warm it in the brief winter months. There were round-headed windows on the west wall, which looked out across the inner bailey, but none in the east wall, which faced the outside, to render it more secure against attack. The end nearest the kitchens was marked by a brightly painted screen that hid the movements of the servants preparing the food behind it, while a dais at the opposite end bore a table at which the Advocate sat with his younger brother, Baldwin. At right angles to the table on the dais were four massive trestle tables, set up at mealtime and then dismantled. The more senior knights sat at the ends nearest the Advocate, while the lesser ones sat farther away.

Geoffrey, Roger, and Hugh found places near the head of the nearest table and helped themselves to watered wine, overripe figs, and hard bread. Two of the Advocate's knights came and settled opposite them: Warner de Gray and Henri d'Aumale, both of whom Geoffrey loathed almost as much as he did the cunning Hospitaller Courrances. Geoffrey stifled a sigh and began to discuss the sword drill planned for that afternoon with Hugh. Meanwhile, Warner began to describe an encounter he had had the day before with a small group of Arabs who had ambushed his scouting party. Geoffrey tried to ignore him, but Warner's voice was strident, and he and Hugh were eventually forced to abandon their own discussion.

When Warner saw he had an audience, he began to elaborate. In many ways, he looked like his cousin the Advocate: both were tall, well-built, and fair-haired. But whereas the Advocate was a thoughtful man and, rumour had it, religious, Warner was brash and arrogant, and he encouraged a lawlessness among his knights that Geoffrey found reprehensible.

"How many of those Saracens were there?" asked Roger, interested as ever in matters military.

"Ten," responded Warner. "Each one armed with a great scimitar and holding a golden idol of Mohammed in the air as they attacked."

Geoffrey stared at him with undisguised dislike. "Moslems do not make idols of Mohammed," he said disdainfully. "They consider it blasphemous."

Warner turned to him with a look of loathing that equalled Geoffrey's own. "I am not conducting a theological debate on Mohammedanism. I am describing an encounter in which I was forced to fight for my life against a band of Saracen fanatics intent on butchering me," he said haughtily.

"No soldier so intent would impair his fighting skills by holding an idol aloft," persisted Geoffrey. "That would be foolish. The whole scene you describe sounds most unlikely."

He felt Hugh's warning hand on his arm, while Roger unsheathed his dagger and casually used it to hack a lump of stale bread from a loaf on the table.

"Are you suggesting I lie?" asked Warner, the colour draining from his face. Around them, conversations began to die away as nearby knights watched the scene with interest. The Advocate's men moved to one side of the table, while Bohemond's and Tancred's moved to the other, anticipating a fight. It would not be the first—nor the last—time that the knights of rival factions pitted themselves against each other. The Advocate, who would certainly prevent such unseemly brawling among his men, was in deep conversation with his brother on the dais, and the noise from the other tables was sufficient to drown out any sounds of disturbance.

"I am suggesting that your description rings false," said Geoffrey, fully aware that he might start an incident that could end in bloodshed, but angered by Warner's ridiculous assertions. "Moslems do not have idols of Mohammed, and no intelligent soldier would willingly use an arm in such a pointless gesture when he would be better to use it to fight."

Warner began to rise to his feet, white-lipped with fury, his hand reaching for the dagger that hung in a sheath from his belt. But before he could draw it, Edouard de Courrances was behind him, both hands pressing down on Warner's shoulders.

"Sit, Sir Warner," he said softly. "I am sure the story of your ambush yesterday cannot yet be fully told."

"There is more?" enquired Hugh drolly. "And us so well entertained by his story already!"

The ironic emphasis on the word "story" almost brought Warner to his feet again, but Courrances's hands on his shoulders were firm, and he subsided. The Hospitaller soldier-monk bent to whisper something in Warner's ear, which was heard with a glittering malice, and then sat next to him on the bench. Geoffrey regarded him coldly.

"To what do we owe the pleasure of your company today?" asked Hugh blithely, voicing the question in everyone's mind as to why Courrances had forgone his usual place on the dais near the Advocate to sit with mere knights.

"I am a monk," said Courrances with mock humility. "I cannot bear to see signs of friction within the ranks of God's knights. I am here in His name to keep His peace."

Roger snorted loudly, and there were sarcastic sniggers from Bohemond's men. One or two of the Advocate's knights came to their feet, but sat again at a glance from Courrances. Geoffrey was impressed at the power of this man, who purported to be a monk, but even now wore the broadsword that the other knights were forbidden to bring into the hall because of past outbreaks of violence. Daggers had been banned too, but this had quickly proved impractical because of the tough nature of most of the food.

"Any further news of the monk—Loukas—who died

yesterday after you and I killed those rioters in the Greek Quarter?" Courrances asked Geoffrey casually. But Geoffrey caught a glitter in his eyes that suggested more than a passing interest. So that was it, Geoffrey thought. *He thinks to pump me for information about the murders that Tancred believes threaten the security of the Holy City.*

He shrugged noncommittally and accepted a rock-hard chunk of week-old bread from Roger. "None that you have not heard already, I am sure," he replied.

"I heard that John of Sourdeval and a monk were dispatched yesterday," said d'Aumale, with what Geoffrey thought verged on malicious glee. "One in the house of a harlot, and the other in a church. That makes five murders now."

Geoffrey gritted his teeth, unsurprised but resentful, that John's death should be a source of gossip for men like Warner and d'Aumale.

"John was not in a brothel," he said to d'Aumale, his voice cold. "He was in the house of a widow in the Greek quarter."

"Oh! A widow!" exclaimed d'Aumale, with a wink at Warner. "That makes it perfectly respectable!"

"Now you listen here," began Roger angrily, not fully understanding the irony in d'Aumale's words, but guessing some slur was being cast on John's reputation.

"Sir Warner, Sir Henri," said Hugh gently. "Our friend is dead, and we grieve for him. Can you not respect our mourning? Do not sully his memory. John was a good man."

Warner and d'Aumale exchanged glances but stood to leave. Warner gave Geoffrey a curt nod before heading off to join the Advocate, on the dais. Geoffrey, seeing a fight had been averted after all, sighed and replaced his dagger in its sheath. Gradually, sensing Courrances had successfully averted a skirmish between Geoffrey and Warner in which everyone else would have joined, men began to drift away. Soon, only Courrances, Geoffrey, Hugh, and Roger were left.

"Be easy, Geoffrey," said Hugh in a low voice. "Warner has

hated you ever since you revealed him for a fool over that business with the Bedouins. He would love to fight you—and kill you."

"He was on the verge of murdering a handful of children!" retorted Geoffrey, still angry. "Quite apart from the question of ethics—fully armed knights slaying children is not the most chivalrous of acts—it would have been foolish in the extreme. The Bedouin would have dogged our every step through the desert until they found an opportunity to slit our throats as we slept."

"I know, I know," said Hugh soothingly. "No one here doubts that the position you took was the correct one—from the tactical point of view, if not the ethical. And that is precisely why Warner loathes you so."

"Aye, lad," put in Roger. "You made him look like a brainless butcher. Which he is, of course!" he roared with laughter. Geoffrey did not join in.

"Men like Warner and d'Aumale have no right to speak ill of John," he said, scowling.

"True enough," said Hugh. "But they are only men, and men will inevitably speculate on the manner of John's death. What was he doing in the Greek quarter in the first place? You must admit, it is curious."

"I personally find this whole business most worrying," said Courrances. Geoffrey jumped. He had forgotten that Courrances was with them, and was unaware that he had been listening to his conversation with Roger and Hugh.

"So you said yesterday," Geoffrey said. Masking his discomfiture, he took a piece of goat from a huge bowl proffered by a servant. He inspected the meat carefully and dropped it back again, sickened by the smell of rancid fat. They had been eating goat for weeks now, even on those religious days when the Church claimed meat was to be avoided. Geoffrey hoped men like Roger, who grabbed the lump Geoffrey had discarded in company with another two that looked worse, would hurry up and finish whatever herd had been cheaply purchased by the citadel cook so they could have something else to eat.

"These deaths are a threat to the very foundation of our rule in this city," continued Courrances. Geoffrey looked searchingly at him. Tancred had said exactly the same. Perhaps they were right. Courrances met his eyes briefly, and then turned his attention to a futile attempt to pare the gristle from his portion of goat. After a while, he gave up in disgust, and flung it from him toward Geoffrey's ever-watchful dog. It was neatly intercepted by Roger, whose powerful jaws were not averse to gristle. The dog's expression changed from gluttonous anticipation, to astonishment, and then to outrage within the space of a moment.

Courrances leaned across the table toward Geoffrey. "The Advocate is also concerned about these murders. If Bohemond and Tancred are half the statesmen I believe them to be, they will be concerned too."

"Your point?" enquired Geoffrey, as Courrances paused.

"My point," said Courrances, turning his strange pale eyes on the Englishman, "is that these deaths are a threat to us all, whether Norman or Lorrainer, English or French, knight or monk. We should work together to solve them. I believe they are the work of Moslem fanatics who are aiming to bring us down by devious means, because their armies cannot defeat ours in battle. The Advocate himself thinks that the Patriarch may know more than he is telling, while the Advocate's brother thinks that the Jews are responsible."

"The Jews?" exclaimed Geoffrey. "They are only interested in maintaining as great a distance as possible from us, and who can blame them? They have neither the motive nor the inclination to become involved."

"Oh but they do," said Courrances smoothly. "Few can deny that they were happier, more free, and more prosperous under the control of the Moslems than they are under us. They would be only too pleased to see us ousted and the Moslems back."

"That is probably true," said Geoffrey, "but it does not mean that they would be so foolish as to attempt to bring it about. Their position is far too vulnerable. If they are in any doubt about what our armies are capable of, they only need to think back to the massacre when the city fell."

"Ah yes," said Courrances, "the massacre. Tancred was misguided in trying to offer protection to the infidel. If he had succeeded in his policy of mercy, there would have been more than the occasional knight or priest murdered in the streets by now."

Geoffrey said nothing. At Geoffrey's insistence, Tancred had attempted to save some of Jerusalem's citizens by gathering them together in a building that flew his standard. But knights and soldiers alike had ignored his orders, and the people who had thrown themselves on Tancred's mercy had been slaughtered like everyone else. Geoffrey had only realised what had happened when he saw the flames rising from the roof as the bodies were incinerated. Tancred had shrugged stoically when Geoffrey, almost speechless with rage and horror, told him what had happened, and promptly put the matter out of his mind in order to concentrate on the more interesting problem of where to loot first. Geoffrey had argued many times with Courrances about this incident, and neither was prepared to concede the other's point of view. Discussing it yet again would only serve to make them loathe each other more than they did already, if that were possible.

"You are something of a scholar, Sir Geoffrey," Courrances went on. "You know Arabic, I am told, and you have made yourself familiar with some of the customs of the Saracens. I approve."

Geoffrey regarded him suspiciously. In the past, Courrances had made no pretence at the scorn with which he held Geoffrey's predilection for learning about Arab culture.

"The point is," said Courrances, leaning so far over the table that the expensive black cloth of his tabard became stained in a pool of spilled grease, "the point is that there are few men here who are suitably equipped to investigate the deaths of these unfortunate men—and John was a friend of yours, after all. You speak Arabic and Greek, and you understand these infidels better than we do. The Advocate would like you to look into the matter."

"What?" exclaimed Geoffrey, aghast. "I cannot undertake an investigation for the Advocate! I am in Tancred's service!"

Hugh began to laugh softly, shaking his head and jabbing at a rough spot on the table with his dagger. Roger looked puzzled.

"I know that," said Courrances soothingly. "But this would be an unofficial matter."

"Are you saying the Advocate wishes me to spy for him without Tancred's knowledge?" asked Geoffrey coldly.

"Yes," replied Courrances, his honesty taking the wind from Geoffrey's indignation. "Because it is in Tancred's interest to have this matter investigated too. I cannot see that he would object."

Geoffrey was thoughtful. There were a number of possible solutions to the case of the murdered men, and investigating them was going to prove difficult, whatever the outcome. If he had the Advocate's blessing, as well as Tancred's, the task would be made immeasurably easier. He could report his findings to Tancred first, and discuss with him what the Advocate needed to be told.

He rubbed his chin and nodded slowly. Courrances gave a quick, almost startled, smile. Geoffrey glanced up to the dais and saw that the Advocate was watching him. For an instant, the eyes of the two men met before the Advocate turned away.

"Are you insane?" exclaimed Hugh. He gaped at Geoffrey as Courrances left to rejoin the august company on the high table. "How can you ally yourself with the Advocate? You are Tancred's man! What will he say when he hears of this?"

"He will know I am acting in the best way to serve him," said Geoffrey calmly.

Roger eyed him with amusement. "So that was where you went last night, lad! Off to see Tancred when all good men slept the sleep of the just."

"Not you, apparently, if you saw me leave," retorted Geoffrey.

"Is it true?" demanded Hugh. "Has Tancred asked you to act as his agent to discover the truth behind these murders?"

Geoffrey nodded. "But you are not the first to guess, evidently. Whoever left the dagger and the pig's heart in my chamber also knew what I have been charged to do."

chapter three

Back in his chamber, Geoffrey pondered the information contained on the scroll Tancred had given him. He sprawled in the window seat, feet propped up against the wall opposite, tapping the parchment thoughtfully with his forefinger. Roger lounged across the bed, paring his nails with his dagger, while Hugh sat on the bench plucking tunelessly at a lute Geoffrey had chosen from the sack of Antioch. The door was firmly closed, and Helbye had been given instructions to allow no one near it. Geoffrey's dog flopped on the stone floor in a vain attempt to cool itself down, and the sounds of its agitated panting filled the room.

"Tell us again," said Roger. "This heat is dulling my brain."

"It was dull long before the heat got to it," muttered Hugh. Roger flung a mailed glove at him, which was retrieved by the dog and returned in the hope of an edible reward.

"The two knights—Guido and John—were in Bohemond's service," Geoffrey began. "The dead monks were Jocelyn, a Benedictine from Conques in France; Pius, a Cluniac from Ripoll in Spain; and Loukas, a Greek. The monks have no connections with each other as far as is known, and they were found in random locations around the city. The only common factor between all five is that they were killed with carved Arab daggers."

"I cannot see another connection between them," said Hugh.

"Although I suppose there must be one." He sighed. "Lord, Geoffrey, what have you let yourself in for this time? This is nothing like the matter of those thefts you solved, you know. Then, the culprit was no one of consequence and he was conveniently dispatched and forgotten. God only knows who might be involved in *this* business."

Geoffrey nodded. He, too, was already having misgivings about becoming embroiled in the matter. It boded ill that the Advocate considered it of sufficient importance that he would consider recruiting an agent whose allegiance lay with another, and anything that secured the interest of Edouard de Courrances was bound to have some sinister twist. But Tancred had gone to some pains to ensure Geoffrey performed this duty willingly. Tancred was a good general, and allowed Geoffrey considerable freedom to use his own judgement, a privilege that neither the Advocate nor Bohemond granted their knights. Geoffrey knew Tancred would applaud Geoffrey's acceptance of the Advocate's commission, since it would grant him access to far more places than Tancred's authority would allow.

"And then there is the matter of the heart," said Roger, looking ruefully at its gnawed remains on the floor between the dog's protective paws. "And of who followed you last night. Speaking Greek, you say."

"There is your answer," said Hugh, snapping his fingers. "Words of wisdom from fools and children. The only clue you have so far is that your would-be assailants are Greek. One of the victims was Greek, also. Begin your investigation with the Greeks."

"The woman you arrested was Greek, too, you say?" said Roger, glancing up at Geoffrey.

"But she was released because another victim was killed while she was being questioned by Tancred," said Geoffrey. "Tancred is quite an impressive alibi. She was telling the truth after all."

"Maybe," said Hugh. "But perhaps her confederates staged another murder while she was being questioned, specifically to show she was innocent."

"They would have to have acted very quickly," said Geoffrey. "And it would have had to have been perfectly timed."

"Well, so it was," said Hugh. "Do you think it odd that so much time lapsed between the first three murders—Guido, Jocelyn, and Pius—but the next two—John and Loukas occurred on the same day?"

Geoffrey considered. But there seemed to be no kind of pattern to the murders at all, and Hugh's point about timing might prove very misleading.

"The first step is to check the information we already have," he said, considering the terse sentences written by Tancred's scribes. "We need to visit the places where these men died, talk to the people who found their bodies, and make enquiries among their friends regarding their habits and acquaintances. That includes questioning the woman I arrested yesterday ourselves. We will see what new information that might bring to light, and if all else fails, we can begin to investigate the Greek community."

"I do not like the sound of this 'we,' " said Hugh disapprovingly. "Do not include me in all this, Geoffrey. Hunting down petty thieves in Nicaea was a far different matter than this sinister business. Nicaea was fun; this sounds like suicide. Hell, Geoffrey, you had not even begun your enquiries before a pig's heart was pinned to your wall by a dagger that looks like the murder weapon, and a group of villains followed you through the street intent on mischief. I am sorry, but there is a limit to the obligations of friendship, and this is it. I will be more than happy to discuss and advise within the safety of these four walls, but count me out of seedy investigations in squalid houses in the company of murderers."

"I had no idea you were so sensitive, Hugh," said Roger, grinning. He uncoiled himself from the bed, his bulk belying the underlying grace in his movements. "I will accompany you around the hovels, Geoffrey. I am not afraid of squalor and murderers."

"I am sure you are only too well acquainted," said Hugh,

surveying Roger's dirty tunic and baggy hose with cool disdain. "Since you hail from the wild lands of the north, I am not in the least bit surprised. And I did not say I was afraid. But it is a poor soldier who rushes headlong into battle without considering his enemy. You two have no information on your enemy to consider."

"Hugh is right," said Geoffrey, although he had a feeling that he knew exactly what he was letting himself in for, and it struck a chill note inside him. "I cannot involve you in this, Roger. You are not even Tancred's man."

"But I am Bohemond's, and until uncle and nephew become enemies, by serving one, I serve the other," said Roger with uncharacteristic insight. "If Courrances is afraid for the Advocate, then I am afraid for Bohemond. And it will be no secret in this hive of bees that we have been closeted here for so long together. Your mission for the Advocate will already be common knowledge, and I do not imagine people will think we have been discussing the quality of the food all this time. I am with you, Geoffrey."

Geoffrey smiled, trying to hide the unease he felt as Roger's words sank in. He had been foolish. It was not easy to gain friends as loyal and trustworthy as these two men, and he should have stopped to think before he involved them. And even if Hugh did have nothing to do with any further investigations, there would be few who would believe him ignorant of the affair, regardless of the truth of the matter.

Hugh leaned Geoffrey's lute carefully against the wall and stood, brushing imaginary dust from his immaculate tunic. Roger stood next to him, slightly stooped, his massive hands dangling at his sides, and his huge size making Hugh, who was slight of build, look like a fragile fair-haired boy. They were chalk and cheese: the one always neatly dressed, clean-shaven, seldom acting without due thought; the other dark and coarse, scruffy, and impulsive. Hugh had been given an abbey education, but Roger, despite his ecclesiastical ancestry, could not even read. Geoffrey knew he could trust these two men with his life—and had done so many times in battle.

He sighed and stood from the window seat. The dog rose from the floor, anticipating an excursion where there might be chickens to chase or people to bite, and wagged its feathery tail eagerly.

"I will oversee your sword drill," said Hugh, "while you go about your dangerous business."

"Oversee mine too," said Roger. "A few hours among the hovels does have a certain appeal after watching my inept crew savaging the art of swordplay." He rubbed his hands together and gave Hugh a leering grin.

Hugh shook his head, laughing, and went to collect his armour. Geoffrey, reluctantly in view of the heat, donned his chain-mail shirt and hauled his surcoat over the top of it. He strapped his sword to his waist and put his dagger in its sheath, calling for Sergeant Helbye and Ned Fletcher to ready themselves. Hugh was right to be cautious, and after the incident of the night before, Geoffrey had no intention of beginning his investigation without armed guards.

He clattered down the stairs, the scabbard of his sword ringing as it struck the walls. Although Norman knights usually rode, Geoffrey preferred to walk within the city. Many of the streets were too narrow for horsemen, and he disliked being forced to ride in single file, feeling it made him vulnerable to attack. Unlike most Normans, Geoffrey was as good a fighter on foot as he was in the saddle, and so the notion of walking did not fill him with the same horror as it did many of his colleagues.

Roger met him in the bailey, similarly clad in chain-mail shirt, surcoat, and leather helmet. Geoffrey's surcoat had seen better days, but it was spotless compared to Roger's, which was so stiff with dirt and grease that Geoffrey wondered if it could walk by itself. They watched their soldiers thrusting and parrying for a few moments, booted feet kicking up clouds of the yellow-white dust that seemed to cover everything in the city.

Hugh walked among them, his few biting criticisms achieving far more than the empty bluster of Helbye. One of Bohemond's most trusted knights, Hugh had been left in charge of a small garrison to guard Bohemond's interests in Jerusalem, while Bohemond himself fought for a kingdom of his own in the north. Fiercely loyal, Hugh took this trust seriously, only too aware that his and Roger's men combined were pitifully few compared to the ranks of those loyal to the Advocate. Tancred had fewer still, most protecting his lands in Galilee, with little more than the small contingency of English soldiers under Geoffrey representing him in the Holy City. While Geoffrey and Roger believed most power would be won and lost in the political games played at the Patriarch's palace and the court of the Advocate, Hugh was uncertain, and he wanted his men ready to fight, should the occasion demand. Geoffrey and Roger humoured him by keeping their own men busy with drills and expeditions out into the desert too.

"Where is your chain mail?" yelled Geoffrey to Tom Wolfram, his youngest sergeant at arms.

"It is too hot . . ." began the inevitable protest.

Geoffrey cut him off abruptly. "Would you care to practice with me without your armour?" he asked, unsheathing his sword.

The young man blanched and took an involuntary step backward. "Oh, no . . ."

"Are you afraid that I might injure you with my superior skills?"

Wolfram nodded miserably. Others had stopped their practice and were watching the exchange with interest.

"Then you are even more foolish than I thought," said Geoffrey, putting his weapon away. "You are in far more danger from these hacking amateurs than from me. I would not injure you deliberately, but one of them might well do so by accident."

The young man blushed scarlet, and Geoffrey felt uncomfortable at berating him in front of the men. Wolfram was not the first soldier to practice in his shirt sleeves, preferring the risk of injury to the intense discomfort of wearing the heavy, stifling chain mail that would protect him. But Geoffrey had warned the young man on several occasions that practising swordplay without armour was not permitted, and yet Wolfram still persisted. Trained soldiers were becoming increasingly scarce, and no knight could afford to lose one through a stupid, wholly avoidable accident.

Leaving Wolfram glowering resentfully, Geoffrey set off with Roger toward the gates, Helbye and Fletcher in tow and the dog worrying about his heels. As always, the gates were closed, and they waited while the soldier on duty hauled the thick bar from the wicket gate to let them out.

Geoffrey and Roger squeezed through the gate and began to walk down David Street toward the Dome of the Rock, where the bodies of Brother Jocelyn and Sir Guido had been found. It was late morning, and the heat was already intense, seeming to encompass the city in a bubble of sizzling silence. Geoffrey's dog slunk after them, dodging back and forth across the road to take advantage of the scant shade. Distantly, the sound of monks chanting Nones rose and fell, giving the city an air of serenity that was far from real.

David Street ran into Temple Street, the road that led to the Dome of the Rock. It was wide and lined with flat-roofed houses that were once a brilliant white, but now the paint was fading and stained. Since the Crusaders had come, it was the practice of the local population to keep their doors locked, whether the occupants were in or not, but the window shutters on the upper floors were thrown open, revealing intricate patterns on the wood in bright colours. Then Geoffrey and Roger passed a mosque, its once-proud minarets cracked and leaning dangerously, and its horn windows smashed by stones.

Toward the Dome of the Rock, Temple Street grew narrower, and the houses seemed taller, looming upward so that the sky appeared as a tiny strip of blue high above. It meant the road was shady, and cooler than the furnace of David Street, and the soldiers stepped forward gratefully. Merchants had their wares on display outside their shops, but their restful positions changed to watchfulness as Geoffrey and his men passed.

Ahead of them, sunlight slanted between the houses, opaque with dust, and creating dark shadows on the walls. Geoffrey smiled to himself. Despite the conflict, the unease, and the fact that a soldier was ill-advised to wander alone in many parts of the city, Jerusalem was a beautiful place. He thought the Dome of the Rock was one of the most splendid buildings he had ever seen, perhaps even more than the fabulous Church of Santa Sophia in Constantinople.

Geoffrey and Roger reached the wall that surrounded the Dome and its gardens, and were allowed in by a Hospitaller. Then they were at the foot of the great Dome of the Rock itself, a massive cupola atop walls of breathtaking blue and turquoise mosaics that dominated the city from its position at the summit of Mount Moriah. Geoffrey stood still, as he always did, to gaze at the gilded dome and the decorative glazed tiling of the walls. Helbye, not anticipating his abrupt stop, bumped into him and exchanged a look of long-suffering incomprehension with Roger.

"We could learn so much from this," said Geoffrey softly, staring at the dome glittering gold against the deep blue of the sky. "We have nothing like this in our own country."

"That is because we are not Mohammedans," said Roger, taking him firmly by the arm and ushering him through the door. He looked around and shuddered dramatically. "And even though this is said to be a church now the Saracens have been ousted from it, it still feels like a heathen temple to me."

Inside, the Dome was cool and cavernous, and somewhere a monk was chanting, his voice echoing serenely through the forest of pillars. Geoffrey stopped again and gazed around in admiration.

"But the Church of Santa Sophia is domed, very much like this," he said, disengaging his arm and moving to inspect one of the slender white marble columns that supported delicate arches.

"Yet we do not use architecture of this type in England or Normandy."

"You mean that big, gaudy church you dragged us round in Constantinople?" asked Roger, remembering the excursion with a distinct lack of enthusiasm. "Aye, lad, but think how ridiculous a contraption like that dome would look on Durham Cathedral."

Helbye and Fletcher nodded wisely, and Geoffrey could think of no appropriate response. He followed them through the entrance porch, and into the inner part of the building, where a bare patch of rock was said by the Jews to be the place where Abraham had almost sacrificed Isaac, and from where Moslems believed Mohammed had risen to Heaven. Geoffrey stared down at it—an ordinary lump of rough rock similar to that in other parts of the city—and wondered if the stories were true. Lost in his flight of imagination, it took a hefty push from Roger to bring him back to the present.

"This here is the man who found that monk-Brother Jocelyn," said Roger, obviously for the second time. "Three weeks ago."

Geoffrey saw a small man wearing the habit of a Benedictine. He had the whitest skin Geoffrey had ever seen, and he wondered if the monk ever went outside.

"Tell me what happened."

The man glanced around nervously, and then looked back at Geoffrey with an ingratiating smile that did not reach his eyes. "There is really nothing to tell. It was nearing dawn, and I was lighting the candles for Prime. I saw a man sitting at the base of a pillar, leaning up against it, with his legs out in front of him. It looked dissolute, to be frank, so I went to tell him to go away. When I drew nearer, I saw it was Brother Jocelyn, and I saw a knife protruding from his back. I pulled the knife out to see if I could restore some spark of life to the man, but he was dead. I ran then to fetch the Prior, but by the time I returned, someone had stolen the knife."

"What was this knife like?" asked Geoffrey.

"Oh, a lovely thing," said the monk with a wistful sigh. "All silver and adorned with jewels. I should have kept it when I went for the Prior. To hand to the Patriarch's men, of course," he added quickly, but unconvincingly.

"How well did you know Brother Jocelyn?"

"Not well, really. He was a secretive man, who seldom spoke. He had occasional duties as scribe for Lord Bohemond on account of his writing being so fine, but most of the time he spent here."

That was interesting, thought Geoffrey. Perhaps being in Bohemond's service was the link between the monks and the knights: Guido and John had been Bohemond's men.

"How long had Jocelyn been a monk here?"

The monk shrugged. "The same length of time as the rest of us," he said. "None of us were here before Jerusalem fell to God's soldiers."

"Did you notice anything unusual about Jocelyn's behavior before he died? Did he meet anyone or disappear without explaining where he had been?"

The monk shrugged carelessly. "No, I do not think so."

"Are you certain? The Advocate will not be pleased to hear his investigations have been hampered by lying monks," snapped Geoffrey, growing impatient with the man's complacency.

The monk glanced at Geoffrey's sudden change of tone. "I did not see him *meet* with anyone . . ." he stammered.

"But you noticed absences?" pressed Geoffrey.

"Yes, well . . . perhaps he was called away by Bohemond to do some scribing. I do not know. He did not sleep in his bed the night he died. He . . . he was nervous and irritable the day before. He shouted at me for letting the inkwells dry out. It is not my fault. Ink dries like water on hot steel in this country . . ."

"What is going on here?" came a sibilant voice from behind them. Geoffrey spun round, disconcerted that he had not heard the man's approach. Roger's dagger slipped silently back into its scabbard as he recognized the Benedictine Prior in charge of the Dome of the Rock.

"We are making enquiries into the murder of the monk, Jocelyn," said Geoffrey. "The brother here was helping."

"It sounded more like an interrogation to me," said the Prior, looking down his long, thin nose at Geoffrey and his men. He nodded at the monk, who scurried away gratefully. "Perhaps I can help you. On whose order do you enquire?"

"On the Advocate's," replied Geoffrey, thinking that it was not such a bad thing to be able to cite such an authority after all. He wondered whether Tancred's name would evoke as much help.

"Our Patriarch has also been investigating," said the Prior, "and I have already spoken to his men. But I will tell you what I told them. You see how empty the church is now?" He gestured round at the great vacant expanse. "It is always like this, except when our community come here to pray, and even then, we are only ten men. It would be easy for anyone with evil intentions to enter unobserved, and hide among the pillars. When I was called, I found Jocelyn dead, and no sign of a weapon. We made an immediate search, but there was no one here."

"What can you tell me of Jocelyn?"

"Nothing much. He performed certain clerkly duties for Bohemond, because his writing was so fine. He was a librarian before he came on Crusade."

"Where?"

"He was an oblate at Conques in France, but he learned his script at Rome when he worked in the library of our Holy Father."

"Jocelyn worked for the Pope?" queried Roger.

"Our Holy Father means the Pope, yes," said the Prior with sickly condescension. "And Jocelyn learned his fine hand from the best copyists in the world."

Geoffrey was beginning to dislike the arrogant Prior. Jocelyn was one of the man's brethren, yet the Prior seemed remarkably casual about his murder. How was Geoffrey to solve the mystery of poor John's untimely death if the witnesses were as complacent as was the Prior?

"And what of Sir Guido, who was also found foully murdered within the lands under your jurisdiction. How do you explain that away? Be careful how you answer: the Advocate does not like liars."

The Prior looked sharply at Geoffrey, and some of the haughtiness went out of his manner. Although the Prior came under the protection of the Patriarch, there was no point in making an enemy of the Advocate. And, the Prior decided, there was something more to Sir Geoffrey Mappestone than to most of the unruly, illiterate bullies at the citadel.

"I found the dead knight three days before Jocelyn died," he replied. "I often walk the grounds here early in the morning—they are cool and silent, and I like to reflect on the pleasures of God's paradise in Heaven."

More like the pleasures of God's paradise on Earth, thought Geoffrey, noting the Prior's handsome collection of rings and his fine robe of thin silk.

"And what did you find, as you so reflected?"

"I saw a man lying under one of the trees behind the Dome. I thought he was yet another of your number sleeping off a night of debauchery, but then I saw there was a knife in his back. I called for help, but there was nothing we could do. The man was quite dead. The Advocate's soldiers came with a cart and took him away."

"And the knife?"

"They took that too. It was a great ugly thing with a wicked curved blade and ostentatious jewels in the handle. I asked my monks if they had heard or seen anything during the night, but none of them had. I have no idea how the knight—Sir Guido—came to be killed here or why."

"Had you seen him before?"

The Prior hesitated. "No."

"If you do not want to tell me the truth here, we can always discuss it at the citadel," said Geoffrey, keeping his face devoid of expression. He had no authority to threaten one of the Patriarch's priests with arrest, but it seemed the Prior did not know that.

The man paled, glanced at Roger, and flicked his tongue nervously over dry lips.

"I am not certain you understand," he said, putting a beringed hand to his breast, "but I think he came here on occasion to walk. The Dome is very fine, and the courtyard and gardens here are most pleasant in which to stroll."

"And how many times did he come?"

The Prior gave him an unpleasant look. "Recently, two or three times a week."

"Did he meet anyone here. Did you ever see anyone with him?"

The Prior shook his head. "Never. He was always alone. He looked . . . bereaved."

Guido *had* been bereaved. Geoffrey, being one of a mere handful of knights who were literate, had read a letter to Guido two months before telling him his wife had died after a long illness. So, if the Prior was telling the truth, which Geoffrey thought he probably was, Guido came to the peace of the Dome of the Rock to mourn, away from the raucous atmosphere of the citadel.

"Do many knights come here?"

The Prior shook his head. "Not really. Perhaps they feel it is still too mosquelike to be a church."

In view of Roger's words moments before, Geoffrey imagined that must be true, although attending any church—mosquelike or otherwise—was not a high priority on the entertainment lists of most knights.

"It is a pity it is underused," he said, looking up at the delicate latticework around the gallery. "It is a very fine building. Peaceful, too."

The Prior softened somewhat. "It is peaceful. Much more so than the Church of the Holy Sepulchre. That is said to be the holiest place in Christendom, but it has the atmosphere of a marketplace."

Geoffrey had to agree. They spoke a while longer and took their leave, stepping out from the cool of marble into the blazing heat of midday that hit them like a hammer. The light reflected from the white paving stones around the Dome and almost blinded them. Eyes screwed up against the glare, they walked back the way they had come and headed for the market near St. Stephen's Street, where Brother Pius had died in the house of a butcher.

"That first monk we spoke to was scared to death," said Roger. "Still, at least you persuaded them both to tell the truth in the end."

Geoffrey began to assess what the Prior had told them.

"So Brother Jocelyn went missing the night before he died—he did not sleep in his own bed. And he was nervous and irritable all that day. It sounds to me as if he knew he was in some danger. Which means he also knew why." Deep in thought, Geoffrey drummed his fingers on the hilt of his sword as they walked. "So he was obviously involved in something sinister. Perhaps something he learned from his duties as scribe."

"Perhaps he had planned to go whoring the night he died, and was nervous and irritable the day before because it was a risky thing for a monk to do," suggested Roger practically.

It was possible, Geoffrey supposed. But it did not explain why Jocelyn had died. Unless his killer was a prostitute who went round murdering knights and monks using daggers with jewelled hilts. He sighed, and thought about their next visit—to the scene of Pius's murder in the house of a butcher in the Greek Quarter.

"Brother Pius, the third to die, was a Cluniac from Spain. As far as is known, he had never been to France, had nothing to do with John or Guido, and did not work for Bohemond."

"Here! Wait a minute," said Roger aggressively, stopping in his tracks and spinning round to face Geoffrey. "What are you implying? Just because you are Tancred's man, doesn't mean to say . . ."

"Easy!" said Geoffrey, raising his hands against Roger's tirade. "I am not saying Bohemond is responsible, only that it is possible that these deaths might be an attack against him—John and

Guido were in his service, and now we know Jocelyn occasionally acted as scribe for him." He took Roger's arm and began walking again. "It is the only real clue we have so far. We must look into it."

Roger conceded reluctantly, and they walked the short distance to the Greek market. Trading in the street dedicated to selling meat was beginning to slow down in readiness for the usual period of rest during the heat of the afternoon. The air was black with the buzz of flies, and the smell of congealing blood and sunbaked meat was so powerful that Geoffrey felt he dared not inhale. He tried to breathe through his mouth like Roger, but this meant he could taste the foulness in the air as well as smell it, which made it far worse. They located the stall of the goat butcher who had discovered the corpse of Brother Pius easily enough: Tancred's scribes had written that Yusef Akira's shop was the one with the oldest, blackest bloodstains in front of it, and possessed the filthiest canopy. It was not difficult to identify.

Resisting the urge to wrap a cloth around his mouth and nose, Geoffrey entered the shop. It was little more than a windowless cave, with several ominous hooks in the ceiling above a gently shelving floor with a hole in the middle. Geoffrey thought his eyes were playing tricks when the floor seemed to move, but a closer inspection indicated that it was crawling with flies and maggots feasting on the drying blood. Fletcher, who had followed him in, beat a hasty retreat, and even Roger stood only in the doorway and would not enter. Geoffrey shifted his feet uncomfortably and longed to leave. He saw his dog chewing on something enthusiastically, and hoped whatever it was would not make him ill. The dog was not pleasant when it was unwell.

In the midst of the filth, a man sat on a stool with his back against the wall to draw on its coolness. He snored softly with his mouth agape, oblivious to the flies that crawled across his face. Geoffrey kicked gently at the stool and watched Yusef Akira return slowly to the land of the living, accompanied by some of the most disgusting noises known to man. Akira drew a grubby hand across his jowls and eyed the knights blearily.

"What do you want?" he slurred in Greek. "Bit o' lean meat? I got some nice stuff round the back."

"No," said Geoffrey quickly, also in Greek, not wanting to venture farther into Akira's domain. "We need information about the death of Brother Pius."

"Oh, that," said Akira, turning sullen. "It'll cost you."

"It will cost you if you do not answer our questions," said Geoffrey, hooking one foot under the leg of Akira's stool and tipping it over. Akira tumbled to the floor and then leapt to his feet with his hands balled into fists. He took one good look at Geoffrey's chain mail and sword, made a quick and prudent decision, and became ingratiating.

"What do you want to know? I already spoke to the Patriarch's men."

"I am aware of that," said Geoffrey mildly. "But now you will talk to me. Tell me what happened three weeks ago when you discovered the body."

"Oh it was a revolting thing," Akira began in a howl. Geoffrey braced himself, wondering what could revolt Akira more than the living hell of his business premises. "I comes from me bed chamber upstairs, and there he was, dead on me floor." He gestured with his hand to indicate where the body had lain near the door.

"How did Pius come to be there?"

"He was dead!" wailed Akira. "With a great carved knife sticking out of his back."

"But how did this happen?" pressed Geoffrey. "How did he come to be dead in your . . ." He gestured around him, wondering what word would best describe it.

"How do I know?" said Akira belligerently. "Old Akira was asleep all night. I comes downstairs at dawn to prepare me shop, and there he was."

"Was the door open? Did you lock it before you went to bed?"

" 'Course I locked it," said Akira indignantly. "I got valuable stock here. The door was open—ajar—when I came downstairs that morning. And that monk was here, bleeding all over me floor."

Geoffrey glanced down at the floor involuntarily, and forced his eyes away before his mind could register its horrors. "Had you met Brother Pius before?"

Akira's eyes became sly. "Maybe, and maybe not."

"And maybe I will ram your head down that hole in the floor if you do not answer," said Geoffrey sweetly.

Akira considered. Geoffrey was a tall man and looked strong and fit. Akira decided he could probably do what he threatened. "Yes," he said reluctantly. "Brother Pius came to buy meat every Monday. He lived with four other monks next to the Church of St. Mary. I didn't know him well, you understand, but I recognised him."

"And what of this dagger in his back?"

"Now there was a curious thing," said Akira. "It was a lovely item indeed. I sees it before I recognises Pius. I was quite shook by finding a corpse on my floor, so I runs out into the street to raise the alarm, thinking to retrieve the dagger later. It would help me greatly in me business, to have a good cutting implement like that. But while I was out raising the alarm, someone comes in and steals it."

"Did you see who it might have been?"

"I did not," said Akira vehemently. "Or old Akira would have paid him a visit and got the dagger back. The monk would have wanted me to have it, don't you think?"

Geoffrey was sure such a consideration would not have crossed Pius' mind, and if it had, the monk would doubtless not have felt comfortable that the weapon used to murder him should be applied with equal vigour to herds of goats.

Gratefully, Geoffrey escaped from the stench of the meat market to the peaceful street in which the Church of St. Mary, Pius's home, stood. Fletcher ran a hand across his brow.

"That place is enough to turn a man to eating grass," he said. "I am going to question the citadel cooks, and if any meat comes from that man, I shall refuse to eat it."

Geoffrey laughed, and pushed open the great door of the church. He could still smell the meat market in the air around him, and wondered if that was why his dog was winding so enthusiastically around his legs. Inside, the church was silent, and he saw a line of monks standing in front of the altar. One of them turned at the sound of someone entering, and came to greet them. Geoffrey, steeling himself for more unpleasant interviewing, was taken aback when the monk smiled in a friendly way and offered them some wine.

"We have come to ask about Brother Pius," he said, wondering if the offer would be revoked when the nature of their visit became clear.

"Poor Pius," said the Cluniac monk, speaking Norman French and shaking his head sadly. "His death was a great loss to us. There are so very few Cluniacs in Jerusalem, you see, and he was invaluable to us in many ways."

"I am sorry for your loss," said Geoffrey gently. "But you understand it is important we discover who killed Pius, and why, and I must ask you some questions."

The elderly monk's eyes glittered with tears, but he nodded acquiescence.

Geoffrey smiled encouragingly at him. "What can you tell me about Brother Pius's death?"

"Only that he was found dead in the house of a local butcher," said the monk. "I do not know how he came to be there in the middle of the night. When we saw he was missing from the dormitory, we assumed he was praying in the church until a messenger came to tell us he was dead. Pius often had difficulty in sleeping, and he frequently came to the church in the night when he was restless."

"What of Pius himself? What was he like? Did he have many acquaintances outside your community here?"

"Not that I know of," replied the monk, reaching out to refill Roger's goblet. "We tend to keep to ourselves, as far away from the disputes and quarrels of the Church as possible. We are just grateful to be here in this Holy City, and we do not wish to spend our time in useless rivalries and arguments."

"Could he write?" asked Geoffrey, wondering if Pius, like Jocelyn, might have acted as an occasional scribe.

The monk smiled and shook his head. "Not at all. Not even his name. He preferred the more physical labours to the intellectual ones. He usually worked in the kitchens and did all the cleaning and cooking. We have not had a clean house or a decent meal since he died." The tears sparkled again, and he looked away.

"He came from Ripoll," said Geoffrey. "Are any other of your brethren from Spain?"

The Cluniac shook his head. "We are all from France. Pius was the only Spaniard. We met with him on the journey here from Constantinople in 1098."

The monk could tell them nothing more, and reluctantly Geoffrey led the way out of the cool shade of the church and into the sun. The day was at its hottest, and the streets were deserted except for the occasional animal and, of course, the flies. The dog whined piteously, and Helbye and Fletcher began to walk more and more slowly. Geoffrey's shirt under his chain mail was soaking, and it began to rub. He considered stopping at one of the refreshment houses until the heat began to fade, but despite its considerable size, Jerusalem was in many ways a small community, and word that the Advocate was now investigating the curious murders of two knights and three monks would soon be all over the city. Geoffrey had a strong feeling that he should question the witnesses to the two remaining deaths as quickly as possible. If Hugh was correct and there was some kind of conspiracy, Geoffrey might never unravel the mystery if he allowed the culprits time to consolidate their stories.

Ignoring the sighs and exaggerated panting of Helbye, Fletcher, and the dog, he walked briskly along the empty streets toward the house where he had seen the body of John the previous day. Their footsteps echoed in the eerily silent roads, and

Geoffrey was aware that their progress was being watched surreptitiously from the windows of the houses they passed. Since so few people were out, four armed men on foot in the heart of the city was an unusual sight.

The sun blazed down with such ferocity that the ground felt uncomfortably hot even through thick-soled boots, and the dust, which had been a minor irritation before, now filled their mouths and noses and gritted unpleasantly between their teeth. Geoffrey's throat became sore and dry, and he thought about goblets of cool, clear water. He saw Roger's face streaked with dust and sweat, and suspected he was imagining the same.

Eventually, they came to the street where they had encountered the commotion the day before. It was deserted, although Geoffrey sensed that they were being observed with interest from several houses. He led the way to the home of the woman he had arrested, and knocked at the door. Helbye was uneasy and stood with his back to the wall and his hand on the hilt of his sword. His anxiety was transmitting itself to Fletcher, who fingered the dagger in his belt with unsteady hands.

No such fears assailed Roger, who pushed past Geoffrey to hammer on the door with the pommel of his dagger. Geoffrey cringed, only too aware that they were on dangerous ground, given the events of the day before. Just as he was considering cutting their losses and visiting the scene where the last of the victims was killed, the door opened and Melisende Mikelos stood in front of them. She was attired in the same widow's dress that she had worn the previous day, but this time her hair was covered by a neat black veil, giving her the appearance of a nun. Geoffrey, recalling how roughly he had handled her, hoped she was not.

"What do you want?" she asked in Greek, eyeing Geoffrey with dislike. "I have no wish to speak with you."

"I would like to ask you some questions about the knight who died here," said Geoffrey, as politely as he could. He guessed instinctively that she was not a person who could be browbeaten into telling him what he wanted to know, especially given the spectacular proof of her innocence the day before.

She gazed at him in disbelief. "You could have done that yesterday," she said, once she had regained her composure. "Instead, you chose to hustle me away, cause the death of three of my neighbours, and bring about a riot."

Geoffrey looked away. She had a point. "May I ask my questions now?"

"You may not!" she spat. "You did not believe me yesterday, and I have no wish to convince you today. Ask Lord Tancred, for I spoke with him at length. And ask the Patriarch, another with whom I conversed long and hard."

"I would rather hear what you have to say from yourself," said Geoffrey.

At his side, Roger gave a warning cough, and Geoffrey saw that people were beginning to gather in the street. He cursed himself for a fool. He should have anticipated the woman's welcome would be far from friendly, and brought a larger force. The dog, sensing the menace in the air, began a low whining, and Geoffrey wondered how he had managed to acquire an animal to whom cowardice came so naturally. It slunk against the side of the building and rolled its eyes pathetically.

"This could get nasty," muttered Roger, fingering the hilt of his sword but not drawing it. "I wonder whether Courrances will ride by and rescue you a second time."

Geoffrey glanced behind him and saw that the crowd was beginning to edge closer. Unlike the day before, he and his men numbered only four, and this time none had bows. The crowd, growing by the moment, was already upward of thirty, and many carried weapons. The riot of the previous day, when those who were unarmed had been killed, had obviously been a bitter lesson, and they were now better prepared for their second encounter with the hated Crusaders.

Geoffrey turned back to Melisende, his mind racing. "Would you have us cut down on your doorstep?"

She shrugged. "You were quite happy to condemn me to the Patriarch's dungeons, and to believe I was the murderer of that poor knight. Why should I be sorry to have my revenge?"

They would find no mercy there. Geoffrey turned from her and drew his sword as the mob drew closer. His colleagues followed suit and drew theirs, standing in a line and preparing to sell their lives dearly. At least it is better than being trampled by Courrances's destrier, Geoffrey thought irrelevantly. He took a deep breath and faced the crowd steadily.

CHAPTER FOUR

S top!" Melisende's voice cut clearly through the ominous silence preceding the fight that was about to begin. "There has been enough killing here already."

"And it was all his fault," cried a man with a long, curly beard pointing at Geoffrey. "He deserves to die."

"So he might," replied Melisende. "But he is likely to take you with him. And more of your family and friends. He is a Norman knight and far more skilled at fighting than you. He may even escape and leave you dead behind him."

There was a mutter of consternation among the people, and a hurried exchange of views.

"We will let the other three go if he stays," said the man with the beard, indicating Geoffrey.

Melisende looked at Geoffrey and raised her eyebrows in an unspoken question. He considered for a moment and then nodded at the bearded man. The chances of the four of them surviving an attack by the mob were not significantly greater than him alone, but if Geoffrey could keep them occupied, Roger might have sufficient time to fetch help from the citadel. Next to him, Roger, Helbye, and Fletcher, understanding nothing of the exchange in Greek, looked bewildered.

"Go," said Geoffrey to them. "They will not harm you. Fetch help from the citadel."

"Are you staying?" asked Roger, confused. "Will she talk to you?"

"Yes, but not with you here. Go."

Roger shook his head. "Oh, no! I do not like this at all, lad. I do not trust her or them. As soon as we are gone, they will turn on you like savages."

Geoffrey squeezed his shoulder. "They will not. I can keep them talking while you fetch help."

"You are a dreadful liar, Geoff," said Roger, standing firm. "I will not leave without you."

"Well, she will not talk to me as long as you are here. Take Helbye and Fletcher and go. Bring Hugh with the men who are practising in the bailey."

Reluctantly, Roger let his sword drop, and he motioned to the others to put away their weapons. Fletcher and Helbye exchanged a look of mutual incomprehension, and lowered their swords, although they certainly had no intention of sheathing them.

Melisende eyed Geoffrey in amazement. "You know they will kill you," she said in Greek. "You must have been walking in the heat too long."

"Let the others go," said Geoffrey to the bearded man. "I will stay."

The bearded man nodded agreement, and Geoffrey gave Roger a shove to set him on his way. Unhappily, Roger began to walk, Fletcher and Helbye following, white-faced but steady. The dog looked at Geoffrey, seemed to hesitate, and then, sensing which option was safest, slunk after the others. The crowd parted to let them through. Geoffrey watched until they had rounded the corner, and turned to face the people, sword at the ready. Perhaps he was destined to be torn apart by a mob after all.

The crowd was still, regarding him silently. He stared back at them, and found that most were unable to meet his eyes. He felt sweat coursing down his back as the sun blazed down, and wondered how he might distract them for sufficient time to allow Roger to dash to the citadel for reinforcements. But already the hostility emanating from the crowd had lessened, and here and there, people had put their weapons away. Geoffrey wondered why. He was alone and surely could not present that formidable a target.

"What are you waiting for?" he asked of the bearded man.

"We must stop this," the man said, so softly that Geoffrey thought he had misheard. He turned to the people around him. "Go home. This is not how we behave. We are not Crusaders!"

For a moment, nothing happened, and then an old lady at the front turned and began to walk back up the street. The sound of a door closing after her was as loud as a clap of thunder in the following silence. Then the bearded man pushed through the crowd and walked away. Others followed, some gratefully relieved that trouble had been averted, and others clearly disappointed in their plans for revenge. It was not long before Geoffrey stood alone in the empty street.

"You were lucky, Norman!" said Melisende behind him, leaning up against the doorjamb and folding her arms. "You should be thankful these are God-fearing people and not like the unholy rabble you call knights, or you would be dead by now."

Geoffrey swallowed, and felt a weakness in his knees. He wondered whether he would have the strength to find Roger before the large Englishman descended on the street with all the fury the citadel could muster. He was surprised to find his hands were unsteady, something that seldom happened, even after the most bloody of battles.

"You are in no danger now," she said, indicating the deserted street with a nod of her head. "You can leave."

"Will you answer my questions first?" he asked.

She put her hands on her hips and gazed at him in disbelief, before letting out a great peal of laughter. Geoffrey felt the unsteadiness in his limbs begin to recede as irritation took over.

"You are incorrigible!" she said. "You are delivered from the jaws of death by a whisker, and you persist in pursuing the very path that led you there in the first place. Very well. What do you want to know?"

It took a moment for Geoffrey to bring his mind back to the

business at hand, and he thrust his hands through the slits in the sides of his surcoat lest their trembling should reveal to Melisende how shaken he was. He took a couple of steps away from her, so that anyone still watching him from the dispersed crowd could not misconstrue their conversation for one that might be considered threatening.

"You say you went out to see your uncle, and when you returned, John—the knight—was dead in your house?"

"Yes," she replied, her voice dripping with sarcasm. "That has not changed since yesterday."

"Tell me again what you did when you came home." He wanted to know whether she had pulled the dagger from the body in horror, as suggested by Hugh, or whether it had been beside the body on the floor.

"I went to pour water to clean my feet," she said, with a heavy sigh, "as I told you yesterday. They were hot and dusty after walking through the city. Then I drank some wine and walked upstairs. The body was, as you saw, lying on its stomach. It was like a nightmare, like something from the scenes when the Crusaders took Jerusalem and killed so many people. I could not believe it was real, and I wondered whether someone might be playing some dreadful practical joke. I took the dagger in my hands and pulled, to see if it were really embedded in his back as it seemed, or whether it was cunningly arranged to look so. I saw it was real, and then I ran outside to call for help."

"What happened to the dagger?"

She frowned. "I do not remember. Perhaps I dropped it in the bedchamber. No! I must have carried it with me. I think I flung it from me at some point."

"So where is it now?"

She glanced around, as though it might appear on the ground in the street. "I have no idea. Someone must have picked it up."

"For what purpose?"

She eyed him sceptically. "I imagine to sell. A year ago, these people lost most of their possessions to looters. Who can blame them if they took the dagger? It was a horrible thing, anyway, covered in big, ugly jewels. Like something a Norman might own," she added defiantly.

"It had a curved blade," said Geoffrey, "and Norman blades are generally straight. I would show you mine if I did not think your neighbours would misread the gesture and rush out to kill me."

She looked at him in surprise and laughed again. Geoffrey looked at her closely for the first time, suddenly aware that she was an attractive woman. She had straight black hair that fell like a curtain down her back, longer than the veil she wore over it, and her eyes were light brown, like honey. When she laughed, and the hard lines around her eyes and mouth disappeared, she looked very young, although Geoffrey judged her to be in her mid-twenties.

"They would not harm you now," she said. "Your courage in saving your friends shamed them into letting you go."

"I was sending them for help," he said. "Do you know no French at all?"

"Enough to know you are not being wholly truthful," she said. "You must have known that you would have been dead long before your friends had time to run to the citadel and return with help."

Geoffrey knew no such thing, since he had detected a hesitancy in the crowd from the start, and had been fairly certain he could stall them from attacking until Roger returned. But Melisende's conviction that he could not made him wonder whether he had been overconfident in his negotiating abilities. Still, he thought to himself, at least he would have delivered Roger and the others from an unpleasant fate had the crowd not shown such unprecedented morality.

"How do you come to know Greek?" Melisende asked. "It is not a skill most of the barbarians in the citadel possess."

"I learned it in Constantinople," he said, wondering whether Roger had reached the citadel and thinking that he might well miss him if they chose to travel different routes. Then Roger would attack the street, and there would be more killing and looting.

"While you were sacking it?" she asked, the laughter gone from her face again.

"No. I find learning conjugations while I pillage very distracting," he replied. "I visited Constantinople long before the Crusaders went there. And why are you here? When did you come?"

"What has this to do with the dead knight?" she said abruptly. She stared at him for a moment. "You may be courageous, and you may be able to learn the languages of the people you oppress, but you are still a Norman, and you still condemned me to the Patriarch's dungeons without a second's hesitation. If that poor monk had not been killed when I was incarcerated, I might have been executed as a murderer by now. Had you thought of that? I was innocent! And please do not patronise me by saying that if I were innocent I had nothing to fear. You know as well as I do that innocence or guilt is immaterial once the doors close behind a prisoner in this city!"

"Quite a speech," he said, deliberately casual to annoy her. The fact that she was correct was beside the point. He wondered what had happened to Melisende Mikelos to make her so aggressive and disagreeable. He had the feeling that she was somewhat disappointed that the crowd had backed away from attacking him, despite her paltry attempts to dissuade them. He had been wrong in arresting her the day before—clearly he had, since she seemed to be innocent of the charge of murder—yet the feeling that she had not been entirely truthful with him persisted. But regardless, he knew he would gain nothing of value from her, and it would be prudent to leave before they annoyed each other any further.

He gave her one of his most winning smiles. "Thank you for your help. I hope this is the last you will hear of this affair. Goodbye."

He gave her a small bow and turned, leaving her standing on her doorstep, her temper boiling at the way in which he had dismissed her grievance so casually. She watched him walk away, aware that all along the street others watched too, some glad they had not killed a knight with the inevitable retribution it would have brought, and others bitterly resentful they had not dispatched all four of them while they had the chance.

What an irritating, arrogant man, she thought, noting the confident stride all Norman nobles seemed to master from birth. But at least he had talked to her in Greek, and not simply spoken French louder and louder until he thought she understood, as most knights would have done—had they bothered to address her courteously at all.

Geoffrey strode up the street, hoping that the weakness he still felt in his knees was not apparent to the people he knew were watching him. He rounded the corner and was confronted by Roger, who was livid.

"What was all that about?" he demanded. "What were you thinking of, sending us off and facing that mob alone? They might have killed you!"

"I told you to go to the citadel for help!" exclaimed Geoffrey in horror. "Why did you not go?"

He imagined the mob closing in on him, while he had struggled to buy time for Roger to come with reinforcements. And all the time Roger would have been watching from around the corner, not understanding a word that was said. The thought made his blood run cold.

"I had no idea what was going on with all that jibber-jabber in Egyptian . . ."

"Greek."

"Greek, then. It is all the same heathen babble." Roger was silent for a moment, and then relented. "So what did she tell you?"

"Nothing," admitted Geoffrey. "Nothing that she did not say yesterday. In fact, it was all a waste of time, and we should not have gone there at all."

"We should have spent the afternoon in one of them cool brothels," said Helbye. "Or in a drinking house sipping cold ale."

"Where are we off to now?" asked Roger, slipping into step beside Geoffrey. "An Egyptian encampment outside the city walls, perhaps, or a snake pit? Somewhere as accommodating as the last place we visited?" He grinned; his fury was clearly forgotten, and for him, the business was over. Geoffrey still felt a residual anger that Roger had not done as he had been asked, and he envied Roger's ability to shrug off ill feelings with such gay abandon.

He gave Roger a weak smile. "We know John lived at the citadel, but according to the notes of the Patriarch's scribes, Sir Guido had recently moved into the Augustinian Priory near the Holy Sepulchre. He was apparently considering giving up knightly duties to become a monk."

"Was he heat-struck or something?" asked Roger, clearly nonplussed. "Why would he want to do anything as stupid as that?"

"He would not be the first," said Geoffrey. "Several knights and soldiers joined the priesthood when they reached Jerusalem. Not everyone came on Crusade for the loot and the fighting."

Roger looked unconvinced, and Geoffrey wondered what the burly Englishman would think if he became aware of Geoffrey's own misgivings about his knightly obligations.

They walked in silence. The sun was still fiercely hot, although its intensity had started to fade. Geoffrey felt slightly light-headed, but did not like to admit so to the others. The effects of his near escape were beginning to take their toll, and he wanted nothing more than to lie down in his own chamber and sleep. Helbye asked that he be allowed to stop to buy water from a man carrying two leather buckets suspended from a yoke over his shoulders, but Geoffrey sensed something untoward in the man's evident enthusiasm for selling it to them, and refused permission. He bought some for the dog, and felt vindicated when the animal declined it after a single sniff.

They were received politely but coldly by the Augustinians at their premises near the Church of the Holy Sepulchre, but at least they were invited to sit for a while in the cool of a marble chamber. While Geoffrey marvelled at the delicate patterns set into the stone, the others sipped appreciatively at the fine red wine they were brought.

"What do you want with us?"

Geoffrey turned at the hostile voice and saw an obese man in the robes of an Augustinian Canon standing in the doorway. The Canon had a bright red face that clashed unappealingly with his greasy ginger hair.

"We are investigating the murder of Sir Guido of Rimini on behalf of the Advocate," replied Geoffrey, coldly polite. "I would be grateful if you would answer some questions."

The Canon's manner softened somewhat. "Ah, yes. Poor Brother Salvatori." He caught Geoffrey's puzzled expression and hastened to explain. "Sir Guido was going to take major orders with us. He had already moved his belongings here, and had taken the name Brother Salvatori in readiness. He spent most of his time here, praying and following our daily routines."

"Did he leave at all? Did he have any visitors?"

"Not that I know of," said the Canon. "He was serious in his intentions and, once he had moved here, he seldom left."

"Seldom? That implies he did leave from time to time."

"Well, perhaps he did once or twice," said the Canon dismissively. "What does it matter?"

"It might matter a great deal," said Geoffrey irritably. "It might help us discover who killed him, and so prevent another man from dying. This is important. Think back to the few days before he died. Did he leave then?"

The Canon screwed up his face in thought. "I think I may recall something. Two days before he died, he was out all night. He returned at dawn and . . . well, he had a man in the room with him."

Geoffrey waited for elaboration, but none came. "Did you know this man?"

"I did not, and I do not condone such activities."

"Can you describe him?"

The Canon sighed heavily. "Not really. He was a Benedictine. And he had eyes of different colours. I heard them talking together in low voices."

"Could you hear what they were saying?"

"No. And I did not wish to. But I heard the scrape of pen on vellum."

Geoffrey was astounded. The Canon pretended that he had only just recalled the incident, but it seemed to Geoffrey that it was clearly vividly etched in the man's mind. He must have been very close to them to see that the eyes of the Benedictine were different colours, and if he had been able to hear one of them writing, then he must also have been listening very hard.

"Have you seen this Benedictine since?"

"Yes. He hovered around outside our premises the morning Brother Salvatori was found dead—that was two days after he had been in Salvatori's room. Then news came of the murder, and he disappeared. I have not seen him since."

"Why did you not mention all this to the Patriarch's men?"

The Canon drew himself upright. "Brother Salvatori was a good man. And I feel he was sincere in his intentions. I did not want his name sullied with the incident of which I have told you."

"But it sounds as though Guido and this monk were only talking and writing," Geoffrey pointed out. "Not engaged in any kind of activity that would besmirch the reputation of either."

The Canon eyed him pityingly, and Geoffrey wondered how the Canon could justify such conclusions from the information he had. He had encountered men like the Canon many times before and knew that a conviction, once held, would never be swayed, no matter what evidence was presented to the contrary.

"Tell me what happened the morning Guido's—Salvatori's—body was found."

The Canon raised his hands. "I received a summons to go to the citadel—Salvatori's body was taken there after it was removed from the Dome of the Rock. The Advocate knew of Salvatori's intention to join the priesthood, and wanted me to pray over his body."

"Was there anything with the body when you saw it at the citadel?"

"What do you mean? Salvatori had no purse or jewellery. He had forsaken such things in favour of a spiritual life," replied the Canon sanctimoniously.

Geoffrey looked from his own strong, tanned hands to those of the Canon who hastily hid them in the sleeves of his habit when he saw the knight's sceptical gaze. The Canon's hands were fat, white, and adorned with rings bearing heavy stones. Geoffrey wondered how the Canon could be so outrageously hypocritical in his piety and still expect to be taken seriously. Geoffrey had seen brave men waver before a battle: perhaps monks wavered when confronted with the easy pickings of the Holy Land.

"I meant was the weapon that killed Sir Guido with his body?"

"Oh, that. Yes. It was there. It was a huge thing, like a Saracen weapon, with a jewelled hilt. I inspected it, but the jewels were not real, only coloured glass."

"What happened to it?"

"It was not worth keeping, so I left it with Salvatori's body." The Canon paused. "When I say it was not worth keeping, I mean I . . ."

"Yes. Thank you. I know what you mean," said Geoffrey, his dislike for the Canon increasing by the moment. He saw he would get no more useful information from him and, somewhat disgusted, he took his leave with curt thanks.

"There is only one other thing," called the Canon to his retreating back. Geoffrey stopped and looked back. "Brother Salvatori was sent a letter that arrived the day he died. We did not break the seal and read it, of course—that would have been most improper. I took it to the citadel myself, because the seal was that of the Advocate."

Wearily, Geoffrey and the others trudged up the Via Dolorosa toward the Church of the Holy Sepulchre, that most holy of Christian places, said to be the site of Jesus' tomb. The Via Dolorosa was the route taken by Jesus at his crucifixion and was a narrow street where the earth underfoot was baked hard and dry. Unlike the rest of the city, this sacred area was full of people, for it was to this road, with the Holy Sepulchre at its end, that pilgrims came to walk barefoot to beg forgiveness for all manner of sins, some petty, most not. Here and there, voices were raised in desperate supplication in a variety of languages—Latin, Greek, French, Italian, and many Geoffrey did not recognise.

He wondered whether crawling up the Via Dolorosa on bleeding knees, or stopping after every step to pray, would really atone for some of the foul acts to which some of these pilgrims were confessing. One man with an unkempt black beard was demanding redemption for murdering his children when he was drunk, and doing so in tones that were anything but repentant. Meanwhile, a woman begged that her husband be struck dead before he discovered how many times she had committed adultery and killed her.

Geoffrey found his answer to the question of redemption in the Church of the Holy Sepulchre itself, which thronged with people, nearly all of them wearing smug expressions in the belief that their sins were forgiven and that they were free to go and sin again. Outside, beggars sat, revealing weeping sores, stumps of limbs, and fingers and toes eaten away by leprosy. Their chorus of demands as the knights entered the church rose furiously, and then turned into curses when Geoffrey's handful of small coins—all he ever carried with him—did not meet their expectations.

The church had been built during the last twenty years, after an older one had been destroyed in an Arab raid. It comprised a handsome dome, not as impressive as the cupola of the Dome of the Rock, but pleasing in its sturdy simplicity. Under the dome was the tomb itself, a small hollow in a rock, around which pilgrims clustered like flies, their hands reaching out to touch.

This church had none of the reverent peace of the Dome or the little church of St. Mary's: a constant babble of voices shattered the silence, wheedling, pleading, demanding, urging, fervent, jubilant, saintly, and ecstatic. Monks chanted constantly, different psalms and prayers for different Orders, all clashing and competing with each other. To one side, a man announced that he had fresh figs to refresh pilgrims weary after their ordeal, while a pardoner offered to sell Geoffrey pieces of the True Cross and hairs from Joseph's beard that would assure his salvation. Geoffrey's dog growled menacingly at the affray, and Geoffrey, knowing that it would be only a matter of time before it found someone to bite, pushed it outside to lie in the shade.

A Benedictine with a pronounced limp came forward to tell them that weapons were not allowed in the Church, and that they would need to leave their arsenal of swords and daggers outside.

"We are not here to make trouble, but we are not here as pilgrims," said Geoffrey. "I want to talk to whoever discovered Loukas, the monk who was murdered last night."

The monk's eyes narrowed. "Who are you, and why do you make such demands?"

"We are here in the name of the Advocate," said Geoffrey politely, wondering how long his good manners would last if forced to deal with yet more offensive monastics. "Please tell us where we might find the witnesses to Loukas's murder."

The monk sized them up for a moment and then, limping, led them away from the dome and along a stone corridor with rooms leading off it. He stopped at one, gestured that they were to wait in the hallway, and slipped inside, closing the door behind him. The entrance opposite was ajar, and Geoffrey pushed it open curiously. It revealed a small chapel filled with tiny burning candles that illuminated it with an unsteady light. Two sheeted bodies lay side by side in front of a rough altar, and several monks knelt next to them, droning prayers. They looked up as he entered, and their voices faltered and then stopped.

Geoffrey walked over to one of the corpses and lifted the sheet to look underneath. The white face of John of Sourdeval stared back at him, his hair washed and neatly combed and the blood rinsed from his body. Geoffrey's stomach lurched as he looked into the face of the man who had been a friend. He stood for a moment, gazing down at the waxen features, memories of many evenings of discussion and debate flooding unbidden into his mind.

He swallowed hard and, muttering a silent apology to John, quickly pushed the body onto its side and measured the wound in John's back against his own forefinger. He eased him down again and replaced the sheet gently, ignoring the half-curious, half-outraged stares of the monks. He turned his attention to the other body.

The man who lay there was small, and even in death his twisted and malformed limbs indicated a hunchback. His face was swarthy too, and although someone had carefully washed and shaved the body, there was a heavy growth of stubble on his chin and cheeks. Assuming it was Loukas, Geoffrey eased the body over, and noted that the gash in its back still oozed a little. He laid his finger next to it, noting that it was longer than the one in John's back. But that meant nothing, for he knew that such wounds could be enlarged if the victim struggled, or fell awkwardly.

"What do you think you are you doing?" came a sharp voice in aggrieved tones. "These men have been prepared to meet God. They died unshriven, and so we must do all we can to ensure their souls reach Him. Your poking and prodding will not help them."

Geoffrey smiled an apology at the surly monk who had ordered him to wait in the corridor, and followed him out of the chapel and into the room opposite. Roger was already seated with a goblet of wine, and Helbye and Fletcher stood to attention behind him.

"This is Father Almaric, who rules the Benedictine community here," said Roger, introducing Geoffrey to the white-haired monk who rose to greet him with a benign smile. "And this here is his secretarius Brother Celeste," he added, eyeing the sharp-voiced monk who had escorted Geoffrey from the chapel with dislike.

Father Almaric offered Geoffrey some wine, and then sat again with evident relief. "Forgive me," he said, "but I have swollen ankles that give me much discomfort. Standing is most painful." He took a grateful sip at the rich red wine in his cup. Geoffrey watched him.

"The Arab physicians say that swollen ankles might be aggravated by red wines," he said. "They recommend sufferers to drink white wines or, better yet, ale or water. And they say a poultice of mud from the Dead Sea brings some relief."

Almaric looked startled at this turn in the conversation.

"Take no notice of him, Father," said Roger comfortably. "He reads all the time and talks to these infidels in the language of the Devil, so it is no wonder that his head is stuffed with such nonsense. I always find red wine soothes pains better than white."

"Does it work, this Arab treatment?" asked Almaric, ignoring Roger.

Geoffrey smiled. "I have no idea—I have never suffered from the complaint. I only repeat what I have read."

Almaric looked at the wine in his goblet and set it down. "I prefer white wines anyway," he said. "And I will ask about this mud poultice. The pain is sometimes unbearable, and all the other remedies that I have tried have failed. But I should not regale you with my problems. I understand you are investigating these dreadful murders for the Advocate?"

Geoffrey nodded. "I would like to speak to the person who found Brother Loukas, and to anyone who knew him well."

"It was Brother Celeste who found Loukas," said Almaric, indicating his surly monk with a nod of his head. "And you are mistaken when you call him Brother. He was no monk or priest. When we Crusaders took over the Holy Sepulchre, most of the Greek community were banned from using the church. Lukas was the only one allowed to remain because we did not know how to rid ourselves of him. He was deaf and dumb, and sorely crippled. When the Greeks left, he simply continued to do his duties here—cleaning floors and doing odd chores around the kitchens. He was physically removed twice, but merely picked himself up and walked back in. I felt an admiration for his dogged devotion and gave permission for him to stay. But although he wore the robe of a monk—some castoff given to him—he was a layman."

"Did he have any particular acquaintances?"

Almaric shook his head. "Not that I am aware. He could not speak, and he could not hear. The brothers here treated him kindly, but he had no particular friends, or even family."

Geoffrey turned to Celeste. "Please tell me what happened when you found Loukas dead."

Celeste looked annoyed. "I have already told the Patriarch's men all I know. Ask them."

"I am asking you," said Geoffrey with deceptive mildness, wondering why so many people were proving to be unhelpful, and beginning to find it aggravating.

Celeste glanced at the benign features of Father Almaric and relented. "It was dark. I was walking around the Church as I always do to make certain all is secure, when I saw someone lying on the floor. It was Loukas, and he had been stabbed in the back."

"Stabbed with what?"

"With a knife," said Celeste heavily. "Like the one you see fit to bring within these holy walls."

"Like this one?" asked Geoffrey in surprise, drawing his dagger and holding it out to Celeste. Celeste gave a sharp, indignant intake of breath, and Almaric intervened.

"Put your weapon away, Sir Geoffrey," he said gently. "Celeste is correct in his disapproval. We do not like weapons in this house of God."

"But was the knife that killed Loukas like this one?" insisted Geoffrey, holding it so that Celeste could see the plain hilt and straight blade.

Celeste glanced at it in exaggerated distaste. "No, I suppose not. It as different somehow. The handle was coloured, and it was bigger."

"What of the blade?" aked Geoffrey. "Was it like this, or different?"

"I could not see much of the blade," said Celeste heavily, "when it was embedded in poor Loukas. But it seemed to be bent, rather than straight like yours. I covered the poor man with one of the blankets we keep ready lest the pilgrims are taken ill—which they often are on entering this holy place after such long journeys—and I called for help. Other monks came, and I went personally to fetch Father Almaric."

"So, someone has been with Loukas's body from the moment you found it until . . . ?"

"Until now," snapped Celeste. "When death strikes so suddenly, the soul is in grave danger. We began a vigil for him immediately."

"And who removed the knife from his back?"

Celeste frowned. "Now there was an odd thing," he said. "The Patriarch's scribes also asked about that. After Father Almaric had finished giving last rites—it is always possible the soul might remain with a corpse for a while and might be saved by granting it absolution, even after death—I went with the body to the chapel to supervise its laying out. When we unwrapped it, the knife was not there. It had gone."

"Did you see anyone remove it?"

"Of course not," said Celeste. "I did not even think about it until the Patriarch's scribes pressed me on the matter."

"So, where is the knife now?" persisted Geoffrey.

Celeste and Almaric exchanged a glance of incomprehension. "I really have no idea," said Almaric frowning. "Oh, dear me. I hope you do not believe it to be stolen. What a terrible crime that would be in this most holy place." He crossed himself quickly and turned to Celeste. "Will you ask among the brethren to see if anyone has seen this foul thing or has some idea what might have become of it?"

"Did you know a monk called Jocelyn?" asked Geoffrey, changing the subject to curb the old man's agitation. "Like you, he was a Benedictine, but he spent his time at the Dome of the Rock."

Father Almaric frowned, racking his brains. "You mean the monk who was murdered at the Dome?" he asked eventually. "No, I do not recall meeting him, although my memory for names is poor. What did he look like?"

Geoffrey had to admit he did not know. He had never seen Jocelyn, dead or alive.

"I knew Jocelyn," mused Celeste. "He came here on occasion. He had curious eyes—one brown, one blue. You knew him Father. He came to you for confession some weeks ago."

The elderly monk looked taken aback. "Did he? Heavens! I must be more feeble-witted than I thought. Curious eyes, you say? I must say I cannot recall anyone of that description."

"What can you tell me about him?" asked Geoffrey of Celeste, leaving the old monk to sit back in his chair looking perplexed.

"Nothing much. He spent most of his time at the Dome of the Rock and came here occasionally to pray. I never spoke to him myself."

"When did you last see him?"

"I really cannot remember," said Celeste. "Not recently, but then he has been dead for three weeks, so that can come as no surprise. Even a knight could work that out."

There was a silence. Father Almaric looked admonishingly at his evil-tempered monk, while Geoffrey studied Celeste intently to see if he could ascertain whether his unpleasant demeanour was usual or whether something in Geoffrey's questions had touched a raw nerve. Almaric attempted to make up for Celeste's rudeness with pleasantries.

"You are Normans from England, are you not? I went to England once, to the shrine of St. Botolph at St. Edmundsbury. It is a Benedictine House, you know. What a beautiful place! So endowed with tranquillity and peace."

"You should see Durham," broke in Roger. "Now there is a house fit for God. Strong too, like a fortress. I could hold it against the Scots easy!"

Almaric looked bemused. "Do you miss it? England, I mean? The cool rain, and the mists, and the great green forests?"

Geoffrey nodded. "I miss it very much," he said softly. He looked away, out of the small window, through which he could see only a wall of baked yellow earth. "If Tancred gave me leave, I would return there tomorrow. I have grown weary of all this heat and dust."

"I miss the ale," interrupted Roger enthusiastically, eager to join in. "And the wenches. These Greek and Arab women are all right, but I prefer a lass who understands what I am saying."

Geoffrey was surprised Roger indulged in conversations of any kind during his frequent bouts of womanising, but saw the monks look shocked and decided Roger's taste in women was hardly a suitable topic to be discussed with two monks in a church.

"Is there anything more you can tell me?" he prompted politely, addressing the monks.

"Nothing," said Celeste, still fixing Roger with an expression of disgust. "I spoke with the other monks, and none of them saw or heard anything that might give a clue as to why Loukas was murdered. Most of the brethren had already retired to bed—it was dark, and there is very little monks can do in the dark except sleep or pray. We are not knights who carouse and entertain women to all hours of the night. And that is all we can tell you about this matter."

He stood pointedly and opened the door for them. Almaric shot him another mildly admonishing glance for his rudeness.

"Celeste is right," he said. "I regret we cannot tell you any more. None of us really knew Loukas. I will think, though, and if I can come up with any more information, I will send word to you."

The knights took their leave of the Benedictines and began to walk back to the citadel. Geoffrey frowned.

"We have learned nothing about Loukas to make matters clearer. But we have our connection between Guido and Jocelyn. The Canon we spoke to earlier said the Benedictine who hung around Guido had eyes of different colours, and now Brother Celeste informs us that Jocelyn had such eyes. The two men spent time in Guido's room at the Augustinian Priory, writing. Guido was killed two days later, and Jocelyn seemed to have learned of his death while hovering outside waiting for him to return. Jocelyn, nervous and irritable, returned to the Dome of the Rock, where he too was murdered."

"But Brother Pius did not visit Guido," Roger pointed out. "He would have been useless anyway, since he could not write."

"So he would," said Geoffrey, "if his Prior was telling us the truth about his illiteracy. But the Prior did tell us that Pius had trouble sleeping at night. Who knows what he really might have been doing while his brethren slept soundly, believing him to be praying in the church?"

Geoffrey, Roger, and Hugh sat together in a shady garden watching the last rays of the sun fade away in a haze of orange. Somewhere in the distance, the mournful wail of a Moslem call to prayer rose and fell, quickly joined by a second and then a third. The garden had a little waterfall, and its pleasant gurgle mingled with the muezzins' voices in a sound that Geoffrey thought he would associate with Jerusalem for as long as he lived.

"Damned caterwauling," grumbled Roger.

The dog lifted his head and uttered a dismal answering howl to the singing. Roger attempted to drown out the dog and the call to prayer by slurping noisily from his tankard of ale.

"The ale is weak, the music appalling, and the women scarce," he complained. "What a place to be!"

Geoffrey looked up to where bats flitted to feast on the clouds of insects that gathered in the trees above. A gentle breeze turned the leaves this way and that in a soft whisper, and wafted the strong scent of blooms around the garden. Geoffrey was reminded suddenly and irrelevantly of his home in the castle at Goodrich, so many thousands of miles away, and of a glade near the river that was always peaceful at dusk. He closed his eyes and inhaled, trying to recall the distinctive aroma of home: wood fires, wet grass, copses of spring flowers. But the memory eluded him, and the familiar smells of Jerusalem pervaded: huge flowers—the names of which he did not know—and dust.

He was jolted to alertness with a start as Hugh splashed a handful of water over him from the fountain, and Roger rocked with laughter.

"Welcome back," said Hugh. "We have been talking to you for at least five minutes, imagining you were doing us the courtesy of listening, only to find you are not at home."

"Sorry," said Geoffrey. "I was trying to remember what it is like in England."

Hugh and Roger stared at him mystified.

"Well, we were discussing what you had discovered today," said Hugh eventually. "You learned that Brother Jocelyn worked occasionally for Bohemond as scribe, and that he was nervous the day before he died. Brother Pius was not a scribe, but was brave enough to shop for meat at the salubrious premises of Akira, where he was dispatched while the redoubtable butcher slept. And Loukas was not a priest at all. It does not seem that there is a link between these three men."

"Loukas sounded short of a few marbles," said Roger, with a significant tap to his temple with a grimy forefinger.

"That may well have been an act," said Geoffrey, "to secure him a position working at the Holy Sepulchre while all the other Greeks were banned. He may well have been a spy for them, pretending to be harmlessly insane to lure them into speaking their secrets when he was around."

"In which case, he may have been killed by someone at the Holy Sepulchre who discovered what he was doing," mused Hugh. "And Jocelyn may have been killed for something he learned while in the employ of Bohemond."

"But it does not fit together," said Geoffrey. "And this dagger business is curious: the same knife, or similar ones, were used for each victim. The monks at the Dome of the Rock and Akira wanted to steal the ones that killed Jocelyn and Pius, but they were too slow on the uptake, and the daggers had disappeared by the time they looked for them. Brother Celeste said he had covered Loukas's body with a blanket when it was discovered, and it was surrounded by a crowd of monks praying for him the whole time. But by the time the body was moved to the chapel, the knife had gone."

"While your woman . . ." began Hugh.

"Melisende Mikelos," put in Roger.

"While Melisende Mikelos took the knife from John's body, and carried it outside with her—just as I suggested she may have done," said Hugh smugly. "And it was stolen when she dropped it in the street. What of the dagger that killed Guido?"

"That was brought to the citadel with his body. I asked to see it, but for some reason it was not kept. No one seems certain what might have happened to it, but you know how soldiers are with valuables. I imagine one of them realised he might be able to sell it, and stole it on the basis that no one at the citadel was likely to want the weapon that had killed a knight. I began to question the men who brought Guido back, but it appears the body was left unattended for some time in the citadel chapel, and anyone could have stolen the weapon then. And the same is true of a letter thought to have been from the Advocate, brought to the citadel by that unpleasant Canon from St. Mary's Church. Guido's friends say there was no letter among his belongings and claim he was unlikely to have one anyway, since he could not read."

"What a mess," said Roger in disgust. "Nothing clear, everything muddled. A priest must be behind all this, because a soldier would never stoop to such subterfuge!"

"So, what will you do tomorrow?" asked Hugh, a smile catching at the corners of his mouth at Roger's remark. "You learned precious little from your enquiries today, except a few facts that confuse the issue more."

Geoffrey sighed and leaned back in his chair, studying the way the leaves were patterned black against the dark blue sky. "I suppose I will go to speak to the Patriarch's scribes to ask about Brother Jocelyn. Then I will attempt to discover where in the marketplace these daggers are sold, and perhaps try to find out more of Loukas from the Greek community."

"Be careful, my friend," said Hugh. "If Loukas was a spy, then the Greeks are hardly likely to admit it, and they will do all they can to prevent you from finding out."

"We should go," said Roger, glancing up at the dark sky. "The curfew bell will sound soon."

The three knights left the garden, said their farewells to the taverner who allowed them to use it, and made their way back to the citadel. Roger bellowed the password for half of Jerusalem to hear, and the guards let them through the wicket gate. As soon as they were inside, a small man scurried toward them, his face streaked with grime and his eyes wide with fear.

"Sir Geoffrey?" he began in a querulous voice, looking at the three knights. Geoffrey raised a hand. "I am Brother Marius," the man said shakily, "one of the scribes employed by the Patriarch to investigate the strange deaths that have been occurring recently. Brother Dunstan, who worked with me, has been murdered."

CHAPTER FIVE

The three knights stared at the trembling scribe in horror as he announced the news of Brother Dunstan's murder.

"How?" asked Geoffrey eventually.

"I did not dawdle to make a thorough investigation, but he looked to have been strangled. It must be something to do with these murders. Perhaps the killer thinks we have sufficient information to solve the mystery, and wants us dead before we can work it out. I am afraid, Sir Geoffrey! Where can I go where I will be safe? How do I know that even now the killer is not watching my every move?"

Marius's voice began to take on the edge of hysteria, and Geoffrey interrupted brusquely. "You are safe in the citadel."

He wondered whether this were true, especially given that a dagger and a pig's heart had been placed so easily in his own chamber. He stared at the frightened monk as he tried to imagine who might have put such a grisly warning in his room. A common soldier would be unlikely to gain access to it without being challenged, so whoever left the dagger and heart had to have been a knight. Yet all the knights at the citadel were under the command of either the Advocate, Bohemond, or Tancred. But both Tancred and the Advocate had asked Geoffrey to investigate the murders, and they would hardly have asked him, knowing his reputation for tenacity, to do so if they were involved themselves. Meanwhile, Bohemond was in his own Kingdom of Antioch in the north, trying to secure his lands.

Geoffrey brought his whirling thoughts under control. "Where was Dunstan killed?"

"At his own desk in the Patriarch's scriptorium," the monk answered miserably.

"Did you see anyone there running away or hiding in the shadows?"

Marius blanched, but shook his head. "No. Dunstan missed his meal, you see, and I was concerned that he may have been ill. I looked for him in the dormitory, in the gardens and in the chapel, but he was not there. I could not imagine why he would be in the scriptorium after dark—we need daylight in which to work—but it was the only other place I could think of. The door was open, whereas it is usually locked, and I sensed something was wrong. I entered, and there he was, lying across his desk with the rope tight around his neck."

"What did you do?"

"Do? What do you mean?"

"Did you examine the body? Did you loosen the rope? Did you shout out?"

Marius looked confused. "I cannot recall. I think I took his hand in mine, but it was cold. Then I ran for my life."

Geoffrey turned to one of the guards and sent him to fetch Tom Wolfram to saddle their horses—he had walked to the Patriarch's Palace the night before, but in view of the fact that he had been followed then, he considered it was probably safer to ride and to keep to the wider, more public streets.

Hugh gestured at Marius. "I will see him safely installed in the chapel. No one will harm him in a church."

"No," said Geoffrey. "Take him to my chamber. Leave the dog with him. Although the mutt might be useless in any kind of confrontation, his barking might prove a deterrent if the killer desires stealth."

"I can do better than that," said Hugh. "I will stay with him myself. I have had rather too much of that excellent wine, but a

Norman knight drunk is still worth ten sober Lorrainers, or Hospitallers, or whoever else might come."

"Careful," said Geoffrey warningly, seeing fear break out on the monk's face. He took Hugh's arm and led him out of the scribe's hearing. "Talk to Marius. See what you can discover. See if there is anything he did not write on that scroll Tancred gave me that he may have considered unimportant at the time, but that may be relevant now."

Hugh nodded, but looked uneasy. "Be careful, Geoffrey. If you have not returned by dawn, I will send out a rescue party for you."

Roger gestured for the guard to open the gates, and they rode out. Wolfram had brought a lamp, and Geoffrey suppressed a sigh of resignation.

"That lamp will provide an excellent target for an archer," he said, riding next to the young sergeant. "And I see you are not wearing your chain mail again."

Wolfram glanced at him guiltily and quickly doused the lamp. "I only thought we might need it to see where we are going."

"Trust your horse, lad," bellowed Roger from behind. "And learn to read shadows."

"Read shadows?"

Geoffrey suppressed his impatience. He had been through this lesson with Wolfram before, but the young man was slow to learn.

"Listen to the sounds about you," he began. "Attune yourself to the noises of the night, so that you will know if they are not right. Feel the mood of your horse. If she is skittish, it might be because she senses a danger you cannot."

Wolfram nodded, and Geoffrey allowed Roger to take over the lesson while he spurred his horse ahead. The streets were pitch black, for the night had become cloudy and the moon was covered. Someone had been watering a garden, and the smell of wet earth was pungent in the air. Somewhere around his head, an insect sang in a high, whining hum, and further down the street, a cat sat on a high wall and yowled soulfully. Geoffrey thought he heard running footsteps in an alleyway off to the right, and strained his eyes in the darkness to see, but there was nothing.

They reached the Patriarch's palace without incident and banged on the front gates to be allowed in. The doors were opened almost immediately, and sleepy-eyed Arab boys were roused to take care of the horses. The guard seemed surprised when Geoffrey told him why he had come, and sent for his captain. The captain looked disbelieving, but obligingly led the way to the scriptorium. Geoffrey supposed that Marius had made his discovery and simply fled through an unguarded side door without telling anyone what he had found.

The palace was a fine building set around a large, square courtyard. On one side lay a small chapel and the Patriarch's sumptuous public rooms, while his private rooms and the accommodation of his retinue were opposite. The scriptorium and the monks' quarters lay between them, a three-storied building with a refectory on the lowest floor, a dormitory above, and the scriptorium on the top floor, built with large windows to provide maximum daylight.

The captain led Geoffrey and Roger up creaking stairs to the upper floor, past the refectory with its smell of stale grease and the monks' dormitory with its smell of stale sweat. The scriptorium was in blackness, and obligingly Wolfram kindled his lamp. Geoffrey took it and entered. It was a simple rectangular room with two long rows of desks positioned to take best advantage of the sunlight. Lining the walls between the windows were shelves bearing great brown-edged books and neatly stacked piles of scrolls. The metallic smell of ink pervaded, and the pale wooden floor was alive with multicoloured splashes where it had been spilled.

Draped across one of the desks toward the rear of the room was Brother Dunstan, like a huge black slug with a great arched body. His head flopped down almost to the ground, while his legs stuck out at an angle. The captain gave a sharp intake of breath and muttered that he would have to report this to the Patriarch. Geoffrey waited until his footsteps had faded, and sent Wolfram to prevent anyone else from entering until the Patriarch came. The captain's incautious flight across the wooden floor had woken the monks in the room below, and already crabby voices were demanding to know what was happening. It would be only a matter of time before they came to investigate, and there were things Geoffrey wanted to do without an audience of monks.

Roger helped him lift Dunstan's body from the desk and lay it on the floor. Quickly, he opened the storage box on the side of the desk and rummaged through it. In it was a jumble of used scraps of vellum to be scraped clean and used again, old and broken quills, leaking ink pots, and a neatly wrapped parcel of the sickly sweet Greek pastries that Geoffrey detested.

"He will not be needing these any more," said Roger, leaning past Geoffrey to grab the package and slip it down the front of his surcoat. "Knightly plunder after violent death," he added in response to Geoffrey's silent disapproval. "And no different at all to what you are doing," he concluded, watching Geoffrey stuff the scraps of used vellum down the front of his own surcoat. Geoffrey replaced what he had taken from Dunstan's box with a handful of scraps from another desk, while Roger watched with raised eyebrows.

Next, Geoffrey knelt by the body and inspected the red weal around the scribe's neck. The rope used to strangle him was still attached, and it coiled onto the floor around him. Puzzled, Geoffrey frowned, and Roger squatted down next to him.

"What is it?" he whispered, casting a glance toward the door. Out in the courtyard, a commotion had broken out, and there were shouts and the sound of running footsteps.

"This rope," said Geoffrey, picking up the end and twirling it in his fingers. "It is very thick for strangling, is it not?"

"It did its job," said Roger soberly.

"I would not use rope like this to strangle someone," said Geoffrey, studying it intently.

"What peculiar things you say sometimes," said Roger.

"Perhaps the killer did not have time to select something more to your approval. Perhaps it was the first weapon that came to hand."

"And I would not tie a knot in it," said Geoffrey, staring down at the corpse. He took Dunstan's head in his hands and moved it about. "His neck is broken! Look at how his head moves on his neck."

Roger leaned over him, fascinated. "God's teeth, Geoffrey! He was hanged, not strangled at all!"

They looked at each other in puzzlement, before turning their attention back to the corpse.

"Come on," said Roger urgently. "The Patriarch will be here any moment. What else can you tell?"

Geoffrey looked at Dunstan's hands. "His wrists are un-marked, so his hands were not tied, and his fingernails are un-broken. Thus, he did not struggle against the rope around his neck." He looked at the end of the rope he still held. "And this has been cut."

A thunder of footsteps on the stairs heralded the arrival of the Patriarch and his officers.

"Anything else?" asked Roger urgently. "The Patriarch might not want this investigated in too much detail. Who knows—a man killed in his own scriptorium? Dunstan might even have been killed by him."

"He has not been dead too long, or he would be stiff." Geoffrey rose as the Patriarch entered.

The Patriarch, Daimbert, was a tall man, slightly stooped, with a cap of pale silver hair smoothed neatly into place with scented goose grease. His expression was perpetually kind, and he always held his hands clasped in front of him in a way that Geoffrey imagined bishops should. Yet, behind his beneficence was both a will of iron and remarkable energy, and there seemed little he would not do to secure power and lands for the Church. Even his friendship with Tancred—who entered the scriptorium in Daimbert's wake—was in the interest of the Church, for Tancred's allegiance to the Patriarch weakened the Advocate's authority.

There were, however, rumours about the Patriarch that were far less flattering. It was said that he was vain, ambitious, and not entirely free from corruption. Two years previously, he had served as papal legate to the King of Castille, and there were those who wondered how many of the gifts that the King had sent to the Pope had actually reached His Holiness, and how many had remained in Daimbert's personal coffers.

Now Daimbert looked down at the dead monk and began to mutter prayers for the dead. He did not look especially moved, but the Crusaders had murdered and massacred themselves a bloody path through a huge chunk of the world, and death was nothing new to any of them. The gaggle of monks behind him crossed themselves and began their own prayers, a disjointed babble of voices, some shocked, some sincere, others merely curious. And one, perhaps, guilty, satisfied, or relieved?

When Daimbert's prayers were completed, he raised his silver head and looked questioningly at Geoffrey.

"Brother Marius came to us," the knight explained. "He said Dunstan had been killed, and we came to investigate."

"On whose authority do you come?" queried Daimbert softly. Only the Advocate had the authority to burst unannounced into the Patriarch's Palace—Bohemond and Tancred, despite their allegiance to Daimbert, certainly did not. It did not take an astute man to detect that an illegal invasion of his property would not be tolerated by the Patriarch, and Geoffrey sensed he was on dangerous ground.

Geoffrey felt Tancred's eyes boring into him, willing him to discretion, but he did not look away from Daimbert's steady gaze.

"The Advocate's authority, my lord," replied Geoffrey politely. He was aware of Tancred's surprise, but still addressed himself to Daimbert. Daimbert, meanwhile, turned to indicate Tancred with an elegant gesture of his beringed hand.

"But you are Lord Tancred's man, are you not?"

"Sir Geoffrey has leave to serve my interests however he sees fit," Tancred intervened smoothly. Geoffrey was relieved, for he was uncertain how he would have answered without revealing that he was already investigating the matter for Tancred, something he sensed Tancred wanted kept from the Patriarch.

Daimbert slowly turned to Tancred. "Is that so? But it is suspicious, is it not, that your man, who freely admits working for the Advocate without your knowledge or permission, comes to my palace and is found standing over the corpse of one of the few men who know details of these peculiar murders?"

The silence in the room was absolute. Geoffrey looked from Daimbert to Tancred and wondered how he had let himself become embroiled in the petty politics of warring lords who wanted power and possessions at any cost. Melisende Mikelos had been right to fear the justice of men like the Advocate and the Patriarch.

"However," Daimbert continued in his soft voice, addressing Geoffrey, "you did not come in stealth, and my captain assures me that Dunstan was already dead when you arrived. I suppose we can deduce you are not responsible for his death. You say Brother Marius came to you?"

Geoffrey nodded, not wanting to add that the scribe had fled the palace because he feared the murderer might still prowl within its walls.

"And what can you tell us about Dunstan's death?" Daimbert continued.

"Very little," said Geoffrey truthfully. "A rope was tied around his neck, and he died." He indicated the body on the floor with his hand. "When we came, he was lying across the desk, looking as though he had been sitting at it when he died, and had slumped forward."

"And you moved him to the floor?"

Geoffrey nodded. Daimbert stooped to look at the face of his dead monk and sighed. "It is a pity. Dunstan had the best hand in Jerusalem, and I am in great need of scribes with good writing. Especially ones that can be trusted."

He glanced back at the monks behind him, not looking at anyone in particular, but causing a great deal of shuffling and blushing. He waited until they had grown silent again, and dismissed them with a wave of a hand that was more contemptuous than paternal. When the last of them had clattered down the stairs to discuss the murder in excited tones in the room below, Daimbert turned to Tancred.

"I am an agent short, and you seem to trust this man. Will you lend him to me to look into this business?"

For once, Tancred was caught by surprise. He opened his mouth to speak, but no words came. Eventually, he puffed out his cheeks and nodded reluctantly.

"Good." Daimbert became businesslike. "You and I are of the same mind. These murders are more than they seem, and I fear that those who are committing these crimes are aiming to undermine the security of our Kingdom here. There are so many against us: the Saracens, the Jews, the Greeks. Not everyone is content with the rule of our Advocate, and this may be a personal attack against him. He obviously believes so, if he has arranged for the matters to be investigated." Daimbert paused. "I am not asking you to serve two masters Sir Geoffrey; I am simply asking that you pass anything you discover about this affair to me as well as to the Advocate. Preferably to me first."

Geoffrey glanced at Tancred, and caught his almost imperceptible nod. Geoffrey wondered when this would stop, and how many more Holy Land princes would attempt to secure his services before the business was resolved. Perhaps he should save the others the trouble and volunteer. There was still Tancred's uncle Bohemond, and doubtless the Greek, Saracen, and Jewish communities would appreciate a well-placed ear.

Daimbert saw his hesitation and misunderstood. He drew a great ruby ring from his finger and held it out to Geoffrey. "You will appreciate that I do not carry much of value around with me in the night, but you may have this. And I will give you another two of similar value when you solve these wicked crimes."

The heavy ring plopped into Geoffrey's palm, and lay there glinting like an evil red eye. Geoffrey saw Tancred smile, and then nodded slowly to Daimbert to show he accepted the commission. Behind him, Roger coughed. Daimbert gave a resigned sigh and felt about in a pocket under his belt. For a man who carried little of value with him at night, Daimbert seemed to be doing admirably. He drew out a silver chain with a pendant and handed it to Roger, who thanked him with a grin and secreted it away under his unsavoury surcoat.

"I have only one thing to add," said Daimbert. "You might wonder why I should take such an interest in the murder of two of Bohemond's knights. I tell you this reluctantly, but I have considered carefully and feel you should be told. Jocelyn the Benedictine was a double agent. He worked for me in the scriptorium, but his writing was excellent, and he had various commissions from other men—including Bohemond. Another person who bought Jocelyn's skills was the Advocate, who needed a man with a fine hand to write begging letters to the merchants for him. Jocelyn, when engaged on the Advocate's commissions, usually took the opportunity to look around, to listen, to read, and to gather tidbits of information for me. I am troubled by his death. He was useful to me."

Geoffrey's heart sank. The business was becoming more complex by the moment. What else would he learn about Jocelyn? The monk spied on the Advocate and had nocturnal meetings with Sir Guido of Rimini. He must have been killed because he was a spy, and since the Patriarch stood to lose out on his death, the most obvious culprit for his murder was the Advocate. And since all five victims seemed to have been killed with similar weapons, it stood to reason that the Advocate was involved in their deaths too.

"Jocelyn worked in the library in Rome," said Geoffrey carefully, his mind racing. "He learned his fine writing in the Pope's scriptorium. Did the Pope send him here to help you?"

Daimbert's face eased into a slow smile that had all the humour of a crocodile about to devour its prey. "Tancred is right about you," he said. "You are thorough and quick-witted. Yes, to answer your question. Jocelyn came here with the express purpose of using his talents to the advantage of the Holy Church in Rome. And of course, that is best achieved through reporting his findings to me, the Patriarch. I commend you on your intellect. Now, it is late, and I have much to do."

Business completed, Daimbert took his leave. Tancred raised his eyebrows and waited.

"Courrances approached me yesterday and asked if I would investigate on behalf of the Advocate," Geoffrey explained. "It seemed prudent to accept when he would soon discover what I was doing anyway, and by serving him, I could use his name to authorise my questions and not yours."

Tancred chewed his lip and then seized Geoffrey's arm. "I have not the slightest doubt of your loyalty to me. And it was no lie when I told Daimbert I trust your judgement in best serving my interests. But this is a dangerous game for a knight to play. Daimbert is an ambitious man, and the Advocate is a desperate one who knows his powers are being leeched away. You now work for three of the most powerful men in the Holy Land. I hope the movements of the other two against each other do not crush you in the process."

So did Geoffrey, especially bearing in mind that Courrances had told him that the Advocate believed the Patriarch's role in the murders was far from innocent. "Is there anything I should know?" he asked.

Tancred gave a small smile. "Only to reiterate my warnings, and my fears that this business involves powerful people—perhaps even one of your other masters. Or it may be simple and just be the Greeks or Arabs. If I knew anything else, I would tell you, because I want this mess resolved as soon as possible. Tomorrow at first light I leave for Haifa. I feel ill at ease in Jerusalem with all these murders. I will be safer in Haifa."

"Haifa?" Geoffrey felt his interest quicken. Haifa was one of the few towns in Tancred's Principality still to hold out against him.

"I plan to force the town to surrender to me. Hopefully, this will be achieved by a frontal attack, but I am prepared to commit to a siege if necessary." He grinned boyishly. "I would rather fight than sit and wait, but I will have Haifa in the end."

"I have read much about Haifa," began Geoffrey enthusiastically. "It is protected on one side by the sea and on the others by walls fortified with watch towers . . ."

"Your learning would be of great value to me," said Tancred, interrupting gently. "Especially if we are forced to lay siege to the town. But I need you here. I will have no Principality to rule if Jerusalem falls, whether to Arab, Greek, Jew, or Christian. Make your reports to the Advocate, and watch him like a hawk. Send your missives to Daimbert, and observe matters here in his palace. But if you discover anything vital, dissemble to them, and get word to me first. We will keep in touch by messenger."

Geoffrey made his obeisance to Tancred and took his leave, with Roger following.

They collected their horses and began to ride back to the citadel. The air was cool after the stuffiness of the Patriarch's palace, and Geoffrey closed his eyes and let the refreshing breeze waft over him.

"I cannot see why you are so relaxed," muttered Roger next to him. "Dozing in the saddle like you are off for a pleasant ride to inspect your Welsh sheep. You have put yourself in a dangerous position. Supposing you find out that Tancred is behind it all? What will you tell Daimbert and the Advocate?"

"Tancred would not let me investigate if he were involved," said Geoffrey, a great wave of weariness flooding over him. He tried to remember the last time he had managed an uninterrupted night's sleep. He had been out on patrol for two weeks, napping in ditches and behind stones, and then all this intrigue had started. He had come close to death twice by an enraged mob, and he had been trudging around the city all day in the searing heat. "And who are you to preach?" he said, turning to peer at Roger in the dark. "You are now in the pay of both Bohemond and the Patriarch yourself."

"But they are allies," protested Roger.

"I would not be so sure," said Geoffrey. "And Tancred is far less likely to engage in treachery than Bohemond. Look what your master did at Marrat an-Numan. He told the citizens that everyone who gathered together in the hall near the gates would be granted an amnesty when he took the city. Then, when they were conveniently in one place, he slaughtered them all."

"But that is honest treachery, and they were the enemy," said Roger earnestly. "He would not engage in all this murky sub-terfuge."

"Not much!" muttered Geoffrey.

"You now serve three men. Not one of them trusts the oth-ers. And any of them could crush you like a fly," said Roger sagely. "You had better hope that Tancred survives this battle at Haifa he seems so gleeful about. You could be in serious trouble without his protection."

Geoffrey was silent for a while. "The rulers of this country are like Greek fire," he said eventually. "A terrible, destructive weapon that burns, and once burning is almost impossible to put out. It is made by combining pitch, brimstone, naphtha, and rosin. Apart, these elements are harmless, but together they are lethal. That is what the leaders in the Holy Land are like."

"Greek fire is a marvellous invention," said Roger admir-ingly. "I plan to take some home to Durham with me to try out next time those Scots come marauding."

Geoffrey raised his eyes heavenward and let the matter drop.

"While you were chatting to Daimbert, I poked around at the back of the room," said Roger after a moment. "There is a door with a great bolt on it. These days, it only leads to a store-room, but before the Patriarch came it was probably a strong room of some kind. Anyway, a rope was tied to the bolt. Judging from the length of what was still attached and what was round Dunstan's neck, I would say that it had been passed from the bolt over the top of the door and used to hang him."

Geoffrey nodded. "I saw that door. And I saw the stool lying on its side next to it. I think Dunstan put the rope over his head and then leapt off the stool to break his neck. The stool was kicked over in the process. Someone, possibly Marius, must have found him there, cut him down, and tried to make his death appear to be murder. But the reality is that Dunstan committed suicide."

"What? Are you sure?"

"Not completely, but it makes sense from the information we have. The rope around Dunstan's neck was tied in a knot, which seems an odd thing for a strangler to do. His neck was broken, which is more consistent with a leap into oblivion than with strangulation. And the rope used was thick and strong—the kind a man might choose if he intended to kill himself and did not want his efforts to be foiled by the rope breaking."

"But why would Marius want to pretend that Dunstan was murdered? Marius said he was strangled, not hanged."

"Perhaps they were good friends, and Marius did not want to condemn Dunstan to a suicide's burial in unhallowed ground. Perhaps he thought we were more likely to believe Dunstan had been murdered by strangulation than murdered by hanging. It is probably quite difficult to hang a man by stealth, especially if the murderer is alone."

"I could do it easy," said Roger nonchalantly. "Force the noose over the head, hurl the rope over a door, and haul like the Devil."

"But you are stronger than most men," Geoffrey pointed out. "And by doing what you suggest, you would choke your victim to death, not break his neck. There was no damage to Dunstan's fingernails, and he would surely have scrabbled at the noose with his hands had he been strangled."

Roger considered. "I suppose so," he said finally, after making the scowls and grunts that always accompanied his attempts at deep thought. "But we do not need to be wasting our time thinking all this out for ourselves. Marius will tell us."

They arrived back at the citadel and saw the horses settled for what remained of the night. Geoffrey's inclination was to go immediately to his room to interview Marius, but Wolfram reappeared breathlessly to tell him that one of the men was ill. Always in fear of a contagious fever that would spread through the garrison like wildfire, Geoffrey went to investigate and found young Robin Barlow groaning and holding his stomach pitifully.

Geoffrey was no physician, but he was able to put the strong smell of cheap Arab wine together with the symptoms of vomiting and dizziness to diagnose that Barlow was suffering from the effects of too much drink. His inclination was to abandon the lad to his misery and assume he had learned his lesson. But the young soldier clearly thought he was going to die, and since it seemed he had never been drunk before, Geoffrey took a few moments to reassure him and to send a comrade to the kitchens for eggs and vinegar.

Roger was waiting for him in the bailey, standing at the well and gulping great draughts of cool water. Geoffrey drank too, for no soldier passed up the opportunity to eat or drink—who knew how long it might be before such an opportunity came again? Together, they walked across the dark bailey toward the torches that flared either side of the entrance to the Tower of David, and climbed the stairs.

Geoffrey's room was stuffy and in darkness, and he imagined that Marius and Hugh had grown tired of waiting for him to return and had gone to sleep. The dog snuffled wetly around Geoffrey's legs, and followed Roger back down the stairs in search of a candle. Geoffrey realized that the room was so stiflingly hot because someone had closed the window shutters. He was picking his way across the floor in the dark to open them, when his foot contacted with something soft and sent him sprawling forward. He landed on his hands and knees and felt something cool and sticky that had spread out across the tiles. He had been a soldier long enough to know the unmistakable texture of blood when he felt it.

As he climbed to his feet, Roger arrived back with a lamp, and light flooded the chamber.

"Holy Mother!" swore Roger softly.

Hugh lay facedown on the bed, the back of his head dark

with blood, while Marius was huddled into the corner with his knees drawn up to his chest. And underneath him was a great puddle of gore that glistened black in the light of the lamp.

After Helbye and Wolfram had been summoned to remove Marius's bloodied corpse to the chapel, and after Fletcher had scrubbed some of the stains from the floor, Geoffrey flopped onto the window seat and eyed Hugh's white face with concern.

"You should let me look at that cut. I read that Arab physicians use a poultice of herbs . . ."

"You tried a so-called Arab poultice on Sir Aldric of Chester after the capture of Antioch, and he died."

"His wound was fatal anyway," said Geoffrey, stung. "The poultice was to ease the pain, not to cure him. But there may be dirt in the wound. It should be cleaned."

"Roger has done a perfectly adequate job," said Hugh. "I feel better already."

"Are you sure?"

"Yes, yes," said Hugh crossly. "For heaven's sake, Geoffrey! All of us have suffered wounds ten times more serious than this in battle, but because I was struck down in a bedchamber, you think I am dying!"

Geoffrey raised his hands. "All right, all right. Tell me again what happened, then."

Hugh sighed heavily. "I was talking to Marius, just as you told me to do, when I saw that hound of yours stand up and wag its tail. I assumed it was looking at someone behind me, but before I could turn, whoever it was hit me on the head. And that is all I remember. The next thing I knew was that you two were hovering over me like demons from hell, and I had a tremendous headache."

"And you saw and heard nothing else?" insisted Geoffrey.

"Nothing!" said Hugh, becoming exasperated. He put a hand

to the bandage that swathed his fair head, inexpertly tied, but impressively large to make up for it, and winced. "That dog is worthless," he said in calmer tones, watching it sitting obediently at Roger's feet, and attempting to lay its head on his knee. "A murderer comes into your room in the depths of the night, and all that thing does is wag its tail! Did you ever train it to do anything worthwhile? Can it hunt? Can it retrieve? Can it do anything other than lie around and eat?"

Geoffrey thought for a moment. "No. What did Marius tell you before he died?"

"Very little, I am afraid. The man was shaking like a leaf, so I went to fetch some wine to calm him down. By the time he was less frantic, some time had passed. I asked him to relate to me what happened, and he was telling me when the murderer entered."

"What exactly had he said?" asked Geoffrey.

Hugh rubbed at the bandage. "That he went looking for Dunstan, but could not find him. He went to look in the scriptorium as a last resort, but did not really expect to find him because there were no lamps lit. Then he saw a dark shape slumped over Dunstan's desk and found that Dunstan had been murdered."

"How could he tell Dunstan had been murdered if there were no lamps? The scriptorium was pitch black, and we had to light Wolfram's lamp," pounced Geoffrey.

"I am only repeating what he said," replied Hugh waspishly. "I am not attempting to defend it. He saw the rope that he assumed had been used to strangle Dunstan, and came running as fast as he could for the safety of the citadel."

"Good choice," said Roger.

"Why here?" said Geoffrey, thinking aloud. "Why not claim sanctuary with the Patriarch? Daimbert was angry at Dunstan's death, and I feel he would have at least tried to protect Marius. How could Marius feel that a journey through the streets at dusk to claim help from men he did not know was safer than remaining with the Patriarch?"

"I do not know," said Hugh wearily. "He must have had his reasons."

"And when we know what they were, we will be closer to solving this," said Geoffrey. He watched his dog pawing adoringly at Roger, who kept pushing it away.

"What is the matter with this thing?" Roger snapped, glaring at it.

"He can smell the cakes you stole from Dunstan's desk," said Geoffrey, leaving the window seat and going to sit at the table. He wanted to write their findings down so that he could consider them logically, but he was afraid that the killer, who had broken into his room twice now, might find any records he made. He remembered the scraps of vellum he had taken, and pulled them out to study them. It was unlikely a clue would emerge from such an obvious source, but he had precious little to go on, and the matter was becoming dangerous. A man had been murdered in his room, surrounded by a fortress full of knights. The killer he was hunting had shown himself to be a formidable force, and Geoffrey could afford to overlook nothing.

Roger's face lit up, and he retrieved the package from his surcoat, smacking his lips in anticipation. The dog drooled helplessly, and its eyes became great liquid pools of temporary adoration. While Roger unwrapped and the dog slathered, Hugh hunted about for some wine.

"I cannot stomach that sweet stuff with nothing to drink," he said. "Geoffrey, do you have no wine in this pit you call home?"

"You must have had it all already," said Geoffrey, looking up from where he was reading.

Roger gave a dramatic sigh and stood to fetch wine from his own supply. The dog weaved about his legs in a desperate attempt to ingratiate, and almost tripped him.

"Greedy, useless beast," he muttered. He saw the dog's glistening eyes fixed on the unwrapped cakes on the bed, and moved them to a high shelf. Relenting, he broke a tiny piece off and dropped it to the floor, where the dog fell on it frantic with avarice.

He returned moments later holding a bottle, and hunted around for the cups without the fungus growing in the bottom. Elbowing Geoffrey to one side, he rummaged around the scraps of parchment with big, hairy hands. The sound of violent retching filled the room, and he and Geoffrey spun around to look at Hugh in alarm. Hugh, startled, stared back. The sound came again, from under the bed.

"It is that revolting dog!" said Hugh, beginning to laugh. "It has been in the refuse pits again."

Roger disagreed. "It must have been that pig's heart he had. Or whatever nasty item it was gorging itself on at Akira's charnel house."

Geoffrey rubbed his chin, and peered under the bed as the dog retched again. "I do not think so," he said, straightening slowly. "I think it was the cake."

chapter six

Hugh and Roger watched in fascinated disgust as Geoffrey forced milk down the dog's throat. The dog struggled, but then accepted the ministrations with soulful resignation. Eventually, all the milk had been drunk or spat over Geoffrey, and the dog curled itself into a ball to sleep off its brush with death.

Geoffrey stroked its head with a caring he rarely felt for it. It had been with him so long, he could barely remember being without it, yet it was usually more a problem than a friend. He had found it eight years before as a puppy, abandoned in a ditch. He took it to young Tancred, having named it Angel due to the halo of dried mud on its head. Tancred had shown scant interest in the fawning creature and had finally tried to rid himself of it by throwing it into a well. Geoffrey had rescued it, but the dog—which had quickly and deservedly lost the name of Angel—had shown little loyalty to him except when hungry, and there was rarely much between them that could be called true affection. Since then, Geoffrey had fed and housed the dog, which had, in turn, graced him with its presence, except on those occasions when there appeared to be a better option.

Roger retrieved the parcel of cakes from the shelf and poked at them dubiously with his dagger, as if he imagined they might leap out of the wrappings of their own accord and strike him dead. Geoffrey came to peer over his shoulder.

"That should teach you not to steal a dead man's food," he said.

Roger shuddered. "I have never had a problem with it before. Are you sure it was the cakes, and not something else? That foul dog has always got something unsavoury in its mouth."

Geoffrey shook his head. "There is an odd smell about those cakes, and, from the dog's reaction, I think there must be a fast-acting poison in them. He is lucky you are mean, and only gave him a little. Had he, or you, eaten a whole one . . ."

"So, the mystery thickens," said Hugh. "Were these cakes sent to Dunstan to kill him? Was he aware that attempts were being made on his life, and he became so frightened that he decided to save the killer the trouble? Or had he had these cakes prepared as a gift for someone else—Marius perhaps?"

Geoffrey took Roger's dagger and poked at the wrappings. The inner ones were a kind of parchment specially designed to absorb grease, but the outer one was of the type used in the market near Pharos Street in the Greek Quarter. The cakes, too, were distinctive, and bore an unusual pattern of crystalised sugar on the crust. Geoffrey thought that it should not be too difficult to trace which of the bakeries near Pharos Street produced the cakes, and perhaps even when. The point at which the poison was added would be more difficult to determine, especially since it might even have been put there by Dunstan himself. But they had to start somewhere, and the bakeries seemed as good a place as any.

He glanced out of the window, and saw that the sky was beginning to lighten. It would not be long before the bakers opened their stalls for business, and he could begin his enquiries. He sighed and stretched, and then turned back to his study of the scraps of parchment from Dunstan's desk. He wished he could have raided Marius's desk too, but he did not know which one had been his, and it would have looked suspicious to have asked.

"What are you doing?" mumbled Roger, half-asleep in what looked to be an uncomfortable position on the wall bench. Hugh was already slumbering on the bed.

"Seeing if there is anything to be learned from the scrap vellum in Dunstan's desk."

"I do not hold with all those squiggles and scrawls," said Roger drowsily. "They only serve to get you into trouble."

Spoken like a true illiterate, thought Geoffrey. As if talking did not have its disadvantages in that way. He peered at one scrap in the yellow light from the lamp, and then put it to one side when he saw it had only been used to clean dirty quills. The next one was a list of scrolls relating to business dealings with a cloth merchant, and the next was a list of loot stolen from a house in the Jewish Quarter. Yet another contained a selection of meaningless words and phrases in a variety of styles, as if Dunstan had been seeing how many different ways he could write. Was this relevant, Geoffrey wondered? Daimbert had praised Dunstan's writing, so perhaps the man had been able to mimic the handwriting style of others. It might be a useful skill for the Patriarch to draw upon.

Geoffrey was becoming sleepy himself, lulled by the soporific flicker of the amber light of the lamp. Then he jolted back into wakefulness when he realised what he had just read. The text was incomplete because the parchment had been torn, but there was enough left to give him the gist of what had been written. And it was in Greek, and so was probably incomprehensible to most, if not all, the other scribes in the Patriarch's service.

". . . you will agree . . . not . . . for others to know . . . damage . . . be irreparable . . . but . . . minimal sums . . . left . . . of the Holy . . ."

Geoffrey rubbed his chin. It did not take a genius to grasp the essence of the letter. It was informing the recipient that the sender was aware of some fact it was better that others should not know, and that would cause or allow some permanent damage to occur. But for a price, the secret could be kept, providing "sums" were left at the Church of the Holy Sepulchre. So, was this a note written *to* Dunstan, or *by* him? And if by him, was it for another or on his own account? Was it an original or simply a rough copy to be written out more tidily at a later date? Geoffrey rummaged in the pile for the parchment on which Dunstan had practised his handwriting, and compared it to the blackmail note. At first, he thought he must have been mistaken, but there, at the bottom, was a line in which the writing was made to slope a little to the right, and some letters were given distinctive ornamentations. Dunstan had been practicing Roman letters in Latin, but the style was as distinctive in Greek.

Geoffrey peered closer, almost setting the parchment alight as he came too near to the lamp, and he saw that there must have been some kind of notch in the nib, for there was a strange irregularity in the writing that would have been invisible to all but the most intense scrutiny. When he looked at the practice sheet, he saw the same irregularity, which suggested that the identical pen had been used. Rummaging in his pockets, he found the scroll that Tancred had given him, containing notes made by Dunstan and Marius on their investigation. It was written in two different hands: one had clear, rounded letters written with a thick-nibbed pen, while the other was a hurried, spiky script with randomly shaped letters. But the telltale irregularities were there that showed that the second section had been written with the damaged quill.

Geoffrey leaned his elbows on the table and stared down at the elusive clues. So one of the two who had written the scroll of findings had also written the blackmail note, and had been practising alternative handwriting styles. Since the note and the practice sheet were in Dunstan's desk, it stood to reason that he was the culprit. In which case, he had sent, or intended to send, the note to someone else. But was Dunstan a blackmailer or simply a scribe? Was the rough note in front of him a dictation? And if so, from whom? Daimbert? Tancred? Bohemond? Geoffrey closed his eyes: if it were a dictation, virtually anyone in the city with the means to pay a scribe might have commissioned Dunstan.

He rubbed the bridge of his nose. He would need to return to the scriptorium later that day and question Dunstan's colleagues about any private clients he might have had, or any mysterious meetings. And whether he regularly received or bought parcels of Greek cakes.

Hugh shifted in his sleep and murmured something. Geoffrey turned to look at him. Perhaps he should be concentrating on who in the citadel had murdered Marius and almost killed Hugh. Helbye swore no one had gone in or out of the citadel, other than Geoffrey himself, after sunset, and Helbye had no cause to lie. He rubbed harder at his nose and tried to think. The obvious candidate who came to mind as villain was Courrances, because Geoffrey detested him and knew the feeling was mutual. The Hospitaller would love to see Geoffrey fall from grace, and might well instigate some unpleasant plot to harm him. But would he kill a monk like Marius, a fellow man of God, to ensure its success? Or harm a knight like Hugh, a colleague from the citadel? Geoffrey decided that he would.

Then there were Warner de Gray and Henri d'Aumale, both of whom had fallen foul of Geoffrey's quick wits from time to time. Geoffrey tried hard not to use his learning to make fools of people, but Warner and d'Aumale sorely tested his good intentions with their bigotry and arrogance. Warner, by dint of his superior talent in swordplay and horsemanship, was the acknowledged leader of the Advocate's knights, backed by the slightly more intelligent, but lazy, d'Aumale. They poured scorn on Geoffrey's academic pursuits, and he despised their proudly maintained ignorance.

He racked his brain for other suspects, but they all fell far short of Courrances, d'Aumale, and Warner. Geoffrey would need to discover where they had been on the nights of the five murders. It should not be difficult to do, since the citadel was crowded to the gills, and it was almost impossible to keep any kind of secret. Doubtless even the story of how his dog had been poisoned would be common knowledge by now, a story that would be related with some glee, since Geoffrey's dog was not a popular resident in the citadel. The unprotected ankles of many knights had fallen foul of its ready fangs, and it had several unendearing habits, chief among which were its penchant for the refuse pits and its ability to seek out edibles that any knight brought to the citadel. Geoffrey leaned down to pat the dog on the head, but withdrew his hand quickly when it sneezed on him.

He stood, walked to the window, and leaned out, breathing deeply of the warm, richly scented air. The sky was now much brighter, although the sun still had not risen. A bird sang a loud and exotic song from the huddle of rooftops below the citadel. People were beginning to stir, and he could hear the rumble of carts as they were allowed through David's Gate for the day's trading. In the far distance, he could hear the wail of the muezzins calling the Moslems to their mosques.

The bell on the citadel chapel began to chime, and Geoffrey decided to go to mass. Courrances was sure to be there, and Geoffrey thought he might be able to elicit some information from him. Geoffrey reconsidered: he would not be able to solicit anything from Courrances without arousing his suspicion, but he might be able to goad d'Aumale or Warner into some indiscretion that would reveal their guilt.

Before leaving, he gathered up the scraps of vellum and went to the fireplace. Some months before, he had discovered a loose stone at the back, behind which was a small crevice. He rammed the parchments into the crevice and replaced the stone so that no intruder should see them and ascertain how much he had learned.

"Is that where you keep your wine? No wonder it tastes so foul!"

Geoffrey smiled at Roger, who was easing the stiffness out of his joints in a series of cracks and grunts. Hugh was still asleep, sprawled across the bed, with his mouth open.

"I am going to mass," said Geoffrey. "I might be able to find out where Courrances, d'Aumale, and Warner were last night."

Roger nodded toward Hugh. "We should let him sleep," he said in a stentorian whisper that was almost louder than his normal voice. Hugh stirred, but did not waken. He had lost the pallor of the night before, and Geoffrey imagined resting would do him more good than any of his or Roger's fumbling ministrations. The dog opened a bleary eye and closed it again with an irritable growl that rumbled deep in its chest.

The two knights walked across the bailey toward the chapel. The citadel was already heaving with life. The great ironbound doors were opening and shutting continuously, allowing a stream of carts through, although each one was allocated a soldier who would stay with it until it left. The Advocate was only too familiar with tales of great fortresses falling to treachery, and he had no intention of allowing his wells to be poisoned, or weevils put in his siege supplies, for the sake of some basic security.

Roger strode into the chapel, blithely ignoring the rule that all weapons should be left in the porch. He bared his big brown teeth at the monk who stepped forward to remind him, and the man cowered back, uncertain as to whether the gesture was friendly or hostile. Geoffrey unbuckled his sword, but kept his dagger under his surcoat.

Mass was just beginning, with monks in the black habits of the Benedictines chanting a psalm. Geoffrey tipped his head back and studied the ceiling as he listened to the rhythmic rise and fall of the plainsong. The mosaics here were fine, too, he thought, depicting scenes from the Bible in brilliant golds, greens, and blues that shone vividly, even in the dull light of early morning.

A group of knights entered noisily, their spurs clanking on the stone floor. Among them were d'Aumale and Warner. The monks, used to such interruptions, did not falter in their singing, even when two Lorrainers began a noisy conversation about horses. Courrances, wearing his robe with the cross that glimmered whitely in the gloom, stood to one side, also chanting, although his pale blue eyes darted here and there, noting who was present and who stood next to whom.

While the monks sang and the celebrant went through the ritual movements of the mass, the knights fidgeted and shuffled. Some chatted, one hummed a folk song loudly to himself, and others sighed and whispered. All stood, although one or two lounged against pillars. D'Aumale and Warner talked to each other, laughing helplessly at some joke, their mirth sufficiently loud to draw disapproving glares from the celebrant. At last it was over, and the knights trooped noisily toward the hall for breakfast. Geoffrey approached d'Aumale and Warner and greeted them cheerfully.

"Good morning," he said, fishing around for a noncontentious subject with which to draw them into conversation. "Helbye informs me that you plan to hold an archery competition. It is an excellent notion. I hope my men will be allowed to compete?"

"I heard your dog was ill last night," said d'Aumale irrelevantly, exchanging a look of amusement with Warner. "I cannot think why you keep that wretched thing. It is wholly devoid of redeeming features."

"Your kindred spirit," said Warner to Geoffrey, and he and d'Aumale howled with laughter. Geoffrey fought not to reply with one of a tide of biting responses that rose unbidden into his mind.

"Poor Hugh was not well either," put in Roger. "Nor was the monk who came to seek the safety of our citadel."

"Probably went too near that dog," said Warner, and laughed again. Geoffrey looked away. It might be easy to beguile them into betraying themselves, but it would not be pleasant.

"The monk, Marius, was not quite dead when we returned," lied Geoffrey. "He described his killer to us."

Warner and d'Aumale exchanged a glance. "Really?" said d'Aumale. "And what did this killer look like? We are all concerned about a murderer within our walls."

"A Lorrainer," said Roger heartily. Geoffrey cringed. Roger was not the right person to be indulging in these kind of games. He was far too indiscreet and brutal. Hugh, on the other hand, would have understood Geoffrey's intentions instantly, and thrown himself into the game with consummate skill.

"You lie!" exclaimed d'Aumale, looking from Roger to Geoffrey. "You slander us all!"

"Do we? Then where were you last night?" demanded Roger.

Geoffrey closed his eyes in despair. He could see the way this discussion would end.

"Well, we were not here!" growled Warner. "We were out and did not return until after you did."

"How did you know when we returned?" asked Geoffrey quickly, "if you were not here to see us arrive back?"

Warner spluttered with rage, although whether because he had been caught in a lie, or because he resented being questioned, was not easy to guess. "We were out!"

"Can anyone vouch for you?" asked Geoffrey with quiet reason.

"Vouch for us? What do you think we are, common soldiers?" shouted d'Aumale, bristling with indignation. "We do not need to discuss our whereabouts with a Norman!"

"True. You do not," said Geoffrey. "But you will save me a good deal of time if you do, and time wasted on investigating a false trail might lead to the death of another man."

"I care nothing about your trails!" snarled Warner. "You are like that fat dog of yours, sniffing around in the garbage, looking for murderers! Call this villain out for a fair fight, like any decent knight should do!" His chest heaved with emotion, and flecks of spit gathered around his buff-coloured moustache.

"You are welcome to try that tactic," said Geoffrey. "But I doubt it will work. Where were you? At a brothel?"

It was not an unreasonable suggestion. There were several institutions where knights were more than welcome, and which formed a mechanism whereby the plunder taken by the Crusaders from the hapless citizens after the city's fall gradually trickled back to its original owners.

Warner was incensed, and the mounting colour in his cheeks told Geoffrey that he had guessed correctly. But that still did not mean that he or d'Aumale had not killed Marius, for the guard on the citadel gates had been a Lorrainer and would never reveal to Geoffrey the exact time when Warner and d'Aumale had returned. In the citadel, most things could be bought and sold, but not a soldier's loyalty to his lord. Not if he wished not to be killed in a weapons' drill by his comrades, or to have his throat slit while on night manoeuvres, or to be selected for every dangerous mission until his luck ran out.

"You are being ridiculous," said Roger glibly to Geoffrey. "What self-respecting whore would sleep with a Lorrainer?"

Warner leapt toward Roger, his face a mask of fury. Geoffrey stretched out a hand, intending it to be a pacifying gesture, but Warner misunderstood, and in an instant, his sword was drawn. D'Aumale's was out too, and so was Roger's. Geoffrey's lay on the pile in the porch, with those of the other law-abiding knights of the citadel.

"Not in a church!" he cried, grabbing Roger's arm and trying to pull him away. "No violence in a church!"

"Are you afraid to fight, Norman?" hissed Warner, advancing on Geoffrey with a series of hacking sweeps of his sword that cut the air as cleanly as a whistle. Geoffrey retreated hastily.

"I will not fight in a church!"

"You will if you do not want to die!"

Geoffrey heard the clash of steel, and saw Roger and d'Aumale already engaged. Roger lunged forward with a blow that knocked the smaller man backward, forcing him to retreat before the onslaught, while d'Aumale defended himself with quick, short jabs that just kept Roger at a distance. Geoffrey felt the whistle of steel slice past his face, and realised Warner meant to kill him, armed or not. He whipped the dagger from his belt, and jerked backward, away from a savage swipe that missed him by a hair's breadth.

Warner was white with fury, and Geoffrey realised he must have angered the man more than he had guessed, for his expression was murderous. Armed only with a dagger, Geoffrey could not hope to win a fight against Warner, a superb swordsman. The best he could do was to try to stay out of reach, and tire his opponent by luring him to hack and sweep. When Warner grew weary from wielding the heavy weapon, Geoffrey might be able to dart through his defences and attack him with his knife.

The sword hacked down, and the tip caught against Geoffrey's mail shirt, slicing through it like a knife through butter and throwing him off balance. He scrambled away and ducked behind a pillar. Warner's sword struck it so hard that sparks flew from the blade, leaving a deep gouge in the smooth white stone. Warner swung again and again, and Geoffrey felt him gaining ground. He ducked and weaved, and dodged this way and that around the pillars, but Warner was relentless. Then Geoffrey was hard up against the back wall of the church with nowhere else to go. Warner's eyes glittered in eager anticipation, and he tensed his arm, ready for the fatal blow.

While Warner prepared to strike, Geoffrey dived at him using every ounce of his strength to drive him off balance. He saw Warner's sword swing round, and felt the upper part of the blade crunch into his ribs. And then the momentum of Geoffrey's lunge sent them both sprawling, scrabbling at each other like a pair of wildcats. Warner fought like tiger, abandoning his sword, and pummelling Geoffrey with his mailed fists. Geoffrey, stunned by a dizzying blow to his temple, felt Warner gaining the upper hand, and with a spurt of strength that verged on the diabolical, Warner heaved himself upright and fastened his hands around Geoffrey's throat.

Warner's strength was prodigious, reinforced by his clear loathing of the Norman. Geoffrey felt his head begin to swim from lack of air, but with calm presence of mind he swung his arm upward and brought the point of his dagger to Warner's throat. Warner gazed in disbelief at the weapon and then at Geoffrey, who could now dispatch him with ease despite Warner's superior position. With a groan of frustration and anger, Warner let his hands go slack, and Geoffrey found he could breathe again. He struggled out from underneath Warner, still keeping the dagger firmly at the Lorrainer's throat and fought to regain his breath.

"Stop this outrage!"

All four knights turned at the sound of the furious voice. Godfrey, Duke of Lower Lorraine and Advocate of the Holy Sepulchre, stood in the doorway of the chapel and glowered at them. For a moment, they were frozen in a guilty tableau of violence, but then weapons were dropped and put away, and the four climbed warily to their feet.

"Are there not Saracens enough to fight that you need to squabble with each other?" shouted the Advocate. "And in a church of all places?"

"We were provoked," said Warner sullenly. "They attacked, and what else were we to do than defend ourselves? They heaped insults upon Lorraine and Burgundy!"

"Which was it, cousin?" asked the Advocate with menacing calm. "Did they attack you first, or did they provoke you to attack them with their insults? You cannot have it both ways."

"We did not . . ." began Roger.

"Silence!" barked the Advocate. "I know you serve Bohemond, and you," turning to Geoffrey, "serve Tancred. But they hold their territories under my liegeship. And while in this citadel and in this city, you are responsible to me! I will not have brawling among the knights. What hope do we have of maintaining peace among the troops when you set this kind of example?"

He scowled at each of them in turn. Behind him, in the gaggle of monks and knights who were in constant attendance, Courrances watched with detached amusement, a small smile playing at the corners of his thin lips. Geoffrey watched him. He knew that a few sibilant words breathed into the Advocate's ever-listening ear would absolve Warner and d'Aumale from blame and bring it all firmly to rest on the shoulders of Roger and him. But Courrances preferred to watch from the sidelines, knowing he had the power to intervene if he felt so inclined, but enjoying the display of disunity between the Normans and the Advocate's men.

The anger went from the Advocate as quickly as it had come, and he raised his hands in a gesture of despair. He fixed Warner and d'Aumale with his faded blue eyes. "Wait for me in my quarters," he said wearily. "I must go to Jaffa again, to conduct negotiations with the merchants from Venice. I want you to organise a guard that will protect me and impress the Venetians, but that will leave sufficient troops here to defend Jerusalem."

Warner and d'Aumale bowed and left, and outside Geoffrey could hear the cheers and laughter of their fellow knights congratulating them on the fight. The Advocate dismissed his retinue with a flick of his hand. No one moved, and it was Courrances who began to usher people out of the chapel. In moments, the chapel was empty with the exception of the Advocate and Geoffrey, while Courrances lurked among the shadows of the pillars, far enough away to be discreet, but certainly close enough to hear what was being said.

"Sir Warner is a hotheaded bully," said the Advocate. "But his loyalty and courage are invaluable to me. Please bear that in mind when you pick a fight with him next time."

Geoffrey met his eyes evenly and said nothing. The Advocate was the first to look away, and Geoffrey noticed how tired and ill he looked. The Advocate's previous visit to Jaffa had ended when he was struck with a mysterious fever—rumours that he had been poisoned were rife—and had to be brought back to Jerusalem to recover.

"What news have you for me about the deaths of the two knights and the monks?"

Geoffrey rubbed his chin, which reminded him he had not shaved for some time, and realised he had very little to tell the Advocate. He outlined what he had learned from interviewing the witnesses the day before, omitting reference to Jocelyn's ambiguous role, and described the death of Marius. The Advocate grew more pale.

"A monk murdered within the citadel, and a knight knocked senseless," he breathed. "This cannot go on! This business is affecting the very roots of our hold on Jerusalem." He pulled hard on the straggling hairs of his long, blond moustache. "So what do you deduce from all this? Do you agree with my brother that the Jews are behind it, with Courrances that the Arabs are responsible, or with me that the Patriarch knows more than he is telling? Or have you an alternative hypothesis?"

Geoffrey did not, and he felt that the evidence to support any theory was weak, to say the least. There was clearly a Greek connection: Loukas was Greek, possibly a spy; John was found dead in the house of Melisende Mikelos, a Greek widow; Dunstan had poisoned Greek cakes in his desk; and the three men who had followed him after his meeting with Tancred had spoken Greek. However, the death of the double agent Jocelyn implied that the business had something to do with the Patriarch, while all three knights—Guido, John and now Hugh—had been in Bohemond's service. Geoffrey decided there was nothing to be gained from telling the Advocate about Jocelyn, and certainly nothing by highlighting Bohemond's connection. He outlined his suspicions that there might be a Greek dimension cautiously, unsure as to how the Advocate might react.

"The Greeks," said the Advocate grimly. "We were foolish not to have slaughtered every last one of them when we conquered the city. Now we have nurtured a viper at our breast."

"Possibly," said Geoffrey, "but this smacks more of the actions of a few individuals, perhaps even one, and not the entire community."

"I suppose I have time to arrange a massacre before leaving for Jaffa," said the Advocate, discouraged only by the effort and time it would take. "If we slaughter the lot of them, we will be certain to kill these individuals of yours, and that will be the end of the affair."

The slaughter of hundreds of innocent people to ensure the execution of a few would definitely not be a prudent political move, thought Geoffrey, frantically scrabbling around for reasons to stay the Advocate's hand. The Advocate, no matter how much he disliked the Greeks, needed their labour and their services, and without them, the city's fortunes would decline.

"This killer is clever," said Geoffrey hastily. "I do not believe killing the entire Greek community would serve to rid you of him—he might adopt a disguise and escape. And I am sure the Patriarch would not condone a massacre."

"The Patriarch does not rule here—I do!" snarled the Advocate, and Geoffrey saw he had touched a raw nerve. "I do not care what the Patriarch condones or does not condone! I am a military leader, and he is a frail churchman bound to the apron strings of the Pope."

The Patriarch was certainly not frail, and Geoffrey doubted very much if Daimbert were tied to the apron strings of any Pope. If the Advocate underestimated his opponents so blithely, he was bound for a fall. Perhaps the murders were aimed against this weak, vacillating ruler after all, thought Geoffrey. Jerusalem needed a powerful leader in these uncertain times, and the Advocate was proving he was not up to the task.

"I may be mistaken about the Greeks," said Geoffrey. "I will investigate these poisoned cakes this morning, and I will try to ascertain who Dunstan was trying to blackmail. We do not have sufficient information to justify massacring the Greeks."

"You have enough information for me," growled the Advocate. "But, very well, I might be prepared to wait a few days to see what else you might uncover. But do not dally. I could grow impatient."

With these decisive words, the Advocate turned on his heel and stalked out of the church. Geoffrey heaved a sigh of relief, and hoped fervently he had not sown a seed of paranoia in the Advocate's mind that might lead to some violent act against the Greek community. He wondered whether the stress of leadership might be too great for the man, and whether he might be losing his sanity. To suggest a massacre on the grounds of a few unproven suspicions was scarcely the act of a rational man—even a Crusader.

Courrances materialised from behind a pillar and glided over to Geoffrey.

"You do not really believe the Greeks are behind this, do you?" he asked.

Geoffrey shook his head. "But I do not know who is."

Courrances put a limp hand on Geoffrey's shoulder, and Geoffrey heard the clank of a weapon under the soldier-monk's robe as he moved.

"You are in a vulnerable position, my friend," said Courrances, so softly that Geoffrey had to strain to hear. "It is difficult to serve two masters, and if you fail to uncover who is behind these deaths, the Advocate will believe you have betrayed him. Even if you do uncover a plot, who knows whether he will believe your findings or not? It depends at whom you will point your finger."

And you were the one who put me in this position, thought Geoffrey. He was suddenly angry with himself. He had allowed himself to be fooled by Courrances, who probably guessed there was something more sinister afoot than a Saracen plot as he had claimed. Courrances was right: who knew where Geoffrey's investigations might lead him, and, even if he did uncover the identity of the killer, who was to say the Advocate would believe him? What if it were Warner? The Advocate had already told Geoffrey that his cousin was invaluable to him: there was simply no way the Advocate would accept Warner's guilt.

Courrances removed his hand, but Geoffrey imagined he still could feel the man's corruption oozing through his armour. The warrior-monk gave Geoffrey a smile that reminded him of the wolves that slunk around soldiers' campfires in the desert, and slid noiselessly out of the chapel. Geoffrey waited a moment before following, his mind teeming with questions and worries.

After a breakfast of flat, dry bread and pickled olives, the most immediate task was to visit the scriptorium, to ask questions about Dunstan and Marius. Roger and Hugh were already practising their swordplay in the bailey, observed by a crowd of soldiers who formed a circle around them. Geoffrey watched them for a moment, admiring Roger's decisive movements and massive strength pitted against Hugh's resourcefulness and speed. Then he went to don his own armour, and set off through the streets to the scriptorium, with Helbye and Fletcher at his heels and the dog slinking behind them.

He was admitted to the Patriarch's Palace by the captain he had met the night before. The captain had apparently been warned Geoffrey might come, for he led him to the scriptorium without asking him the purpose of his visit.

The scriptorium was not yet light enough for the monks to write, but they were already busy, mixing inks, sharpening pens, and scraping vellum. The large room was full of their chatter, mostly about the death of Dunstan the night before. Talking to a Benedictine at the far end of the room was the Patriarch, who spotted Geoffrey and strode to greet him.

"Marius was murdered last night too," said Geoffrey without preamble, watching the reactions of the Patriarch carefully. "He was stabbed in my chamber at the citadel while I was here."

The Patriarch dug strong, slender fingers into Geoffrey's arm and led him out of the scribes' hearing. "In the citadel?" he echoed. "Marius was murdered in the citadel?"

Geoffrey nodded. "Which points to the likelihood that the murderer is a knight, for it is not easy to gain access to the citadel at any time, but it is especially difficult after dusk."

"My God!" breathed the Patriarch. "This is becoming more sinister by the minute. So now I have no one investigating this business but you. You had better take care!"

Geoffrey did not need to be told.

"Do you have any idea who might be responsible?" the Patriarch asked, after a pause.

Geoffrey shook his head, unwilling to give voice to his suspicions about Courrances, Warner, and d'Aumale without adequate proof. "But I need to question your scribes. I want to know more about Dunstan and Marius. Did they have any particular enemies? Or friends?"

The Patriarch steepled his fingers and looked across the scriptorium at the gossiping monks. "Marius was very popular;

Dunstan was not. Brother Alain is the best person for you to talk to. He is the scriptorium's biggest gossip, and he was great friends with Marius."

He clicked his fingers imperiously and pointed at a large, balding man who sat apart from the others, biting his nails. The man swallowed hard and, looking like a lamb to slaughter, came toward Geoffrey and the Patriarch.

"This is Sir Geoffrey Mappestone," said the Patriarch to the nervous monk. "He has questions that you will answer fully and honestly."

The monk nodded miserably, and the Patriarch strode away, calling out orders to his clerks. Geoffrey took Brother Alain's arm and led him to a window seat near Dunstan's desk. He could feel the man trembling, and noted that there were fine beads of sweat all across his glistening pate.

"Now," said Geoffrey when they were seated. "Why did you help Marius make Dunstan's death appear like murder?"

The man gazed at him aghast, and Geoffrey knew his intuitive guess had been correct. He had based his assumption on the fact that if the man was as great a gossip as the Patriarch had inferred, then very little would have kept him from the hubbub of excitement that Geoffrey had detected as he entered the scriptorium. But Alain had been sitting apart, eyeing Geoffrey and the Patriarch with much the same expression as a mouse sighting a swooping owl.

"I do not know what you mean. I . . ."

"Brother Marius was murdered last night," Geoffrey said brutally. "At the citadel. For your own safety, I recommend that you tell me the truth."

All colour fled from the monk's face, so that, with his bald head and bloated features, he reminded Geoffrey of a drowned corpse.

"Marius dead?" Alain gave a great sigh and turned to gaze out the window at the fountains in the courtyard. "I would say Dunstan killed him, but Dunstan was dead already, killed by his own hand."

"Why would you think Dunstan was responsible?"

"Dunstan was a vile creature, greedy in all things. Everything he did bespoke avarice. He always took more food than everyone else, even at times when there was barely enough to go round, and he was always out at the Greek market buying extra. He stole, too. Several of the brothers found things missing—inks, gold leaf, bits of jewellery—small things of no consequence, but we all knew it was him. We think he sold them at the market, because under his bed, he has a great chest of coins."

"A fine medley of traits for a monk."

Alain looked at him sharply, uncertain how the knight's comment was intended to be taken. Geoffrey met his gaze and smiled encouragingly.

"Over the last three or four days, Dunstan became much worse, and he became irritable too. He was constantly devouring those Greek cakes. We all wondered if it were overindulgence that was making him so irascible—all that sweetness disturbing the balance of his humours. He and Marius had arguments. At first, they were nothing much, just the usual disputes between colleagues working closely together. Then the fights began to be serious. Yesterday afternoon, they had a blazing row that could be heard all over the palace. Then Dunstan became maudlin, and he began to say he would take his life if Marius did not recant some of the things he had said. Marius refused. Dunstan sat here and moped for the rest of the day. When he did not appear for dinner, I knew there was something wrong. I found him hanging on that door. He had taken his life as he had threatened. Marius is . . . Marius . . ."

"You must tell me the truth," said Geoffrey as the scribe's voice trailed off miserably.

Alain took a deep breath. "Marius is important to all of us here," he said, gesturing round at the other scribes, who were watching them intently. "He has to be told!" he yelled suddenly. Several monks shook their heads, and others appeared anxious, while some would not look at Alain and Geoffrey at all.

"Told what?" asked Geoffrey, mystified.

"Marius is important to us because he provides things . . . ladies . . ."

"Marius arranges for women to visit the scriptorium?" asked Geoffrey, hiding a smile. "Do not look so morose, Brother. I will not tell the Patriarch."

Alain's relief was tangible. "Every Thursday night," he said. "He arranges for some ladies to come to us. They have been coming for months now, and we have all . . . grown fond of them. I knew that if Dunstan was found to have committed suicide after proclaiming so loudly that Marius would drive him to it, then Marius would be sent away. And I would never see Mary again!"

"Mary is one of these women?" asked Geoffrey.

Alain nodded. "I cut Dunstan down and put him over his desk. I thought to make it look as though he had been murdered, and had not taken his own life. I thought the Patriarch would assume he had been killed because he was investigating these strange deaths. Marius was with others all day at the library, and so had a firm alibi and would not be blamed for any murder."

"But you misjudged the situation," said Geoffrey, feeling a certain pity for the plump monk. "Marius saw the body, immediately assumed, as indeed you had intended, that Dunstan had been murdered—by someone at the palace—and fled in terror to be murdered at the citadel."

Alain nodded and turned away to gaze out of the window. "I was foolish to have attempted such a rash plan. But when I saw Dunstan hanging there, all I could think about was that Marius would be blamed. And none of us here knows how to contact these ladies but Marius. He ran errands for the Patriarch, you see, and this enabled him to be out and about a lot. The rest of us live and work here, and we seldom leave the palace premises. Marius not only brought the ladies here, but he knew which of the guards could be trusted not to tell . . ."

"This explains why Dunstan's suicide was dressed up as murder, but not why he was driven to suicide in the first place," interrupted Geoffrey, before the conversation swung too far away from the business at hand. "Have you any ideas?"

Alain took a deep shuddering breath. "Perhaps his evil dealings became too much for him. He was always in the church confessing his sins, so they were obviously beginning to weigh heavily on him."

"What evil dealings?"

"He could change the style of his writing, and he knew Greek. He did all sorts of scribing for various merchants who paid him far too well for his work to have been honest. Then there was something going on at the Church of the Holy Sepulchre. Marius and I usually attend mass there on Sundays, and we saw him at least twice. I saw him poking round the back of the altar in one of the chapels."

And Geoffrey knew exactly why. Dunstan had been searching for the blackmail money that he had instructed should be left there. So that cleared up another mystery—that Dunstan was definitely blackmailing someone.

"Was there anyone who wished Dunstan harm? Someone who might have driven him to his death?"

"Oh yes," said Alain. "All of us, for a start. He made us pay him to keep the secret of the ladies from the Patriarch. Then there are all the merchants he cheated. And I was beginning to wonder whether the Patriarch knew about him, and decided it was time for . . . well, you know."

So Dunstan had been a thief, a cheat, and a blackmailer with scores of enemies. Any one of them could have left the poisoned cakes in his desk; from the sound of him, Dunstan was sufficiently greedy to have eaten them without questioning where they had come from. Dunstan had been a doomed man long before he saved others the bother of killing him.

"Are you aware that he was blackmailing anyone other than all the monks in the scriptorium?"

Alain frowned. "We wondered about that," he said, gesturing again to his colleagues. "Our suspicion is that he tried to blackmail someone, but the someone was too powerful for him. We think Dunstan's intended victim turned against him, which explains why, for the last three or four days, his behavior was so odd. He never left the palace, and he was moody."

"Do you have any idea who might harm Marius?"

Alain shook his head, and Geoffrey was horrified to see the sparkle of tears in his eyes. "None at all. And now I will never see Mary again," he said.

CHAPTER SEVEN

Geoffrey returned to the citadel, gave Hugh and Roger a brief description of his findings, and prepared to leave again for the Greek market. Hugh looked well-rested and healthy, but claimed a headache. Geoffrey suspected it had more to do with the fact that it was his turn to supervise the repairs on the city walls, than with the blow on the head the previous night, for it had not affected his sword practice with Roger. The knights loathed "wall duty," which involved overseeing large work parties of soldiers and local labourers to repair the damage caused when the Crusaders took Jerusalem. The soldiers and locals were apt to quarrel at the slightest provocation, and both slacked at the heavy labour as soon as the knights' attention was elsewhere. Wall duty was hot, dirty, and unrewarding, and the knights thoroughly resented its necessity.

Geoffrey, Roger, Helbye, Wolfram, a trio of soldiers from Bristol, and Geoffrey's dog set off toward the market in the Greek Quarter. The business day in Jerusalem was already well under way. Carts clattered along the packed-earth streets, and the gutters ran wet with night waste. Blankets were draped out of windows to air, and shutters were thrown open to allow the clean morning breeze to circulate. A few flies buzzed around their heads, but not in the swarms that massed in the heat of the day. The cold unease that had lain leaden in the pit of Geoffrey's

stomach since his conversation with Courrances began to recede, and his natural optimism began to shine through in the
freshness of the new day.

The Greek market was seething with activity. Brightly
coloured canopies were rigged outside every house, while owners laid out their wares on the street in the shade, so that there was
barely enough room to walk between them. Everywhere, voices
were raised, advertising goods and arguing about prices, and
gangs of children, idle while their parents haggled, whooped and
shrieked and weaved in and out of the stalls. The first street contained the spice-sellers, with huge mounds of brightly coloured
powders and seeds laid in neat piles across blankets spread on the
ground. The sweet smell of dried peppers mixed with the pungent aroma of garlic and coriander. The dog wandered over to a
lurid heap of turmeric intent on mischief, but beat a retreat
when a preliminary sniff made it sneeze.

The next street was where the cobblers plied their trade, and
their stalls had great piles of shoes and boots ready to be stitched
to individual requirements. The smell of leather was not quite
strong enough to dispel the powerful wafts emanating from the
nearby butchers' shops. Beyond were the candlemakers and beyond them, the bakers, with the rich scents of cakes and bread.

Geoffrey left Helbye and the others at the corner, while he
and Roger went to investigate alone—he did not want to
frighten anyone who might provide him with information by a
show of excess force. Slowly, and with Roger offering to sample
the wares from each stall, Geoffrey walked along the street,
searching for the sweet cakes with the distinctive pattern. Although the street was full of people, they maintained a wary distance from the knights, whose reputation in the city was, not
without cause, that of undisciplined violent louts who sought
fights with little provocation. Roger stopped to purchase cakes
from a baker who seemed to specialise in goods twice the size of
those of his colleagues, and Geoffrey strolled on alone.

As he neared the end of the street, he thought he was going
to be unsuccessful and that he would need to begin buying cakes

so he could identify the style of wrapping paper. Then he saw them on the very last stall in the row. He paused at the corner and looked up and down the alley that ran to the left and right. It was dingier than the bakers' street, and there were one or two stalls selling what looked to be broken pots and pans. The alleyway disappeared into shadows in either direction, and Geoffrey felt uncomfortable not knowing where they led. His military training told him he ought to explore them before speaking to the baker—for it was a foolish warrior who did not know his escape routes—but, he decided reluctantly, this might merely serve to arouse suspicion.

The stall owner had her back to him, busily wrapping bread for an elderly man who was complaining about his sore gums in a high-pitched, tremulous voice. When she turned, Geoffrey was startled to recognise Melisende Mikelos. She recognised him at the same moment, and her reaction was far from flattering.

"You! Not again! Will you pester me forever?"

Geoffrey hoped not, but the way she was appearing in the most unexpected of places suggested otherwise. He felt a sudden surge of disappointment that, after all they had been through, she was guilty after all. He had come to accept her innocence after Loukas had been killed while she was in custody, but her clear link with the poisoned cakes gave him cause for serious doubts. Even if she had not committed the murders herself, she must surely be involved. She met his gaze with her clear gold-brown eyes, and Geoffrey's disappointment intensified. She was an attractive woman—if her personality was not taken into account—and it seemed a shame that she had embroiled herself in the unpleasant business of murder.

He smiled politely. "I have come for some cakes."

She shot him a disbelieving look. "For your elderly mother?" she jibed.

"For my dog," he retorted, and regretted it instantly. He was not going to gain information from Melisende Mikelos by being offensive. The dog, meanwhile, had recognised the scent of the cakes that had caused him so much discomfort the night before;

it paused only to nip Geoffrey hard on the ankle to repay him for the force-fed milk, before sloping away up the street with its tail between its legs. Melisende watched it go, while Geoffrey surreptitiously rubbed his ankle.

"Your dog has no more sense than you do," she said. "What do you really want?"

"Do you know a scribe named Dunstan?" Geoffrey asked, deciding a direct approach might work better than subterfuge with this outspoken woman.

"No. Why? Does he like cakes?"

"He did. Before he died."

"Died? You mean murdered?"

Geoffrey looked at her curiously. "No, I mean died. Why do you ask if he was murdered?"

Melisende shook her head impatiently. "Because that is what seems to obsess you. Murder. And you said you are investigating the murders of the knights, so I assume there must be a connection."

Geoffrey could not fault her logic. "These cakes of yours," he said, changing the subject. "Do you make them yourself?"

"I do not, as a matter of fact. My skills lie in bread, not cakes. These are made by my servant, Maria. Do you want to interrogate her here, or bear her off to the dungeons?"

"Here will do," said Geoffrey. "Where is she?"

Melisende eyed him with disapproval, but called to a passing urchin to tell Maria Akira that a knight was waiting to speak with her.

"Akira? Is she a relative of Yusef Akira, the butcher?" And the man in whose shop the body of Brother Pius had been found, thought Geoffrey.

"We usually refer to Crusaders as butchers," she retorted. "And Akira as a meat merchant."

Was she fencing with him to gain time to think, or was she simply unable to resist the ample opportunities he gave her to insult him? he wondered.

"You have not answered my question."

"Yes," said Melisende with sudden exasperation. "She is his daughter. But they are estranged. He does not know she works for me, and I would rather you did not tell him. I might have known that thieving reprobate would be the kind of person with whom you would associate."

"He is a very dear friend," said Geoffrey. "He taught me everything I know."

She glanced at him sharply and smiled reluctantly. "I suppose you met Akira because one of the priests was killed in his house. Like a knight was killed in mine. But of course *he* was not arrested and dragged off through a riot to the citadel prison."

Geoffrey's patience was beginning to wane. He decided he preferred to question witnesses when they were afraid of him, rather than when they clearly regarded him in the same light as a loathsome reptile. He glanced up the street, heaving with bakers and their customers, and conceded reluctantly that rearresting Melisende so that he might gain some honest answers from her was out of the question. Fate would be unlikely to deliver him from a furious mob a third time—although he was sorely tempted to put her under lock and key.

"It is interesting," he said, turning back to face Melisende, "that Maria is connected to the deaths of John and Brother Pius because she is acquainted with both you and Akira."

"So are half the people in this market," she said with a dismissive wave of her hand.

"Not to the same extent," he said. "Akira is her father, and you are her employer."

"So what?" she said with contempt. "That means nothing at all. Akira has other relatives: I employ one of them to tend my garden."

That Melisende knew something about the murders was obvious to Geoffrey. How to prise it from her without causing a riot was less clear. A thought suddenly occurred to him.

"Was he blackmailing you? Dunstan?"

She gazed uncomprehendingly at him, eyes vivid in the sunlight. "What? Who is this Dunstan? And what could he blackmail me about?"

"All manner of things," he replied with a shrug, seeing Roger walking toward him beaming broadly and proudly bearing someone on his arm. "Perhaps an unwanted birth, or selling undersized loaves to your customers, or a string of male visitors . . ."

She spun round, her hand moving fast to clout him around the face, but his reactions were quicker, and he caught her arm before it struck him. Her eyes flashed in fury, and she was shaking with rage.

"How dare you! How dare you say those things!"

"Oh, come mistress," he said, maintaining his grip on her arm. "Do not pretend to be shocked. Here is your servant, Maria Akira, better known as Maria d'Accra to every knight in the citadel who knows his brothels."

Roger reached Melisende's stall and stood with Maria Akira's delicate hand resting gently on his brawny arm. Melisende looked from Geoffrey, to Maria, and back to Geoffrey again. For once, she was at a loss for words.

"Good morning, Sir Geoffrey," bubbled Maria Akira, flouncing up to him. "I did not know you were partial to cakes, or I would have brought you some."

"I like cakes," announced Roger loudly.

Maria looked up at him and giggled. "Then I shall see you have some next time."

"Next time?" queried Melisende, finding her voice. "What is going on? Maria?"

Maria smiled prettily, while Geoffrey watched the exchange with interest.

"Maria is a favourite of all the knights at the citadel," said

Roger, making Maria blush modestly. "She works at Abdul's Pleasure Palace on Friday nights."

"And every other Saturday," added Maria helpfully. "When I have time off from working for Mistress Melisende."

Melisende's jaw dropped, and Geoffrey began to laugh. Maria, ever fun-loving, laughed too, but Roger was unsure where the humour lay.

"Maria is very good," he protested valiantly. "One of Abdul's best. All the knights agree!"

Melisende's jaw dropped further still, and she gazed at Maria in stupefaction. Geoffrey laughed helplessly, while Roger remained confused.

"How could you?" Melisende managed eventually, although whether her comment was addressed to Maria for being a prostitute, or to Geoffrey for laughing at her discomfiture, was unclear. "I no longer require your services," she said coldly to Maria, before turning abruptly on her heel and striding away.

"No!" Maria was horrified. "I need this job! Abdul can only keep me two nights a week at most. What will I do?" She watched Melisende's upright figure striding away down the alley, her dainty hands clasped at her throat. Maria gave Roger a hefty shove in the chest which made no impact at all. "This is your fault!" she wailed, and turned and fled.

"Catch her," said Geoffrey to Roger, still struggling to bring his laughter under control. "Bring her back. I will talk to Mistress Prickly."

With long strides, he caught up with Melisende who had made good progress down the alley, away from the market. She was rigid with anger and shock, and ignored him as he fell into step beside her.

"You should not abandon your shop," he said gently. She stopped and spun round to face him, seeing the laughter still playing about in the depths of his green eyes, although his face was quite serious.

"Leave me alone! Every time you appear, trouble follows!"

"It is not my doing that your servant has other occupations in her spare time," said Geoffrey reasonably. "As far as I know, she has worked for Abdul for several years. If this has not affected her service to you up until now, where is the problem?"

"Where is the problem?" she echoed in disbelief. She shook her head. "A typical Norman response! I am a respectable widow—or was. Now I have murders committed in my house, and I discover my faithful servant is a harlot in her spare time." She turned from him, and Geoffrey saw tears glitter in her eyes.

"So that is not what Dunstan was blackmailing you about?"

She tipped back her head and took a deep breath. "No," she said, once she had regained control of herself. "I was not being blackmailed. I know no one called Dunstan. And . . ."

"And?" he asked, seeing her hesitate.

"Dunstan," she said, looking away. "A fat man with a tonsure?"

This was not a helpful description in a city where most monks ate well.

"Black, wiry hair, and a thin scar on his upper lip," he supplied, trying to imagine Dunstan's bloated features as they might have been before he had hanged himself.

"Yes," she said, screwing up her face as she thought. "Yes. I think I do know a man of that description and name. Not well. But he buys cakes from me from time to time."

"When did he last buy them from you?"

She shook her head slowly. "I am not sure. Not this week."

"He had some wrapped up in a parcel in his desk."

She shrugged. "Many of our cakes are soaked in honey, which preserves them. He may have had them for a week or more, and they would still be perfectly all right to eat."

"Did you prepare the packets of cakes for him in advance, or did you wrap them for him when he came to your stall?"

"The latter. He did not come on a regular basis. I imagine, like most people, he only came when he felt like eating cakes."

"The cakes in his drawer were triangle-shaped with diamond patterns iced on them. There were perhaps ten of them in the one parcel."

"Ten? Oh no. He did not buy that many. And he usually wanted a selection of different ones, not ones of the same kind."

Geoffrey regarded her sombrely while he thought. Was she lying or telling him the truth? He had never experienced such difficulty in distinguishing lies from honesty before, and Melisende had him perplexed. The poisoned cakes were definitely from her stall: Geoffrey recognised them, and Melisende had sold cakes to Dunstan by her own admission. But did she poison them? Did Dunstan really buy different types of cake, or was she cleverly trying to throw him off the scent by confusing the issue? And had she only admitted to selling Dunstan cakes now because denying it would merely look suspicious in light of the evidence she must know he had?

"So now what do I do?" she said, regarding him as intently as he was studying her. "I have just lost a servant whom I considered a friend. I am hounded by the Advocate's men because I was unfortunate enough to have had my house chosen as the scene of a murder, and now you think a fat clerk is blackmailing me because I sold him some cakes."

"If you truly value Maria's friendship, you will talk to her and come to some mutually acceptable agreement," said Geoffrey after a moment's thought. It seemed unfortunate that Maria should lose her job because of Roger's indiscretion, although Maria seemed rather proud of her talents, and he wondered how Melisende could not have known. But Abdul's Pleasure Palace was mainly stocked with Arab girls, and Maria was the only Greek. Perhaps that was why Maria had chosen to work for Abdul's establishment. Even though the population of Jerusalem was small, the different communities were insular and tended to be exclusive, so Geoffrey supposed it was possible that the Greeks were unaware of Maria's actions in an Arab-run brothel serving Crusader knights.

He began to walk with Melisende back toward the market. "Is there anything else you can tell me about Dunstan?"

"Nothing," she replied with a shrug. "I have probably said too much already. I should have denied knowing him so that you would go away and leave me alone."

145

"Then I will go away and leave you alone now. Once again, thank you for your help. I am grateful we were able to speak without inciting a riot."

Geoffrey gave a bow and left her, retracing his steps back up the alleyway toward the bakery, leaving her staring after him in confusion. He was arrogant, spoke with carefully chosen words, and knew exactly how to infuriate her without even raising his voice. Yet, there was more to him than most of the brutish knights who swaggered around the city, and Melisende could not condemn him for the single-mindedness of his enquiries when she possessed that exact same quality herself. She felt her anger evaporate as he rounded the corner. Although he was certainly not classically handsome, with his rugged features and his surcoat stained from innumerable battles, he possessed a certain strength of character and wry humour that made her hope that they would meet again—for bandying words with him was far more interesting than selling cakes in the market.

Roger had retrieved Maria, who sat weeping uncontrollably while he made clumsy attempts to soothe her. Geoffrey told her to talk to Melisende, and they took their leave. As they walked back up the street, a vision of Melisende's mortified face came unbidden into his mind's eye, and he began to laugh again. He had admirably resisted the urge to respond rudely to her jibes, he felt, but it had been gratifying to see this articulate, unfriendly woman at a loss for words. Roger shot him a mystified look, but said nothing until they rejoined Helbye, who gave Geoffrey a glare of such malevolence that the knight stopped dead in his tracks.

"Your vile dog has upset a baker's stall and bitten two people," Helbye growled. "It cost me a week's pay, and those people are still livid. Look at them."

Geoffrey looked and saw they were the object of attention that was far from friendly. The dog, knowing it had transgressed, lay on its side and raised a front paw, exposing its chest in submission. Geoffrey regarded it with exasperation. He wondered, not for the first time, how he had become encumbered with such a worthless, greedy, cowardly animal. He hoped Warner had not been right when he had said the dog recognised a kindred spirit.

"So to conclude," said Hugh, pulling uncomfortably at the bandage that still swathed his skull, "the cakes came from Melisende Mikelos, but she thinks Dunstan did not buy them himself because he usually preferred a selection to ones all of the same kind. That statement could simply be a ruse to keep you from knowing that Dunstan bought the cakes and that she poisoned them."

Geoffrey thought about what Huge was saying. His investigations had been brought to an abrupt halt when news came of a Saracen attack on a group of pilgrims on the Jerusalem to Jaffa road. Knowing that the Advocate was going to be travelling that way in the near future, a large contingent of knights and soldiers had ridden out to clear away any of the enemy. But by the time they arrived at the scene of the attack, the Saracens had long since disappeared back into the desert.

On their return, Geoffrey and his men had met Warner de Gray, who had been stricken with fever on his way to Jaffa with the Advocate's advance guard; he was being returned to Jerusalem on a litter. Warner reported seeing horsemen riding in the distance toward Ibelin, so Geoffrey led a small party in hot pursuit. However, after two more gruelling days of riding through the desert, the horses began to fail. With the Sirocco blowing a fury and baking all in its path, and with his men worn out mentally and physically, Geoffrey turned his company around, and the men gratefully headed back toward Jerusalem.

Geoffrey had concentrated completely on the task at hand, and he had not allowed himself time to consider the mystery of the murders. He knew from bitter experience the dangers of allowing one's mind to wander when in a land surrounded by hostile forces. So, upon his return after five days in the desert, he felt the need to review what he had learned of the mystery with Hugh and Roger. Now they lounged in the shade of the curtain wall mulling over what had happened before their recent excursion.

"I still cannot see why that Melisende was so appalled at Maria working for Abdul," said Roger, not for the first time since their talk had begun. "She is very good."

"So you told Melisende," said Geoffrey. "I am sure your recommendation of Maria's sexual prowess will go a long way in restoring her position as servant to a respectable widow."

"Do you think so?" said Roger, pleased. "Good. I like Maria. I do not like Mistress Melisende, however. She is unpleasantly aggressive, like the Scottish women I meet on occasions at home. But that Maria . . ."

"Melisende must be involved in all this." Hugh interrupted Roger's eulogy before it became graphic. "There are too many coincidences for comfort. And you said you had the impression she was lying, or not telling you all she knew."

"She was most definitely holding something back," said Geoffrey. "Could she have killed poor John? She is aggressive enough certainly, and it requires no great strength to stab a man in the back. But then she must also have killed the others, for the method of murders has been identical in each case. And we are left with the conundrum of Loukas, killed while Melisende was talking to Tancred."

"Perhaps she has an accomplice who killed to give her an alibi," said Hugh. "She seems a clever woman, and would easily be capable of arranging for another murder to be committed in the event of her arrest."

"But if you are correct, it was very foolish of her to kill John in her own house," said Geoffrey. "Why not in someone else's house—like Akira's again, or someone unconnected?"

"Perhaps she is more devious than you imagine," said Hugh. "Perhaps she knew she might be traced through Dunstan's cakes—if he ever ate them and died of poisoning—or that she might be connected to the murders through Akira, whose daughter works for her. Akira was never considered a suspect when a victim was found in *his* house—perhaps she assumed she would be regarded as an innocent bystander, like Akira was, if John's body was discovered in *her* home."

"It is a risky thing to do," said Geoffrey. "Such a plan could go badly awry."

"It did," said Hugh. "Horribly awry. As she went through the motions of appalled revulsion for the benefit of the neighbours, she was unfortunate in her timing, for you happened to be going past. Instead of sending for the monks at the Holy Sepulchre— or even fat old Dunstan, her customer—she found herself confronted with a contingent of soldiers. You arrested her so that the Advocate could question her. She had miscalculated. The monks, who doubtless would have been far more sympathetic to a pretty and distraught widow, would never have arrested her. No wonder she loathes you. You seriously interfered with her carefully considered plans."

"She might be a witch," said Roger. "That would explain all this plotting and murdering. I would have her arrested again and let the Patriarch's prison warders question her. They know how to get confessions from witches."

"I am sure they do," said Geoffrey. "But I would be happier with the truth than with some confession wrested out of her by the prison warders." He thought hard. "But even if all our suppositions are correct—and we certainly have nothing to prove them—we are left with the problem of why. Why would a Greek widow feel the need to murder monks and knights and send poisoned cakes to Dunstan?"

"Well, we know Dunstan is a blackmailer," said Hugh. "So that is easy. Although you will need to find out what secret of hers he had managed to discover. And the Greek population here despise us. They were grateful at first, when Jerusalem was conquered by Christians and the Saracens were expelled, but their lives changed very little in reality. They simply exchanged one brand of slavery for another. So, the Greek community is being avenged for its bad treatment by this forceful widow."

"Maria said Warner and d'Aumale were at Abdul's the night Dunstan killed himself," said Roger casually, picking at his teeth with his dagger.

"What?" said Hugh. "Are you saying they have an alibi for that ruthless attack on me and poor Marius?"

Roger scratched his head. "Well, she said she saw them there, but she did not see what time they left."

"Damn!" said Geoffrey. "That does not help us at all. Did anyone else see them?"

"There was some kind of celebration that night, and it became rather rowdy by all accounts," said Roger wistfully. "Virtually everyone was drunk, and it is almost a week ago now, so I imagine the chances of getting an accurate estimate of when those two bravos left will be fairly remote."

"Damn!" said Geoffrey again. "That means they could have left at any time, neither proving nor disproving their innocence of Marius's murder. Which means that we still must consider them suspects. And if this occasion was as debauched as you say, then one, or even both, may have slipped out of Abdul's and returned there later, after Marius's murder."

He stood up and began to pace back and forth restlessly, rubbing his chin. "I can make no sense out of all this," he said eventually. "We have a host of theories, but no facts. And if Melisende is the murderer, then who killed Marius and knocked you senseless? She certainly did not do that: there is simply no way she could get into the citadel without being seen, even if the guards did let her past the gates on the sly. It just does not make sense."

"It is a muddle," agreed Hugh. "I am glad it is for you to solve and not me. I am concerned about what Courrances said to you in the church last week, though. He has tricked you cleverly. All I can say is that I will try to help you reason it out, and may even be persuaded to go out and about with you, since it appears your life might depend on it. What is your next step?"

"Abdul's Palace. Tonight," said Geoffrey promptly. Roger looked pleased. "I want to see if we can raise some serious doubts about the alibi of d'Aumale and Warner. And I want to talk to Maria, if she is there, to see whether she can tell us anything about Melisende. Good servants, which Melisende maintains Maria is, are unobtrusive, and their presence is often unnoticed by those they serve. Who knows what Maria may have seen or heard? Such as why Dunstan may have been blackmailing her mistress."

For the rest of the morning, Geoffrey cleaned his weapons and mended minor damage to his chain mail. He could have ordered Helbye, Fletcher, or Wolfram to do it, but, like every knight, he had once learned to do it himself, and now he trusted his own care of the equipment that might save his life over that of others.

Roger and Hugh sat with him in his room, chatting idly about what they planned to do with the treasures they had amassed during three years' Crusading. Roger honed his sword as they spoke, testing the sharpness of the edge with his rough, dirty thumb. Hugh lay on the bed with his arms under his head, staring up at the ceiling. The bell summoned them for a meal of the inevitable goat in a strongly spiced sauce, with flat bread and piles of underripe figs that Geoffrey suspected were the major cause of intestinal disorders among the knights of the citadel.

After the meal, as the afternoon heat began to make the horizon shimmer and the city boil, a temporary peace settled, and only the flies showed any signs of activity. Geoffrey, having missed most of his sleep the night before, handed his filthy clothes to Wolfram to put through the process of dirt redistribution he called washing, and retired once more to his room.

Moments later, Helbye arrived with a message from Tancred. Geoffrey scanned through it, but it said nothing of relevance to the case in hand. It told him in exuberant terms about the plans he had for attacking Haifa, and of a sad sight he had encountered on the way. The highly respected Sir Guibert of Apulia and a small band of his soldiers had been attacked by Saracens east of Caesarea, and had been killed to a man. Tancred's soldiers had buried them in the desert. Such an event was nothing unusual, because journeys outside Jerusalem were always dangerous although Tancred questioned why Guibert should have been so far from home.

Geoffrey lay on the bed, but after a moment he rose again to retrieve the fragments of parchment he had taken from Dunstan's desk. Sleepily, he tugged at the stone, wondering how he had jammed it back into place so hard that it was difficult to remove again. He slipped his hand into the hole, then snapped out of his pleasant drowsiness with a shock. The hole was empty; the parchments were gone.

He backed away from it, bewildered, looking from the stone in his hand to the hole in the wall. Then he took a candle stub, lit it, and peered into the little cavity, half-expecting that he was mistaken. But he was not, and the hole was empty. He backed away a second time and sat heavily on the bed. It was impossible! No one knew of that hiding place but himself! He caught his breath, and his stomach churned so violently that he clutched at it. A clammy sweat broke out on his forehead and down his back as he recalled putting the parchments in the hiding place. Hugh had been sprawled across the bed, sleeping deeply after his knock on the head, but Roger had seen him! When Geoffrey had turned from replacing the stone, Roger had been awake and stretching and had made some comment about him keeping his wine there!

Heart thumping painfully, Geoffrey tried to bring his tumbling thoughts into order. He was being unfair and ridiculous! Roger would never steal from Geoffrey's room! And even if he did, he could not read, so how would Dunstan's scribblings be of any value to him? Perhaps he had stolen them to give to someone else, came the unsettling response to his question. But that was even more ludicrous. Firstly, Roger knew what was in the parchments, because Geoffrey had told him, so why would he need to take them? And second, who could Roger have given them to? His friends in the citadel were Geoffrey and Hugh.

Geoffrey stood abruptly and began to pace around the room. His movements woke the dog, which eyed him with malevolence at the injustice of being woken at the hottest point of the day, and growled softly. Another thought sprang into Geoffrey's mind. The dog was an unfriendly creature, yet no one had reported it barking or causing a disturbance when Marius had been killed and Hugh injured. Which may well have meant that the killer was someone whom the dog knew, and did not perceive as a threat. Someone like Roger. He recalled Hugh's words. "I saw that hound of yours stand up and wag its tail."

But that was impossible, Geoffrey told himself sternly. He had been with Roger all that night, and they had entered his room together to find Marius dead. Geoffrey closed his eyes and felt sick. But that was not true either. Geoffrey had been called to tend to young Barlow, terrified by his first experience of poison by alcohol. Roger had not been with Geoffrey then; he had waited in the courtyard, or so Geoffrey assumed. He recalled vividly Roger's massive frame etched against the dark night sky as he drank water from the well.

Was that the answer? That the killer in the citadel was Roger? Geoffrey sat down again and turned the stone over in his shaking hands as he thought. On the way back from the Patriarch's palace, he and Roger had discussed the case in detail, and Roger had questioned the validity of trying to understand why Marius should disguise Dunstan's suicide when Marius would tell them what they wanted to know anyway. Geoffrey recalled thinking that Roger had been right and that such speculation was pointless when they would soon have answers. But perhaps Roger knew that they would not have answers, or was afraid that they would. When Geoffrey went off to tend Barlow, a godsent opportunity presented itself: Roger could slip up the stairs to Geoffrey's room, knock Hugh unconscious, and stab Marius. He could easily have been back outside drinking at the well by the time Geoffrey returned from Barlow's tent.

Or could Hugh have killed Marius? But that really was ludicrous, for Geoffrey had seen the blood oozing from the back of Hugh's skull from the blow that felled him, and it was difficult for a man to hit himself on the back of his own head. And anyway, Hugh had an intense loyalty to Bohemond stretching back over many years: they had been friends since boyhood, and Hugh would never consider doing anything to betray him.

But Roger, although in Bohemond's service, owed no such loyalty: he had simply been available and had joined up with the first Crusade leader he had met. Geoffrey squeezed his eyes tightly shut and remembered the many conversations he had had with Roger, in which the big knight had confided that he did not like Bohemond and did not approve of many of his tactics. The conversations were never in front of Hugh, of course, and Geoffrey had put Roger's confessions down to too much drink and a tendency to consider all things not English, including the French Bohemond, as suspect. But now it seemed there might be more to them than Geoffrey had possibly imagined.

So, Roger had had the opportunity to kill Marius. He had known Geoffrey was about to question the scribe, and knew that it would only be a matter of time before Geoffrey had the answers to his questions. So, Roger had decided to kill Marius before he could speak. But that was risky. First, how could Roger know that Marius had not already told Hugh everything he knew? And second, what would he have done if Hugh had not been sitting so conveniently with his back to the door? The answer, again, was unpleasantly clear. Roger had not intended to stun Hugh, he had intended to kill him, so that Marius's secrets would remain untold. The room had been dark—Geoffrey had later waited while Roger fetched a lamp. Roger must have assumed, because there was plenty of blood from the wound on his head, that Hugh was dead, and the room was too dark and time too short to check further.

Geoffrey recalled with a sickening clarity that Roger had tried to persuade him to go for help while he, Roger, stayed with Hugh. Geoffrey, anxious and guilt-ridden that his friend had been injured while doing him a service, had refused, and Roger had gone instead. And in so doing, Geoffrey had probably saved Hugh's life, as Roger had been unable to complete the job he had started. Then, when Hugh awoke and revealed that Marius had been far too jittery to tell him anything, Roger's anxieties would have been over. He would have had no need to kill Hugh. What if it had been different, and Hugh had claimed that Roger had struck him and killed Marius? Geoffrey could imagine Roger declaring Hugh's story the invention of a fevered mind, a man rambling and out of his wits. And at some point, Roger would have been left alone with Hugh, who would then simply have "died in his sleep," or become raving and "killed himself."

Sleep now seemed out of the question. Geoffrey leaned back against the wall, stretched his legs out on the bed, and began to go through his analysis again step by step to see if there was some way in which he might have been mistaken. But he was not, of course, and the more he thought about it, the more it seemed to make sense. Roger could also have left the replica dagger and the pig's heart in his room. No one would have questioned Roger if he had been seen entering or leaving: he and Geoffrey were good friends, and were constantly in and out of each other's quarters to borrow wine. But why should Roger have become involved in such treachery? Roger, like most of the Normans, was acquisitive, and had come on Crusade with the sole intention of making his fortune. A chest of booty looted from cities all across Asia Minor stood in his room—not as large as Hugh's, but bigger than Geoffrey's. So, was that his motive? Was someone paying him to kill?

Could Roger also have killed the priests, and Guido, and John? Geoffrey decided that he could. None of the knights had many regular duties, and it was easy to leave the citadel for hours at a time without being missed. Geoffrey had no idea where he had been himself when the first murders were committed three weeks before, and it would be impossible to prove whether Roger had been at a particular place at a specified time so long after the event. Many of the knights who lived in the citadel were drunk half the time and would probably not recall where they were the previous day, let alone weeks before. Geoffrey studied the fireplace stone in his hands gloomily. No wonder Courrances had been so gloating in the chapel the morning Geoffrey had fought Warner. Perhaps Courrances had already surmised that Roger was involved, and had recruited Geoffrey out of sheer malice.

Geoffrey looked from the stone out the window to the brilliant blue of the sky. What should he do now? He was reluctant to involve Hugh any more than he had to—Hugh had already risked his life for this business. And he certainly could not confront Roger with his findings until he was certain where they led—he did not want Roger to warn any accomplices he might have that Geoffrey was coming close to the truth. And if Roger had already tried to kill Hugh, he would have no compunction at all in killing Geoffrey.

But even the knowledge of Roger's role in the affair did not clarify matters. There were still many unanswered questions— what was the link between Dunstan and Melisende? Did she send him the poisoned cakes, or did Dunstan poison them ready to send to someone else? If the latter, then to whom? Roger? Why were the monks and knights killed? Who was Dunstan blackmailing? And perhaps most vital of all, who was behind all this? Roger himself? Melisende? Courrances? Warner and d'Aumale? Or was it Bohemond, whom Roger served and whose knights were being killed, or the Patriarch, whose devious ways were notorious all over Christendom?

Geoffrey had planned to go to Abdul's Pleasure Palace that night to try to ascertain the whereabouts of Warner and d'Aumale, but in view of his discovery about Roger, this seemed unnecessary. Yet Geoffrey supposed that Roger must have accomplices, and knew that he should determine whether Warner and d'Aumale had left the brothel the night of Marius's murder— unlikely though an alliance between Roger and the Advocate's knights might seem.

With questions buzzing around in his mind like the flies that cruised around his head, Geoffrey did not think he would fall asleep. But the room was hot, he had slept very little the past few days, and the basic need to rest finally overwhelmed him. He slept fitfully, his dreams teeming with visions of Roger stalking through Jerusalem's streets with hands that dripped blood.

When his eyes opened and he saw Roger leaning over him, he gave a yell of shock and reached for his dagger. But he had removed his belt to sleep, and belt and dagger hung over a hook on the wall. He was defenceless! Roger leaned closer, and Geoffrey watched him in horror, acutely aware of his vulnerability while Roger towered over him. He felt the stone underneath his leg and reached for it, wondering whether he would be able to crack open Roger's skull. Just as Roger had attempted to dispatch Hugh—with a hard blow to the back of the head.

"Easy, lad!" Roger said, concern etching his large, blunt features. "Are you fevered?"

A heavy, sweaty hand clamped down across his head, and Geoffrey tried to prevent himself from cringing. His heart thumped more loudly than it had ever done in battle, and he wondered when he had felt so afraid. Now! Do it now! A voice clamoured inside his head, and his fingers tightened on the stone.

"Aye, you do seem a bit hot," said Roger, removing his hand. "I will nip down to my quarters and bring you some wine."

He saw Geoffrey's hand clutching the stone, his fingers white with tension. Roger looked puzzled.

"What have you got there? Is this the latest warfare technology from you southerners?"

He guffawed with laughter, and stood upright. Still laughing uproariously at his own joke, he left the room. Sweat-soaked and shaking, Geoffrey watched him go.

CHAPTER EIGHT

Geoffrey did not want Roger's company when he went to Abdul's Pleasure Palace, but Roger had set his heart on going and was not to be deterred. Geoffrey was reluctant to raise objections that were too strong, lest he arouse Roger's suspicions, and he considered asking Hugh to go too. But Hugh was too fastidious to take his enjoyment from a place like Abdul's, and Geoffrey decided the less Hugh had to do with the whole affair, the safer he would be. The dog had tried to follow them out, but Geoffrey had shut it in his room, ignoring the outraged howls that issued forth as they left. So Geoffrey and Roger set out together later that night, moving quickly down the silent streets, their swords clanking and their boots stirring up the dust from the baked ground.

Roger was in a buoyant mood and hummed as he walked. He had been to some trouble to render himself more desirable: he had shaved; his hair had been hacked short with a knife; and the rim of greasy dirt that usually encircled his thick neck was almost gone. He wore his best shirt too, under his chain mail, a fine garment of pale blue silk that he had rescued from the corpse of a merchant after the siege of Antioch. There was a crudely mended rent in the back, surrounded by a sinister dark stain, but Roger considered the shirt a fine thing and nearly always wore it when visiting brothels.

Next to him, Geoffrey trudged along laden down with his doubts and fears. The one thing that had been constant during the three-year Crusade to Jerusalem—through intense heat, freezing cold, debilitating diseases, flies, and continuous shortages of food and water—had been his friendship with Roger and Hugh. Now one had tried to kill the other, and Geoffrey was thoroughly sick of the Holy Land and the Crusades, and of the politics that caused a good man like Roger to turn traitor.

Since it was already late, activities at Abdul's were in full swing. Even from the end of the street, high-pitched squeals of delight, men's laughter, and the thump of loud music could be heard. Abdul saw Geoffrey and Roger enter, and he hurried over to greet them himself, welcoming Roger, in particular, like an old friend. Roger, eyes darting in all directions at the women who draped themselves across elegant couches or danced provocatively to the sound of drums and rebecs, was off in a trice. Geoffrey was relieved. He did not want to question people about Warner and d'Aumale while Roger listened. He watched Roger weave his way across the room with surprising grace for a man of his size, and then he found a stool at the edge of the room from which he could observe the scene for a while before beginning his enquiries.

Abdul's establishment comprised a large room on the ground floor, with a maze of small rooms on the upper floor that might be hired for private use. But it was the lower-floor room that boasted the action. A trio of sweating musicians pounded out a cacophony of noise, the rhythm of which was mesmeric. Over the din, men yelled and laughed as they enjoyed the company of the women. Geoffrey remembered Roger's words about how he preferred women who spoke his own language, and he wondered whether Abdul's music was deliberately loud so that the knights would not realise the women did not understand a word they said.

Abdul's Pleasure Palace was exclusively for knights: lesser soldiers, no matter how much booty they might produce, were simply not allowed inside. Abdul employed several hulking men

whose strength was reputed to be prodigious, whose dual purpose was to ensure no one was admitted who should not be
there and to collect appropriate payment from the knights. There
were probably about thirty knights, mainly Normans, in the
lower room, and about the same number of women. The women
were scantily clad, as women in brothels generally were in Geoffrey's experience, and the knights wore bizarre combinations of
chain mail and undergarments.

Geoffrey sipped wine from a handsome jewelled cup and
watched the revellers. He looked for Maria, but she was nowhere
to be seen. Perhaps Melisende had accepted her back on the
condition that she give up her alternative career. A knight lunged
drunkenly past and stumbled over Geoffrey's feet. He struggled
to stand, decided it was too much effort, and went to sleep where
he lay. Others around the room were in a similar condition,
sprawled in chairs with their heads back and mouths open, or
face down on the tables. In the morning, most would clearly
have only the haziest of memories of their night out, and Geoffrey despaired. How could he possibly expect reliable answers
about the whereabouts of Warner and d'Aumale from this
crowd? And tonight was a normal one, whereas the evening in
question had been a party, doubtless far more rowdy and drunken
than it was now.

Abdul slithered up to him, rubbing his oiled hands together
and giving a leer with curiously white teeth. Geoffrey wondered
if they had been applied with whitewash.

"You look sad, my friend," Abdul said greasily, his eyes looking anywhere but at Geoffrey. "Perhaps I can bring you someone
who might cheer you up?"

"Is Maria d'Accra here?"

Abdul's expression became predatory. "She might be. But
her mother has been ill, and she has seven brothers and sisters to
feed and . . . that should help, thank you sir." As Abdul did a disappearing trick with the coins, Geoffrey followed him through
the tangle of gyrating bodies to the stairs on the other side of the
room, ignoring Roger's indiscreet waves and winks.

Abdul led the way up the stairs and along several narrow corridors, before asking Geoffrey to wait in a small vestibule lined with benches. A few moments later, a young man slunk past, casting resentful eyes at Geoffrey, and Abdul returned, rubbing his hands together like a fly. He beckoned Geoffrey to follow him until he stopped outside a door with a handsome inlay of green marble. As Abdul prepared to open the door, Geoffrey grabbed his arm.

"Were Warner de Gray and Henri d'Aumale here six nights ago?"

Abdul looked startled; then his eyes narrowed craftily. "Everyone was here *that* night, Sir Geoffrey," he said. "But perhaps my memory might be jogged if I were not so concerned about my sick mother . . ."

"Is there anyone in this Palace without a sick mother?" asked Geoffrey, handing over more coins.

The coins were quickly bitten and secreted away somewhere on Abdul's oily person. "Warner and d'Aumale were here," he said.

"All night?"

"They arrived after dark and left in the small hours."

"When, exactly?"

Abdul spread his hands. "I do not remember. There were probably a hundred knights here then. I cannot recall them all. Sir Warner and Henri d'Aumale were here, and I remember they left after the unfortunate incident with the snake charmer. But I cannot recall the exact time."

"Perhaps I can talk with this snake charmer? He may remember."

Abdul looked shifty. "If he did, it is probably the last thing he remembered." He looked up to the ceiling and crossed himself clumsily, back to front and upside-down.

Geoffrey was obviously going to get no further with this line of enquiry, so he opened the door to Maria's room and stepped inside. Abdul made to follow him in, but Geoffrey closed the door firmly and hung his gauntlets over the panel in the door through which he was sure Abdul peered. There was a hurt silence, and then footsteps receded down the corridor.

The room was whitewashed and tastefully decorated with blue marble tiles, lending it a clean, cool appearance. Several bottles stood on a low table, near a large bed draped with blue covers. Geoffrey saw no sign of Maria, and sat down on the bed to wait. A few moments later, he was aware that the bed was shaking. He leapt to his feet and hauled the covers away, revealing Maria huddled into a ball and laughing uncontrollably.

He waited while she brought her mirth under control, and wondered at his own surliness. His dreadful suspicions of Roger seemed to have robbed him of his sense of humour. Maria, still giggling, scrambled off the bed and came to stand next to him at the window.

"What is the matter with you?" she demanded playfully. "You usually do not mind a joke."

"Why are you here?" he countered. "I cannot imagine Mistress Melisende would approve."

Maria grimaced. "You will not tell her, will you?"

"No. But others might. If the job you have with her is more important to you than what you do here, you should consider your position more carefully."

"Both are important to me!" pouted Maria.

"I meant financially," said Geoffrey. "But it is none of my business." He took her by the hand and led her over to sit next to him on the bed. "I need to ask you some questions about Mistress Melisende. Will you answer them?"

"What questions?" asked Maria suspiciously. "And since when do Norman knights ask so politely when they can simply demand?"

"You sound like your Mistress! I will demand if it makes answering easier for you," said Geoffrey, with a reluctant smile. "Now. How long have you worked for her?"

Maria raised her hands. "That is easy! Since she arrived here."

"And when was that?"

"A year ago, when your crowd took the city."

"A year?" repeated Geoffrey, puzzled. "She came with the Crusaders? I imagined she was in the city when it fell, and that was when she was widowed. She certainly gives the impression that she was here then."

"Oh no," said Maria. "She came when you did. She posed as an Italian so that she might travel here with the Crusaders, but she is really a Greek."

Geoffrey was more puzzled still. "Why would she want to come to a city where Greeks are treated so badly? What happened to her husband?"

Maria's eyes lit up, and she leaned nearer to him so that she could whisper conspiratorially. "Do you know, I do not think she is a widow at all! I think her husband is alive somewhere. Perhaps he was violent to her, or a criminal! But I think she came on the Crusade to escape him!"

It seemed a rather extreme way to escape, but if a woman were desperate and had the means to make herself a new life at the end of it, Geoffrey supposed it would not be impossible. He wondered what kind of husband would drive the aggressive, self-confident Melisende to such ends, and decided it would be a man he had no wish to encounter.

"She absolutely hates Normans," Maria went on blithely. "So perhaps *he* was a Norman. Like you," she added for his edification, raising her huge brown eyes to look at him. "That must explain why she does not like you."

"I think I may have managed that all on my own . . ."

"No! I am right!" exclaimed Maria, clapping her hands together gleefully. "It all makes sense now! That is why she told me to tell her whenever I saw you. I had to note who you were with and what you were doing. And why she asked my sister, Katrina—she works as a kitchen maid in the citadel—to watch you too."

"Did she?" said Geoffrey, thinking fast. "I wonder why?" It had to be because Melisende was involved in something sinister! Was she Roger's accomplice? Or he hers? Ends began to come together in his mind. The men who had followed him back from his meeting with Tancred had been speaking Greek—they must have been sent by Melisende to watch his movements, just like Maria and Katrina had been instructed to do. In which case, he had been right in thinking she had some kind of secret. Perhaps she had murdered this monstrous husband of hers, and that was the reason why she had to engage in such a desperate flight. And having attained a taste for killing, she was busy again, murdering priests and knights. It was beginning to fit together. Or was it? Why would Roger be in her employ?

He leaned back and considered, while Maria went to the table and began picking at a plate of nuts. Melisende could be the killer, and Roger, he knew, had killed Marius. But why? And Melisende clearly could not have killed Loukas when she was in custody at the citadel. So did Roger kill the monk for her, to prove her innocence? But somehow Geoffrey could not imagine the blustering Roger stealing into the Holy Sepulchre, and lying in wait for a crippled lay brother to slay. Perhaps he had been waiting to kill someone else, though, a real monk, and had panicked and killed poor Loukas by mistake. That would explain why the murder of Loukas seemed to represent a break in the pattern: a member of the Orthodox Church, rather than a Latin.

"Will you tell Mistress Melisende you met me tonight?" asked Geoffrey, standing and wandering to the window again.

"Well, I would," said Maria bluntly, "had I met you anywhere else. But if I told her I had seen you, she would pester me with questions, and she would be bound to find out where we met in the end. And then I would lose my job for certain."

"Do you know a scribe called Dunstan?"

"Dunstan? Oh yes. He often visited Mistress Melisende."

Geoffrey raised his eyebrows. "In her house? For what purpose?"

I would not know," said Maria, with a ridiculous air of false innocence. "Buying cakes, I should imagine. Dunstan likes cakes."

"Did you know he had died?"

"Who? Dunstan?" she asked, startled. She thought for a

moment. "He has not been for cakes for more than a week now. But he came irregularly, so we would have no reason to assume any harm had befallen him."

"There was a box of your cakes in his desk that made my dog very sick."

"You gave our cakes to your dog? That horrible black-and-white thing? They were probably too rich for it. They are made with the finest ingredients."

"I think, in Dunstan's cakes, poison was one of these fine ingredients."

She looked at him for a moment with her mouth agape, and then went into peals of laughter. "Now you are more your old self! Joking and teasing. I was worried about all this seriousness."

"I am not jesting with you. Dunstan's cakes were poisoned."

The laughter faded from her face. "You are serious!" She swallowed hard. "I make the cakes, and Melisende makes the bread, but I did not poison any of them. Perhaps Dunstan put the poison there himself. Perhaps he planned to make a gift of them to someone he did not like. And then me and Melisende would be blamed for the murders, not him," she concluded gloomily.

"Do you know of anyone Dunstan might want to poison?"

She shook her head. "He was not a pleasant man. He was always grumbling about someone. I cannot imagine he was popular. But he never mentioned anyone specifically he did not like."

Geoffrey walked to the table and fiddled restlessly with one of the cups. Even with Maria's empty-headed information, he was still no closer to establishing a motive. Was it possible Dunstan was visiting Melisende's house to blackmail her over the business of her mysteriously absent husband, and that she slipped him a box of poisoned cakes as he left? But what blackmailer was likely to accept such a gift from his victim? Perhaps Dunstan did poison them himself, intending to use them for someone else. But whom? And why? Did he intend to give them to Roger? Did Roger know exactly what they were when he stole them from Dunstan's desk and saw an opportunity to poison Geoffrey—the man who was investigating his crimes? But Roger knew that

Geoffrey hated sweet Greek cakes, and would not have eaten any when offered. Roger had been most definitely planning on eating them himself, so perhaps he really had not known that they would have killed him.

Geoffrey was becoming tired. His head throbbed from lack of sleep and the weight of his discoveries, and he longed to be in his own chamber, away from the artificial joviality of the brothel. He turned from the window, made his farewells to Maria, and opened the door. At that moment, there was a particularly loud yell from the carousing knights downstairs, so loud that neither Geoffrey nor Maria heard the thud of the arrow that smashed into the wall where Geoffrey had been standing.

Geoffrey intended to leave Abdul's Pleasure Palace and let Roger find his own way home. Roger probably had no intention of leaving anyway, not when there was still wine to be downed and women to be accosted. As Geoffrey reached the head of the stairs, he glanced up a corridor that ran at right angles to the one he had just walked down, and paused. Someone was lying there, partly propped up against the wall. Even from that distance, the dull sheen of oil that glistened on the man's face told Geoffrey that it was Abdul.

He approached cautiously, aware that if Abdul had imbibed too much of his own wine, he might prefer to sleep off his indignities in private. But Geoffrey strongly suspected Abdul was not foolish enough to drink the sour wine he served the knights, and that there was another reason why he should be prone on the floor. Geoffrey glanced around quickly to make sure it was not some kind of trap to catch him unawares, and quickly knelt next to the rotund brothel-keeper.

Abdul stirred when Geoffrey shook his shoulder, and then he groaned softly.

"What happened to you?"

"Jerusalem is not the city it was," bemoaned Abdul, clutching at a lump on the side of his head, already turning dark with the beginnings of a bruise. "Between you and me, I preferred the Saracens to the Christians. They were not so greedy and not so aggressive."

"Did you see who hit you?"

Abdul shook his head and tried to struggle to his feet. Geoffrey helped him. "But it is not the first time I have been robbed in my own house. At least I still have this."

He raised a hand, and in it Geoffrey saw the chain and locket that the Patriarch had given Roger in payment for his spying services. Abdul inspected it carefully in the light from a torch on the wall.

"That villain!" he exclaimed. "This is not even silver! Look! It is nothing but base metal!"

Geoffrey smiled grimly. Perhaps there was justice in the world after all. Roger had been paid for his traitorous services with imitation jewelry, and the scheming Abdul had been duped by his own greed. Abdul grunted and put the necklace in his purse. "I will give this to Maria. She will not know it is of poor quality."

"Did Roger hit you?"

"Oh lord, no. The attack came from the direction of the back stairs. Sir Roger was already ensconced in a room with Eveline. Eveline is . . ."

He stopped in midsentence as another tremendous crash came from below, accompanied by shouting. Abdul groaned anew.

"It is not my night, Sir Geoffrey. First I am hit on the head, and now your comrades riot."

"Do they often riot?" asked Geoffrey as Abdul braced himself to enter the fray.

"They most certainly do," replied Abdul with resignation. "And from the noise, I see tonight they are in earnest."

He hurried away, while Geoffrey crouched down to peer at the scene below from the top of the stairs. A table flew past his line of vision, smashing to pieces against a wall. Men ran here and there in various stages of undress, while women screamed. Abdul's voice rose in a reedy shout above the chaos, appealing for calm, but either the knights did not hear or they did not care. From the rooms upstairs, more knights and women emerged, jostling past Geoffrey to join in the chaos.

Geoffrey had expected Roger to be one of the first to rally to the call, since the big knight was never one to pass up the opportunity for a fight—armed or unarmed or, Geoffrey imagined, clothed or unclothed—but there was no sign of him.

A Lorrainer was weaving down the corridor toward Geoffrey, and took a swing at him as he passed. Geoffrey ducked it with ease and heaved the Lorrainer head over heels down the steps. He saw the tumbling knight knock over two more who were attempting to climb the stairs, and then he headed toward the room that Abdul had said Roger had hired. He knocked softly and called, but there was no reply. He hesitated, wondering whether to abandon Roger and slip away—fights between knights were notoriously violent, and he had no wish to become involved in a brawl that was none of his making.

The shouting from below was growing louder and sounded as though it might be spreading to the street. Geoffrey knew he had to make up his mind quickly, or he would end up fighting whether he liked it or not. He turned the handle, pushed open the door, and gasped in horror.

The room was very much like the one in which he had seen Maria, except that its decor was green not blue. And the covers on the bed were stained a deep crimson.

Two people lay there, and Geoffrey edged forward, his heart thudding. Eveline lay on her back, her eyes staring vacantly at the ceiling, while a blossom of blood oozed from a wound in her chest. Next to her, also on his back, was Roger, his mouth agape as he snored lustily, an empty wine goblet in his hand. Geoffrey felt sick. For a moment, all sounds receded, and he was aware only of Roger's snores and the dead woman on the bed. Then a particularly loud bang from downstairs brought him to his senses. He edged away, but as he moved, Roger opened his eyes, groaned loudly, and called Geoffrey's name.

Geoffrey froze as Roger lifted his head from the pillow.

"I feel awful," the burly knight slurred. He raised himself a little higher. "What is happening? What is all that noise?"

"A fight," said Geoffrey tersely. "I am leaving."

"Wait for me. God's blood!"

Geoffrey watched as Roger came face to face with the body of Eveline. The Englishman started violently, and his big brown eyes widened in horror. Slowly, he reached out a hand and touched her on the shoulder, as though she might waken if he shook her. Then he snatched his hand away, lurched from the bed, and was violently sick. Geoffrey was impressed. It was quite a performance from a hardened killer.

Eventually, Roger turned to look at Geoffrey, his face ashen. "What happened?" he whispered, his voice hoarse. "Who did this to her?"

"It looks very much as though you did," responded Geoffrey coolly.

"Me?" said Roger. "I barely remember coming here." He gestured helplessly. "I do not even have my dagger—I left it downstairs as instructed by her. By Eveline." He looked at the dead woman again, his face a mask of pity.

"Are you saying someone waited until you fell asleep, and then murdered your whore?" asked Geoffrey incredulously.

Roger nodded. "I hope you believe me." He grinned weakly, but the smile faded as his eyes fell again on Eveline. "Oh God, Geoffrey! Who would do this?" He looked up at Geoffrey, still standing in the door. "You do not believe me, do you?"

He looked so hurt that Geoffrey was cut to the quick. He remembered Abdul, struck by someone coming up the back stairs as he was returning from showing Roger to his room. Was Roger innocent? Could the scenario Geoffrey had outlined with such sarcasm actually have occurred? Eveline had demanded that Roger leave his dagger behind. Was that because she was already nervous about him? Or had she been so instructed by whoever wanted Roger found in these compromising circumstances?

There was shouting in the corridor now. Any moment, someone would burst in and find them. Roger might not have a dagger to implicate him in Eveline's murder, but Geoffrey certainly did, and he was not going to wait around to be caught in the net that was tightening around Roger.

He went to the window and saw that it overlooked a narrow alleyway. He dashed over to the bed and grabbed Eveline's arm, gesturing for Roger to take the other one. He did not relish what he was about to do, but the shouts and crashes from outside were coming closer by the moment, and he was running low on ideas.

"Drop her out of the window."

"What?" Roger was aghast. "Are you insane? Whatever for? That is desecration! You can go to hell for that!"

"Just do it," grunted Geoffrey, as he struggled to manhandle the limp body to the window alone.

Roger stood in front of him. "I will not let you do this," he said quietly. "It is not right."

"Listen," snapped Geoffrey, pausing in his battle with the whore's body. "Did you kill her?" Roger shook his head. "Well, you will hang for it unless you take steps to prevent it. We have very little time. I propose we get Eveline out of this room and abandon her on the street somewhere. Then it will be assumed that she died during the fighting. If we leave her here, then Abdul will say, quite truthfully, that you were her last client, and you will be blamed, innocent or otherwise. Eveline is quite dead. Whatever we do now cannot hurt her. Help me drop her out of the window."

Ashen-faced, Roger complied, turning quickly and covering his face with his meaty hands as a soggy thump came from below. He moved toward a jug of wine that stood on the table, and poured himself a goblet with shaking hands. Geoffrey knocked it away and shoved him toward the window.

"Roger! There is no time for that. Quick! Jump!"

As Roger walked morosely to the window, Geoffrey gathered

the bloodstained sheets into a bundle. He noticed wine on his sleeve where it had spilled as he had knocked it from Roger's hand, and saw that the stain was surrounded by a fine white residue. But there was no time for speculation, and Geoffrey pushed past Roger to throw the covers into the street below. The big knight clambered inelegantly out of the window and let himself fall, and Geoffrey glanced quickly around the room. There was nothing to indicate that a violent death had occurred. Roger had no knife with him, and there was not one in the room. Unless he had had the foresight to hurl it out of the window, there was a possibility that he was telling the truth, and the whole episode was some bizarre plot to land him in a horribly compromising position. But why? Was it Melisende, realising that Roger was a dangerous ally and that she would be safer without him?

There was a heavy thump on the door, and Geoffrey saw the thin wood bow inward. Any moment now, the men outside would enter, and if Roger truly were innocent, then they would know exactly what they would find, and they would pretend to be aghast at the sight that confronted them. Geoffrey considered remaining, so that he could see who burst through the door. But he had visions of Roger being discovered under the window clutching the body of Eveline, and decided against it.

He scrambled onto the windowsill and let himself fall, landing lightly on his feet and rolling to one side. Roger stood immobile, and Geoffrey had to punch him hard on the arm to get him to pick up the body and walk with it, while Geoffrey carried the covers rolled into a ball. They kept to the shadows. He was aware that the door to Roger's room had been smashed open, and that someone was looking out of the window into the alley below. They did not have much time.

"I will create a diversion," he whispered. "You must use it to dump Eveline's body in the road and escape. You must not be seen. Can you do it?"

Roger was grey with shock. He stared dumbly at Geoffrey, who began to wonder if he was capable of doing anything at all.

"Roger! Can you do it?"

"I did not kill her, Geoffrey!"

"I know," Geoffrey lied. "But we can discuss it later. Now we must act. For Heaven's sake, man! Pull yourself together! This is not the first time you have encountered violent death."

"It is the first time I have encountered it in my bed!" muttered Roger. "I feel sick."

Geoffrey was heartily wishing he had left while he had had the chance. Now, here he was helping a man—of whose innocence he was by no means certain—to escape justice. He looked down the alleyway and wondered if he should run and leave Roger to sort out his own muddle.

"What are you going to do?"

Roger seemed to have pulled himself together somewhat. Geoffrey peered into his face and saw a resolution there that had been missing before. Perhaps Roger would manage after all.

"I am going to set fire to that stable over there . . ."

"What about the horses?" interrupted Roger in horror. A knight was of no use without his mount, and like all Normans, Roger had a healthy respect for horses.

"They will be fine. When you hear the alarm, dump the body in the road, and go straight to the citadel. You must not wait for me, or you might be caught. Your best chance to escape all this is to be as far away as possible."

Roger nodded understanding, his usual bumptious bonhomie gone. Geoffrey had never seen him so morose, and he wondered if that was how all murderers acted within moments of their crime.

While Roger watched from the shadows, a pathetic, hulking figure in a shabby surcoat and an incongruous pale blue brothel shirt, Geoffrey made his way across the street toward the stables. The main road outside Abdul's Palace was now a seething mass of fighting men, some armoured, others not; some using swords, others daggers. Geoffrey watched curiously for a moment, wondering how the noisy but amicable evening could have erupted so quickly into violence. There were more knights than the thirty he had seen earlier, and he imagined a rowdy group of Lorrainers must have entered and picked a fight with the Normans already there.

He reached the stable unnoticed and slipped inside to the warm smell of damp hay and manure. A horse snickered at him, shifting uneasily in the straw, and Geoffrey patted its nose to soothe it. Like Roger, he was fond of horses, and he would certainly avoid roasting the beasts alive. A quick survey told him that there were only three of them—two destriers that probably belonged to knights intending to spend the night at Abdul's, and an ancient nag with sad eyes.

The destriers were restless, made nervous by the commotion outside. Geoffrey slipped the bolts on their stalls and began to kindle a fire in some lose straw. As the fire caught and white smoke poured out, he pushed the bundle of bloodstained covers on top and watched them smoulder. As the acrid stench of burning filled the stable, the horses began to panic, kicking back against the stall doors. Finding themselves unexpectedly free, the destriers bolted out, crashing among the fighting men and adding to the havoc. Nonchalantly, and with admirable panache, the nag followed, backing sedately out of its stall, and even finding time to snatch a mouthful of hay before ambling at a leisurely pace into the road, and heading not for the fighting, but for the freedom of the city streets.

By now, Geoffrey's fire was well under way, and the stable was filling with a choking smoke. Geoffrey's eyes smarted as he kicked the burning hay to make it burn faster. He turned to leave just as the stable door slammed firmly shut. He was not overly concerned, imagining the wind had caught it—until he heard the sound of a bar being dropped into place on the other side. He gazed at it in disbelief, before beginning to yell at the top of his lungs and hurling himself against it with all his might. It held fast. It was becoming difficult to breathe, and he dropped to his knees to inhale the clearer air near the floor. As he knelt, he glimpsed a flutter of material caught against the door at waist level. It looked like material from a knight's surcoat, torn when someone had leaned his weight against the heavy doors to close them. Behind him, a timber post, well and truly alight, crashed down in a shower of sparks, and he had to hurl himself backward to avoid being hit. It fell sideways, blocking the door. Geoffrey regarded it in dismay. He would certainly not be leaving the burning stable that way!

The burning post set more hay alight, and the flames began to roar and crackle. Geoffrey could not have put it out now, even had he tried. The release of the horses must have alerted someone that mischief was afoot, and the door had been closed on the arsonist as a kind of instant revenge. Or was it more sinister than that? Was the person who trapped him in the burning building Melisende, or one of the Greeks she had ordered to follow him?

He coughed hard, his lungs rebelling against the choking fumes he was inhaling. A distant part of his mind told him that the identity of the person responsible for locking him in the stable really did not matter much, and that he would be better served seeking another way out. The stable was a small building, low and single-storied. He tried to focus his smarting eyes on the roof, but it was dense with smoke, and the stillness of the fumes indicated that there were no gaps to the outside that he could exploit. He tried to stand to grope his way round to the back of the stalls, but he became dizzy through lack of air and dropped back onto his hands and knees.

Slowly, becoming weaker by the moment, he crawled along the floor until he reached the back wall. He hammered half-heartedly, but the wood was solid. He moved on further, hoping to find a gap, or even some kind of door. Just as he was beginning to despair and to feel it might be easier to give up, his fumbling fingers detected an irregularity in the wood. It felt as though one of the planks had rotted, and rather than go to the expense of replacing it, someone had simply nailed another over the top. If he could prise the new plank away, he might be able to break through the rotten wood and escape.

But whoever had nailed the plank in place had done a thorough job, and after several abortive attempts, Geoffrey knew he would not be able to get it off. Above him, the roof began to burn, flames running in ribbons up the timbers to the dried mud roof. Another supporting pole crashed to the floor, showering Geoffrey with sparks, and he saw his surcoat began to smoulder. Now he could barely breathe at all, and his head swam. As another pillar began to collapse with a tearing groan, darkness descended over him.

CHAPTER NINE

Through a hazy blackness, Geoffrey heard the screech of tearing wood, and then felt himself seized by the shoulders, and manhandled through a hole in the wall, the ragged edges of which ripped at his hands and face. He was dragged away from the searing heat and found himself breathing cool, clean air. As he gasped for breath and fought to open his eyes, which still burned and stung, he was heaved like a sack along a dark alley and over a wall.

Gradually, he regained his senses. His breathing ceased to rasp, his eyes cleared, and the acid, sick feeling in his stomach caused by the smoke receded. He opened his eyes and saw the explosion of glittering stars in the night sky, blocked immediately by a large, anxious face.

"Roger!" he croaked. "You should be in the citadel."

"I know how you like a fire of an evening, and I thought you might get carried away," said Roger. But although he smiled, the humour did not reach his eyes. Roger looked like a man who had been on a battlefield.

"What happened?" asked Geoffrey, struggling to sit up. Roger helped him.

"I did as you asked, and poor Eveline now lies in the street. I even took the knife of the knight who lay next to her, and plunged it into her wound. So people will now assume that Sir Henri d'Aumale killed her."

"D'Aumale is dead?" asked Geoffrey, his mind whirling.

"I could not tell," said Roger, "but he was unconscious at any rate. I am not surprised that those Lorrainers are involved in all this. And I would not be surprised if it were them who killed Eveline in the first place."

Was that it? Was Geoffrey making a mistake in assuming all these incidents were connected? Perhaps this was merely the latest step in the war of attrition the Norman knights had waged with the Lorrainers since the Crusaders had taken the citadel a year before. Geoffrey took a deep breath and coughed violently.

"Shh," said Roger, looking over his shoulder. "We are in someone's garden, and we do not want them raising the alarm."

"Sorry," said Geoffrey. "What happened then? Did anyone see you?"

Roger shook his head. "Two destriers came thundering down the road, and since they were loose and unmarked, they were considered fair game. Most of the knights went tearing after them, and those who did not were watching the fire. Then there was some kind of hubbub at Abdul's, and everyone who was left went racing back inside. I thought I would wait for you, since the streets had emptied and there was no hue and cry raised for us. But then I saw an odd thing."

He paused. Geoffrey waited until he thought Roger had forgotten what he was going to say. "What did you see?" he prompted.

Roger gazed at him sombrely. "When all those knights ran into Abdul's, one went instead to the stables. Smoke was pouring out of the door, and I wondered whether you might emerge and bump into him. But you did not come out, and I saw him heave the doors closed. At first, I assumed he was trying to contain the fire, but then I saw him bar them."

"Did you see who it was?"

Roger continued to gaze. "It was smoky and dark. But he looked very familiar."

"Who?" demanded Geoffrey impatiently.

Roger shook his head uncertainly. "I cannot swear to it, lad, but I thought it was Courrances."

Geoffrey said nothing, but looked at the piece of material he still clutched in his hand: the scrap of cloth that had ripped from a surcoat when someone had leaned against the rough wood of the heavy doors to force them closed. It was an expensive black linen and still clean, even after what it had been through. Geoffrey knew of only one person whose surcoat was black and spotless, and that was Courrances.

He told Roger, and the big knight blew out his cheeks unhappily. "Looks like he does not want you to investigate after all," he said. "Despite having gloated at the position you were in a few days ago."

"Perhaps he did not know there was anyone still in the stables," said Geoffrey uncertainly.

Roger raised his eyebrows. "Maybe. But it was pretty damned obvious the fire was started deliberately, especially since someone had taken the trouble to let the horses out first. He may not have known it was you, of course. Maybe he just does not like arsonists."

Geoffrey rubbed his eyes, feeling them gritty and sore under his fingers. He wondered when he had last felt so physically and emotionally battered, and slowly climbed to his feet. He wished he could awaken in the morning and find all his suspicions were just dreams, and he could go back to his position of trust with Roger. But even as the wish flitted through his mind, he knew it could never be fulfilled; from now on, he must regard Roger with as much caution as he did Courrances.

"When Courrances had gone, I went to undo the gates, but they had jammed from the inside," continued Roger, solicitously slipping a burly arm under Geoffrey's elbow. "I assumed you would be looking for another exit, and came across that weak spot at the back. It was getting unpleasant, with smoke pouring off the roof, and sparks everywhere, but then I thought I heard a scratching sound above all that cracking and roaring. I battered the wall in, and you were just inside."

"I was lucky you thought to look round the back," said Geoffrey, trying to clean his begrimed face on his sleeve.

"I know how you think," said Roger with a sudden grin. "Friends do after a while."

Geoffrey felt an uncomfortable twinge of guilt.

"We cannot return to the citadel looking like this," he said brusquely, sniffing cautiously at the acrid burning smell that pervaded his clothes. "It might give us away."

"I know a bathhouse round here that is reasonably clean," volunteered Roger.

Geoffrey balked at the word "reasonably," but allowed himself to be led down a maze of twisting alleyways in the general direction of the Patriarch's palace. Roger moved through the shadows like a great cat, almost as light and fleet of foot as the smaller, more agile Geoffrey. They made little noise, and melted into the shadows when they heard or saw someone coming the other way. By unspoken agreement, every so often one would stop and hide while the other went on ahead to see if they were being followed, but there was no suggestion that they were. Geoffrey was often cautious while out at night, but Roger seldom was, and Geoffrey imagined the events of the night must have shaken him indeed to make him depart from his usual confident complacency.

Eventually, Roger stopped in front of a nondescript house, and looked around carefully before knocking. The door was opened immediately, and the two knights were ushered inside. They were given a quick look over, and then led along a tiled corridor without a word being spoken, and down some stairs to a room in a basement. It was cool, almost chilly, and contained several vats of water that, while they were certainly not freshly poured, were sufficiently clear that Geoffrey could see the bottoms. Just.

The bath attendant eyed Geoffrey and Roger dubiously, and poured a hefty dose of fragrant oil into the water.

"We will smell like whores," muttered Roger disapprovingly, but stripped off his dirty clothes and presented them in an unsavoury bundle to the bath attendant. Geoffrey did likewise, and climbed into the bath, screwing up his face at the agonising coldness.

"I hate doing this," he grumbled to Roger, trying to stop his teeth from chattering.

"My father took a bath once," said Roger conversationally. "He said it was an experience every man should have once in his lifetime."

"Why?" asked Geoffrey, peevishly. "To mortify the flesh? To curb physical desires?"

"So he would know better than to do it again," said Roger with a roar of laughter that echoed around the basement room and brought the attendant running in alarm.

"Right," said Geoffrey, beginning to climb out, "that is enough."

"You need to put your head under the water," said Roger, wallowing like a pig. Geoffrey looked at him in dismay. "Your hair stinks of smoke. You need to get it right under." He nodded at the attendant, and Geoffrey felt powerful hands begin to push him down. He squirmed and struggled, but the oils made the sides slippery, and he was helpless until the attendant pronounced himself satisfied.

"Ordeal by fire and water," he muttered, climbing out onto a floor that was awash.

While they waited for their clothes to be cleaned, they sat draped in towels, dripping onto the already saturated floor. Geoffrey pretended to be dozing, because he was confused by the information he had collected: he was disturbed by the notion that while Roger attempted to kill Hugh, he had risked his own life to save Geoffrey from the fire. It made no sense. Perhaps Roger was not the one who had killed Marius after all. Perhaps it was Courrances, who had shown his murderous streak by locking

Geoffrey in the burning stable. But all knights had murderous streaks, he reasoned, for that was what warfare was all about. Even Geoffrey had been seized with the occasional burst of bloodlust, especially after a long siege or if the opponents were Lorrainers.

Their clothes were returned washed, brushed, and smelling sweeter than they had done since Geoffrey had set off on Crusade. It was an agreeable feeling, and Geoffrey determined not to wait four years before taking his next bath. Outside, the air was still pleasantly cool, although dawn was not far off. Geoffrey breathed deeply and coughed, aware of the lingering effects of the smoke deep in his lungs.

As they walked along the street where Melisende's house was, Geoffrey melted deeper into the shadows, and Roger, unquestioning, followed suit. Lights were burning dimly in her upper and lower windows, although Geoffrey realized it was not unusual for bakers to be up and busy long before dawn. Nevertheless, he was curious, and edged closer to see if he could see through the shutters.

Fortunately for Geoffrey, there was a split in the wood that afforded him an excellent view of the room within. He saw Melisende and Maria sitting at the table together. Maria had been crying, and there was a vivid bruise on her cheek, while Melisende appeared to be listening to what she was saying. It did not take much imagination to detect that Maria had fled straight from the riot at Abdul's to the safety and comfort of Melisende's clean and welcoming home. Maria must have confessed her whereabouts—for Melisende was no fool and would see an immediate connection between Maria's battered face and a night of fighting at Abdul's. Which meant, thought Geoffrey, that Maria had probably also told Melisende that she had spoken to him there, and that he had asked her all manner of questions. After all, why should Maria keep his trust when it was no longer necessary for him to keep hers?

He glanced behind to see what Roger was doing, wondering how he might react to seeing his accomplice spied upon, but

Roger was doing exactly what he would normally have done—he was prowling the shadows to make sure they were not observed. Satisfied for the moment, Geoffrey put his eye to the crack again and strained to hear what was being said. But however hard he listened, he could hear only the occasional word, and nothing of any note. The two women seemed to be discussing cakes, for words like "raisin" and "almond" cropped up. Then Maria stood and moved toward the window. Her next words brought a whole new flow of questions racing through Geoffrey's mind.

"Well, if you did not poison them, who did?"

Geoffrey darted back into the shadows as the door opened, and Melisende stepped out, followed by another, taller, person who was swathed in a dark robe. Geoffrey glanced around, and saw that Roger too had made himself invisible. Melisende looked quickly to left and right, and set off up the street, the hooded figure walking beside her.

Roger spoke softly in his ear. "Shall we follow her?"

"I will follow her," whispered Geoffrey. "You stay here and see what Maria does."

Roger nodded, although it was too dark for Geoffrey to read his reaction. Was he aware that Geoffrey's ploy stemmed from a lack of trust, or did he think Geoffrey really considered watching the airheaded Maria important? And more to the point, would he do it, or would he simply follow Geoffrey? Well, we will find out, thought Geoffrey as he trailed after Melisende through the dark streets. As he walked, he tried to remember where he had seen someone with a gait similar to that of Melisende's companion, but the memory eluded him.

Their progress was slow, verging on the stately, and Geoffrey began to grow bored. They made their way toward Pharos Street, and then plunged into the labyrinth of alleys that lay to the east between St. Stephen's Street and the Dome of the Rock. Then it was more difficult to follow them, for the streets were short, and if Geoffrey came too close he ran the risk of being seen, while if he stayed too far behind, he was likely to lose them.

He realised they were heading for the jumble of alleys near the Gate of Jehoshaphat, where many of the houses had lain empty for a year. Compared to the Jewish Quarter and to those parts of the city occupied by the Greek community, these houses were palatial. But people were superstitious, and it was not easy to forget the slaughter that had occurred there. Geoffrey had heard that renegade soldiers who had deserted from the Crusader armies inhabited sections of the area, and he knew it was also peopled each night by merchants interested in buying and selling items on the black market. But he did not need rumours to tell him that it was a dangerous place to be at any time, especially in the dark.

They zigzagged deeper and deeper into the maze, and Geoffrey became aware that someone was behind him. He was not surprised, since he had half-expected Roger to follow him. Perhaps Melisende's tortuous route had even worked to his advantage, he thought, having made it so difficult that Roger had given himself away. At the same time, Geoffrey was not unduly worried by Roger's presence behind him, since if Roger had meant him harm, he would not have rescued Geoffrey from the fire.

Thus, he was wholly unprepared for the attack when it came. The first indication that all was not well was when a stone from a slingshot thudded into the wall above his head. Startled, he stopped and swung round in time to see a swordsman racing toward him with his weapon at the ready. Geoffrey whipped out his own sword and took up a defensive position. He was surprised to note that it was not Roger who bore down on him like a madman.

He parried the blow that sent shocks down his arm and drew a grunt of pain from his opponent, and he made a quick jab toward the swordsman's legs before he could recover his balance. The man went down in an inelegant pile of flailing limbs, and Geoffrey turned to face an attack from the other direction. Like the first man, he hurled himself recklessly at Geoffrey, who blocked the hacking swipe and used the momentum to drive the second man stumbling over the first. Then there were two more, not attacking wildly like the first ones, but advancing one from each side, dividing Geoffrey's attention. When the first man recovered and joined the affray, Geoffrey knew he was in trouble.

But he had faced worse odds in the past, and had certainly encountered far better swordsmen than these. Deciding his best chances lay in attack rather than in defence, he gathered his strength and went on the offensive. With an ungodly howl learned from the Saracens, he leapt at his attackers with great two-handed sweeps of his sword, driving them before him like leaves before the wind. One of them dropped his weapon and fled in the face of the onslaught, and the others wavered. Sensing their weakness, Geoffrey drove again, breaking into a run as they scattered before him. The first man tripped, and Geoffrey pounced on him, thinking to ask him some questions. He had stretched out a hand to haul him to his feet, when a stone from the slingshot hit him on the shoulder, glancing off his chain mail but causing him to lose his balance.

He crashed to the ground and saw the swordsman scramble to his feet, weapon in hand. Geoffrey was not prepared to be dispatched by a mere novice, and he lunged for his opponent's ankles, abandoning his own weapon as he did so. The swordsman fell again, and Geoffrey tried to clamber to his feet. He was aware that the man with the slingshot was directly behind him, and that the other attackers were returning, rallying their courage now that they saw Geoffrey was unarmed. One of them hacked at him, while another hurled himself at Geoffrey's knees to bring him to the ground. As he struggled to free himself, Geoffrey drew his dagger. But there was a dull ache in his head, and then nothing.

Geoffrey opened his eyes slowly, aware that hands were moving over him, pulling him this way and that. Gradually, he focused on the face of Melisende, who was searching him expertly, her face a mask of disdain. He was glad he had taken a bath and that his clothes were clean.

He tried to sit up. Immediately, there was a jangle of weapons, and he found himself staring up at four swords and a cocked bow. It was, he thought, flattering, that even flat on his back and, he ascertained quickly, weaponless, these people regarded him with sufficient awe that they considered it necessary for five of them plus Melisende to guard him. And there was another, staring down at him with a curious mixture of irritation and dislike. Brother Celeste from the Holy Sepulchre. Of course! thought Geoffrey. It was Celeste he had seen limping recently as he had led them to talk to old Father Almaric about the death of Loukas in the Church of the Holy Sepulchre.

Contemptuously, Geoffrey pushed the weapons away and sat up, blinking as the world around him tipped and swirled, and then settled again.

"You smell of that disgusting whorehouse!" hissed Melisende with contempt. "Maria told me you had been there asking questions."

Geoffrey doubted she would believe the fragrant smell came from bath oils and his freshly cleaned clothes, so he offered no explanation. He rubbed his aching shoulder, and raised his eyebrows. "So now what do we do?"

"You are so arrogant!" said Melisende furiously. "I should have brained you properly."

"That was you, was it?" he asked. "Well, that makes sense. These poor specimens of soldiers could not have done it."

The first swordsman moved toward him threateningly. Melisende laid a restraining hand on his arm. "Easy, Adam. He is deliberately trying to antagonise you. Do not give him that satisfaction."

Geoffrey had seen Adam before, and he understood perfectly well the young man's passion. It was Adam who had been ousted from Maria's room at Abdul's Pleasure Palace to make way for Geoffrey.

Melisende turned back to her captive. "They would have bested you eventually," she said, eyeing him with the utmost disdain.

"How?" he asked incredulously. "They had run away! They only came back when they saw I was unarmed. And incidentally, hitting someone on the head from behind when he is outnumbered six to one does not constitute a fair fight."

"And since when have Normans ever engaged in fair fights?" she asked coolly.

So there they were again, back at her favourite topic. Perhaps Maria was right about Melisende's husband, because something had to account for her abnormal hostility toward Geoffrey. He raised his hands in a gesture of defeat, knowing this was one battle he could not win.

"Where did you get this?" she demanded, holding up the red ruby ring that the Patriarch had given him in payment for his services. Geoffrey glanced up at the sky and saw it was still dark. He could not have been stunned for more than a few moments, but it had been sufficient time to allow her to search him quite thoroughly. The ring had been in a pouch sewn into the inside of his surcoat. In fact, Geoffrey had forgotten it was there. He had been meaning to ask Helbye, who was astute in such matters, to sell it or exchange it for something more useful—Geoffrey found rings interfered with his sword grip, and he never wore them himself.

"I took it from a church," he replied. He could hardly tell her the Patriarch had given it to him in payment for an investigation into murders that Melisende may well have committed, and yet his reply held a grain of truth—Daimbert represented the Church in Jerusalem.

Her eyes narrowed. "That has an element of honesty about it," she said bitterly. "For no Norman would hesitate to steal from a house of God. Yet, I know you are lying."

He doubted she would have believed him even if he had felt compelled to be straightforward with her. And there was a certain justice in the situation, given that he had been equally sceptical of her honesty at various times in the past.

"We will take him with us," she said to the swordsmen. "Guard him well. You have seen what he is capable of. He fights like the Devil himself."

"The Devil against the angels," he muttered, pulling his arm away from Adam, who made a nervous attempt to hold him.

"We cannot take him!" protested Celeste. "He will be a hindrance all the way. And what will we do with him when we get there?"

"Well, we certainly cannot dispatch him here," said Melisende. "This place may have an abandoned feel to it, but, believe me, there are people watching our every move even as we speak. They will not interfere with us as long as we do nothing to bring attention to these alleys. But it would be disastrous to everyone who uses this place to have a knight killed here. The area would be seething with the Advocate's men for weeks, and all business would have to cease. No, Brother, I am afraid we have no choice but to take him with us."

"We could kill him here and take the body with us," suggested Adam enthusiastically.

Melisende considered. "No," she said eventually. "He is too heavy. It is better to have him walking."

Geoffrey was far from reassured by her words, and it was small comfort to know that the only reason he was not being murdered there and then was because someone—possibly involved in even more sinister dealings than Melisende and her companions—might see. He wondered whether this was what had happened to Guido, John and the monks—had they been taken to a different area to be dispatched quickly by a dagger in the back?

"If you attempt to run, my archer will shoot you down," said Melisende, coldly. "Regardless of who sees. So please yourself. It makes no difference to me."

She turned and flounced away, leaving the jittery swordsmen and the archer to bring Geoffrey. He was not unduly worried about the archer, for the man was using entirely the wrong arrow tips to penetrate chain mail, and Geoffrey could see his

bow was poorly strung. But regardless, Geoffrey would not run—
not from fear of the bowman, but because it was very difficult for
a knight to run at speed for any distance wearing heavy chain
mail and surcoat. He could manage quick bursts over a short distance, and he could maintain a reasonable marching pace for
miles, but he would never be able to outrun his guards.

Melisende led them through yet more streets, until Geoffrey
was completely disoriented. He glanced up at the stars to gain
some sense of direction, and he knew they were moving generally in a southeasterly direction, but it did him no good, since he
did not know exactly from where they had started. He wondered
where Roger was: Geoffrey had made what was now an obvious
error of judgement in assuming it had been Roger who was following him, and he was angry with himself for not paying more
attention.

Finally, Melisende halted in front of a shabby house and
opened the door with a key. Inside, she kindled a lamp, opened
a door that led to some damp stairs, and led the way down. The
first flight was wooden, then they turned and descended another
of stone. Soon, they stood in a cellarlike room with walls that
glistened with water and green slime. To one side lay a long tunnel that sloped downward at a sharp angle. At its steepest points,
there were rough steps hewn into the rock, but for the most part
it was smooth. At the sight of its black, gaping maw, Geoffrey felt
a cold sweat break out all over him, and he was seized by a rising panic.

Melisende lit two more lamps, handed them to her men,
and gestured for Celeste to precede them down the tunnel. Geoffrey swallowed hard and clenched his fists to prevent his hands
from shaking. He recalled nightmares from his childhood of dark
tunnels like this, swelling to fill the entire room and sucking
everything down to a bottomless pit. And he remembered even
more vividly helping to dig a tunnel to undermine the walls of
a castle in France. The walls had collapsed while Geoffrey was inside the tunnel, and he still had nightmares about the long hours
spent in the dark, with water rising steadily around him and the

air turning foul. He would wake after these dreams feeling weak with a helpless terror that was never equalled by the anticipation or aftermath of even the most ferocious of battles.

Celeste had already disappeared, and the others were waiting for Geoffrey to follow. He contemplated the chances of success if he grabbed the weapon of the nearest swordsman or simply ran back up the stairs, but Melisende seemed to read his thoughts. She seized a dagger from Adam, and waved it at Geoffrey with a menace her swordsmen could never achieve.

"Down you go," she said.

He swallowed again and forced himself to move his legs, deliberately avoiding meeting her eyes lest she saw the fear he was sure was apparent. At the mouth of the tunnel he faltered, unable to help himself. Melisende gave him a hard poke with the dagger, and he inched forward, walking stiffly, so that he stumbled twice before he was even out of sight of the cavern.

"Where are we going?" he asked to break the eerie silence.

"Have you not heard of the caves and tunnels under the rock on which Jerusalem stands?" she asked. Geoffrey had, of course, but had certainly never entertained the notion of visiting them. "We use them for all sorts of things—communication between different parts of the city, storage, even dungeons."

Geoffrey's heart turned to lead. Not that, he thought, not left in a tiny cell thousands of feet below the ground in the pitch blackness, with water rising higher and higher, and the air becoming thin . . .

"What is the matter? Afraid of the dark?" sneered Melisende, and the contempt in her voice steeled his nerve. He made himself unclench his hands, and used them for balance against the walls. He tried not to think about the great weight of rock pressing down on the tunnel roof, nor of the fact that the cave seemed to be becoming narrower as they descended. It was growing lower too, so that he could feel the rock brushing the hair on the top of his head, and once he cracked his skull painfully.

The water dripping down the walls became an ooze and then a trickle. It lapped around his ankles, seeping icily into his boots. Then it was up to his calves, while the height of the tunnel forced him to walk hunched over. He wondered how there could be enough air to breathe with seven people in such a tiny space, and he began to cough uncontrollably.

"Stop," said Melisende, catching his arm. "What is wrong with you?" She peered at his face as if looking for weaknesses, and he pulled away angrily to begin walking again. He tried to take long slow breaths to control the trembling in his knees, but he felt as though the atmosphere was growing thinner. However deeply he breathed, he could not seem to draw enough air into his lungs.

The water rose sharply; the bottom of the tunnel dropped away completely; and then the water was over his head, enclosing him in total blackness. The chain mail weighed him down, and he felt himself sinking, down and down in black water that was shockingly cold. Hands grabbed at his hair and the scruff of his neck, and he was hauled gasping and spluttering to the surface by Melisende and the archer, to find the water reached only to his waist. Melisende and Adam exchanged a grin of amusement.

"If you had been watching Brother Celeste," said Melisende, "you would have seen he did not plough through this pond like a great ox, but took the path that curves around the edge of it."

Geoffrey began shivering uncontrollably. When, earlier that night, he had decided to take baths more frequently, he had not intended that it be within hours. He sloshed out of the pool and along the path that Melisende had indicated, realising that she had known perfectly well that he would fall in the water without a warning. Well, perhaps that repaid him for the terror he had imparted to her when he had provided her with an escorted visit to the Patriarch's dungeons. And she clearly had had good cause to be terrified then, since Geoffrey knew she was guilty of something untoward, even if it were not the murders.

On the other side of the pool, the tunnel was little more than a hole, and Geoffrey realised he would have to crawl on his hands and knees. Celeste's light had already disappeared into the darkness, and there was nothing but an impenetrable blackness. Keeping his eyes firmly closed Geoffrey dropped to his knees, and made his way along the tunnel, feeling it grow smaller and smaller until it forced him to lie on his stomach. He felt a rising panic as he opened his eyes and could see nothing at all—no light ahead, and none behind—and the cold realisation came that they had tricked him into entering a blind alley. Melisende would now block the open end with stone, and he would end his days where he was, in a thin tube with the great mass of rocks pressing down from above, with water trickling in to fill it, and the air becoming more and more difficult to breathe. He stopped and tried to catch his breath, and could not stop coughing.

"Hurry up!" shouted Melisende impatiently from behind him. "I do not like this part, and I resent being holed up here while you mess about."

Geoffrey never thought he would be so relieved to hear a human voice again. Still coughing, he edged forward and found that the tunnel suddenly expanded so that he could stand. He hauled himself upright and tried not to lean against the wall in relief. One by one, Melisende, the swordsmen, and the archer emerged from the crack and stood brushing themselves down. Experience had taught them where to tread so as not to get wet, and so none were as sodden and bedraggled as Geoffrey. Shaking with cold, he began to think wistfully of the searing heat of the desert.

Melisende urged him on again, and he rounded a corner that led into a vast cavern, like a huge cathedral, lit with torches around the edges. At one end, a number of crates were stored, along with bales of cloth, great boxes of nails and tools, and barrels of wine. The unmistakable aroma of spices bit the cold air too, along with the sharper tang of fruits. Some of the goods bore Greek letters, while others had Arabic script. Here, then, were the illegally imported goods, sold without taxes in the seedier parts of the city. It was this black market that was undermining the Advocate's power in the city, forcing him to make crippling trade agreements with the Venetian merchants in Jaffa. The Advocate, thought Geoffrey, would give his eyeteeth to see these mountains of illegal imports.

Geoffrey was too exhausted and too shaken to put this information to good use, other than the casual thought that John, Guido and the monks had possibly died because they had stumbled upon this great cache of black-market goods. Was this what Dunstan had blackmailed Melisende about? Her smuggling career? Geoffrey wondered how she could justify being morally harsh with Maria, when her own personal life was so deeply embedded in crime.

Melisende began to deliver orders to her men, who scurried about like ants across the uneven floor of the cavern. Celeste eyed Geoffrey with suspicion.

"What do we do with him now?" The Benedictine shook his head. "It would have been better for everyone—including him—if we had dispatched him in the street."

Geoffrey, recalling the terrifying journey—and with his stomach sick with anticipation of worse to come, was inclined to agree.

"Even if we had succeeded in killing him without being seen and had successfully hidden the body, it would have been found eventually," said Melisende, shaking her head and regarding Geoffrey dispassionately. "Imagine the reprisals there would have been had we been suspected of killing the Advocate's man. Geoffrey Mappestone is a nuisance, but Uncle will know how to deal with him."

The way she said it, "Uncle" was a sinister title. Geoffrey imagined some small, fat Greek merchant sitting surrounded by his illegal goods in an underground palace somewhere, issuing a continuous stream of orders to hundreds of scurrying servants.

"How will you manage him?" asked Celeste doubtfully, looking Geoffrey up and down like a piece of suspect meat.

Melisende laughed, her voice ringing about the chamber to be thrown back as echoes. "Him?" she said with disdain. "He will be no bother! Look at him!"

Geoffrey was sure he was no longer the picture of sartorial

elegance he had been when they had started this journey to hell, but he was still a knight and still larger and stronger than any of Melisende's motley crew. He began to cough again and then sneezed. Celeste nodded.

"I see what you mean. But you should tie his hands."

Melisende agreed, and Geoffrey's arms were tied behind him with unwarranted enthusiasm by Adam, who, judging from the time he took, was determined to do a thorough job.

"Thank you, Adam," said Melisende, when the young soldier had finally finished.

"I do not trust him," said Adam, moving toward Geoffrey belligerently, displaying exceptional confidence now that the knight was helpless. "He might overpower you or attempt some trick."

"There is little he can do," said Melisende. "Even if he managed to break away, he would never find his way out. And what would he do with no light and no food? Anyway, he does not present a threat to me. He is a thoroughly miserable specimen."

Celeste and Adam went off to attend their own business, while Melisende turned to Geoffrey.

"Now. We have another little trip to make, you and I. You heard what I said to Adam. It is perfectly true. You are most welcome to run if you like—it would certainly make matters easier for me—but if you do escape from me, you will die here without question."

He nodded understanding, and Melisende peered at him closely. "You do not like these caves, do you?"

"I have been in more pleasant places," responded Geoffrey carefully. He did not want to provide her with ammunition with which to torment him on their next journey by telling her there was little that could unnerve him like a dark cave.

"You are quite white," she said, turning him roughly to face the light, so she could see him better.

"I am quite cold."

"No," she said, narrowing her eyes. "It is more than that."

"I have not slept well for days; I have been locked in a burning stable; I have been in several fights; half of my scalp has been left on that tunnel roof; and I have had two baths," he said. "Perhaps that explains it." He did not mention the sickening discovery that one of his closest friends was a murderer, or that being underground came second to nothing on his personal list of horrors.

She grinned. "Typical Norman," she said. "Soft. Now, you go first, and I will follow. I will use this dagger without hesitation if I think you are up to no good. We are going to see Uncle."

Geoffrey forced his icy limbs to move, and Melisende directed him across the cavern to the other side. He was uncertain whether to be relieved or afraid that they were to take another route. She directed him to one tunnel of several in a row, and they set off, the light from her lantern creating monstrous patterns on the dripping walls. Unlike the last journey, this one appeared to require some navigating. Every so often, the passageway would fork, and Melisende would pause before making her choice. Geoffrey forced himself to concentrate on what she was doing, and quickly grasped the pattern she was following: at each tunnel entrance, a series of letters in different alphabets was carved, and Melisende merely chose the passages whose letters spelt the word "Kristos" in Greek.

He trudged wearily ahead of her in a variety of directions, which had him wondering whether they were travelling in circles. The passageways all looked the same to him: slender narrow cylinders of roughly hewn rock, some natural, others created by people, but all damp, cold, and airless. At one point, his tiredness led him to select the correct tunnel before Melisende had finished reading the letters, and she eyed him with distrust.

"That did not take you long to work out," she said with grudging admiration.

"But it will do me no good," he said, "for I do not know where we are going."

"To see Uncle," she said brightly, grabbing his arm and pushing him on.

"But I do not know whether I will like Uncle."

She laughed behind him. "No. You probably won't."

Geoffrey banged his head once again on the low roof, and then slipped in the slime that seemed to grow in all the tunnels Melisende chose. He noticed that the cave walls were becoming narrower again. Melisende bumped into him when he paused, and he skidded a second time. It was difficult to retain his balance with his hands behind him, but he was determined to avoid the indignity of being helped to his feet by the appalling Melisende.

The walls of the passageway were clearly converging, and the roof only just cleared the top of his head. He was forced to turn sideways; and then that too became tight, and he was in the unpleasant position of having one side brushing his face and the other scraping at his hands. Ahead, the tunnel narrowed into a black slit of nothingness, and he stopped. The air was still, damp, and had the chill of the grave. He wondered how long it had been there, unrefreshed from outside, and breathed again and again by the smugglers who used the tunnel. He had heard of poisonous air in caves, and he began to wonder whether the staleness he detected might be attributed to deadly fumes. On cue, he began to cough. He lost his footing and slipped forward, plunging between the narrow walls. He found himself jammed tight, the combined bulk of surcoat and chain mail wedging him so firmly he could not move at all.

He began to struggle, panic sweeping in great waves as he realised he could neither move forward nor backward. Behind him, Melisende insulted, urged, threatened, and finally pleaded, but her voice was a mere babble to him. Finally, she took a handful of his hair and pulled it hard.

"Take a deep breath," she ordered. "Close your eyes, and count to ten or something."

He did as she directed, and felt the passage walls recede slightly, so that they no longer felt as though they were crushing him.

"Good. Now take a step forward."

"I cannot," he said, trying to keep his voice steady. "I am stuck."

She gave a heavy sigh and leaned all her weight against him, while he struggled more and more frantically.

"Wait," she said, leaning down to inspect his hands. "I see. There is an old hook here. The rope is caught on it. No wonder you cannot move."

He took a deep, shuddering breath. "So cut the rope."

She glanced at him uncertainly, but bent, holding the knife at an awkward angle, and began to saw. The teeth-jarring sounds of metal on stone filled the air, accompanied by Melisende's increasingly impatient sighs. "I cannot cut it," she said eventually. "Adam did too good a job."

Geoffrey regarded her with undisguised horror, and the walls began to close in again.

"Do not struggle," said Melisende crossly. "You will make it worse." She shook her head in irritated resignation. "I cannot squeeze past you, so I suppose I will have to go back for help."

The light began to fade as she retraced her steps along the passage.

"No! Wait!"

In a distant part of his mind, Geoffrey wondered whether the agonised yell that rent the air was truly his, or whether some tormented demon prowled the sinister tunnels to give voice to his terror. Melisende came back.

"I will not be long," she said, in a more gentle tone than she had used with him before. "Adam and the others will be able to pull you free."

"No," he said in a calmer voice. "Try cutting the ropes again."

"I cannot without cutting you."

"I do not care. Please try."

With a shrug, she bent, and the sounds of scraping echoed around the tunnel once more. He felt his hands become slippery, although whether from blood or sweat, he could not tell. After what seemed like an eternity, she straightened.

"That might work. Try moving forward."

He tried, but he was held fast. Melisende shook her head. "I am sorry, I cannot do it. The angle is too awkward."

"Burn it off then," said Geoffrey, his panic-ridden mind casting about for any solution that would not leave him trapped between the walls in the pitch dark. "Use the lamp."

"That is a desperate measure," she said. "It will be better, and much less painful for you, if I go back. All we need is a saw to cut through the hook, and you will be free."

But she might be gone for ages! She might consider his release secondary to selling her cakes in the market, or seeing Uncle, or killing another knight. She might leave him there for hours or even days. That thought filled him with such terror that he strained forward with every fibre of his strength. There was a sharp snap, and suddenly he was free, stumbling forward by the momentum of his lunge. He dropped to his knees and tried to catch his breath.

"The hook sheared off. That was quite a feat of strength," she added admiringly. "She how thick it is?"

Geoffrey did not want to look. He found the rope was loose, and wriggled his hands free. Melisende helped him stand, but he was too shaken to notice the indignity of it all.

"It is not much further now," she said, patting his shoulder as she might a small child. "The tunnel widens in a moment."

He began to walk again, more easily now that his hands were free, and saw she was right. The tunnel became more like a corridor, and within moments they came to a flight of steps that led upward. He began to climb, steadying himself with a hand against the wall. Eventually they reached a stout door, and Melisende handed him a key with which to unlock it. Then there were more stairs, this time of wood, not stone, and Geoffrey felt the air growing steadily warmer and fresher.

A second sturdy door led to a dark corridor, and Melisende gestured that he was to lead the way along it. A mouse darted in front of them, and Geoffrey knew he was back above ground level. The relief was so great that he felt as though he could simply lie down where he was and sleep for a week. The corridor led to a hall, where two clerks rose from a bench as they approached. Recognising Melisende, they allowed her past with smiles, and she knocked at the door outside which they had been sitting. A voice called for her to enter.

"Melisende!" exclaimed the Patriarch in pleasure, rising to greet her.

"Uncle," she responded, with equal warmth.

CHAPTER TEN

Seeing them embrace, Geoffrey was surprised he had not noticed the resemblance before: the haughty expression, the olive complexion, the ruthless way in which they dealt with people. So that was it, he thought, trying to stir some life into his numbed brain. Uncle was no Greek merchant, but Daimbert the Patriarch, who stood holding his niece's shoulders in a fatherly way as he listened to her speaking in rapid Italian. Geoffrey had spent a number of years in Italy with Tancred, so he understood the conversation.

The Patriarch became aware that his niece had not come alone, and his eyes widened in horror as he recognised Geoffrey.

"Melisende," he said, aghast. "What have you done to my agent?"

"Your agent?" she said in confusion, looking from the Patriarch to Geoffrey. "You are mistaken, Uncle. This is Geoffrey Mappestone, a Norman knight from the citadel, who is in the pay of the Advocate."

"And also the man I chose to investigate the murders for me," said Daimbert, a little irritably. "Anyway, he is Tancred's man, not the Advocate's. I draughted him into my service recently."

"But we have been at odds!" protested Melisende in dismay. "He might have been useful to me! Why did you not tell me?"

"I did not think you needed to know," said the Patriarch. "Sir Geoffrey is in a dangerous position—ostensibly serving the Advocate, but also working for me. And doubtless passing information to his real master, Tancred, too," he added dryly. "I wanted to protect him as far as possible."

This was too much, thought Geoffrey. The Patriarch may indeed have wanted to protect him, but it would not have been for Geoffrey's sake, but to ensure he completed the task for which the Patriarch had commissioned him.

"The ring!" exclaimed Melisende. She reached into a small pouch that dangled at her waist, and drew out the gaudy bauble. "You gave him your ring!"

"I did indeed," said the Patriarch. "I assumed he would wear it since it is such a fine thing, and that those of my people who saw it would guess he was in my employ."

"I guessed he had stolen it," muttered Melisende. "That is why I brought him to you. Celeste wanted to kill him where he stood, and I was hard pushed to come up with a reason why he should be spared. You are too obtuse, Uncle."

The Patriarch smiled and turned his attention to Geoffrey. "Well? Have you unravelled this mystery yet?"

Geoffrey felt a twinge of unease. He had almost convinced himself that Melisende and her men were the killers, aided by Roger. But in the light of the knowledge that she seemed to be a much-loved relative of the Patriarch, he was uncertain. Was this what Courrances knew? That the killer was a person close to the Patriarch? And did he know that this knowledge might cause the Advocate to turn against the Patriarch, and plunge the city into civil war? Geoffrey needed time to think, and he was certainly not about to discuss his findings with Daimbert and his niece before he had consulted with Tancred. He temporised.

"The evidence is mounting," he said cautiously. "But I still need the answers to certain questions." Such as what you are up to, he thought. And do you know your niece might be a killer?

Daimbert smiled paternally. "So there is some progress?"

Briefly, Geoffrey outlined his reasoning that Dunstan had

committed suicide—blaming Marius, not Alain, for tampering with the evidence, since Marius was dead anyway and he had felt sorry for Alain. He mentioned his discovery that Dunstan was blackmailing someone, possibly the murderer, omitting any mention of Roger's role in the affair, but describing how someone had locked him in the burning stable. Daimbert listened carefully, his dark eyes never moving from Geoffrey's face. Melisende also listened attentively, her forehead crinkled in a slight frown. When Geoffrey finished, the Patriarch nodded slowly.

"So how will you proceed now?"

Geoffrey considered, trying to force his numbed brain to think clearly. "I plan to make further enquiries in the citadel among the friends of Guido and John," he said finally. He had already done this, and had been told nothing useful, but in view of the fact that it was probably Melisende's men who had followed him from his first meeting with Tancred, he was reluctant to reveal too much about his future movements. What he really intended to do, after he had slept, was to concentrate on Dunstan's movements for his final few days and to try to ascertain to whom he had sent the fatal blackmail note.

The Patriarch pursed his lips. "I suppose you know the best course of action," he said ambiguously. "Unfortunately, my niece has put me in something of an awkward position. You now know about my small foray into the world of trade, and you will have established that it is because of the black market—run by me—that the Advocate is forced to make debilitating deals with the Venetian merchants. That you know all this makes me feel somewhat vulnerable."

Not as vulnerable as me, thought Geoffrey, meeting the Patriarch's dark, unreadable eyes with a level gaze. The Patriarch continued.

"I am forced to make a choice. I can either let you go to continue your investigation for me. Or I can keep you here to ensure my secret is kept." He tapped his teeth thoughtfully with a long forefinger.

"Sorry, Uncle," said Melisende. "I did not envisage you

would be faced with such a problem. I thought you would want to question him because he had stolen your ring, and I did not want Celeste or Adam to murder him in the streets."

"Really, Melisende," said Daimbert, without rancour. "Your loyalty commends you, but your logic does not. What if he had stolen my ring? Then you would have presented me with a thief who knows all about our little operation. What would we have done with such a man? Would you have had me kill him?"

Melisende had clearly not thought of anything beyond presenting her uncle with a thief, and she regarded Daimbert in horror. Geoffrey watched her closely. She was intelligent and quick-witted, but she was also impulsive and did not bother to consider the implications of her rash actions. She glanced at Geoffrey and then back to the Patriarch, and Geoffrey had the impression that she did not really wish to bring about his death. Perhaps she just wanted him under lock and key in her uncle's dungeons, so that she could come and go at her leisure and they could argue and insult each other, and so continue their relationship the way it had begun.

"Well," she said finally, still gazing at her uncle. "You had better keep him alive if he can be useful to you. He can be reasonably discreet if he wants, and can probably be trusted to keep our secret."

"Probably is not good enough," said Daimbert. He turned to Geoffrey. "However, I know you will maintain your silence because of your loyalty to Tancred. If I lose my authority in Jerusalem, so will Tancred lose his. If you report the location of our supplies to the Advocate, you will strengthen the Advocate's position in Jerusalem, and so weaken mine and Tancred's. I do not for an instant trust you for my sake, but I know I can trust you for Tancred's. Therefore, it is in my interests, to let you go to continue your investigation into these murders. I hope the false trail that has led you here has not inconvenienced you too greatly?"

"Not at all," said Geoffrey dryly.

The Patriarch eyed him appraisingly. "You look quite dreadful. My niece is not always as gentle as most of her sex." He took Geoffrey's arm and turned him so that he could see him more clearly in the gloom. "Perhaps you will allow Melisende to prove she can be mannerly if she pleases, and stay for some refreshment before you leave?"

Geoffrey started to shake his head, wanting to be away from the Patriarch and other members of his corrupt family as soon as possible.

"Good," said the Patriarch, donning his paternal smile and clasping his slender hands in front of him in his bishoply way. "Now, if you will excuse me, I leave for Haifa later today to join Tancred, and I have much to do. I will, of course, carry a missive from you to Tancred should you wish to report your progress to him."

Geoffrey was sure he would, and considered writing Tancred a message that would deliberately mislead the Patriarch. But these were powerful men, and Geoffrey did not want to spend the rest of his life waiting for a knife to be slipped between his ribs because he had fed the Patriarch false information. He declined Daimbert's offer to act as messenger on the grounds that he had written to Tancred the day before.

Melisende led the way out of the Patriarch's room to a chamber nearby, where she offered Geoffrey wine and gestured that he should sit on one of the wide benches that ran round two of the walls. Instead, he walked across to the window and threw open the shutters as far as they would go, breathing in the warm morning air as deeply as he could. Melisende watched him.

"I have met others who have a fear of underground places," she said quietly.

"I am not afraid of them," said Geoffrey, twisting around to feel the first rays of the morning sun on his face.

"Yes, you were," she said. "If I had known, I would not have forced you down there."

Not much! thought Geoffrey, but said nothing. The horrors of the underground caves were already receding, and the sun flooding into the room was easing the chill from his bones. He leaned his elbows on the windowsill and watched the scribes walking across the courtyard to the scriptorium opposite.

"We should talk," said Melisende, coming to stand next to him and reverting to speaking Greek. "There is probably much we can tell each other."

"I am sure there is," he said without enthusiasm. "But why would you tell a Norman anything?"

She cast him a sidelong look that oozed mischief. "I had to ensure my true identity was concealed," she said. "By professing a profound dislike of Crusaders, no one would ever guess my ancestry is as western as yours."

"So you only pretend to be Greek?"

"Yes. Uncle was horrified at what he saw when he arrived in Jerusalem. The Greek population had been so maltreated, that it seethed with unrest. Uncle needed someone to infiltrate that community so that he could be informed of their plans and thoughts."

"Is it not dangerous for you? What if you were caught?"

"I almost was," she replied with a grin. "By you. When you arrested me, you very nearly undid in an instant what it had taken me months to establish."

He turned to face her. "Hence all the antagonism?"

She smiled again. "That was partly for the benefit of the Greek community, but partly genuine. I was furious to think that your senseless arrest of me might expose me as a spy."

"Your disguise is very convincing. How did you learn to speak Greek so well?"

She turned to stare out of the window. "In Rome, where I lived with my uncle, I had a Greek nurse. Uncle insisted she speak Greek to me so I would grow up knowing that language as well as I do Italian."

"Really?" said Geoffrey in surprise. "Did Daimbert anticipate he might need a Greek-speaking spy so long ago?"

She whipped her head around to glare at him. "He did not insist I learn it for that reason! He wanted me to learn simply for the sake of my education!"

"Then would Latin not have been a better choice?" reasoned Geoffrey. "Surely there are many more Latin texts in Rome from which to learn than Greek?"

"My education is none of your business!" snapped Melisende, but her outburst lacked the conviction of her earlier outrages, and Geoffrey guessed she might have been wondering along the same lines herself.

"Are you a widow?" he asked, to change the subject. "Or is that a part of your disguise?"

"I was married while I was still a child—to a Norman, actually," she said. "He owned rich estates in the south of France, and several castles. Uncle arranged it. It was a good marriage for me, and since my husband was more than sixty years old when I was fifteen, I did not have long to endure the match."

"And I suppose when this wealthy Norman died, Uncle, as your guardian, took control of these estates and castles?" asked Geoffrey with an innocent expression.

Melisende looked at him through narrowed eyes. "What are you saying?" she said coldly. "Do you imply that Uncle was using me to improve his own fortunes? I can assure you, that is quite untrue."

But Geoffrey strongly suspected otherwise, and from the way Melisende refused to meet his eyes, guessed that she thought so too. So, loving Uncle Daimbert had used his niece to amass a fortune for himself in the south of France, and then he had insisted on her learning Greek so that she might be his eyes and ears to aid him in the growing schism between the Latin and the Greek Orthodox churches. Perhaps Daimbert envisioned himself as Pope one day, and knew he would need an interpreter he could trust. Whatever his motive, it was obvious that Melisende's personal development had little to do with it.

"How did your uncle come to put you in the dangerous position you hold in the Greek Quarter?" he asked, curiously. "Did you travel to Jerusalem specifically to be his spy?"

"No! Of course not! I travelled here of my own free will with Uncle. When he was made Patriarch, he expressed a concern over the unrest in the Greek Quarter. I volunteered to act as his agent." She sniffed, and faced him with a haughty expression. "I like to use my talents as much as you like to use yours."

He shrugged. "But I am not a spy. I am exactly as I appear— a knight investigating the murders of two of my comrades and three monks."

She turned away again. "But women cannot become knights. And in many ways, I am better suited to my work than a man would be. Who would suspect that I am the Patriarch's niece? You did not, and you are more astute than most. Maria helped me in that respect. She got it into her woolly head that my professed dislike of Normans was because I had a brutal Norman husband."

Geoffrey said nothing, and Melisende shook her head in amused disbelief.

"How could Maria think that I, of all people, would flee some brainless thug! I would be more likely to send *him* off on Crusade while I stayed at home! Anyway, people seemed to believe her gossip, and I let them think I had witnessed the slaughter when the Crusaders took Jerusalem. It took a little while, but they accepted me in the end. With Brother Celeste's help, I was able to recruit a small group of men who assist me—chiefly they carry messages back and forth between me and Uncle."

"Like that loutish Adam?"

"Yes, he is one of them. I have about ten in all. But we have been talking about me. How did you become involved in all this?"

"Uncle made me an offer I could not refuse," said Geoffrey, leaning further out of the window and inhaling deeply. "I have a penchant for big, gaudy ruby rings."

"Really?" said Melisende flatly. "Then why did you not ask for it back when Uncle took it away with him just now?"

So he had, Geoffrey recalled. Crafty old Patriarch! He began to laugh. Melisende watched him bewildered, and for a while, neither of them spoke.

"So what do you know about the murders that unsettled Uncle sufficiently to employ me?" asked Geoffrey eventually.

She continued to look out of the window. "Very little. I have asked questions in the Greek Quarter until I am blue in the face, but I have ascertained nothing at all. The culprit lies elsewhere."

"The night I arrested you, I was followed as I returned to the citadel from here. When they lost me, I heard them speaking Greek. Was that Adam and his motley crew?"

She nodded with a sigh. "When the body of that knight appeared in my house, I just assumed it was someone making a covert threat against Uncle—making a statement to him that they knew who I was and what I was doing in the Greek Quarter. Uncle's main opponent in the city is, of course, the Advocate, for whom you work. As soon as I was released, I ordered Adam and the others to follow you wherever you went. I should have known better. They lost you on the first journey, and now it seems as if you even overheard them. They are quite worthless!" she concluded with a disgusted sigh.

"Yes. You would do better with a few Normans."

She glanced at him sharply and then laughed. "True. With a handful of men like you, I could take the city myself!"

"Then Uncle had better be grateful he set you to infiltrate the Greek Quarter and not the citadel."

She laughed again, but then became serious. "I still have no idea why that poor knight should have met his end in my house."

"Were you really shocked to find him?"

"You are damned right I was shocked!" swore Melisende vehemently. "You probably thought all that horror was an act, but I can assure you it was not."

"Why so? You must have seen worse sights on your journey here."

She shook her head. "Not at all. I travelled with Uncle, and he tends to keep well away from battles and slaughter, and although his men usually join in the looting, they do not fight themselves. We had plenty of supplies and travelled very comfortably, although I understand it was different for most."

It certainly was, thought Geoffrey, recalling days of marching across the searing floor of the desert with no water, and weeks when food was so scarce he had been able to think of little else.

"So, you see," she continued, "I really saw very little on our journey to distress me. That dead man in my bedchamber was the first body I had ever seen. I have not been able to sleep in that room since."

Geoffrey regarded her intently. "But if you are so adverse to violent death, why did you not try to stop the crowd outside your house from attacking me? And you seemed quite happy to deliver me into the hands of Uncle when you thought I had stolen his ring."

"I had no choice!" she protested. "If I had tried to save you from the crowd after you had arrested me, they would have suspected I was not all I seem. And I did try to stop them, if you recall. I told them if they attacked you, more of them would die. And as for handing you to Uncle, it was a choice between letting Adam kill you in the alleys, or bringing you here. I assumed Uncle would just lock you away until it was safe to release you again. He has others similarly incarcerated. It did not cross my mind that he might kill you."

Geoffrey supposed what she said was true, although he wondered what other false impressions she still harboured about her ambitious, scheming uncle. He said nothing and watched bald Brother Alain the scribe trailing disconsolately across the courtyard to begin his day of scrivening.

Melisende continued talking. "I still have nightmares about the body of that young knight. When I pulled the dagger from him, his hand moved, and I thought he was still alive. I bent to look at his face, and I saw his expression! He looked so shocked! And so young!"

Geoffrey refrained from pointing out that being stabbed in the back came as a shock to most people, and settled for saying, "He was twenty-two. And a friend of mine."

"Oh. I am sorry." She looked genuinely sympathetic, but Geoffrey was not about to lose sight of the fact that Melisende came from the same stock as Daimbert and might well have inherited, or learned from him, his superb acting abilities and innate cunning.

"Do you have any notion as to who killed Loukas, the Greek who was murdered at the Holy Sepulchre while you were under arrest?"

She shrugged. "No more than I know who is killing the others. It was fortunate for me that the man died when he did. Uncle would have been obliged to hand me back to the Advocate when he returned, and time was running short."

Hugh had suggested that one of Melisende's people had killed Loukas to "prove" she was not guilty of the other murders. It would, of course, have been in Daimbert's interests for her to be released, so that she could go on spying for him. But did Melisende know that a death had been arranged so that she might go free? On balance, he decided it had probably not crossed her mind: her improbable illusions of Uncle's essential benevolence went too deep. He thought also that she had seemed genuinely shocked when the Patriarch had suggested Geoffrey should die for what he knew, and reluctantly conceded that she had had no direct hand in Loukas's death.

She continued. "The rumour in the Greek Quarter is that the Advocate is killing Bohemond's knights to prevent an uprising against him. I was confused, though, why you should be investigating for the Advocate if that were true. Meanwhile, I was worried about Uncle. He has allied himself with Bohemond, and the attacks against Bohemond's knights are, indirectly, attacks against him. If I had known you were working for him, I would have warned you not to waste time looking in the Greek Quarter, but to concentrate elsewhere. As it was, I thought you were working for the Advocate, so I was only too pleased to see that you were wasting your time with the Greeks."

"What about Dunstan? Did you know him, or not?"

She shrugged. "What I told you in the market was true. He bought cakes from me."

"Maria told me he came to your house many times."

"What? But that's ridiculous! Why should he do that?"

"Because he knew your real identity, and was threatening to tell?"

She frowned. "You have asked me before if this Dunstan was blackmailing me, so, I think I can assume from this that Dunstan was a blackmailer. But you must believe me, Sir Geoffrey, when I say that I would never allow some fat, slimy toad like Dunstan to come between me and my work in the Greek Quarter! He would not have left my house until Uncle had been told exactly what he was about!"

Looking at her flashing eyes and determined chin, and bearing in mind his own experiences of her temper and abilities, Geoffrey had no doubt she was telling the truth. So the partial note Geoffrey had found in Dunstan's desk demanding money for secrets kept had not been intended for Melisende, but someone else.

"Did you know Dunstan worked for your uncle?"

"Did he?" She seemed startled, and Geoffrey wondered whether the Patriarch deliberately kept his niece in the dark lest she be uncovered by the Greeks: what she did not know, she could not tell potential enemies.

"So was Maria lying about Dunstan's numerous visits to your home?"

"Well, yes. She is very . . . impressionable. She probably imagined it."

"But you used her to spy on me."

"What? Maria? Are you serious? I could not possibly use her! She is far too unreliable. She would manage to concentrate for a few moments, and then she would be off with some man. She is an excellent cakemaker, but short on wits."

"What about her sister, Katrina?"

Melisende raised her hands. "You seem to know more about her from her job at this horrible brothel than I do as her employer. I did not know she had a sister. She told me she was Akira's only child."

"Did you discuss Dunstan's poisoned cakes with her last night?"

She looked surprised. "Yes, I did." Her eyes narrowed. "You were eavesdropping on us!" When he did not respond, she gave him a withering look and continued. "She told me you had been asking questions about me, and I told her some of our cakes had been poisoned and sent to Dunstan. We sat together trying to work out who might have done such a thing."

"I think we may have gravely underestimated Maria," said Geoffrey after a moment. "I think there is more to her than she lets on."

"Maria? Not a chance!" said Melisende dismissively. Then she looked at Geoffrey appraisingly. "But tell me why you think so."

"Akira for a start," said Geoffrey. Melisende looked blank. "One of the five murdered men appears in the house of Maria's much detested father, and another in the house of her employer, who makes no secret of the fact that she considers Maria a witless wanton."

"Are you suggesting that Maria killed those men and put them in our houses for malice?" asked Melisende in disbelief.

"Yes. I am not sure if she killed them herself, but it is certainly possible it was she who arranged for them to be slaughtered in those particular locations."

"But that is . . ." She faltered into silence. Geoffrey waited. "I had a note that afternoon. From Uncle, wanting to see me. But when I arrived here, Uncle said he had sent the note several days before, and that he had been wondering why I had not come sooner." She looked up at him, her honey-brown eyes blazing. "Maria must have found the note and kept it, so that she could send it later and get me out of the house when it was convenient for her! She betrayed me!"

"She probably feels the same way about you," said Geoffrey reasonably.

"What are you saying?" she demanded.

"Come on, Melisende! You are an Italian noblewoman who has infiltrated the Greek community in order to pass their secrets to the Patriarch! How is that different from what she has done to you?"

Melisende was silent.

"I suppose she uses Abdul's Pleasure Palace as a means of

gaining information from the knights," he said, reflecting. "Even Roger told me he liked Maria because she could speak his language. So the chances are that the knights talk to Maria, and who knows what secrets they might tell her?"

"She came with recommendations from Father Almaric at the Church of the Holy Sepulchre," said Melisende. "And he is a saintly man whose loyalty to Uncle is absolute."

"Well, she fooled him too," said Geoffrey, recalling the benign, rather bewildered old Benedictine he had spoken with about the death of Loukas. "But what about these cakes? The poisoned ones that were sent to Dunstan? Do you have any idea who might have tampered with them?"

She shook her head. "It was not me. It must have been Maria. When she got back from the fight at this . . . Abdul's"—she gave a shudder, and Geoffrey suppressed a smile—"she told me that you said you have evidence that it was *me* who poisoned these wretched cakes."

"She told you that? I can assure you, I have no such evidence."

Melisende looked sombre. "So it is Maria who is behind all this! Silly, empty-headed, flirtatious Maria."

Geoffrey said nothing, but gave a huge sigh, dispirited by all the intrigue and lies. It had been a long night, and it was beginning to take its toll. He ached all over, felt tired and battered, and wanted nothing more than to return to his chamber in the citadel and go to sleep. He made his excuses to Melisende and agreed to meet her the following day.

As he left, she took his hand and smiled at him beguilingly. He wondered what Tancred would say if he knew his most trusted knight was already looking forward to his next encounter with the Patriarch's devious niece. He took his leave, striding gladly through the warm, dusty air, and breathing so deeply of it trying to eradicate the last vestiges of the underground atmosphere from his lungs, that he made himself dizzy.

He approached the citadel with relief and made his way to his own chamber. Hugh was waiting for him and leapt from the window seat with a grin of relief. The dog opened a disinterested eye, and went back to sleep. Geoffrey imagined that someone must have risked life and limb to feed it, or it would not be greeting him with such bored lethargy.

"Thank God!" said Hugh, rising to thump him on the shoulder in a comradely way. "We have been worried sick about you. Where have you been?"

Geoffrey told him, briefly, as he began to remove his armour. Hugh gave a whistle.

"Hell's fires! Daimbert plays a dangerous game."

Geoffrey tugged off a boot, releasing a thin stream of water onto the floor, and then removed the other. "So do we all."

Hugh looked at him strangely. "What do you mean?"

Geoffrey was inutterably weary and longed only to rest. But he could not, in all countenance, sleep while Hugh remained in danger from Roger. He did not want to embark on a long explanation there and then outlining his reasons for Roger's guilt, and he settled for an explanation that would satisfy Hugh, but that would put him on his guard too.

"I think I know the identity of the killer," he said. "And it is not one of the Advocate's men. Be careful, Hugh. I will not be long in exposing the murderer."

Hugh looked as if he would ask questions, but Geoffrey pushed him firmly from his room and closed the door. He rummaged around for a dry hose and lay on the bed. After a moment, he rose and dragged the heavy chest across the floor to block the door. Then he unsheathed his dagger and lay it on the bed near his hand, and was asleep the moment his head touched the covers.

Later, the handle of the door began to turn slowly; the door eased open with the same deadly care. And then it stopped. The killer pushed a little more, but the door would not budge. He pushed harder still, and the chest gave a protesting crack. Through the partially opened door, the killer saw Geoffrey stir in his sleep, and noted the dagger near his hand. He grimaced. Time was running out: he had already failed to kill Geoffrey with the arrow fired at him at Abdul's Pleasure Palace the previous night; Geoffrey had survived the attack by Greeks in the old Saracen Quarter; and now he would live because the killer could not enter his room without the heavy chest giving him away. But there would be other opportunities.

Meanwhile, the dog watched curiously, then went back to its dozing.

The angle of the sun slanting in through the window told Geoffrey it was late afternoon and that he had slept most of the day. He heaved himself stiffly off the bed and went to the garderobe, where he splashed water from a jug over his head and body, and shaved quickly. The dog came to slather expectantly, nudging Geoffrey toward the box in which unpleasant tendrils of dried meat were stored for occasions such as this. As he had done hundreds of times before, Geoffrey yet again earned the dog's eternal devotion—an eternity that would last until it finished whatever morsel it sat chewing noisily. Geoffrey excavated a fresh shirt from an untidy pile on a shelf, poured himself a goblet of wine, ignored the dog's whines for more food, and sat down to think.

He went over the facts he knew for certain. The knight, Guido, and the monks, Jocelyn and Pius, had been killed within four days of each other. Guido had been bereaved and had taken to walking alone near the Dome of the Rock; he was also having doubts about the morality of his knightly duties and was considering a monastic vocation. Meanwhile John of Sourdeval was a serious young man, who perhaps spent too much time philosophising. So each in his own way was vulnerable. Guido, it seemed, had discovered something that prompted him to contact the Advocate's scribe Jocelyn. Jocelyn had probably written whatever it was down for him because Guido was illiterate and the monk had then been in a state of nervous agitation from the time Guido's body was discovered until his own death two days later. After his death, Guido had been sent a letter from the Advocate that had been addressed to Brother Salvatori, which meant that, in all probability, what he had dictated to Jocelyn had been a letter to the Advocate, and the Advocate had acknowledged his letter by responding to the name Guido planned to choose when he took his monkish vows.

Pius, the third victim, had been murdered in the house of Maria Akira's father, but had no known connections with the Patriarch or anyone else in power. Could his death have been a mistake then? Or a random killing to take attention from the fact that there had been a very good reason for the deaths of Guido and Jocelyn? The more Geoffrey thought about it, the more that seemed to be plausible. He had been told from the beginning how random the murders seemed to be: the three priests were not the same nationality, not from the same Order, and seemed to have no connection with each other.

Except the daggers. Geoffrey had seen the carved dagger that had killed John, and he had been told that similar weapons had been used to kill the other victims. Some witnesses had considered the weapon beautiful, others gaudy, depending on their taste. But all five weapons had disappeared, either at the scene, or later, so that Geoffrey could not compare them with the one that had been used to pin the pig's heart to his wall.

And the last victim, poor Loukas, had been conveniently dispatched while Melisende languished in the dungeons of her uncle. It was perfectly clear that Loukas's death had been arranged, as Hugh had said from the beginning, to prove Melisende's innocence. Loukas was killed in the Holy Sepulchre, and was a poor madman whom nobody would mourn—the most readily dispensable of the monks at the Church and the one selected as a sacrifice for Melisende. The body was found by Celeste. And Geoffrey now knew that Celeste worked for the Patriarch and was deeply involved in his black-market business. Celeste would probably also know—from the Patriarch himself—about the kind of dagger used by the murderer. But Geoffrey only had Celeste's word that such a dagger had been found on Loukas: the body had been covered with a blanket before the other monks had come, and Celeste claimed the dagger had later disappeared.

So, there was the killer of Loukas, thought Geoffrey. Nasty Brother Celeste, working possibly under the Patriarch's instructions so that Melisende could be freed to continue her work in the Greek Quarter. It also explained why Loukas was so different from the others—he had merely been available when Celeste had needed a victim in a hurry. So did Celeste kill the others too? Geoffrey thought back to the bodies in the Holy Sepulchre. He had made a rough measurement of the wounds in John and Loukas, but they had not been the same. The wound in Loukas had been bigger, which Geoffrey had attributed to tearing. But it was equally possible, even likely, that it had not been caused by the same kind of weapon.

He considered his list of suspects. At the top was Celeste, whom Geoffrey was now certain had killed Loukas. Yet, it seemed Celeste did not actually have a dagger that would tie Loukas's death to the others, and he had simply pretended that Loukas had been killed with one. So, it was possible that Celeste was not the murderer of the others. Geoffrey compared the lame monk to the victims: illiterate Pius, who did the shopping for his brethren, including braving Akira's slaughterhouse; and the two knights, trained in combat from youth. The Crusade had not been an easy journey, and those knights who had survived it owed their lives to their superior fighting skills and finely tuned instincts. Stabbing men in the back required no great strength, as Geoffrey himself had pointed out to Hugh when they discussed Melisende's possible guilt, but it might well require speed. Having followed Celeste down the tunnels under the city, Geoffrey knew he was not a speedy mover.

The next suspect was Melisende, the aggressive, single-minded niece of the Patriarch. If Celeste had killed Loukas, then had Melisende killed the others? Perhaps Celeste genuinely believed Melisende's guilt when he had murdered Loukas to free her. Geoffrey rubbed his sore eyes. But was that really necessary? Why could the Patriarch not simply release her? But the answer to that was clear in the light of Melisende's revelations in the palace that morning: the Greek community would have been rightly suspicious of an unexplained release, and she would not have been able to carry on passing their secrets to Uncle to the same extent. Loukas's murder was a sufficiently spectacular and public statement of her innocence to allow her release without question.

Geoffrey thought hard. The third potential culprit was the Patriarch himself. But then Daimbert would hardly have released Geoffrey to continue his investigation when he had been presented with an ideal opportunity to rid himself of him—especially since Geoffrey now knew about his black-market dealings. Reluctantly, Geoffrey crossed the Patriarch off his mental list of murder suspects, although he remained unconvinced that his involvement was entirely innocent.

And then there was Roger. Geoffrey knew the big knight well enough to know that he would not have had the patience or deviousness to plan all these deaths. If he had committed the murders, then it would have been under the orders of another. But whom? Celeste? Melisende? Geoffrey already had ample evidence that Roger could have killed Marius, and perhaps Eveline. Yet, the big Englishman had saved Geoffrey's life by helping him escape from the stable. Roger would know that the chances of Geoffrey uncovering the identity of the killer increased with every day he was alive to investigate, So, if Roger were guilty, why had he saved Geoffrey? Why not let him die?

Unless he were innocent, of course. Geoffrey rubbed his eyes again and moved on to Courrances, who had urged him to investigate for the Advocate and then locked him in the burning barn. Courrances was devious, and he would certainly be capable of laying false trails and leaving misleading information to make Geoffrey stumble around. He would also love to see Geoffrey fall from grace. The warrior-monk would kill monks or knights without compunction and would probably have had the opportunity to murder Guido, John, Jocelyn and Pius.

There were also, of course, Warner de Gray and Henri d'Aumale. But if Roger were responsible for killing Marius inside the citadel, then Geoffrey could think of no reason why the

Lorrainers should be involved and, like Roger, neither had the cunning or intelligence to plot with such deviousness. Based on Roger's claim that d'Aumale was unconscious after the riot at Abdul's Pleasure Palace, Geoffrey was not yet even sure if d'Aumale was still alive. Reluctantly, Geoffrey dismissed the unsavoury pair as suspects.

And finally, there was Dunstan and Marius, scribes in the pay of the Patriarch, like Jocelyn. Perhaps Dunstan was the murderer and had then committed suicide in remorse? But Dunstan was a blackmailer, and blackmailers were not remorseful people. So why had he killed himself?

Geoffrey had to admit to himself that, even with all he knew, he was still as far from learning the identity of the killer as he had been when he started. He had a fine assembly of possible culprits, but no evidence. He could hardly go to the Patriarch or the Advocate with a list of suspects—one of whom was a trusted scribe of the Patriarch and one of whom was the Patriarch's niece, while another was the Advocate's most valued adviser—and tell them to take their pick. And if he did, he knew they would chose Roger simply because it would be the solution that would cause the least damage. Geoffrey took a sip of wine, leaned his elbows on the table, and began to despair of ever finding an answer.

There was a thump at the door, and the dog gave a deep-throated growl.

"Are you in there? Let us in, lad!" Roger's peeved tones must have been heard all over the citadel. Reluctantly, Geoffrey stood to move the chest, but such an object was of no substance to Roger, who heaved at the door until he could squeeze through. He saw the chest and nodded approvingly. "Good idea, lad. You cannot trust anyone these days."

Hugh appeared in the doorway and eased himself lithely past the chest.

"What have you been doing?" Hugh asked Roger, as he settled himself comfortably on the bed, "while the phoenix and his vile dog have been sleeping the day away?"

Geoffrey shuddered involuntarily at this reminder of his near escape from the fire, and sat down abruptly. Roger also sat on the bed, grinning smugly at Geoffrey. "Well, ask me how I got on?" Geoffrey looked blank, and Roger was disappointed. "With what you sent me to do yesterday."

"Oh, yes." Geoffrey had quite forgotten his ruse of the night before to rid himself of Roger while he followed Melisende. "What happened?"

"You can ask Maria yourself," said Roger proudly. "I brought her here."

"You brought a whore to the citadel? Are you mad? She will never get out alive!"

"Not to the citadel, to the prison." Roger preened himself. "I have solved the mystery for you," he said with infuriating smugness. "I know who killed those priests and knights!"

CHAPTER ELEVEN

Roger made his announcement regarding the identity of the murderer with pride.

"But it cannot be him, Roger," said Geoffrey patiently. "The plot is too complex, and he simply does not have the wits."

"Now you look here, lad," said Roger, becoming self-righteous. "Just because men cannot write and read does not mean they are stupid. You are too arrogant by half about that learning of yours. I tell you again, your murderer is Warner de Gray. And it was him who killed Marius too!"

Was this Roger's idea of proving his own innocence, wondered Geoffrey, to blame a man he did not like to make the whole business go away?

"Tell me why you think Warner is the culprit," he said with resignation.

"Why?" echoed Roger loudly. "What kind of question is that? Because he is a murderer, of course! Why else?"

Geoffrey wondered how he could contrive to send Roger on some spurious mission so that he could confide his fears and knowledge to Hugh. If ever he needed the quiet support, advice, and thoughtful logic of the Norman knight, it was now.

"I do hope you are right Roger," drawled Hugh, laconically. "That would be a most fitting end to all this ugliness, and we can all get back to the real business of good, honest slaughter."

"Hear, hear," said Roger fervently.

"But what more can you tell to enlighten us about this miserable affair?" asked Hugh of Roger.

"It was Warner," responded Roger with finality.

"So we understand," said Hugh patiently. "But what are the reasons behind your accusations?"

"Reasons!" spat Roger in disgust. "You sound like old book-brain here. I plan to challenge Warner to a duel before God. God will strike him down because he is guilty!"

Geoffrey stared at him. Roger took the business of duelling with utmost seriousness, and although certainly not a pious man, was far too superstitious to risk calling the wrath of God down on his own head if he did not have absolute trust in his convictions. Geoffrey's thoughts tumbled together in an impossible jumble, and he longed for Roger to be gone so he could talk to Hugh. But Geoffrey did not want Roger to leave if his intention was to accost Warner and challenge him. That would get them nowhere at all.

"Tell me about Maria," he said, to change the subject.

"Maria?" asked Hugh. "Now who is she?"

"Maria d'Accra," said Roger. "The whore I arrested last night."

"You did what?" said Hugh, startled. "Whatever for?"

"I have not told you that part of my story yet," said Roger. Hugh leaned forward on his stool and listened with fascination.

"After Geoffrey had gone after that dreadful Greek woman, Maria also left the house, so I followed her, like he told me to. She went straight to the Church of the Holy Sepulchre. And she was up to no good at all, for I have never seen such a furtive mover in all my days. The Church, of course, was all locked up, but this did not stop Maria. Over the roof she went, like a monkey. I followed as best I could, although I was slower and less silent. Anyway, she ended up in this little garden, and someone was talking to her there. It was that nice Benedictine, Father Almaric. They talked for a while, and he handed her a scroll. Then she was off over the roof again and back to her father's butcher's shop, where I arrested her."

"What did she do with this scroll?" asked Hugh.

"She hid it," said Roger regretfully. "Somewhere in the butcher's horrible premises, I suppose. I could not find it, and she would not tell me where it was."

"And when did all this happen?" drawled Hugh with evident amusement.

"Last night," said Roger. "But I only brought her here a short while ago. First, I took her back to that Melisende's house, thinking to wait there for Geoffrey. But he was so long in coming, I had to bring her here instead, because I was growing hungry and there are only so many sweet cakes a man can eat before his stomach craves meat."

"Well," said Hugh, leaning back against the wall. "It is an exciting story, Roger, but hardly one that will convict Warner of murder. And it does not really justify arresting this Maria Akira. She is Abdul's whore, you say? Perhaps the monk she met in the garden is one of her lovers, and she was merely taking advantage of the absence of her mistress to earn a little extra money."

"Aye," said Roger, suddenly deflated, "I suppose you might be right at that."

Geoffrey was baffled. What was wrong with Roger? He did not usually give up his bigoted opinions with such ease. Geoffrey handed his cup to Hugh to fill. He had to talk to him alone.

"My hands are sore from all that business in the caves last night," he said to Roger, displaying fingers that were multi-coloured with cuts and bruises. "Do you have any goose-grease salve?"

"No," said Roger, settling down on Geoffrey's bed. "That bloody dog of yours ate the last of it a month ago."

"I have some somewhere," said Hugh, rising.

For Roger to stay and Hugh to leave was not what Geoffrey had intended at all. "It does not really matter," he said. "But I would like some of that wine you had the other day, Roger."

"That stuff has long gone," said Roger, leaning back more comfortably on the bed. Hugh signalled that he would be back, and slipped out. Geoffrey cursed under his breath.

Roger was up in an instant, and had closed the door. Geoffrey reached for his dagger. Was this it? Was this how he had killed Marius? Geoffrey came to his feet in a fighting stance as Roger reached inside his surcoat and drew something out. Roger looked at the dagger with a sad, reproving expression, and held out a scroll for Geoffrey.

"I lied to Hugh," he said softly. "Maria did not hide the scroll. I took it from her and forced her to read it to me."

Still holding his dagger, Geoffrey cautiously took the scroll from Roger, alert for any trickery. Roger let his hands fall to his sides while Geoffrey read. It was a letter bearing the Advocate's seal, and it was addressed to Brother Salvatori. Geoffrey looked at Roger in amazement.

"It is the letter that the Canon of St. Mary's said had arrived for Guido after he died," said Roger. "Remember the Canon saying he brought it to the citadel?"

Geoffrey nodded. He scanned through the scroll, then read it aloud.

" 'From Godfrey of Bouillon, Duke of Lower Lorraine and, by the Grace of God, His Advocate of the Holy Sepulchre in Jerusalem, to Brother Salvatori. I am much interested in what you have written, and I have passed the information to Sir Warner de Gray to deal with as he sees fit. You will know that there are many who seek my death, but I am appointed by God, and only He will decide when the time is fit to remove me.' "

He looked at Roger, bewildered, while Roger gazed back at him steadily.

"Guido warned the Advocate that there was a plan afoot to kill him," Roger said. "He could not write himself, so he hired Jocelyn to write for him. Then they were both murdered."

Geoffrey shook his head slowly, staring down at the letter in his hand. "Guido wrote as Brother Salvatori," he said slowly. "Not as Sir Guido of Rimini. So of course the Advocate had no reason to associate a message from an Augustinian monk called Salvatori with the murder of Guido." He sighed and shook his head. "But I do not understand the connections. How did this letter come to be in the possession of Father Almaric? And why did he give it to Maria?"

But even as he spoke, details were becoming clear in his mind. Maria, the spy spying on the spy, pretending to be flighty and empty-headed so that she would not be suspected. He had decided that Maria may well have arranged for John and Pius to be killed in the homes of her employer and hated father, respectively. And now she had come into possession of a vital piece of evidence that had disappeared.

Roger swallowed and looked away. "I will tell you what I think, but you have to let me finish all of what I have to say. Will you listen without breaking in?"

Tendrils of unease uncoiling in his stomach, Geoffrey nodded.

"When I mentioned Maria d'Accra, Hugh acted like he had never heard of her." Roger raised his hand to stop Geoffrey from speaking. "Listen to me!" he snapped. "We do not have much time. Then Hugh referred to her as Maria Akira, although I called her Maria d'Accra—her whore name. And I did not say she were one of Abdul's women, but Hugh knew."

"So what?" said Geoffrey when Roger paused. "You know he can be a snob. He probably did not want to admit that he frequents the same whorehouses as you do."

"Then you hid them scraps of parchment in that hole in the fireplace." Roger rummaged around inside his surcoat and produced one that was still recognisable, but partially burned. "I found this in Hugh's fireplace yesterday. You see, I saw he had lit a fire, and he never does that—you are the one who likes fires, not him—and I was curious. I found this scrap and thought it looked like one of the ones you stole from Dunstan's desk, although they all look alike to me."

Geoffrey took it, his thoughts in turmoil. Was Roger, having failed in his attempt to implicate Warner, now trying to blame Hugh?

"I saw you put them parchments in that hole," said Roger

heavily, "while Hugh looked like he was still asleep on the bed. But I happened to glance at him as you did it, and his eyes were wide open. He saw where you put them as clearly as I did."

"But he did not knock himself on the head when Marius was stabbed," said Geoffrey harshly.

"Did anyone?"

"You saw the blood! You bandaged his head for him!"

"Aye, lad. I saw a good deal of blood," said Roger somberly. "It was all around poor Marius. But I saw no great gash on Hugh. He fussed and squirmed when I was trying to clean it, and would not keep still. I did not see his head clearly, because he would not let me. But I would have seen a serious wound. And use those wits you are so proud of, Geoffrey! If you were Hugh and you had a serious wound, would you rather have you tend it, with your scraps of medical knowledge and clean hands, or me, with my great clumsy fingers and ragged fingernails?"

It had been something that had rankled at the time, and that had been nagging at the back of Geoffrey's mind ever since. He had always been the one to tend their various wounds in the past, and it had surprised him that Hugh had asked Roger to do it in his stead. Roger was rough and scarcely dextrous.

"I can see you do not believe me," said Roger quietly. "But I can also see that you have had your suspicions. Believe me, I wish I was wrong!"

Geoffrey looked from the burned parchment, to Guido's letter, to Roger. Now what? he thought wearily. "When Hugh comes back with the goose grease . . ."

"You will see no goose grease," said Roger with certainty. "Hugh will be off to find that incriminating scroll in Akira's shop."

Geoffrey did not believe him for an instant.

"And what about that dagger and the pig's heart?" he asked. "I suppose Hugh put them in here too?"

Roger scowled in thought as he sifted slowly through the evidence. Eventually, he pulled a face and admitted defeat. "No, lad. You have me there. I asked around the kitchens to see if Hugh had brought them a pig, but pork is expensive here, and only Courrances eats it regularly."

Geoffrey stared at him. "Courrances?"

Roger nodded. "Aye. Pigs are not common here, as you pointed out earlier, but Courrances often gets a pig delivered because the Advocate is fond of a bit of pork . . ."

Geoffrey snapped his fingers. "Courrances left the dagger and the pig's heart! Of course! It was after the so-called warning that Courrances asked me to investigate these murders for the Advocate. And Courrances not only knows where to buy a pig, he knows the style of weapon used on the murder victims. He described one to me after the riot near Melisende's house. He did not intend it to be a warning at all! He hoped it would make me curious enough, or frightened enough, to comply with the Advocate's request that I investigate."

"I do not understand why he wanted you involved at all," said Roger. "He does not like you in the slightest."

"But that is exactly why," said Geoffrey, thinking quickly. "He already had his suspicions that a knight might be involved in all this, and he did not wish to put himself at risk by investigating, so he recruited me instead."

"You must have made his day then," said Roger, "when you agreed to do it almost immediately."

Roger was right, thought Geoffrey. The reason he had agreed so readily was because Tancred had already asked him to investigate, and the Advocate's request actually made the situation simpler for him. But Courrances had not known of Tancred's charge, and far from being relieved that he had passed the dirty work to a much detested comrade, his suspicions would have been roused. He must then have wondered whether Geoffrey was responsible for the murders; hence, Courrances's attempt to kill Geoffrey in the burning barn.

He stood abruptly, pushed past Roger, and headed for Hugh's room on the floor above. It was, as always, meticulously tidy, with his clean shirts piled neatly on one shelf and some carefully washed goblets on another. Geoffrey began to poke around.

"Nothing!" he said to Roger eventually. "There is nothing here to indicate that Hugh is responsible for what you are suggesting."

"Well, he is hardly going to leave it in full view, is he?" said Roger reasonably. He elbowed Geoffrey out of the way and made for the locked chest on the floor. Here, Geoffrey knew, was where Hugh stored the booty he had collected along his arduous journey from Germany. Before Geoffrey could stop him, Roger had drawn his sword and was levering off the locks.

"He will be furious . . ."

"He will not be back!" snapped Roger. "He has gone after bigger prizes than these tawdry baubles." The locks broke, and Roger threw up the lid. Both knights peered inside. The exquisite cups of silver, the heavy gold coins, and the wealth of rings, bangles, and necklaces that they knew were stored in the chest had gone. All that was left were some old shirts.

Geoffrey watched as Roger rummaged. Then Roger's shoulders slumped. Geoffrey leaned over him and saw what the shirts had concealed: three long, curved daggers with jewelled hilts, two of them still stained dark with blood. And although they were certainly similar to the one Courrances had left in Geoffrey's room, they were not identical.

Geoffrey sat down on Hugh's bed with a thump, and swallowed hard.

"Hugh?" he said, meeting Roger's eyes. "It was really Hugh?"

Roger nodded. "I wish I was wrong. But I put things together—the burnt parchment; the fact that he would not let you see to his wound; the fact that the blood was still warm on Marius when we got back, but Hugh claimed Marius had not had time to tell him anything; and the fact that although he would not go out to investigate with you, he still wanted to know what was going on. He wanted to know how long he could let you live before he was forced to kill you too."

Geoffrey felt sick. "How could I have been so wrong? And all the while, you were working things out so easily!"

"Hardly that, lad," said Roger with a rueful smile. "It took some hard thinking, I can tell you, and I gave myself aching wits in the process!"

"I warned him," said Geoffrey, remembering his conversation with Hugh earlier that day when he had been so exhausted. "I told him I was close to solving the murders, and that it was someone in the citadel. I meant him to beware of you, but instead I probably told him it was time to kill me!"

"I saw him!" exclaimed Roger suddenly, sitting back on his heels. "When you were asleep, I saw him outside your chamber. He told me he had lost a coin, and we looked about for it, although we both knew we would find none."

Geoffrey regarded Roger soberly. "You are right, of course," he said. "Marius's body was still warm when we found it, yet Hugh said Marius had only just started to talk to him. And we were gone a long time. Marius's story as told by Hugh had inconsistencies—he said Marius claimed to have seen from the door that Dunstan had been strangled, but the scriptorium was far too dark for him to have seen that far, even with a lamp."

Roger nodded slowly. "Hugh was simply repeating Marius's gabbled story that he gave when he arrived."

"Which must mean that he and Hugh had said a great deal to each other before Marius was killed. And it explains why Hugh volunteered to stay with Marius in my chamber."

"But you said it was that other monk—bald Brother Alain—who made Dunstan's death look like murder instead of suicide," said Roger. "So, what did Hugh and Marius talk about?"

Geoffrey thought, watching Roger play idly with one of the daggers. "When Alain thought he would make Dunstan's suicide appear as murder in a feeble attempt to protect the popular Marius, his plan had exactly the reverse effect. Marius must have believed that Dunstan had been murdered because of what he knew of the deaths of Guido, John, and the monks—and Dunstan certainly knew more than he had written down for Tancred, because he was using the information to blackmail the killer. The reason Dunstan's and Marius's investigation met with so little success was that they knew the identity of the killer from the start—or perhaps had discovered it, and were persuaded to go along with his plan. So Marius fled the palace and came to the citadel in terror, because he thought Dunstan had been killed for this knowledge, and he imagined he might be next."

"And Hugh talked to Marius to lull him into a false sense of security," said Roger. "Then Hugh stabbed him because Marius running here—on the surface of it to you, but really to Hugh—was a liability. And Hugh is not a man to allow a panicky monk to upset his plans."

Roger was right there too. There was a ruthless streak in Hugh that would have no compunction in dispatching a weak-willed monk in order to carry out his own business. While on desert duty, Geoffrey had once seen Hugh kill a small child to ensure it did not cry out and reveal their hiding place. They had later quarrelled bitterly about it.

Roger took a deep breath. "What a foul business! He was our friend. What do we do now?"

Geoffrey sat back on the bed and tried to think. Of all the knights at the citadel, Hugh was the very last one he would have imagined to be the killer. They had been friends for more than three years and had saved each other's lives on so many occasions that Geoffrey could scarcely recall them all. And of Roger and Hugh, Geoffrey had far more in common with the literate, intelligent Hugh than with the ignorant, slow-witted Roger. He found his hands were shaking, and he felt weak and sick. Perhaps there was some other explanation for all this. Perhaps Courrances had taken the loot from Hugh's chest and put the daggers there, much as someone—Courrances again, no doubt—had tried to have Roger found in bed with a dead prostitute.

"Come on, lad," said Roger, standing up suddenly. "If *your* wits are failing you, mine are still working. It is obvious where we go next. Hugh thinks the scroll from Brother Salvatori is hidden in Akira's house. He will be searching there for a while, because obviously we have it here. If we hurry, we might catch him in the act. And who knows, perhaps we can talk some sense into him."

There was no point in using horses to reach Akira's shop. The streets in that part of the city were too narrow, and it would only take a lumbering cart, or an uncooperative rider, to block their passage completely. Clad in half-armour—light chain-mail shirt and leather leggings—Geoffrey set off on foot, confident that he could make better time running than Hugh could make on horseback. Hugh, like most knights, never walked when he could ride.

Roger yanked at the bar on the gate, while Geoffrey fretted impatiently.

"Off somewhere nice?" came a silky enquiry at his shoulder. Geoffrey saw that Courrances was watching their movements carefully, his sharp, clever mind considering what they might mean.

"The most salubrious establishment in the city," replied Geoffrey, breaking away from Courrances to run after Roger, "Akira's meat emporium." The black-robed Hospitaller thoughtfully watched him dash away.

People scattered as the knights ran through the narrow streets. Geoffrey heard an outraged howl and saw that Roger had rushed into a fruit barrel, and oranges were rolling in every direction; a few were crushed by Geoffrey running behind, but many more stolen by quick-fingered children. Roger, ahead of him, was unfaltering, and made his way purposefully toward the butchers' alleys. Eventually, they skidded to a halt at the corner of the butchers' street. There was no sign of Hugh's horse, and the street looked deserted. Breathing heavily, they walked cautiously down the road and looked into Akira's shop.

Inside, the floor was still dark with the stains of his trade, and the flies and maggots still feasted. Except that this time, Akira had joined the ranks of the victims and hung from one of the hooks in the ceiling, slowly rotating this way and that. Geoffrey started to lean back against the wall in defeat, but thought better of it when he saw the splattered blood. Roger surged past, his sword in his hand, and thundered up the stairs.

"Empty," he said, returning a few moments later. "And now Hugh will know I tricked him. Nothing could be hidden up there. It is bare."

Geoffrey walked over to the dangling corpse, and looked up at it.

"Help me, Roger!" he said urgently, sheathing his sword, and grabbing Akira's legs. "He is still alive!"

Roger lowered the hook on its chain, while Geoffrey supported the greasy bundle that was Akira. The rope, Geoffrey realised, had been passed under Akira's arms, not round his neck as Geoffrey had supposed, and Akira's feet were swollen, so he must have been hanging there for quite some time. The butcher began to regain consciousness.

"Whoreson!" he muttered.

"Ingrate!" retorted Geoffrey.

Akira forced his bloodshot eyes open, and fixed them blearily on Geoffrey.

"Oh, it's you," he said in tones far from friendly. "What are you doing here?"

"We came to see if a friend of ours was visiting," said Geoffrey. "But what about you? Will you live? Shall I send for a physician?"

Akira struggled into a sitting position and reached out a bloodstained hand to grab Geoffrey's shoulder. Geoffrey winced at the powerful aroma of old garlic that wafted into his face.

"You must tell the Patriarch that they tried to murder poor Akira," he moaned.

"I will indeed," said Geoffrey, trying to extricate himself from Akira's powerful grip. "I am sure he will be deeply shocked to hear of your accident."

"Accident!" snorted Akira, shifting his hold on Geoffrey's shoulder to one that was stronger yet. "They tried to kill me. Not even quickly like that poor monk, but slowly."

"Who?" asked Geoffrey absently, racking his brain to think of places Hugh might go.

"Maria and her vile lover. Adam is his name."

Geoffrey was puzzled. "It was not Sir Hugh of Monreale who did this to you?"

Akira snorted. "If you mean that skinny, fair-haired knight, he was here before you, but didn't even pause to see if I was alive. And you," he said, turning suddenly and fixing Roger with a baleful eye, "didn't heed Akira's pitiful calls when you came to arrest that treacherous whore."

"I thought you had arrested her inside the house," said Geoffrey to Roger.

Roger shook his great head. "Outside. She was about to enter, but I got her outside. I do not like the smell of this place very much. No offence," he added to Akira.

Akira, using Geoffrey as a crutch, heaved himself up and lunged on unsteady legs to his stool near the window.

"Why did Maria do this to you?" Geoffrey asked.

"Oh, she hates old Akira," said the butcher in a nasal whine. "She told me last night, when I was hanging there like a trussed goat, that she wanted me to be blamed for these vile murders. She wanted to pay me back." He began to weep crocodile tears, and Geoffrey sensed the war of attrition between the wily old butcher and his scheming daughter had been waged over many years, and that no love was lost between them. Akira's false tears now were probably aimed to make the knights feel sorry for him and leave him some money.

Akira continued his sorrowful tale. "But those priests were kind, and didn't arrest old Akira when I found Brother Pius in my shop. Then yesterday, that Maria says she's leaving the city with her lover. Adam."

Geoffrey wondered whether it was Adam or Maria who had led the other to betray family and friends. Maria had tried to kill her father and had tried to implicate him and Melisende in the murders; meanwhile, Adam was a Greek spying on his own community under Melisende's command. What a pair!

"She brung me cakes once," said Akira, blubbering with self-pity, "but when I gives one to old Joseph, he dropped down dead. So, she's tried to kill me before!"

"Old Joseph?" queried Geoffrey, hoping this was not another priest or knight.

"My cat!" wailed Akira, fresh tears welling down his cheeks. "I tried hard with Maria. But after all I did, she still finds me repulsive!"

Really? thought Geoffrey, unable to stop himself glancing at the sordid room and its shabby inhabitant, I wonder why? But if Maria had sent poisoned cakes to her father, she had probably also sent them to Dunstan. Melisende, it appeared, was blameless for that part of the mystery after all. And with sickening clarity, Geoffrey suddenly realized exactly how Maria had done it. Marius had smuggled whores into the scriptorium on Thursdays, and the one Alain loved was called Mary. It was probably Maria, and she had left the cakes for Dunstan at the same time. And sweet old Father Almaric, who had given Maria the scroll addressed to Brother Salvatori from the Advocate, was the same trusted associate of the Patriarch who had recommended Maria to Melisende!

"Is this making any sense to you, lad?" asked Roger, rubbing at his head tiredly. "Because I am flummoxed!"

"That does not surprise me in the slightest," came the soft voice they knew so well from the doorway. Geoffrey whirled round, his sword already out of its scabbard, but Hugh had two archers with their bows at the ready at his side and Geoffrey faltered. Hugh saw his hesitation and nodded. "You are wise to be cautious, Geoffrey. I have come too far to be stopped now, and if you make the slightest move toward me, these men are under instruction to kill you."

Geoffrey felt sick. So far, the notion of Hugh's treachery had been a distant thing, something with which he had not yet had to come to terms. Now, Hugh was standing in front of him, threatening to kill him as easily as he had killed the Bedouin child in the desert.

"Hugh . . ." he began, taking a step forward. Immediately, both archers swung their bows round to face him, and Geoffrey saw their wrists begin to draw back. He stopped.

"Throw down your weapons," ordered Hugh of Geoffrey and Roger. Geoffrey hesitated, but saw the resolute expression on Hugh's face. He dropped his sword and then heard Roger's clatter to the ground behind him. "Now your daggers. Both of them," he added for Roger's benefit. "And move back against that wall."

Geoffrey and Roger backed away until they stood side by side against the far wall. Akira slouched with them, moaning softly, while Hugh's archers were ranged opposite, their eyes never leaving Geoffrey and Roger. Hugh made a motion with his hand, and others clustered into the small room, one of which was the gentle Father Almaric, who smiled beneficently at Geoffrey. Another was Adam, who made a threatening gesture toward the cowering Akira.

"Please," Akira whispered. "I got nothing to do with all this. I'm only a poor butcher. Let me go, and you won't be sorry. I got some nice lean meat round the back, and I'll keep you supplied for as long as you stay in our lovely city."

Hugh looked around him and shuddered. "It is a tempting offer," he said. "But I am afraid I must decline."

"Did you kill them, Hugh?" asked Geoffrey softly. "Did you kill John, Guido, and the monks?"

"Not Loukas, the last one," said Hugh. "That was none of my doing. But I was forced to kill Guido and John. I offered them a chance to join our select group to replace this vacillating Advocate who festers on the throne of Jerusalem with a strong king, but they declined. Since I had already given them details of our plan, they had to die."

"Why them?" asked Geoffrey, a sick feeling spreading through him as he imagined the young, impressionable John at the mercy of such ruthless cunning as Hugh's.

"You already know," said Hugh. "I need strong and intelligent soldiers for my plan to work. Guido was grieving for his wife and was considering taking the cowl; I needed him because he was an excellent strategist. I killed him as he strolled in the gardens at the Dome of the Rock, which had become a habit of his. And John was intelligent and a man of integrity; he would have been an asset to our cause. I had Maria lure him to her mistress's house, where I, not a welcoming lover, awaited him. But others listened and have joined with us—all good, strong men who want to see Jerusalem remain in Christian hands, not taken back by the Saracens just because the present Advocate cannot keep it."

"And Jocelyn and Pius?"

"I had to kill Jocelyn because he helped Guido write a missive to the Advocate outlining our plans. Fortunately, Guido refrained from mentioning me by name and was stupid enough to sign with his monkish name. Had he signed himself Guido and not Salvatori, I might have been in serious trouble. Jocelyn was also a double agent for the Patriarch and was simply too dangerous to be allowed to live."

"And Pius?"

Hugh shrugged. "Jocelyn was very careful during the two days after Guido's death—he knew he was in danger. I followed him one night and killed him just as he reached the Dome of the Rock and thought he was safe. On the way, I saw him stop and talk to a monk. I could not take the risk that Jocelyn had told this monk our secret, so I killed him too. Maria opened the door of this place so I could leave the body here. You see, I had to create a smoke screen to prevent anyone seeing a pattern in the deaths. I used those cheap daggers from the market so that people might believe the killings were ritualistic, and I even managed to retrieve them on occasion to thicken the mystery. But the one I used on John was stolen from his corpse. You cannot trust anyone in this city."

Geoffrey regarded him sombrely. "Poor Pius had trouble sleeping. I am sure Jocelyn told him nothing. Pius was probably only making idle chatter with a fellow monk out in the night."

"I cannot help that," said Hugh abruptly. "One cannot be too careful in these political games. But I am innocent of that Greek monk's death. The word is that the Patriarch had him killed, although I cannot think why."

"And Maria helped you hide the bodies?" asked Geoffrey.

"Maria, Adam, and Father Almaric, among others. It was Almaric who was able to warn me about Guido's letter to the Advocate outlining our plans."

Father Almaric stepped forward and, beaming benignly, sketched a benediction at Geoffrey and Roger. Geoffrey wondered if he was in complete control of his wits. It was Almaric who had recommended Maria to the Patriarch as a maid to Melisende: a spy to watch over a spy.

"I know," said Geoffrey. Hugh looked startled, and Geoffrey explained. "Jocelyn used Father Almaric as confessor, presumably because Almaric professed to be one of the Patriarch's most loyal subjects, and Jocelyn assumed anything passed to Almaric would not only be under the seal of confession, but safe because Almaric was the Patriarch's man. But when Celeste reminded Father Almaric that the monk with the distinctive eyes came to him for confession, Almaric pretended to have forgotten him."

"But it is true, my son," said Almaric, earnestly. "I forgot so much because of the incessant agony in my feet. But since I tried the remedy you recommended, I have been much better. I am able to walk, and the pain is so much improved that I am able to sleep much better at night, and so wake refreshed and sharp-witted in the mornings."

Wonderful, thought Geoffrey. He had guilelessly acted as physician to a man who was attempting to murder the Advocate.

"The letter the Advocate wrote to Guido?" asked Geoffrey. "How did you come to have it, Father?"

Hugh sighed and closed his eyes. "Does it really matter?" he said, wearily. "Sir Armand of Laon—he is one of us—appropriated it when it was delivered to the citadel. He gave it to Almaric for safekeeping when you began your enquiries. I sent Maria to fetch it when I decided it was time to put our plan into action. Father Almaric has been a good ally, but he is forgetful, and I wanted the letter in my possession lest my plan, for some reason, failed."

"And Dunstan? How did he find out all this?"

Hugh gave a hearty sigh. "Do you think I have nothing better to do than to satisfy your curiosity? Dunstan found notes made by Jocelyn in Jocelyn's desk in the scriptorium. Dunstan was foolish enough to believe he could blackmail us. I simply arranged that Maria send him some of her cakes, but not before I had a quiet word about what happened to men who tried to blackmail me. I suppose I literally frightened him to death."

That would explain Dunstan's increasing agitation in the days before his death. Foolish, greedy monk. If he had gone directly to the Patriarch with his findings, he would still be alive, and so, probably, would Marius. And Geoffrey would never have been dragged into the investigation, and Hugh would be safely behind bars, along with his seemingly formidable force of supporters.

"And of course, you killed Marius and pretended to have been attacked in the process."

Hugh shrugged. "What else could I do? I had recruited him to our cause when he began his so-called investigation with Dunstan. But he was foolish enough to come running to me when he thought Dunstan had been murdered. He was simply too much of a liability. I talked with him for a while, to make certain he had made no written records of what he knew, and then I stabbed him. I smeared the blood from his wound onto my head to convince you I had been hit."

"Why did you do all this, Hugh?" Geoffrey asked softly. "Was it worth the price?"

"Oh yes," said Hugh, surprised by the question. "And it would have been worthwhile for you, too, given time. You are my friends. I would have looked to your interests."

"But I would not want to profit from such crimes," said Geoffrey coldly.

"You would," said Hugh earnestly. "Why not join us! We plan to kill the Advocate within the next two days, and hold the throne for Bohemond. This city needs a man like Bohemond. The Advocate is a weakling, and even his own men admit it. We have seven of his knights in our ranks, and every one of them is with us because they know the Advocate is a poor leader." He left his men and moved nearer to Geoffrey. "Come with us, Geoffrey! You have been on desert patrols, and you know that the Saracens are waiting out there like wolves as the Advocate's rule grows steadily more chaotic. If we are to keep this land Christian, we need Bohemond on the throne."

Geoffrey said nothing, and Hugh turned to Roger.

"You come with us, then!" he said. "You are Bohemond's man! You owe it to him to help us rid ourselves of this pathetic Advocate who is killing our hold on the land."

"All right, then," said Roger agreeably. "Might as well swing for a sheep as for a lamb! I am with you, if it is for Bohemond you are working."

"No, Roger!" cried Geoffrey. "This is treason! How do you know Bohemond is even aware of these plans?"

Hugh grinned at Roger and thumped him on the back in delight. "Good man! I should have known I could trust you."

"Aye, lad," said Roger, returning Hugh's smile. "You should have had me in on all this before. I would have been an asset to you."

"You still will be, Roger," said Hugh. "Now, we have wasted enough time answering Geoffrey's questions, and we have a lot to do." He turned to Akira. "You have a cellar, I believe?"

Akira looked astonished. "How the hell did you know that?" Then his expression hardened. "That bloody Maria!"

Hugh smiled. "Open the door, if you would. You and Sir Geoffrey are going to spend some time together."

Geoffrey's heart sank as he saw Akira fumbling around in a distant, fetid corner to haul open a heavy trapdoor that had been concealed under the moving red carpet of his floor. Roger helped him haul it open, and Hugh took a lamp from Adam and peered down into the yawning hole.

"That should do," he said, satisfied. He straightened up and looked across to Geoffrey and Akira, gesturing elegantly to the hole in the floor with his hand. "All yours, gentlemen."

"Now, you just wait a minute!" blustered Akira. "I'm not going down there! That trapdoor's heavy and can't be reached from down below. How do I know you'll come back and let us out?"

"My dear fellow!" exclaimed Hugh. "I assure you I have no intention of letting you out. I am afraid this is the end of the road for you, Akira. Your daughter tells me your customers are few these days, but that the trapdoor is sufficiently thick to muffle any cries for help anyway. She tells me you left her there on several occasions."

"That was years ago!" protested Akira. "And I'm an old man now! Please let me go . . ."

"Shall I kill them?" asked Adam, stepping forward eagerly.

Hugh shook his head. "Down in the cellar is better—no mess to clear up, you see." He looked around him in disgust. "Not that it would make much difference here."

"Think about what you are doing, Hugh!" said Geoffrey, desperately. "If you fail, you will die as a traitor."

"Believe me, Geoffrey," said Hugh, "I have thought about little else since this notion came into my head about three months ago. The Advocate must die. You are either with us, or against us, and you have made your position abundantly clear. We have been friends, and I do not want to watch you die. Now, jump down the hole, if you please."

Adam gave Geoffrey a shove that sent him staggering toward the cellar. Geoffrey glanced down at its black depths and gave Hugh an agonised look. Hugh wavered. He had forgotten Geoffrey's intense dislike of underground places.

"I would rather die now, up here," Geoffrey said quietly.

"No, you would not," said Roger, wrapping his arms around Geoffrey in a powerful grip that rendered him helpless. Geoffrey felt himself lifted like a rag doll, and then he was bundled through the trapdoor before he could offer more than a token resistance. He was not sure how far he fell, but he landed hard on a stone floor, jarring his ankle and cracking his arm painfully against a roughly hewn wall. There was a yowl like a mating cat, and Akira landed on top of him, driving the breath from his lungs.

"See you in hell!" Roger shouted down after them with a diabolical laugh, before the door was dropped back into place and Geoffrey and Akira were plunged into total darkness. Immediately Akira sprang up and howled in such a dreadful way that it served to force Geoffrey out of his own terror in order to make the butcher desist. Geoffrey took a shuddering breath, noting that not the merest glimmer of light could be seen through the edges of the trapdoor. No wonder Maria hated Akira if he locked her in here. He swallowed hard and crawled across to the screeching meat merchant.

"Akira!" yelled Geoffrey, grabbing at his clothes. "Be quiet! I cannot think with all that noise!"

Akira clutched at Geoffrey, and seemed to become calmer at human contact.

"We'll die here!" he snivelled.

"How tall is the room?"

"Taller than you," sniffed Akira. "And taller than you with me on your shoulders, so don't think we can get out that way."

Geoffrey released Akira and sat back. He put his hands in front of his face, but could see nothing. It had been like this when the tunnel had caved in on him in France. And the air in Akira's cellar was rank, as though something had died down there. Geoffrey recalled Maria's claim that she had a sister called Katrina who Melisende had never heard of, and felt a cold fear grip like an iron band around his chest. He forced himself to crawl on hands and knees to feel the walls, partly to see how big the cellar was, but partly to reassure himself that no skeletons lurked in its gloomy depths.

"Here! What are you up to?" queried Akira suspiciously.

"Just trying to see how far back the cellar goes," said Geoffrey, his voice far from steady. He took a deep breath. Now, not only one friend had turned traitor, but two! Not only traitor, but they had wanted him dead. Neither had had the courage to kill him outright, and they had condemned him to die in the very way they both knew he dreaded more than any other. He found the wall and leaned his hot forehead against its chilly roughness.

"Well, wait a minute, then," said Akira. "I got a candle."

He rummaged around for a few moments; there were some scratching noises accompanied by some foul language, and then the cellar was alive with dancing shadows.

"I always keeps a candle down here," said Akira. "I stores me valuables down here, you see."

"How do you get out," asked Geoffrey, instinctively moving nearer the light.

"I lets a rope ladder down," said Akira, "and then I climbs back up it."

Geoffrey looked around their cell. Akira had been right when he had said they would not reach the trapdoor, for the ceiling was indeed taller than his and Akira's height combined. No wonder his ankle ached viciously from where he had landed on it. The cellar was the same size as Akira's room above, large enough for two men to lie end to end in either direction. It was empty, except for a strong wooden box in one corner and various rags and bones strewn about the floor. Geoffrey remembered Katrina and scrambled to his feet.

The underground room was hewn out of solid rock, and so they would never be able to tunnel their way out. Geoffrey began to feel the familiar tightening around his chest when he imagined lying in the sealed chamber with Akira, with the air growing thinner and thinner . . .

"What else do you have in here?" he asked, only to hear the sound of Akira's voice, not to solicit information.

"None of your business," snapped Akira, walking over to the wooden box and covering it with one of the rags from the floor. "This is all your fault," he said, suddenly aggressive. "If you hadn't hung around old Akira's house, then I wouldn't be down here now, suffering."

"Sorry," said Geoffrey. "I should have been more thoughtful." He sat down on the stone floor and rubbed his ankle. "Do you have any more candles?"

"I got one more," said Akira, fishing it out of his pocket. "But it won't do us no good."

"I suppose there is no other way out of here?" said Geoffrey, looking up at the dark rectangle of the trapdoor high above them.

"Well, yes, as a matter of fact," said Akira.

Geoffrey stared at him in amazement.

"But that won't do us no good neither," the butcher continued. "There's a tunnel, but it can only be opened from the outside."

"Where is it?" said Geoffrey, leaping to his feet and peering around into the gloom as though it might suddenly make itself apparent.

Akira gave a heavy sigh and heaved himself upright. "But it won't do us no good," he insisted. "You can't open it from the inside."

"But we have to try," said Geoffrey. "Anything is better than sitting here in the dark waiting to die."

Akira grumbled his way into a dark corner and poked about. "That bloody Maria! She sold me out, she did. It was her who told that blond knight about this place, knowing that we couldn't get out once we were down here. Bloody Maria! I suppose you don't have friends what might come for you?" he asked Geoffrey, suddenly hopeful. His optimism faded as quickly as it had risen. "No. Your fine friends are the ones that shoved us down here in the first place, and old Akira hasn't had no friends since poor Joseph was took. And poor Joseph couldn't have done much, him being a cat."

Geoffrey picked his way through the bones on the floor. "Did you have a daughter called Katrina?" he asked.

Akira turned round to glare at him. "No, I did not, thank God! One bloody daughter is more than enough for poor Akira." He gave an enormous, wet sniff, wiped his nose on his sleeve, and continued to prod. "Here we are." He pulled at a large ring set in a second trapdoor and revealed a narrow tunnel disappearing into a sinister slit of blackness.

Geoffrey regarded it in horror. "Is that it?" he asked in a whisper.

Akira nodded. "I suppose we could try it," he said listlessly. "But it's a bit of a tight squeeze for old Akira these days."

Geoffrey looked from the great stone room to the narrow tunnel, and felt as though he were being offered a choice between two alternative routes to hell. He swallowed and took the candle from Akira with trembling hands.

"How far is it?"

"Not far, or bloody miles, depending," said Akira, taking the candle back again. "Follow me."

Geoffrey closed his eyes in despair as Akira's bulky form disappeared sideways into the narrow slit. If it were possible, this was even worse than the journey with Melisende, since the light was dimmer, and the tunnel horribly narrow from the outset. For a moment, he could not force his legs to move, but then the cellar grew darker and darker as Akira's candle went further into the tunnel, and he entered at a run.

The tunnel was a split in the rock and was a natural, rather than a man-made, feature. Geoffrey began to wonder how safe it was, and felt sweat coursing down his back and face as he envisaged the walls suddenly caving in from the pressure of the mass of rock above. Akira's grunts and mutters ahead told Geoffrey that the butcher was having problems easing himself along, and Geoffrey began to feel sick. He clenched his hands into tight fists and drove everything from his mind except Akira's golden wavering light ahead.

Geoffrey had no idea how long they travelled. The split grew wider, but just when he allowed himself to feel relief, it closed in again, even tighter than before. He and Akira had moments when they became stuck, and one had to help prise the other forward. Geoffrey's shirt was drenched in sweat, and his legs would not have held him up if it were not for the fact that the walls pressed so closely against his back and chest. Just when he thought it could grow no worse, the candle went out.

The silence was absolute.

"Light the other one," he said in a voice that had an edge of panic to it.

"Can't," said Akira. "Didn't bring the tinder with me."

Geoffrey felt like strangling him, but he had lost the strength in his limbs, and knew his arms were far beyond doing anything so useful.

"No matter," said Akira. "I knows where this tunnel goes." He moved forward, and then Geoffrey could only hear the sounds of his own ragged breathing and his thudding heart.

"Akira!" he yelled. "Tell me about Maria! Tell me about your cat!"

"What?" came Akira's startled voice from the blackness. "What for? You afraid of the dark or something? Why would a knight be interested in old Akira's cat?"

Akira's voice droned on, and Geoffrey followed it gratefully along the narrow split. He lost track of time completely: he might have been in the tunnel for a matter of moments, or for hours. Each step forward seemed to take an eternity, and he tried not to let himself think that if they could not open the other exit from the inside as Akira claimed, then they might have to make their way back along the tunnel to the cellar again.

Just as Geoffrey was slipping into semiconsciousness, where all he was aware of were Akira's mindless monologue and the laborious process of putting one foot in front of the other, Akira stopped.

"Here it is," he announced. "There's steps here, so watch out."

Geoffrey edged forward carefully, feeling the walls widen suddenly so that he could put his hands out in all directions and feel nothing. Then he was tumbling down the steps, a helpless jumble of arms and legs, and landed in a heap next to Akira.

"Clumsy devil," muttered Akira. "Told you to watch out. Here's the entrance."

It took a moment for Geoffrey to register that he could see

Akira's dim shadow poking around. At first he thought it must be the effects of banging his head when he fell down the steps, but he blinked hard and found he could still see. Unlike the trapdoor in the cellar, this door allowed the tiniest sliver of light to percolate through. He heaved himself upright and looked at it. It was made of wood, and sturdy, and light was seeping in along its bottom. And if light could come in, then so could air, and at least he would not die of slow suffocation in the cellar.

"Where does this come out?" he asked Akira, calmer now that he knew the outside was almost within his grasp.

"A garden," said Akira. "It used to belong to a cloth merchant, but now some knight owns it, and he don't like old Akira using this door. He blocked it off with some stones so I can't get it open."

Geoffrey put his shoulder to the door and pushed with all his might. Nothing happened. He took hold of a ring that acted as a door handle, and pulled. The door remained fast. Taking a deep breath, he grasped the ring a second time, braced his foot against the doorjamb, and pulled with every ounce of his strength. He felt the blood pounding in his ears, and the muscles stretching nastily in his arms, but still he hauled. Then there was a resounding rip, and he went crashing backward, the ring still in his hand.

"You must be strong," said Akira with admiration. "You ripped the ring right out of the door. Of course, it don't help us none.' He gave another wet sniff, wiped his nose against his shoulder, and sat down next to the disconsolate Geoffrey. "Told you it don't open from the inside," he said.

"Is there a house nearby?" asked Geoffrey, rubbing the base of his spine, where he had fallen. "If we shout, will anyone hear?"

"Oh, they'll hear all right," said Akira morosely. "But it won't do us no good."

"Must you keep saying that?" cried Geoffrey in exasperation. "Why will shouting not help?"

"Because the knight what lives there is called Sir Armand of Laon. And he's a good friend of that skinny, fair-haired knight what threw us down here in the first place."

Akira wanted to return to the more spacious cellar, but Geoffrey refused to budge from the sliver of light and hot breath of fresh air that occasionally oozed underneath the door. The knight lay flat on his stomach, but could see nothing except some brownish weeds. Akira had told him that the garden was fairly large, and the chances of anyone hearing shouts for help from the road were remote. And even if they did, no one was likely to investigate cries coming from the garden of as powerful a knight as Armand of Laon. Geoffrey lay on the chill stone floor and watched the light fade from under the door.

He did not think he was likely to fall asleep, but he did, exhausted by the events and tensions of the last few days. He awoke cold, stiff, and disoriented in total darkness. He was immediately seized by panic, and leapt to his feet struggling for breath. Akira, who was kicked awake in the process, grumbled in protest.

"Quiet!"

It did not sound like Akira's voice, and Akira went obligingly silent. Geoffrey leaned against the wall, trying to bring his breathing under control, and heard the scrape of stone on wood. Someone was moving the rocks from the door! He wanted to cry out in relief, but how could he know it was not Armand coming to finish him off quietly under cover of darkness? But that was ridiculous! Armand had no need to do anything so risky, when all he had to do was wait patiently for a few days.

The sound came again, accompanied by a grunt in a familiar voice. Roger! Geoffrey pressed further back against the wall, wondering what was happening now. He was unarmed, having been made to drop his dagger and sword in Akira's shop; there was no way he could best Roger in an unarmed fight at any time, but especially now when his limbs felt like jelly and he was gasping for breath like a landed fish.

Then the door was thrown open, and the sweet, warm air of Armand's garden wafted into the tunnel. Geoffrey saw Roger's great bulk silhouetted against the pre-dawn sky, and tensed himself.

"Geoff? Are you there, lad? It is me, Roger!" He took a step inside. "Geoffrey!" he called urgently.

"I'm here," came Akira's ingratiating voice from near Roger's knees.

"Where is Geoffrey?" demanded Roger, reaching down and hauling Akira to his feet with a fistful of his grimy tunic. "If you have done anything to him, I will kill you!"

"There he is!" came another familiar voice, accompanied by a pointing finger. Melisende! Geoffrey saw Roger peer into the darkness, and then felt his arm grabbed as he was dragged outside.

Geoffrey was unresisting, wondering what was to happen next.

"Here you are, lad," said Roger, thrusting a water bag at him. "Now, take some deep breaths. Are you all right? If that foul butcher has harmed you, I will tear him into little pieces . . ."

"I didn't do nothing to him!" protested Akira. "He's scarcely said a word to me the whole time we've been here, regardless of the fact that I've been telling him everything about me!"

"I am sure he has been right entertained," said Roger dryly.

"You are making too much noise!" whispered Melisende urgently. She turned to Geoffrey. "Drink some water. You will feel better in a moment."

"We do not have much time," said Roger, glancing up at the sky. "Geoff? Look lively! We have work to do!"

Geoffrey sipped at the water, staring up at the speckle of stars in the lightening sky, wondering if he were dreaming. He took a deep breath, then another, and felt the strength returning to his limbs. This process was speeded along by a sudden and unexpected thump on the back by Roger, which brought tears to his eyes.

"Come on, lad, pull yourself together!" hissed Roger urgently.

"I don't understand," said Geoffrey, confused. "Why are you not off with Hugh?"

"How else would we have escaped?" whispered Roger. "I thought they meant to run us through there and then, and my sole object was to get a sword to protect us. Did you not understand the message I shouted to you?"

"See you in hell?" queried Geoffrey, his mind working sluggishly.

"Yes!" said Roger. "I thought you would work that out, you being so learned and all. You told me once that your vision of hell was being lost in deep airless tunnels. So, I shouted that I would see you in one, to let you know I would come for you. You did not understand?" He looked crestfallen.

"It was rather obscure," said Geoffrey, weakly. He supposed he might have grasped Roger's hidden message had he been anywhere but a cave, since he found caves were the last places in which he could think clearly.

"Well, I could not exactly shout 'Hang on, lad, I will be back for you later,' could I?" said Roger, somewhat belligerently. "I intended to come before now, but it has been chaotic at the citadel. Hugh has had all his men mount up and head out—he says for a desert patrol, but he means to kill the Advocate. He has scarcely let me out of his sight, since I think he was suspicious of the way I abandoned you at Akira's. But as they rode out, I was able to slip away. I really did come as soon as I could," he said gently, patting Geoffrey's arm in a rough gesture of affection.

Geoffrey looked into Roger's blunt, honest features peering down at him in concern, and wondered how he could have been so utterly wrong about his friends. Melisende stood to one side, watching him anxiously. He rubbed tiredly at his eyes and took another deep breath.

"But how did you know to come here?" he asked, gesturing at the garden.

"Hugh levered the ring-pull out of the trapdoor in Akira's shop," said Roger, grudgingly admiring. "Cunning devil knew that no one would ever prise that great block of stone up without it. But while I was waiting for you to come back to Mistress Melisende's home yesterday, Maria and I had a long time for chatting. She told me that Hugh and Adam had hauled Pius's body along some tunnel to dump it in Akira's house, while she went to open the trapdoor in the cellar. But she refused to tell me where the tunnel came out. As soon as I could get away from Hugh, I went to see if Mistress Melisende here might know."

Melisende gave a shrug. "Fortunately, Maria had mentioned it to me once, when she told me some story of how she had escaped from the cellar after Akira had locked her in. I came with Sir Roger to make sure he found the right garden." She smiled at Geoffrey, who forced himself to smile back.

"That Maria!" began Akira, with a shake of his greasy head. "But we shouldn't hang around here. That Armand don't like Akira in his garden."

"Armand has gone with the rest," said Roger, "but you are right—we have no time to waste. Follow me."

Geoffrey, Melisende, and Akira fell in behind Roger, who led them around the edge of the garden to a tree next to the wall. He scaled it quickly and prepared to drop over the other side.

"Here! Wait a minute," squeaked the butcher. "Akira can't get up that!"

While Geoffrey pushed from underneath and Roger heaved from above, Akira disappeared over the wall in a cacophony of curses and groans. Melisende was up the tree like a monkey, hauling up her skirts to reveal strong, white legs. Geoffrey followed them over and saw he was in the street next to the one where Akira had his shop.

"Is this as far as that tunnel went?" asked Geoffrey in bewilderment. "It felt as though we were virtually outside the city walls."

"I told you it wasn't far," said Akira with a sloppy sniff. "And I told you it could be miles, depending on how you takes to that sort of thing. You took to it worse than anyone I've ever brought there—you probably expected to come out in Normandy!"

He gave a guttural chuckle and scuttled away into the night. After a moment, he came back.

"Where shall I go?" he asked, helplessly. "That Maria is still at large, and that Adam might come back to get me."

"Maria is locked up at the citadel, and Adam has gone with Hugh," said Roger. "You will be safe at home, Akira."

Akira gave him a grin revealing some impressively worn teeth. "Akira likes you," he said to the large knight. "You ever need a nice bit o' lean meat, you know where to come."

He slithered away into the darkness a second time.

"Well, he likes me. That *is* a relief," said Roger, watching the hunched shape disappear down the shadowy street.

"You had better send word to Uncle Daimbert," said Geoffrey to Melisende. "Tell him that Hugh plans to kill the Advocate, and that we will try to stop him."

"Are you sure that is the best course of action?" asked Melisende. "It might be better for the city to have a change in leadership. Everyone is discontented with the Advocate because he is so weak, and as long as he is in power, the city remains vulnerable to attack from the Saracens. Think about how the Crusaders slaughtered the Arabs when the city fell. If the Saracens attacked us now, there would be no quarter for any Christian in Jerusalem—man, woman, or child."

That was certainly true, thought Geoffrey. The shock and outrage at the bloody massacre of innocent Arab citizens by Christians a year before would be avenged ruthlessly by the Saracens. If the city fell, there would not be a Christian left alive to tell the story.

"Your friend—Sir Hugh—is not to be trusted, obviously, but he is right on this count," Melisende continued. "We need a strong leader to rule."

"But Hugh is talking about murder," objected Geoffrey. "And he says he will put Bohemond on the throne, but Bohemond is away in the north—he is not here to take advantage of the vacant crown. Neither is your uncle, who is also away from Jerusalem. Nor even is Tancred. The Saracens will not hesitate to attack the city if they know it does not have a leader. The murder of the Advocate could well bring about the very massacre you hope to avoid."

She studied him intently, a slight frown on her face, and then shrugged. "You could be right," she said eventually. She gave him a wry grin. "As usual. Uncle left for Haifa yesterday morning. I will send word to him and to Tancred too. But in the meantime, will you hunt this Hugh down?" Geoffrey nodded. "Then be careful." She leaned toward him, gave him a furtive kiss on the cheek, and was gone into the night, heading for the Patriarch's Palace.

"You are in with a chance there, lad," said Roger, beginning to stride toward the citadel. Geoffrey fell into step next to him, his strength and composure returning in leaps and bounds.

"That is twice you have saved my life in as many days," he said to the burly Englishman.

"You have done the same for me in the past," said Roger comfortably.

"Oh God!" said Geoffrey as they walked. "What a mess! I doubted you. And I could not have been more wrong."

"Aye, lad," said Roger. "I sensed something was up when we went to Abdul's together. But even with doubts about my innocence, you still got me out of that mess with Eveline. I bear you no ill feelings for suspecting me of being the killer."

Roger's easy forgiveness made Geoffrey cringe with guilt.

"That business with Eveline was probably Hugh's doing, too," said Roger, when Geoffrey did not reply.

"No," said Geoffrey. "That had to be Courrances. He had probably come to believe that one, or all, of us three was responsible for the murders, and he wanted us out of the way. He planned that you should be found fast asleep with a dead whore by your side, while I was to be killed during the riot. Had Hugh been with us, doubtless there would have been something arranged for him too. But I know you. You do not usually fall asleep on your whores—especially after paying for them. As we left the room through the window, some wine spilled on my sleeve, and there was some kind of white powder in it. I am fairly sure it was drugged, which also explains why you were sick and pathetic when we dealt with Eveline's body. And it was peculiar that a fight should break out so unexpectedly. The knights in the lower room were quiet when we arrived. I think it was started deliberately by Courrances and d'Aumale."

"I saw d'Aumale at Abdul's Pleasure Palace," said Roger, "but not Courrances."

"Yes, you did," said Geoffrey. "Running to lock me in the burning stable."

"But how could they know we would be there?" asked Roger. "It is not as if we have a regular visiting time. How could they plan so quickly?"

"Because Hugh probably told Courrances what we were doing," said Geoffrey. "And he could have worked it out anyway. We knew Warner and d'Aumale were at Abdul's the night Marius was killed, because Warner admitted as much to us in the chapel. Courrances would guess we would want to check their alibis and so would pay a visit to Abdul."

"But why did Courrances want us out of the way all of a sudden?"

"Because he, like us, has concluded that the person behind these killings was a knight at the citadel. Not an Arab, as he kept insisting. Not the Greeks. Not the Jews. I have no idea what his evidence might be, but he must have narrowed down his list of suspects to you and me. And perhaps to Hugh too. I suppose he considered the murder of Marius in my chamber to be the most vital clue, and went from there."

"When I was waiting for you at Melisende's house, I did a lot of thinking," said Roger. "I just assumed the business at Abdul's Pleasure Palace was Hugh's doing. It was obvious you were getting close, and then he would have no choice but to get you out of the way. And me too."

"And we told him our findings every step of the way," said Geoffrey bitterly. "As long as we kept talking to him, he knew he had nothing to fear. He would probably far rather we were investigating, telling him exactly what we had discovered, than any of the Patriarch's scribes."

They walked in silence for a while, Geoffrey still breathing deeply, forcing the memory of Akira's tunnel from his mind.

"Now that Hugh has fled," said Geoffrey, thinking about the slender Norman's emptied chest, "the Advocate will be safe as long as he remains in the citadel. Even all Hugh's soldiers will not be able to attack him successfully if he stays within the castle walls. So, why are we rushing to apprehend Hugh now?"

"But the Advocate is not in the citadel!" said Roger, turning to look at him in sudden concern. "He left for Jaffa while you were out chasing Saracens. And Hugh means to kill him as he and his retinue travel back to Jerusalem."

Chapter Twelve

At the citadel, all was in chaos after the hurried departure of Hugh and his men. Geoffrey winced when he recalled how Hugh had drilled his soldiers rigorously, while most of the knights let sword drill and archery practice slip. Hugh had apparently decided to take the fate of the Holy Land into his own hands months before the murders had occurred. And Geoffrey's investigation had forced him into action before he was ready, since it would have been better for him to have had Bohemond waiting in the wings, rather than far away in Antioch. But it had probably taken little organisation: his troops were ready, and the empty chest in his room suggested he had been packed and ready to act for some time.

Geoffrey called for Helbye, and ordered him to prepare his men and Roger's for immediate pursuit of Hugh's cavalcade. The bailey erupted into activity once more, and several knights, intrigued by the second spurt of activity, came to see what was going on. Some were Bohemond's men, and friends of Roger. When Roger explained what had happened, they shouted orders to their own men to make ready, for everyone knew a vacant throne would do Bohemond no good at all when he was not there to take it.

"I suppose we should talk to Maria before we go," said Geoffrey, as he and Roger ran to their own chambers to don full armour and grab as many weapons as they could realistically carry. "She might be able to fill in some details about this vile business."

"I left her in the care of Tom Wolfram and Ned Fletcher," said Roger. "I had a feeling Hugh might try to visit her too, so I told them to let no one see her but me. You know Fletcher—he will take that quite literally, and Hugh will not get past him."

Still buckling his padded surcoat over his chain mail, Geoffrey strode across the bailey, followed closely by Roger, to the low arch beyond which a narrow flight of steps led to the citadel prison. When he saw the gloomy opening and the rock-hewn walls, he was horribly reminded of the tunnels under the city, and almost turned back. But Roger pressing behind him, and the knowledge that the prison comprised three well-lit and reasonably large rooms, gave him the courage to enter.

The cells were relatively empty and totally silent. Geoffrey was wary. The cells were seldom silent. They were not only used for criminals from the city, but for soldiers who transgressed the Advocate's few, but rigidly enforced, rules. There were some soldiers there now, standing together in a soundless huddle in the furthest cell.

"They left with the first cavalcade," one called, peering at them through the bars on the door. "You might yet catch them if you hurry."

"God's teeth!" swore Geoffrey, staring in horror at the body of Ned Fletcher. He glanced into the cell and saw that Maria was dead too, her head twisted at an impossible angle and her pretty face marred by glassy eyes and gaping mouth. Around her neck glittered the cheap metal locket that Daimbert had given Roger, and that Roger had exchanged for a night of pleasure with the unfortunate Eveline.

Roger took a hissing breath and turned to the prisoners.

"You might still catch them," urged one of them.

"Them?" asked Geoffrey, his shock turning to a cold anger. Ned Fletcher had been from his home manor of Goodrich, and he had grown fond of the sturdy, reliable soldier over the years.

"Sir Hugh and Tom Wolfram," the prisoner replied. "He

stabbed Ned, and then went in and broke that lass's neck. She screamed at him to let her live, but he had no mercy!"

"Who was it?" demanded Geoffrey. "Which of them killed Ned?"

"Tom Wolfram!" chorused the soldiers in exasperation. One of them continued. "Then Sir Hugh came in, saw what Wolfram had done, and started going mad. He yelled and shouted at Wolfram that he was a fool. Then he and Wolfram were off."

"This is my fault!" said Roger bitterly, turning to Geoffrey. "If I had thought more carefully, I would have guessed that Maria would never be safe here—although she did not seem overly concerned when I arrested her. She probably believed Hugh would rescue her. If I had been more cautious, she and Ned would still be alive!"

"I doubt it," said Geoffrey with quiet fury, giving vent to his own anger and frustration. "Hugh is not the only traitor here it seems. Wolfram too is guilty. Maria was doomed the instant she stepped into the citadel."

"Wolfram!" said Roger, his voice hoarse with the shock of it all. "And how has he come to be involved?"

"The same way as the others," said Geoffrey angrily. "Seduced by the promise of rewards beyond his wildest dreams. Or perhaps I drove him to it by my insistence that he wear his chain mail! Who knows?" He slammed one mailed fist into the other. "But I should have guessed! It was Wolfram who told me to go to see Barlow when the lad was drunk. I thought then that you had seized the opportunity to kill Marius, but the incident afforded Wolfram the opportunity to buy time to tell Hugh that we were back. Perhaps it was even Hugh's idea, so that I would begin to suspect you."

"Sir Hugh was yelling at Tom Wolfram that the woman could still have been useful," called the prisoner helpfully. "But Wolfram said it was because Maria had been captured that they were forced to act sooner than they wanted. What did he mean?"

"Can you ride?" asked Geoffrey. All but one of the soldiers nodded. "Then come with me, and you will find out."

As Roger fumbled with the keys to release them, Geoffrey knelt next to Ned Fletcher and eased his twisted limbs into a more decent position. He took a last look at the man who had been with him since his youth, and stood abruptly, anger seething inside him. Roger followed him up the stairs and waylaid a monk to see about removing the bodies to the chapel.

"We will get Hugh for this, lad," said Roger, pulling on his gauntlets. Geoffrey nodded wordlessly and surveyed the flurry of activity in the bailey. He had perhaps fifteen knights and about thirty soldiers, hurriedly rounded up from the camp within the citadel walls. Only those who could ride had been chosen, because the little cavalcade would never catch up with Hugh with foot soldiers trailing behind. Geoffrey nodded with satisfaction when he saw that his three best archers were among the numbers.

He strode over to his own horse, already saddled and with his spare sword and mace strapped to its sides. He yelled to Helbye to check that all the water bags were full, since he was not going to ride after Hugh only to be thwarted by the intense heat of the desert—even if the men could be made to go short, the horses could not if they were to be of any use. As he swung himself up into the saddle, Courrances and four of his Hospitallers rode through the gates. With them was d'Aumale.

Courrances surveyed the scene in astonishment. "Another foray into the desert?" he queried. "Two within a day, and with such a show of force?"

Roger said nothing, and Geoffrey wondered whether Courrances were a part of Hugh's plan to kill the Advocate. But if the Advocate died, then Courrances would lose the power he had so carefully amassed. Geoffrey was debating how truthful to be, when d'Aumale spoke up.

"There have been a number of threats to the Advocate's life," he said. Courrances shot him a foul look, but d'Aumale went on. "He read me a letter from some monk outlining details of a plan to kill him. Is that what this is about?"

"D'Aumale!" shouted Geoffrey, exasperated. "Why did you

not tell me this earlier? Much time might have been saved, and Ned Fletcher might not be dead!"

"Because I have only just been told you have been investigating these murders on behalf of the Advocate," said d'Aumale with a disgusted look at Courrances. "Warner and I were under the impression you were doing Tancred's bidding. And since, under the right circumstances, Tancred might benefit very greatly from the Advocate's death, we did not think to confide in you! Had we known, we would most certainly have told you about this monk's letter."

"This monk was Sir Guido of Rimini," said Geoffrey, exasperated. "He signed himself Brother Salvatori because he was planning to take the cowl."

D'Aumale blanched and glowered at Courrances again. "Why did you not tell us sooner that Sir Geoffrey was working for the Advocate? We might have joined forces and averted all this!"

"Joining forces would not have been wise," came Courrances's oily voice. "And you should not be speaking with him now. Geoffrey Mappestone *is* Tancred's man. How do you know it is not Tancred's agents who are plotting to kill the Advocate, so that Tancred might be ruler of Jerusalem? Or Bohemond," he added with a glance at Roger.

Roger bristled. "Lord Bohemond would not stoop to such depths," he declared, although everyone, including Roger, knew perfectly well that he would. Bohemond stood to gain more than anyone from the Advocate's demise. And Tancred would benefit too, and the Patriarch, and possibly even the Advocate's brother Baldwin, away in the Kingdom of Edessa.

"I imagined the Greeks were behind it all," continued d'Aumale urgently, ignoring Courrances. "Meanwhile, Courrances believed it was a Saracen plot; Warner, who is in the hospital with a fever, thought the plot had to be Bohemond's or Tancred's. And then, who should begin asking questions and be seen in curious places—but you two and Sir Hugh."

"Hugh was never with us," said Roger. "Geoffrey and me went alone."

"I saw Sir Hugh several times in the Greek Quarter," said Courrances. His face became sharp. "He has gone, hasn't he—to Jaffa? He is on his way to murder the Advocate!"

"The evidence is far from clear," said Geoffrey, wanting time to think it out. Helbye gave a shout to say that all was ready. Geoffrey took the reins and wheeled his horse round to face the gates, raising his arm to order his men to prepare to leave.

"Wait!" said Courrances. "We are coming with you!"

The four Hospitallers and d'Aumale, like Courrances, were already fully armoured. They prepared to follow.

"Not a chance," said Geoffrey, pulling on the reins to control his restless horse. "We do not want to be found in compromising positions with dead whores in brothels, or killed in burning stables."

Courrances blanched. "I was mistaken."

"You were indeed," said Geoffrey, standing in his stirrups to cast a professional eye over his troops as they arranged themselves in a thin column, two abreast.

"I drew a conclusion based on the evidence presented. I was wrong to have accepted it so readily," said Courrances, lunging and grabbing Geoffrey's surcoat. "Several days ago, while you were in the desert, Hugh told me that he was concerned that you were involved in something that might prove detrimental to the Advocate. He told me you were working in league with the Patriarch. I made enquiries and found it to be true—both you and Roger are in the pay of the Patriarch. Hugh was plausible—acting as a grieving friend who was deeply shocked at a betrayal of loyalties. I took him at face value and arranged the business at Abdul's when he told me you were planning to go there. As it turned out, the entire thing was a fiasco, and d'Aumale could have been killed when he was knocked down by one of the horses you let out, which was racing down the street. I have apologised to him, and now I apologise to you. But Hugh duped me every bit as much as he did you."

"Not quite," muttered Geoffrey bitterly. "And was it you who left the dagger and pig's heart in my chamber?"

Courrances nodded. "I had to make you feel as though it was in your own interests to investigate the murders for me. Had you declined to take up the case, I had planned to leave similar items in the rooms of Roger and Hugh. But you agreed—far more readily than I had expected—so readily, in fact, that I became suspicious, and began to entertain the notion that *you* were the killer. After all, no one was murdered in the two weeks you were out on desert patrol. Then the minute you step back in the city, John was killed. And then Hugh came, and told me his reasons for suspecting you . . ."

His voice trailed off. "But a pig's heart?" said Roger, with a shake of his great head.

Courrances shrugged and then gave a rare smile. "To begin with, I thought all this was the work of Moslem fanatics. I left a pig's heart to point you in their direction, since the pig is considered unclean by them." He saw Geoffrey's bemused expression. "Too obscure, I see."

Geoffrey's men were ready, and the horses, sensing the excitement, were restless and prancing. The bailey was filled with low clouds of dust kicked up by their hooves, and already Geoffrey was beginning to bake inside his armour. He donned his metal helmet, with the long nosepiece, and signalled for the men to begin filing out.

"We must come with you!" Courrances insisted, watching the mounted soldiers ride past. "I saw Hugh's force when it left earlier. He has at least twice the men that you have. You need us!"

Geoffrey made a quick decision; it was in Courrances's interest to save the Advocate, and the Hospitaller was right in that Hugh probably had a considerably larger force than had Geoffrey. The addition of Courrances, his Hospitallers, and d'Aumale would provide much-needed reinforcements to his small army.

"Come on, then!" he yelled, clinging with his knees as his horse reared, impatient with the delay.

Roger looked at him aghast. "What are you doing? We do not want Hospitallers with us!"

"First, it is better to have Courrances where we can see him," said Geoffrey in a low voice, watching the warrior-monk run to his own mount and give terse orders to his men. "And second, we are going to need all the help we can get. If Hugh succeeds, Bohemond will be held responsible whether Hugh is acting on his orders or not. And I suspect he is not, because Bohemond is too far away to take advantage of an empty throne if Hugh strikes now. If Hugh murders the Advocate, we will need to combine all our forces to prevent the city from plunging into civil war. And if we fight among ourselves, the Saracens will be on us in an instant. Believe me, Roger, we need Courrances just as much as he needs us."

The horsemen thundered down the winding path that led down through the Judean Hills to the coastal plain and Jaffa, a prosperous city that was some thirty miles distant as the crow flew. The predominant colour of the countryside around Jerusalem was a pale buff-yellow, which became deeper when bathed in gold by the setting sun. It was midmorning, but the heat was intense, making the scrubby hills shimmer and shift. Here and there, small desert plants eked a parched existence from the arid soil, providing a meagre diet for the small herds of goats that roamed the area with their Bedouin masters.

Dust rose in choking clouds under the horses' feet, so that the soldiers not at the front of the cavalcade were blinded by it. Geoffrey felt it mingling with the sweat that ran down his face, and forming gritty layers between skin, chain mail, and surcoat. The dust worked its way into his eyes, ears, mouth, and nose, so that his whole world seemed to comprise nothing but the thud of hooves on baked soil and the bubble of rising grit that engulfed him.

He spurred his horse, so that he rode level with Roger, screwing up his eyes against the glare to squint ahead for any sign of Hugh. They reached a tiny oasis, where gnarled olive trees huddled around a shallow pool of murky water, churned to mud by the feet of the animals that came to drink. Curious Bedouin watched the horsemen from the shade of the trees, and exchanged looks of mystification as to what could be so important as to warrant such frenzied activity in the desert heat. With bemused shrugs, they went back to their storytelling and their gossip.

Beyond the oasis, the path sloped upward and rounded a bend, providing a view of the countryside that stretched like a blanket ahead. Geoffrey reined in, clinging with his knees as his agitated horse reared and kicked. An excited bark from below told him that the dog had followed them, although how the fat, lazy beast had kept up, Geoffrey could not imagine.

"There!" he yelled, pointing.

Far in the distance was another group of horsemen, strung out in a long black line across the yellow floor of the desert. There were, Geoffrey estimated quickly, at least a hundred of them, riding toward Jaffa. Hugh had no reason to suspect that Geoffrey had escaped and raised a counterforce, but he must have missed Roger from his troops, and was making good, but not furious, time on his journey.

Courrances reined in next to him, narrowing his eyes at the distant black dots of Hugh's army. "A hundred and twenty, I would say," he said. He looked at Geoffrey's men. "And we number perhaps fifty." He looked back at Geoffrey, fixing him with his expressionless pale blue eyes, and spurred his horse after his Hospitallers.

"He is right," said Roger. "This will be no well-matched battle, Geoff."

"But Hugh does not know we are coming," said Geoffrey. "We have the element of surprise."

"Do not fool yourself," said Roger. "He knows all right. He has left too many clues behind him for someone not to follow—if not you and me, then Courrances."

Geoffrey did not answer, and he set off again as fast as he dared without destroying the horses. The main road went steadily west, heading for the ancient settlement of Latrun, before continuing northwest to Ramle and then on to Jaffa. Geoffrey knew this region well, having taken many scouting parties out to scour the desert for Saracen bandits, and he knew that by bearing farther north, he could cut in a straight line across the desert and rejoin the road at the tiny settlement of Ramle. Such a shortcut would serve the dual purpose of slicing several miles from their journey, and of masking their pursuit from Hugh and his men.

He yelled his plan to Roger, who grinned in savage delight. D'Aumale forced his way through the milling soldiers, his face tight with tension.

"If we cut directly across the desert, we might yet intercept Hugh," Geoffrey explained.

"Then what are you waiting for?" yelled d'Aumale, spurring his horse off in entirely the wrong direction. Geoffrey and Roger exchanged amused glances before kicking their own mounts into action, and the chase was on once more.

The route across the desert was not as easy as that provided by the main road. It was rocky, and deeply scarred with great cracks caused as the land shrank away from the ferocity of the sun's heat. The soldiers were forced to negotiate steep ravines caused by the winter and spring rains, when great sheets of water fell briefly on the dry land, only to run off it again in churning brown torrents that headed straight for the sea. But despite the rough terrain, they made good time and lost only two of their number due to lame horses. Geoffrey dispatched them back to the citadel to see if reinforcements might be raised. Geoffrey's dog panted along with them, easily able to maintain the slower pace forced by crossing the open country.

There was a tiny spring, little more than a muddy puddle, that Geoffrey knew, about halfway along their route. He called a halt and ordered men and horses to drink—but sparingly, for he knew the horses would be unable to run with overfull stomachs. Then they were off again, refreshed, and ready for the gruelling second leg of their race across the furnace of the desert.

Geoffrey felt his face burn and his head pound as he became hotter and hotter. Beneath him, his horse began to wheeze from the dust, and the dog, still trotting at his side, had its tongue out so far it was almost scraping the ground. Another rider fell behind as his horse began to limp, and Geoffrey wondered whether, even if they did catch up with Hugh, they would be able to fight him. For fight Hugh would. The sardonic knight had no choice now but to follow the path he had taken to its bitter end. Even if he gave himself up, the Advocate would hang him as a traitor.

Geoffrey forced thought from his mind, and concentrated on guiding his horse around the great lumps of shattered rock that strewed the desert floor, and urging it to leap across the maze of ravines that gouged through the baked earth.

Eventually, after the sun had reached its zenith and was beginning to dip into late afternoon, they saw a thin line of green in the distance, and Geoffrey knew Ramle was in reach. The sun cast shadows across the desert that were growing steadily longer, and there would soon be very little daylight left. Geoffrey urged his men on with shouts of encouragement that made his voice hoarse. But they needed little urging, for they too had seen Ramle on the horizon and sensed battle was imminent.

A dry riverbed cut through the desert toward Ramle, and Geoffrey led his men down into it. The bed was relatively smooth, and so they were able to pick up speed. And there were banks on either side that would shield them from sight, so that Hugh would not see them coming. As they drew nearer to the trees, Geoffrey raised his hand to bring the main body to a halt, and while he and the knights continued to advance at a more sedate pace. Who knew what precautions Hugh might have taken, and the last thing Geoffrey needed was to ride headlong into an ambush. D'Aumale began to speak, but Geoffrey silenced him with a glare, and the gentle pad of hooves and the occasional clink of metal were the only sounds as they rode forward.

They reached the flat-roofed houses on the outskirts of Ramle, which had been their target. The villagers, seeing the advance of heavily armed knights, had already fled into the desert, abandoning homes, belongings, and livestock. Geoffrey saw several of the men take acquisitive looks at the houses, and knew he would be hard-pressed to prevent them from looting later. Not that there would be much to take, for the houses were poor and the livestock scrawny. Even Geoffrey's dog, infamous killer of the citadel chickens and goats, appeared uninterested and slunk away to find somewhere shady to recover from its exertions.

An old woman, too frail to run with the others, watched their approach with a mixture of resignation and fear. She saw Geoffrey looking at her, and pulled a thin, black shawl tighter around her shoulders, as if she imagined it might protect her from him.

"Greetings, mother!" he called in Arabic. "We mean no harm to you."

She gaped at him, startled by the curious notion of a Crusader knight speaking her own tongue, albeit falteringly.

"Can you tell me how long it has been since the other soldiers passed this way?"

She recovered herself and came toward him, her toothless jaws working in time with her doddering footsteps.

"No soldiers have passed this way today," she said when she reached him.

Geoffrey's hopes soared. "No group of horsemen? More than a hundred of them?"

She shook her head. "No." She gestured to where the road wound through the grove of olive trees, toward the main settlement of Ramle and then on through the desert to Jaffa and the sea. "You would still see the dust if they had passed recently."

Geoffrey saw that was probably true. So they were ahead of Hugh! The fair-haired knight and his retinue of traitors must have been making slower time than Geoffrey had imagined, perhaps considering that no force large enough to confront them could be raised so quickly. So now, despite his inferior numbers, Geoffrey had the advantage.

"Thank you, mother. These other men will pass soon and there may be fighting, so one of my soldiers will take you out of harm's way."

Quickly, he translated the news to the others. He dispatched Helbye as lookout and began setting up an ambush. Barlow was charged with carrying the old woman away from the village to the shade of the olive grove, much to Courrances's amazement.

"She is an infidel! We need Barlow here."

"She is an infidel who has just given us the powerful weapon of surprise," retorted Geoffrey. "Without her information, we would now be riding to Jaffa with Hugh behind us. Then he would have surprised us. Besides, what I do with my men is none of your business."

Courrances bit back the reply he would dearly have loved to make, and went to help d'Aumale. Geoffrey's plan was simple. The road through the houses was narrow, like a gully. When the first of Hugh's men was almost through the village, Barlow, wrapped in the old woman's shawl, would drive goats across the road at a prearranged signal from Helbye, who was watching the road from a tree. When Hugh's soldiers slowed to avoid the blockage, a group led by Roger would attack the rear of the column. As Hugh's men turned to deal with this, a second unit led by Geoffrey would attack the front. And in all the confusion, Courrances, d'Aumale, and the Hospitallers would harry the middle section trapped in the narrow road, with the aid of Geoffrey's archers.

The men were well-trained, and it took only a few moments for them to take up their positions. Then all was silent except for the worried bleating of goats and the yapping of a small, ratlike dog. Geoffrey sat on his horse behind the last of the houses in the village, wiping away the sweat that trickled from under his conical helmet. He caught the eye of one of the soldiers from Bristol and smiled encouragingly. The young man tried to smile back, but was clearly frightened and managed only a grimace. Geoffrey appreciated why he was nervous. They were outnumbered more than two to one, and they had no idea of the composition of Hugh's army. If Hugh had fifty knights, they were doomed, despite Geoffrey's carefully considered tactics.

Geoffrey took a deep breath of hot desert air and cleared his mind of everything but the battle ahead. Then, faintly at first, but growing louder, he heard the drum of hooves on the road. He strained his ears and concentrated. Hugh's men were advancing at a steady pace, not the breakneck gallop that Geoffrey had forced across the desert. Good. The slower they went, the greater were the chances of trapping the entire group between the houses, because they would not be as strung out. He risked a glance up the street, and saw the first knight trotting toward him. Then the plan swung into action.

Helbye waved to Barlow, dropped out of his tree, and went racing off to join Roger. Barlow began to move his goats forward, but the creatures scattered and milled about in every direction except the road. Geoffrey's hand tightened around the hilt of his sword as he watched Barlow's hopelessly inadequate attempts to control the animals. Barlow waved his arms about in desperation, frightening them, so that they ran in the opposite direction to the one he intended. The first horseman was already halfway through the village, and there was not a goat in sight. Barlow began to shout, and Geoffrey gritted his teeth in exasperation. Hugh's men would hear Barlow yelling in English and would know he was no Bedouin. Then they would guess there was a trap, and Geoffrey and his men would be unable to hold them.

Hugh's knight was now two-thirds of the way through the village, his comrades streaming behind him in a nice, tight formation that would have been perfect for Geoffrey's plan. But Barlow had failed miserably with the goats, which were now moving in a nervous huddle away from the road toward the desert.

Then it happened. In a furious flurry of black and white, Geoffrey's dog appeared, sharp, yellow teeth bared in anticipation of a goat repast. With terrified bleats, the goats first scattered, and then clashed together in a tight group that wheeled back toward the road. The dog followed, snapping and worrying at their fleeing legs.

The goats hurtled across the road just as the first of Hugh's men reached the end of the village. It could not have been more perfectly timed. The goats, far more in terror of the ripping jaws that pursued them than of the mounted knights, plunged down the street, cavorting and weaving about the horses' legs. The first few knights were helpless, hemmed in by a great tide of bleating, dusty bodies. Meanwhile, the dog had felled a victim and was engaging in a vicious battle that caught the interest of Hugh's men.

One of them, however, was more interested in the dog than in the blood sport. Geoffrey saw puzzlement cross Hugh's face, and then an appalled understanding as he recognised the animal. At that moment, chaos erupted at the far end of the village. Roger was in action, wheeling his great sword around his head at the hapless soldiers who came within his reach. Some tried to ride further into the village, away from Roger, where the three archers poured a lethal barrage of arrows down into the body of trapped men. The press from behind caused further confusion in the middle of the column, and Courrances and his men entered the affray, emerging from the houses with blood-curdling battle cries.

Hugh gave a great yell and kicked his horse forward, away from the chaos of goats. Several others followed, trying to break free to gallop to the open road ahead. Geoffrey and fifteen men from his small army left their hiding places and tore into the battle.

Hugh saw Geoffrey, and his face dissolved into a mask of hatred and loathing. He wheeled his horse around and drove at Geoffrey, oblivious to everything but the man who was attempting to foil his carefully laid plans. Geoffrey raised his shield to parry the blow, and felt himself all but dislodged from his saddle. Hugh swung again, the impact cleaving a great dent in Geoffrey's shield. Then Geoffrey jabbed straight-armed at Hugh's side and heard him grunt with pain.

Another man joined the affray: Wolfram, who had been Geoffrey's man. Geoffrey had a brief vision of Ned Fletcher and rode at him hard and low, aware that despite all his nagging and encouragement, Wolfram was still not wearing full armour. He caught the young man a hefty blow with his sword; in blocking the well-placed swipe, Wolfram was knocked out of his saddle and fell to the ground.

Geoffrey whirled around as Hugh struck again and again, taking the brunt of the blows on his shield. Geoffrey was stronger by far than the smaller Hugh, whose skills lay in carefully executed swordplay rather than brute strength. But Hugh was fighting like a fool, letting his hatred blind him into exhausting himself before the fight had really begun.

But Hugh had not survived numerous battles while on Crusade by being stupid, and his innate sense of survival forced him to regain control of his temper. With a final lunge, he wheeled away and regarded Geoffrey from a distance. Hugh and Geoffrey knew each other well and had matched their fighting skills against each other many times in sport. Hugh was quick and cunning; Geoffrey was strong and intelligent. In their mock battles, Geoffrey imagined that they shared a more or less equal number of victories. His own success against Hugh now was far from secure.

In the brief respite, he felt a searing pain in his leg and looked down to see Wolfram at his side, armed with a dagger. Impatiently, Geoffrey kicked him away as hard as he could, and with a yell, rode at Hugh, using his superior strength to drive him backward, hoping to force him off balance. Hugh took the blows on his shield, reeling in his saddle at their force. Then he kicked out suddenly with his foot, catching Geoffrey's horse with a stunning kick in the throat. The horse reared in pain and terror, forcing Geoffrey to use his sword arm to control it. While Geoffrey tried to calm his bucking mount, Hugh attacked with a series of quick jabbing thrusts, at least one of which pierced Geoffrey's chain mail, sending a dull aching sensation through him. Geoffrey tore his horse's head around and forced it away. Hugh followed.

Geoffrey sensed Hugh's raised sword behind him, poised to strike at his back—like poor John of Sourdeval and the scribe Marius, Geoffrey thought suddenly, attacked from behind—and he whirled around in his saddle, raising his shield and swinging his own sword at the same time. It was not a wise manoeuvre, placing him awkwardly in the saddle, and without lending any real strength to his sword arm. But it was also not a manoeuvre Hugh anticipated, and his shield went skittering from his grasp. He recovered quickly and swung at Geoffrey, sitting unsteadily in his saddle, with a violent swing that took both of his hands. Geoffrey raised his shield, but the force of the blow unseated him, and he went tumbling to the ground, his helmet flying from his head.

He scrabbled to his feet as Hugh drove his horse forward, trying to trample him under its hooves. Geoffrey ducked and dodged, and escaped by the skin of his teeth at the expense of a painful kick on his leg. He gripped his sword and turned to face Hugh. Hugh now had the considerable advantage of height, and he rode at Geoffrey wheeling his sword like a windmill. Geoffrey dropped to the ground and scrambled away, feeling the whistle of the sword the merest fraction away from his bare head. He climbed to his feet again and considered running away. But then Hugh would break away from the melee and ride for Jaffa to kill the Advocate, and everything Geoffrey had worked for would have been for nothing.

Meanwhile, Wolfram had recovered and was also advancing on Geoffrey with sword drawn. Geoffrey looked from Wolfram to Hugh, trying to ascertain who would attack him first. Geoffrey spun round and raced at Wolfram, forcing the young man to retreat rapidly to avoid being hacked to pieces by Geoffrey's expertly wielded weapon. Wolfram would know he could never beat Geoffrey in such a confrontation, but Wolfram had Hugh. Hugh spurred his horse forward a second time, driving the terrified beast to where Geoffrey sparred with the young soldier. At the very last moment, Geoffrey threw himself to the ground and covered his head with his hands. One of the horse's hooves smashed into his thigh, but he was otherwise unharmed.

Yelling with savage delight, Wolfram dived at him, while Hugh brought his horse in a tight circle to bear down on them again. Geoffrey was still off-balance, and Wolfram's graceless lunge knocked him to the ground again. Then Hugh was on them, his sword whirling and slashing, and the hooves thundering into the ground all around them.

Wolfram went limp. Geoffrey struggled out from underneath him and saw that one of Hugh's wild swipes had cut deeply into the young soldier's back.

"Should have been wearing your chain mail," Geoffrey muttered as he rolled the lifeless body away and struggled to his feet yet again. Gritting his teeth, he turned to face Hugh. He could see the glitter of Hugh's eyes under his helmet, and saw that he smiled. As far as Hugh was concerned, this contest was already won: Geoffrey was limping and had lost his helmet. Hugh knew that Geoffrey's chances of besting a mounted knight of Hugh's experience and skill were remote. He began to relax.

Geoffrey hurled his sword away and drew his dagger, leaping toward the back of Hugh's horse where Hugh could not see him. Roaring with fury, Hugh wheeled his horse around in a tight circle. But Geoffrey moved with it, using his dagger to hack and slice at the leather straps that anchored the saddle to the horse's back. The horse reared in terror and pain, and Hugh fought to control it. A flailing hoof caught Geoffrey a glancing blow on the chin and sent him sprawling. Within moments, Hugh was with him, crashing to the ground with his saddle tangled about his legs.

Now is the time, Geoffrey's instincts screamed at him, while Hugh struggled to free himself from the saddle and its clinging stirrups. But the blow to his chin had left him dazed, and it was all he could do to climb groggily to his feet. He made a feeble lunge at Hugh with his dagger, but Hugh punched him away and succeeded in freeing himself. When Geoffrey's vision cleared of the exploding lights that blinded him, he found he had dropped dagger and shield, and faced Hugh unarmed. Eyes glittering, Hugh advanced with his sword and raised his arm for the strike that would rid him of the man who had thwarted all his plans. Geoffrey met his gaze unflinchingly.

The blow never came. Hugh's expression changed from one

of twisted malice to one of surprise, and his sword descended slowly. Behind him stood Roger, and Hugh buckled and fell to the ground. In his back was a curved dagger with a jewelled hilt.

"Took a fancy to this when I saw it in his room," said Roger, bracing a foot against Hugh's back and retrieving it. He showed it to Geoffrey, turning it in his hands. "Fancy, eh?"

Geoffrey tore his eyes away from the bloody dagger and back to Roger. "Have we succeeded?"

"Aye, lad. Courrances and his monks wreaked havoc in the middle part, and the trapped men trying to escape hindered the fighting at the back and the front. I killed that treacherous Father Almaric—he was wearing chain mail, would you believe, and he had a sword! And I got Maria's lad, Adam, too, and Courrances killed Armand, among others." He paused, looking at the bodies strewn across the road in satisfaction. "Those goats worked a treat."

Only just, thought Geoffrey wearily. He looked around for his dog and saw it gnawing something bloody between its paws. He hoped it was only an animal. He glanced toward the village, and saw Courrances and d'Aumale rounding up the few remaining soldiers in Hugh's army, and setting them to gather up those who had been killed. It appeared to have been a massacre, and Geoffrey suddenly felt sick.

"It is not as if we have nothing better to do," he said to a bemused Roger. "This whole land is surrounded by hostile Saracens, and all we can do is kill each other! Perhaps we are not fit to be here at all and should give up our claims to others."

"Don't talk daft, lad," said Roger. He gestured at the slowly growing heap of corpses in the street. "The world is a better place without the likes of them in it."

On the ground, Hugh gave a soft groan and forced himself onto his back. Geoffrey and Roger exchanged a glance and looked down at him dispassionately. Hugh saw them and smiled.

"I always thought it would be glorious to die in battle with my friends."

"But you expected to be in battle *with* your friends, not

against them," said Roger, slightly indignantly. "Besides, we are not dying."

Hugh's smile widened, showing teeth that were stained with blood. Geoffrey knelt next to him, repelled by the whole treacherous business.

"Was it worthwhile, Hugh?" asked Geoffrey softly. He gestured to the pile of soldiers' bodies. "Your men are dead, and you will soon follow them."

"It was worthwhile," Hugh responded. "I sent word to Bohemond two weeks ago that I was going to kill the Advocate, and that he should be ready to step forward to claim Jerusalem. Even as we talk, he will be massing his troops in anticipation."

"But he will find the Advocate alive," said Geoffrey. "And no one will support Bohemond if he tries to snatch the leadership by force. The Advocate was crowned in the Holy Sepulchre by the Patriarch himself."

"Yes, yes," said Hugh wearily. "But the Advocate is weak, and even his own men are wavering in their loyalty to him. You think you have won because I am dying. But there are others who think like me and it will only be a matter of time before one of them succeeds. And regardless, Bohemond will come soon with a great force, and you two will have no choice but to fight for him."

"How do you know he will come?" asked Geoffrey. "He might decide he wants no crown won with blood."

"Oh, that will not bother him," put in Roger cheerfully. "Bohemond is no lily-livered monk."

"I sent word to him with a man whom I know will be able to persuade him of his best options," Hugh whispered. "Sir Guibert of Apulia took my message that Bohemond should prepare himself two weeks ago."

Geoffrey gazed at him. "Sir Guibert is dead," he said softly.

Hugh's eyes grew round with horror, but then he dismissed Geoffrey's claim. "You lie. Guibert would not fail me or Bohemond."

"Doubtless not," said Geoffrey. "But Guibert and his soldiers were attacked by Saracens before they ever reached Bohemond, and were killed to a man. Tancred told me about it in a message he sent from Haifa. He was curious as to why Guibert should be in the desert at all, and thought it sufficiently odd to mention in his letter. Bohemond did not receive your message."

The colour drained from Hugh's face, and he closed his eyes.

There was a shout of warning from Helbye, whom Roger had posted to watch the road for any reinforcements that Hugh might have had stashed further away. Roger dashed for his horse, while Geoffrey snatched up Hugh's sword, anticipating another skirmish. There was no time to arrange a second ambush: they would simply have to do battle as they were.

Helbye strode forward to intercept a small party of soldiers that was riding toward Jerusalem, and Geoffrey watched as the sergeant engaged in a hurried exchange of words. Geoffrey saw Helbye's jaw drop, and then the sergeant seemed to collect himself. He came racing toward Geoffrey.

"The Advocate!" he gasped. "The Advocate is dead!"

Geoffrey looked from Helbye to the soldiers who had just arrived. One was Sir Conrad of Liege, a knight who Geoffrey knew well, who was one of the Advocate's staunchest supporters.

"It is true," said Conrad, fixing Geoffrey with exhausted, red-rimmed eyes. "He died of a fever early this morning." He looked at Geoffrey and Roger, and then at Courrances and d'Aumale, who had come to see what the commotion was about. "What happens now?"

Geoffrey looked down to where Hugh lay, smiling with the last of his dying strength.

"Was it you?" Geoffrey asked in a whisper. "Did you poison him?"

"You will never know," replied Hugh, his voice so weak Geoffrey had to kneel to hear him. "You will never know."

ḣISTORICAL NOTE

During his year as Advocate of the Holy Sepulchre, Godfrey, Duke of Lorraine, proved himself to be an honourable and pious, but ineffectual and unwise, ruler. The problems for the young kingdom caused by external threats and challenges from all sides and by the Advocate's lack of ability were compounded by intrigues, quarrels, and power struggles between the Advocate, Daimbert the Patriarch, and the other leaders of the Crusade who had remained in the Holy Land: Raymond of Toulouse; Bohemond; Tancred; and Baldwin, the Advocate's younger brother. These internal struggles were particularly problematic because Daimbert, who wanted control of both the city and Kingdom of Jerusalem, not only officially represented the Catholic Church, with the supposed backing of the Pope, but was clearly allied with the Normans, under the leadership of Bohemond and Tancred.

The Advocate continually needed more supplies and men to maintain his tenuous hold on the Kingdom, and he was forced to make a number of debilitating agreements in order to do so. In June 1100, he initiated contact with the Venetian fleet—an enormously powerful organisation from both a merchant and military standpoint—which had put into Jaffa. He attempted to gain military support and supplies from the Venetians in return for trading rights and part tribute from every town they helped to capture.

On July 18, 1100, while in a second round of negotiations for these treaties in Jaffa, the Advocate died of a fever. As soon as the news was received in Jerusalem, Warner de Gray, himself a dying man, occupied the Tower of David and manned it with Lorrainers and the other men who were most loyal to the Advocate. He then sent messages to Baldwin to come and assume his inheritance. Exhausted by his efforts, Warner died on July 23, but the citadel, the military key to Jerusalem, was held for Baldwin until he arrived in November.

At the time when the Advocate died, Daimbert was with Tancred, besieging Haifa, which fell on July 25. Daimbert had been named in the Advocate's will to succeed him as secular leader in Jerusalem, and Daimbert did not think that the Advocate's followers had any strong leaders remaining. So, despite knowing that he would need help to realize his claims, he did not feel obliged to hurry back to the city. When Daimbert returned to find troops loyal to the Advocate in command of the citadel, he sent a message to Bohemond—at that time far north in his Principality of Antioch—inviting him to come take the throne—under the fatherly eye of Daimbert, of course. At the same time, Daimbert restrained Baldwin from coming to Jerusalem. The message never reached Bohemond, because in the interim he had been captured by Turks while on an expedition to the upper Euphrates; he was held prisoner by them until the spring of 1103.

Thus, when Baldwin arrived in Jerusalem, and Tancred withdrew to his lands in Galilee, Daimbert had no powerful backers, and had little choice but to accept Baldwin as the Advocate's successor. On Christmas Day in 1100, Daimbert crowned Baldwin King of Jerusalem, a title he held until his death in 1118. In the long run, Baldwin proved himself the ablest and soundest of the Crusade leaders, and never again did Daimbert—who died in 1107—come close to making Jerusalem a theocracy under the control of the Church.